ANIMAL FARM 2

by Martin Knox

First Published – 2021
This edition published 2021 by Novel Ideas
Brisbane, Qld Australia

Copyright © Martin Knox 2021

A catalogue record for this
work is available from the
National Library of Australia

The National Library of Australia Cataloguing-in-Publication

Creator: Knox, Martin, author.

Title: Animal Farm 2 / Martin Knox.

ISBN: 978-0-6489930-2-5 (paperback)

Subjects: Fiction.
                 Satirical fiction.
                 Humorous fiction.

Typeset in Times New Roman 12pt by Donna Munro Graphic Design.
Cover artwork by Donna Munro Graphic Design.
Printed and bound in Australia by Ingram Spark.
Copyright © Martin Knox 2021
htttps://www.martinknox.com
mpknox46@aapt.net.au

DEDICATION

This book is dedicated to my family: Zoe, Tessa, Amani, Uly and Dorian, hoping that through my writing others will better respect, understand and conserve the World they will inherit, with more caring for living things, especially humans, animals and environments, through philosophies of freedom, voluntary responsibility, reason and science. I appreciate their support but opinions and any errors are my own.

REVIEWS

ANIMAL FARM 2 (2021)

Pre-publication review by Brad Ahern, Science Educator.

Following Orwell's masterful satire, *Animal Farm*, Martin Knox continues the story in the aftermath of the Animal Revolution up to modern times, with an insightful account of the progress and difficulties of the Socialist Animal Collective. An action-packed story of farm animals seeking liberation. They mine coal and their work is restricted by bourgeois management and superpower influence. They discover and carefully explain a paradigm shift within climate science. Another prescient and engrossing cautionary fable satirising the threats posed by modern-day totalitarianism and globalism.

TIME IS GOLD (2020)

Readers' Favorite 5-stars December 11 2020
Reviewed by Romuald Dzemo

Time is Gold by Martin Knox is a brilliantly plotted and well-written novel that centers on a strong and original concept. Maxi Fleet wants just one thing: to run faster than any female has ever run before. She is training to beat the world. Stan has offered a lot of support, supervising and guiding her as she trains to compete in a future marathon. Maxi is determined to push herself beyond the limits and achieve her dream, and there is a strong support system to help her as she pursues this dream. Jack Cram is a PhD student in physics who is working on a revolutionary concept of stretching time. In Maxi, he finds the best opportunity to experiment on his theory, and if he succeeds, it will be a breakthrough for him and the scientific community. Can his idea of "extreme-flow" improve Maxi's performance and produce the desired results?

This is a wonderful story with elaborately developed themes, including love, ambition, hard work and pain, the drive for success, performance, and friendship. Set in the future, it has strong psychological and scientific underpinnings. The story is told in an absorbing first-person narrative, a style the author uses with mastery and it establishes a real connection between readers and the characters. The story has a premise that got me hooked right off the bat and I loved the bold ideas developed in this novel, especially the concept of "extreme-flow." This concept stipulates that anyone can perform better by getting into the flow that is extremely engaged. Hence marathon runners and others who embrace endurance with cognitive vigor can bolster their time, bit by bit, crossing finishing lines earlier, inserting additional accomplishment and staying younger. Time is Gold is a classic novel, speculative in style, hugely engaging, and featuring tight and excellent writing. While I loved the plot points, it was the depth with which the characters are written that had me turning the pages.

SHORT OF LOVE (2019)

Readers Favourite, August 5, 2019
Review by K.C. Finn Rating: 5 Stars
Short Of Love is a work of picaresque satirical fiction penned by author Martin Knox, which explores the notion of love and relationships, and how we treat other human beings when we view them as commodities for love rather than as individuals.

Author Martin Knox has created a fascinating parody of modern love and its effects on life, whilst also managing to stay true to the nature of many relationships where competition becomes a feature over compassion. Overall, Short of Love will interest any reader who enjoys dissecting relationships and the notion of romance itself.

Online Bookclub Review, January 15, 2020
Review by Stephanie Elizabeth
Short of Love by Martin Knox is a fascinating piece of satirical fiction. It explores love, relationships, and the moral impact of viewing people as commodities, rather than individuals. The story revolves around the exceedingly selfish Tom Archer, a student with his eyes fixated on a future as a successful engineer. But his focus wavers when he meets Vicki Hillstone. He becomes so wholly consumed by his desire for her, that he is driven to a whole new level of distraction.

Readers Favourite July 31, 2019
Reviewed by Vincent Dublado

Martin Knox's Short of Love is an unconventional love story that spans decades dating back from the Jungian nightmare cycles of the 60s. First released under the title Love Straddle, this new and abridged version does not take away the essence and ambiance that make the story endearing. Every day we read a love story with a cookie-cutter leading man that sweeps readers (especially women) off their feet. But this novel offers something different with a misfit protagonist that we would find complicated except that his predicaments are downright understandable. Short of Love reads like a cross between a romantic story and an Idiot's Guide reference on relationships--an insightful delving into balancing love and a career.

Book launch address. September 15, 2019
Editor Vesna McMaster

Short of Love is a complete re-working of an earlier work, Love Straddle. This predecessor was presented as a first-person narrative and was almost twice as long. One of the outcomes of this reduction in volume is that the pace of the novel is relentless. You won't be falling asleep over this one: it's been distilled to 100 proof.

Which takes me to the question of the novel's genre and place among literary works. I'm assuming most of you haven't read it yet. I'd describe it as a combination of Tom Jones, Catcher in the Rye, and St Augustine's Confessions, with a Beatles soundtrack. Tom Jones for the rapscallion, picaresque aspect, and endless parade of jaw-dropping events. Catcher in the Rye for the unabashed use of raw unacceptability, dragging unsavoury things out of the shadows and into common view for scrutiny. And the Confessions for the overall aim (I think) of creating a malleability and a weakness in the reader, via the abasement and frankness of the creator, towards a consideration of acceptance and reconciliation.

I'd encourage you to take a punt on it, and be in on that first wave that gets to respond to a text before all the other critics with fat weight behind their names come in on the game. You get first pick. So if you haven't already done so, go and buy the book.

Thanks very much for listening.

PRESUMED DEAD (2018)

Readers' Favourite January 6, 2019
Reviewed by Grant Leishman; Review Rating: 4 Stars

Presumed Dead is a classic "whodunit" and author Martin Knox does a very credible job of describing in detail the investigative techniques of crime scene analysis that the character had developed in his years as a police forensic scientist. The story is well constructed, with possible "red herrings" thrown in at appropriate points.

The two principal characters of Jane and Phillip are well drawn and easy to relate to and empathize with. It is interesting that, as in real life, Knox has sought to bring two people with polar opposite personalities together in a romantic relationship. Jane, the firebrand extrovert with a passion for politics, and Phillip, the quiet, methodical, introvert who struggles to relate to people on a personal level.

I particularly enjoyed the political undertones of the story and the ideals of what truly constitutes democracy. The idea of scrapping political parties and independent politicians voting on their conscience every time has been floated often and I think even trialled occasionally. It brings a real modern-day relevance to the story – one only needs to look at the political turmoil in the US at present to see the dangers of partisanship and party politics. All in all, a very satisfying read and one I can recommend.

OnlineBookClub May 21, 2020
Reviewed by Abacus; 4/4 Stars

The pace of the book is sedate, allowing for time to experience all the investigative techniques and the political power plays – so like politics today. Another intriguing aspect was Phillip's ability to understand Jane's mind by the movement and appearance of her left or right eye. The author was able to describe for us the conflicting emotions experienced by someone who suffers from post-traumatic distress syndrome (PTSD). The love story between Phillip and Jane also progresses during the chaos of fighting the council. We need a Jane and a Phillip now to solve the partisan American swamp politics.

I rate Presumed Dead **4 out of 4 stars**, for creativity, its focus on science, and the investigative techniques. It was a joy to read – educational and humorous. There are some detailed descriptions of an autopsy which may be too much for some readers.

I recommend this book to lovers of science, politics, crime investigation, love stories, authentic characters, and people who love a unique approach to a crime thriller.

Warm Witty Words, November 12, 2018
Reviewed by Donna Munro

I've read all Martin Knox novels, and Presumed Dead is a standout. Though I'm not a political person, I felt what it was like to be amid councillors, throwing words in heated discussions on public concerns, bouncing them across the floor like ping pong balls.

It's impossible to tell which politicians are lying and who abducted Jane. The story twists and turns, particularly after part 4. The reader will be right alongside Phillip as he tries to solve the crimes and his faithful bunch of friends, give us some hope that honourable, devoted politicians actually care about their community and the greater good. Anyone who has an interest in politics will love this masterful story."

Pre-publication review September 8, 2017
Reviewed by Phil Heywood, former Associate Professor and Head of Urban and Regional Planning, Queensland University of Technology.

'. . . a convincing and interesting story line on topics of currently seething public interest, including over-development of coastlines, political corruption and the roles of individuals and the media within contemporary society'

LOVE STRADDLE (2014)

Reviewed by Ian Lipke, October 4, 2014.
Editor of Media-Culture Reviews at Queensland University of Technology; author.

This novel by Martin P. Knox is vast in scope, scintillating in the brilliance of its conception and staggering in the creation of its hero. This is the work of a major talent

The concept is a straddle, a manipulation of the market in commodity futures:

'...an investor in commodity futures wants to spread the risk between commodities that are substitutes for each other... when the price of one goes down, the other goes down as well.'

Selwyn then applies such a concept to women and their affections to comical effect. It is in the teasing out of this idea into human behaviours that the originality of Knox's writing appears.

The last words in this review have to be delivered by the irrepressible Selwyn. Vicki has given him his marching orders and he has taken up with Helen.

'Vicki knows what I'm like. Her place in my straddle allows her full freedom. If it becomes possible, I still want to close out my short on her and exchange my love for hers, at my best price.

Until then, I also have a long position and am invulnerable.'

What a hoot! This book is recommended very highly. Get hold of a copy from Amazon. You'll enjoy it as much as I did.

THE GRASS IS ALWAYS BROWNER (2011)

Reviewed by Venero Armanno, December 10, 2011. Lecturer Creative Writing, University of Queensland; author of 9 best-selling novels.

'Martin Knox is the type of writer who knows how to tell a wonderful story and pose thought-provoking questions about life and the future. In his book The Grass Is Always Browner, Knox has managed to craft a political thriller, a romance and an allegorical tale of one man's prophetic journey towards enlightenment, all within the umbrella of a deeply satisfying work of speculative fiction. This is a novel to savour and Martin Knox is a writer to watch.'

AUTHOR BIO

Martin Knox grew up on a farm in Somerset, UK and graduated as a chemical engineer from Birmingham University. He worked in the petroleum industry in Canada. He researched alternative systems of government at Imperial College, London and emigrated to Australia where he worked in planning mine development projects. At age 40, he became a high school science teacher and wrote textbooks published by the Queensland Department of Education.

He has been writing fiction novels full time since 2013, with findings from his research of government, politics, crime, endurance running, democracy and satires about love and climate science. He has proposed an underground railway for Brisbane. He meets with groups to discuss writing, current issues and philosophy readings. He writes letters, zooms, plays the guitar, sings badly, plays chess and does outdoor gym.

He is divorced with children and grandchildren.

CONTACTS
mpknox46@aapt.net.au
Blog: https://martinknox.com

Contents

CHARACTERS

Names in order of first appearance.

Human	Presidents of Caruba	Felix Younucko, Natalia Alphancourt
Pig	Boar Presidents	Lords Napoleon, Nikos, Leonard, Miguel, Borat, Dimitri
	Sows	Gertrude, Hyacinth, Andrea, Monty, Algy, Charlotte
	Other	Ivan, Archie, Giraud
Cattle	Bulls	Tosser, Rondo, Earl, Henry, Jack, Arnold
	Favourite cows	Milk Bar, Pamela, Dolly, Jolene, Rose, Laura
	Other cattle	Buttercup, Clarabelle, Cynthia, Claudia, Simone, Myrtle, Hugo, Christine
Sheep	Rams	Scrote, Noddy, Eugenia, Harvey, Stanley, Norman, Barry, Amos
	Favourite ewes	Sharon, Trudy, Sophie, Dinah, Juliet, Barbara
Llama	Ewe	Hannah

Goats	Billy	Wizard, Artemis, Dionysus, Fred
	Nanny	Mellie, Coral
Horses	Stallions	Horace, Tiny, Goliath, Domino, Brandy, Jigsaw
	Favourite mares	Titani, Gloria, Lucy, Fiona, Blondie, Grace, Bella
	Other horses	Lucy, Scottie, Violet
Donkeys	Jacks	Mokey, Oscar, Dynamo, Dongle, Pickle, Eeyore
Mules	Jacks	Muffin, Big Ears, Biscuit, Jasper, Dougal
	Jenny	Muriel
Hinney	Jack	Jasper
Poultry	Cockerel	Solo, Gregory, Upstart, Glock, Randy, Andy
	Hen	Nestle
Sheepdogs	Bitches	Keep Me, Molly, Penny, Ruby, Lady, Missy
Cat	Tom	Asshole, Ammo, Hunter, Chester, Ranger
Raven	Male	Patriarch

ACRONYMS

EGHE: Enhanced Green House Effect
GHG :   Green House Gas
SR: Social Republic
DU: Democratic Union
ICBM: Intercontinental Ballistic Missile
UV: Ultraviolet
IR: Infrared
IPCC: International Policy Committee for Climates
RED: Renewable Energy Deal
ENSO: El Niño–Southern Oscillation
CO_2:   carbon dioxide
H_2O: water
CH_4:   methane
N_2:   nitrogen
O_2:   oxygen
BSE: bovine spongiform encephalopathy
AI: Artificial Insemination
pv: photovoltaic
PC: politically correct

PROLOGUE

When the worker animals had first peeped in at the pigs' party in the farmhouse seized from Farmer Jones, the hosts stood on two legs, mingling with their guests, with pigs and men indistinguishable. The pigs were celebrating with neighbours the success of the animals' revolution. They heard voices raised and saw a melee of carousing, with swilling of tankards of ale, pigs and men pushing, surging, yelling and falling about. Dismayed, the animal workers crept away from the window, wondering what would befall them next.

Seeing the pigs in human roles had made the worker animals uneasy. Their rebellion had been against human ownership, but although they had ousted Farmer Jones and proclaimed 'Animal Farm' theirs, the living conditions were no better now than before. They had to work at the limits of their endurance, received insufficient food and slept in damp, cold and draughty buildings.

Animal Farm could have been one of many farms on Caruba, an island near the equator, 1000 kilometres long and 200 kilometres wide. Caruba was 400 kilometres from the coast of the Democratic Union (DU), a superpower having 250 million, operating under economic precepts of capitalism espoused by Adam Smith, John Stuart Mill and others. It had political ties with the distant Social Republic (SR), a superpower also with 250 million, operating under socialism based on later philosophies of Karl Marx and Vladimir Lenin.

The human population of Caruba was 10 million. Half the island was hilly or mountainous, with the remainder under tea and coffee, with grazing for livestock. Businesses congregated in Salton, the capital, with a population of 1.2 million. The Caruba Government was led by President Felix Younucko. Despite the DU's resentment at Caruba's alignment with the SR, it supplied the island with diesel oil, manufactured goods and tourists.

Old Major, an obese crusty North Caucasian boar, had announced before the revolution on Caruba that animals would overthrow humanity. When the muddling drunken owner of Manor Farm on Caruba neglected his animals' food and living conditions, they had revolted and run amok over the farm. Farmer Jones had fled to a neighbouring farm, where he led other farmers in retaliatory attacks to recover his property. They had made two forays but were repelled by animals wielding farm tools as weapons. Several humans were injured and a few of the rebel animals were killed. Humans had attempted to repossess Jones' farm and when they failed, it became known as 'Animal Farm', operated by livestock animals. Neighbouring farmers viewed it with foreboding, in case animals tried to take over their own properties.

After the revolution, two pigs, Napoleon and Snowball, imposed central authority, enslaving the other animals, denying them rights and forbidding them to express wants.

Napoleon in Orwell's book was a huge Berkshire boar, black with white legs, white face, white tail and pink skin. His heavy body was deep-sided with a strong, arching back, a muscular firm build and blocky legs. Seen from the side, his face had a dish-shape, an upturned nose, a large jowl, short snout, short neck and erect ears. He had boisterous charm. His revolution had succeeded in destroying the old order, but issues of trust prevented creation of a new one. He suppressed opposition by surveillance and punishment. His planning was disastrous.

His rival Snowball was a boar of a different type: a Large White, large-framed, with light shoulders, a stretched appearance, deep sides, long legs and small hams.

Napoleon ousted Snowball and gained absolute power, managing Animal Farm for the benefit of the pigs alone, elevating them to a ruling class and enabling them to live a life of luxury. Among the animals there was whispered conjecture regarding the whereabouts of Snowball, but anyone mentioning his name was punished, so he was soon forgotten.

2

Napoleon had appointed himself Lord of Animal Farm. He aligned with the Caruban and Social Republican governments, wanting pigs to be the future rulers of the world. He monopolised information and personally interpreted world events, pretending he had high level connections with superpower leaders that enabled him to serve the animals' interests. He ensured his leadership was obeyed and exalted, ruling brutally over the other animals.

Lord Napoleon had ousted Snowball and gained power, managing Animal Farm for the pigs' benefit, enabling them to live a life of luxury. He led the Animal Party for nearly 40 years, first as secretary, then as treasurer and then as absolute leader of Animal Farm.

Central planning determined every aspect of life. All the animals, except for the pigs, worked long hours under harsh conditions and without reward. The workers were too fearful and ignorant to complain. The only machinery on the farm was a tractor and a windmill. Most tasks were done manually.

'Your conditions are not ideal but you must put up with them,' Lord Napoleon had said to the animals. 'They expect us to fail. You must ensure that we succeed. When they see our success, belief in Animalism will spread to neighbouring farms and outwards to bring the whole World under our control.'

The animals grew food for Caruba's markets. The Farm became known for high quality farm producte.

Lord Napoleon had surrounded himself with a pig oligarchy, with advisers, sycophants and informers, including an optimistic dog, Keep Me; a pessimistic cat, Asshole; and Patriarch, leader of a treachery of ravens who controlled the other animals' socialisation, information sources and expression of opinion. The structures of farm life that had enabled animals to cope under Jones collapsed. No social groups existed and the workers were unable to discuss their bad conditions.

From before the Revolution, the Ravens had opposed animal learning.

'You have no need for knowledge about how to lead your lives on the Farm,' Patriarch said. *'That has been the role of we Ravens to*

3

advise, since time immemorial. Our information is the best. We fly to distant places, meet Ravens there, find out about human and animal living conditions and bring back what we have learned to present in sermons at our services. It is most important that every animal comes to our services. You won't need to worry about ideas that are still being worked out, like science, technology and economics. We Ravens understand them and will provide all the advice you need.'

Lord Napoleon's secret police and militia had induced terror that transformed the Farm into a totalitarian state. Older worker animals realised Lord Napoleon had imported totalitarianism from the Social Republic. His regime imposed communism and tyranny, suppressing individualism, democracy, market capitalism and liberalism. Every worker animal felt isolated and expendable.

The commandment: 'ALL ANIMALS ARE EQUAL' had been written large on the barn wall after the revolution, but it had been changed mysteriously with words added: 'BUT SOME ANIMALS ARE MORE EQUAL THAN OTHERS.' The pigs distinguished between the various animal species for their compliance and utility, with pigs rated highest, horses next and goats lowest. The pigs maintained control by practicing terror frequently and arbitrarily.

Periodic purges eliminated victim groups judged to be incongruent with Lord Napoleon's world-mastery plan. Sent to the abattoir were: incurably sick; insane; critics; dissenters; animals tied by family marriage or friendship to critics of the regime; social misfits such as strays; nomads; refugees; asylum seekers; foreigners; followers of foreign religions and animals unfit for labour on the farm, due to disability, illness or inherited predisposition. Piggish ill treatment crushed the worker animals' psyches, even without violence and torture. The persecution was so brutal it could not be opposed. When there was resistance or rebellion by one animal, the pigs would retaliate viciously against the entire group. The worker animals were crushed into an obedient mass of conformity.

When the pigs took over, Lord Napoleon stereotyped and reviled the goats, victimising and persecuting them.

4

An aggressive farmer nearby had started invading his neighbours, trying to expand his domain to dominate his locality on Caruba island. His fighters were human mercenaries and animal conscripts. Farms in the district joined forces to fight back and Animal Farm suffered heavy losses in the fighting. By the time the invader was turned back, Animal Farm had swallowed several neighbouring farms and become a powerful agricultural conglomerate. There were tensions between the allies as they eyed each other's territories jealously and prepared to defend their borders.

The story continues a decade after Orwell's book, Animal Farm, ended in 1944. The pigs had resided in luxury in the farmhouse formerly Manor Farm and consolidated control over neighbouring farms.

'Leadership is demanding and we pigs share the work,' Lord Napoleon said. 'That is why title to the farm's lands has now been transferred into the pigs' names jointly.'

About this time, Old Napoleon chose his deputy, Nikos, to succeed him when he retired.

'Citizens of Animal Farm, under my leadership as your president, you have survived and enjoyed good lives,' he said. 'In the near future, Lord Nikos will succeed me. He will follow the traditions of Animalism, aligned with communism in the SR.'

When Old Napoleon died peacefully in his sleep, the workers felt his oppression lift off them. They hoped that Lord Nikos would improve their abject conditions.

CHAPTER 1 NIKOS

The animals were waiting in the farmyard for Lord Nikos to speak to them for the first time as Farm president. He was a British Saddleback boar with a large, black deep body and a white saddle over his shoulders and forelegs. He was the preeminent animal present, reclining on a *chaise longue,* on a makeshift platform left by Farmer Jones when he fled. He gazed over his audience confidently. The animals either sat on the ground, or lay with their legs folded under them.

He was from peasant stock, a rough-living pig who frequently swore foully and was out of his depth in ruling over bourgeois pigs and a proletariat of livestock species. They would enjoy seeing him humiliated.

Gertrude was Lord Nikos' favourite sow. She had tip-toed through the farmyard mud in high heels and made a sensational appearance. She had a red shoe fetish and had taken to wearing clothing items she had found in Mrs Jones' wardrobe. Today she wore a flowery skirt at mid-thigh, her belly swollen with piglets.

She ensconced herself in a bed of straw to one side of Nikos' platform.

'The turnout this afternoon is good,' she said to him.

'They don't have any choice,' he said.

The farmhouse had a telex machine and Lord Nikos had earlier sent messages notifying the SR high command of his accession, to ingratiate himself with them.

He had a commanding view of the animals and scowled from his jowls at the disarray in the audience before him. At his side was Keep Me, his faithful Border Collie, dangling her pink tongue. She was black with white shoulders and a white stripe down the centre

6

of her face. Lord Nikos rested a languid trotter on his black cat, Asshole, stretched out like a panther along the armrest of the *longue*. Half Siamese, he was glossy black with green eyes and a white tuft on his chest. Crouched growling beside Lord Nikos were four Rottweilers, his bodyguard and death squad. They were large strong dogs, with black bodies, their muzzles, throats and lower legs brindle.

At the front of the audience a row of corpulent pigs reposed, side by side. Behind them were crouched poultry and geese. In the next rows were lambs, then sheep and calves and a large red kangaroo. Behind was a row of cattle, a donkey and a mule, with horses at the back. On one side, intentionally shunned and shamed by separation, were goats. Small wild animals, rabbits, rats, mice, frogs and lizards, peered out from openings between hay bales.

The excitement of the crowd was taken up by the pigeons roosting in the eaves. They trod their perches excitedly, cooing, pirouetting for their amours, trying to climb on, occasionally allowed to mount, then losing interest and winging away to another dalliance.

Lord Nikos stood up heavily, erect on two legs. He over-filled a dark grey suit, with a white shirt, his tie loosely knotted and his flabby neck bulging from his unbuttoned collar. He raised a trotter.

'Quiet!' a goose hissed from the front.

'Animals,' he snorted gutturally. 'Napoleon appointed me as his successor before he died. I am your new president. I will lead you and together we will overcome problems. As you know, we are in danger from the thugs and cowards of the Democratic Union.'

Their island home, tiny Caruba, was in dispute with the neighbouring DU superpower.

'We must prepare to defend ourselves,' said Lord Nikos. 'Some of you workers will help President Felix Younucko with manufacturing for Caruba's armaments industry.'

They showed their agreement with Lord Nikos with a murmur of grunts and sighs. When the DU was mentioned, several young pigs squealed with indignation and impatience.

'The DU could attack us at any time,' he said. 'They would destroy our crops, our buildings, kill us and occupy our land. They

7

want us to stop competing for markets, resources and followers. They are jealous of Animal Farm's success under Animalism. Our distant benefactor, the Social Republic, has its eyes on Animal Farm too, demanding we on Caruba stop using agricultural chemicals and respect the rights of wild animals. They say pesticide use endangers wild animals. A DU report we have received says it is not true and makes more work for us. Anyway, because our friends the SR government want it, we will be cautious and stop using pesticides.'

He paused and glared around. Rats and rabbits shrank back between the bales and under the floorboards. Pigeons exploded from the rafters and flew outside.

'Your hard work and our management, comrades, have made Animal Farm prosperous, the first farm ever worked by animals, for animals. Humans resent our success and are arming to attack us. They want our land for themselves. We must stop them!' He ended with an angry squeal.

The dogs growled and bayed menacingly.

Led by bleating sheep, the workers chanted: 'Stop the humans! Stop the humans! Stop the humans!'

'We must get ready to fight,' Lord Nikos said.

The older animals had heard this before. The conflict with the DU had gone on for many years.

'They will come from the sea, as they did when Farmer Jones and the DU tried to take back the farm in the Gulf of Pigs attack,' said Lord Nikos. 'In the battle, Napoleon and I were in front. That traitor Snowball gored me, as I blocked his escape. Comrades, we must prepare to fight again, giving our lives if necessary. We must do as Winston Churchill said: 'We will fight them on the beaches and we will never surrender."

'Napoleon hid at the rear,' recalled Mokey. He was the oldest animal, a donkey jack, dark grey with black ears, cautious, melancholy, wise but cynical. *'The scratches on Nikos's back were not from Snowball's teeth but from crawling under a hedge to get away. The pigs were routed and fled. We worker animals stayed and fought. Many of us were injured.'*

8

'Snowball is still at large, plotting with our enemies to attack us,' said Lord Nikos. 'I am setting up a team who will design and assemble bombs, bazookas and missiles, to repel the DU when they attack. Defence is our top priority. Every animal is needed to work and every pig to supervise them.'

At this moment the sheep started bleating: 'Four legs good, two legs better.'

'It used to be 'two legs bad,' Tosser the bull said quietly to his favourite cow, Milk Bar. 'They changed it when the pigs stood up on two legs.'

Tosser was a massive Friesian, with a deep-bodied Bison front end, tapering to a narrow muscular rear, enabling him to turn quickly. He was black with white patches, white legs and feet, small horns, with a white shield emblazoned on his forehead.

'Two legs better! How ridiculous,' Milk Bar said. 'The pigs imagine they are humans . . .'

'Shh! We'll talk about it after,' he said.

Lord Nikos announced: 'Here are changes to your rosters.'

He read out a list of animals' names and their fieldwork assignments.

'To increase output, starting times this week will be half an hour earlier, finishing half an hour later.'

He sensed their resentment but was gratified by their obedience. They would realise that their time and every other aspect of their lives were under his control.

After, as they were dispersing to their workplaces, Milk Bar said: 'The pigs have forgotten they were once like us. We were all animals together then, equals.'

'I don't know what we can do to oppose them,' Tosser said. 'They seem to have taken over, behaving like humans.'

'It would be okay if it they were benefitting us,' said Milk Bar. 'But it is the opposite. I feel vulnerable.'

'You have every reason to feel anxious,' said Tosser. 'The rest of us are anxious too.'

9

'I can't go on like this,' she said. 'My ancestors passed on to me a desire to live under a tree in the grasslands. Wolves I can deal with, but not the insidious machinations of pigs.'

'We can survive if we adapt to the new conditions, without being provoked to rash actions.'

'I can't escape from worrying about this pig malignancy,' Milk Bar said. 'We don't know what will happen to us.'

'It's the thought that you might be able to do something to improve your lot that is upsetting you,' said Tosser. 'But you can't. All we can do is be ready to take our chances when they arise. Cattle on farms have always led unpredictable lives, controlled by others.'

'Cows are cared for in India, until they die of natural causes.'

'That is an ideal,' he said. 'To achieve that, humans would have to regard us as sacred. It could happen, but not soon. We must be patient.'

'I have to go and be milked,' said Milk Bar, heading for the cowshed.

Milk Bar was a large Friesian, a milk factory, from her broad muzzle, long flat back, and deep rear end to her large pendulous udder. She was quiet, caring and wise, a true partner with Tosser, the cattle's unofficial leader. Whereas he was gruff and abrupt, she spoke fluently and sweetly, simpering only a little.

When his friend Titani was given more work to do, the unfairness to her during pregnancy annoyed Tosser. Titani, an enormous black draft horse, was the largest animal on the farm. She had been traded for three cows, to work in a pair with Horace, second largest animal, a bay Clydesdale bred on the Farm. They ploughed from dawn to dusk, until exhausted, without any concession for her condition.

'It risks my foal to have to work so hard. I should get lighter work but the pigs don't care.'

Tosser was annoyed that the welfare of the foal could be threatened by the stress, but there was nothing he could do. Titani had another concern.

'My other worry is what will happen to my foal after it is born,' she said. 'The pigs sold my last foal after only two months.'

10

Horses were valuable because their work was at the centre of farming activity.

'Why are horses large?' Pamela, a calf, asked Milk Bar, her step-mother. She had been imported as a calf to diversify the cattle gene pool.

'I wasn't born on the Farm,' Pamela thought. *'I can hardly remember my mother and where I came from. But I feel like I belong here even though conditions are bad. The animals are friendly and smart. We have learned to talk with each other. Different animals have interesting points of view. I love studying science and discussing the farming issues.'*

'Humans have selected large horses to breed from.'

'Why are they so tall?'

'They are the heaviest and strongest farm animal, with large feet, for pulling ploughs and carts,' Milk Bar answered her. 'A carthorse can keep a plough turning up the ground without faltering. They can also kill an enemy with a kick. Beware their backlegs.'

'But Lucy is a small horse.'

Lucy was a Shetland pony.

'She was selected for work in underground mining, in low tunnels.'

Milk Bar had come to Animal Farm from a neighbouring farm, in a swap. Tosser had grown up with her and preferred her company to the other dozen cows in his harem. She allowed him to attend to the others, when they came into season, but she was loyal to him, refusing the younger bulls. She was almost continually pregnant and produced milk constantly year after year. It was a gruelling life and she was thin, her ribs like piano keys and her pin bones prominent. Feeding her calves and watching them grow could have brought her satisfaction, but the pigs weaned them early. Only one son, Rondo remained, the others having been traded off the Farm. Pamela was kept from her with the yearlings.

As Tosser's favourite cow, Milk Bar made sure she could match his information and analysis with her own. She relied on a network of animals to keep her informed of the workers and pigs doings as well as news from the outside world.

11

Milk Bar convened meetings of the Farm's livestock. She was respected as a positive and persuasive leader. Sometimes Milk Bar's life seemed to her to be too hard to bear and she became sad and uncommunicative. At these times Tosser would stay with her until she unwound and relaxed into the rhythm of the Farm. Her closest friend was Sharon, a ewe. She would visit her and divert her attention. They would chat together for hours.

Tosser was the largest of the cattle, the predominant male. Like most herd bulls, he was determined and could become impassioned. He felt responsible for the safety of the animals. He had been born on the farm and had never known any other home. The pigs allowed him to serve all the females, provided he kept younger bulls away. Already there were a couple of youngsters vying to be next in line for his position. They wouldn't tangle with him yet, respecting his seniority, greater size and dark aspect.

Domination by the pigs was unpleasant, but Tosser's grandparents had told him how the pigs had seized control after the revolution. He had taken over from a line of bulls going back to a grandfather who had chased Farmer Jones out. The pigs ascendance was well-established now and challenging them unthinkable. He sometimes wondered what he was supposed to do. He felt responsible for his cows and their young, but it wasn't obvious how he could protect them from hunger, hard conditions and the pigs' bullying.

The life he wanted would be free of pig control. As a herd animal he could accept predators taking the old, the sick and even the weak young, but the pigs' sending of animals to the abattoir was intolerable. But he knew if he attacked a pig it would be the end for him.

CHAPTER 2 IDEOLOGY

The ethos of their revolution bound the animals together and was revived at farm community meetings.

'Let us sing,' snorted Lord Nikos.

They sang together these words.

Animal Farm, Animal Farm,
Never through me shalt thou come to harm!

The animals joined in, singing the traditional patriotic words with gusto. After the singing, Lord Nikos stomped down off the stage, ending the meeting. The worker animals went silently with bowed heads to their work in the fields.

In the first days after the revolution, there had been a spirit of camaraderie on Animal Farm, with all the animals, even the pigs sometimes, working together to secure their future. That spirit had been lost when the pigs established themselves as despotic rulers and the farmhouse became their exclusive domain.

Pigs came down to the cowshed to milk the cows. The pigs had sold the calves to buy whisky. They took away the pails of foaming milk to the farmhouse, to make their mash.

Farmer Jones had operated a *laissez-faire* farm organisation, lubricated by fear and favour. Instead of the classless society Napoleon had promised, he kept the fear and favoured a ruling class of pigs. The pigs deployed the animals as mobile labour units, under whatever conditions of labour the pig guards chose. Animals' wants could not be voiced and they received barely enough food. The leader's ideology was arbitrary and fickle. Control was central, remote and insensitive to individual differences.

At night, pig guards were rostered to patrol the sheds and places where the animals slept, on an hourly schedule. If animals were talking, they would be warned and if it continued, pigs would beat up the offenders, injuring or even killing them. The worker animals countered by posting lookouts.

Religious, cultural, recreational and social groups had been eliminated. Lacking community, workers were atomised and felt superfluous. Napoleon's leadership offered them their only hope of recognition as individuals, from association with the success of Animal Farm. Animals declared unwanted for the running of the Farm were sold to the abattoir.

When the expected attack by Snowball did not occur, Lord Nikos had switched his attention from external threats to domestic matters. Whereas Napoleon had searched local farms for enemies, Lord Nikos fostered good relations with neighbours and stopped torturing and killing their animals. He terminated his secret police. He sent pigs to take over at adjacent farms and Animal Farm became the centre of a prosperous trading bloc.

Lord Nikos ended the purging that Napoleon had begun, sending supposed traitors and dissenters to the abattoir. But the slavery continued. The animals were owned by and controlled by the pigs and did not dare complain openly. In his last years, Napoleon had set up a Farm security agency that had jurisdiction over the animals' thoughts and talk. Lord Nikos expanded it, recruiting animal spies, with promises of large rewards.

The pig's hegemony could not be contested. Worker animals were unable to meet socially or unite. Species or interest group meetings and protest events were forbidden, arrests were made without hope of a trial and disappearances were common. The only political organ allowed was the Animalist Party.

Pig self-interest, greed, covetousness, resentment, lust for power and cowardice were rampant. The pigs conducted cruel experiments on worker animals to discover tolerances for starvation, for crowding in accommodation and ability to endure hard labour. The pigs exploited the strengths and weaknesses of the different animal breeds, making speciesism their main ideological weapon of class control.

'Some species are parasites,' they said. 'They take without giving.'

The goats' loyalties continued to be suspect and they were excluded or imprisoned.

'Treatment of the goats is shameful,' said Tosser to Milk Bar. 'Why are they picked on?'

'In the Bible, humans redeemed themselves by laying the sins of the people upon a goat and sending it into the wilderness,' she said.

'They are sacrificing scapegoats to expiate their sins against us,' Tosser said.

'Lord Napoleon had a scapegoat several years ago,' said Keep Me.

'What happened to it?' said Asshole, perched on a pile of bricks in the corner of the barn, doing a cat stretch.

'It escaped,' Keep Me said.

'I don't blame it,' said Tosser. The pigs allege goats eat more food and return less work than any other animal species. It's not true. Farmer Jones used to rely on them to keep his flocks of sheep together and lead them to new pastures when required. They had privileges, such as access to rich grazing in the orchard.'

'The other animals were envious of goats and have kept the prejudice alive,' said Asshole.

'The pigs keep us in fear by bullying the goats,' said Scrote, an active and creative ram. 'They force the goats to work ever-longer hours, starve them and shut them inside ruined farm buildings without shelter from cold and wet.'

When a group of goats tried to escape, the dogs hunted them down and they were whipped with knouts, in some cases to death. The treatment of the goats inculcated terror in the Farm's animal population.

'If you don't work faster,' a pig said to a sheep, 'we will send you to the abattoir.'

The pigs spread the terror and created division by having the animals select who to send.

15

The pigs' bullying knew no bounds. Young boars liked inter-species sex with sheep or with yearling cattle, of either gender. In small groups, boars gang-raped their victims. The penalties for non-cooperation were brutal. Animals who had been violated were traumatised but there was nothing the other animals could do to stop it. Tosser had asked Keep Me to take a complaint to Lord Nikos, but there was no response.

For relief from the brutal conditions, animals turned to religion. Patriarch led a treachery of Raven clergy, whom the pigs had exiled and persecuted, driving the Ravens' religious activities underground.

'What hope does Paradoxy give your followers?' Tosser asked Patriarch.

'It opposes totalitarianism with hope and search for truths,' the Raven said. 'It connects with the remnants of their religion from times past.'

Patriarch magnified pig virtue in his religion's dogma and so the pigs tolerated Paradoxy. Keep Me and Asshole lived in the farmhouse with the pigs and were complicit in their domination of the workers. Keep Me, like all dogs, was a sycophant whose main aim was to be spared from the cooking pot when the next of the regular famines beset the island. The farm had always had a sheepdog. Male dogs were preferred because they did not get pregnant, but they were rougher with sheep, more liable to bite, rather than nip as bitches did. Dogs mated with all-comers and as there was no demand for mongrels, the litters were tied in a sack with a rock and thrown into the dam.

Asshole wanted the pigs to feed him regularly. To escape the cooking pot in a famine, his strategy was to return to the wild and live by hunting. He was the only cat allowed on the farm. Females were driven away because kittens were unwanted.

'I don't need female company,' Asshole said. 'I have friends on other farms.'

He was a fiercely independent cat.

'You can be sure those two pets report our talk to the pigs,' Tosser said. 'They are spies and dangerous. But don't let them know we are on to them.'

16

One day when Milk Bar was there, Tosser told Keep Me: 'We need to know what Lord Nikos is planning to do with our animals who are too sick to go to work. If he won't provide medical care, all the animals will go on strike. Keep it quiet.'

It was his test to expose Keep Me's spying.

'If animals fall sick, their work has to be done by the others,' said Lord Nikos at a gathering of the animals. 'If sick animals complain, they will be taken to the hunt's kennels to be fed to the hounds. You would be wrong to imagine we would address your wants if you went on strike. We would take the ringleaders to the abattoir.'

Tosser knew that Keep Me had leaked his threat to Lord Nikos.

'What are you going to do about Keep Me?' Milk Bar asked him.

'Punishing her would drive her further away from us. Perhaps we can get her on our side somehow.'

'She might tell us what the pigs are up to.'

'You could ask her to warn us of any raids or purges,' Milk Bar said. 'If she is loyal to us, she will want to head off these injustices.'

Napoleon had used trials, confessions, assassinations and purges to enforce his ideology. Lord Nikos's judicial system was more lenient but more secretive, with harassment, demotion and exile. Keep Me began to supply Tosser with information she overhead from the pigs but her true allegiance was secret. She endeavoured to be everywhere at once and to her credit, succeeded. She always knew what was going on and both the workers and pigs relied on her.

CHAPTER 3 BOARDOM

Titani was a Shire heavy horse, descended from the legendary stallion Boxer. She was kindly and willing, strong-boned and muscular, with large feet for ploughing, the oldest and hardest working animal on the Farm. She was reaching the end of her working life but the pigs made no allowances. They had given her more and more ploughing to do with Horace, until their legs had buckled. She had foaled alternate years, pulling a plough while heavily pregnant. Pig rule was arbitrary to ensure an animal's contribution to the community was minimised and unfairly rewarded, as part of the terror that maintained pig control.

After harvest, Horace and Titani began the cultivation process, continuing for several months until replanting with barley seed. They walked side by side pulling a single furrow moleboard plough that cut off a long slice of turf and turned over the top foot of soil into the previous furrow using a shaped moleboard. Horace walked on the unploughed land, with Titani down in the furrow beside him, because she was taller. Each wore a padded collar around their neck with a breast strap between the front legs, connected to a pole passing back between the horses to a whippletree across behind them, tugging on the plough. Another horse, Queenie, followed behind, raising the plough on to a wheel holding a lever in her mouth, swinging it around when they reached the headland.

The team of three took great pride in their precise straight and parallel ploughing. They would plough across a field, furrow after furrow, taking several days to reach the other end. The yellow stubble and green weeds would be transformed into dark brown ridges, straight and gleaming, polished by the metal mole board of the plough.

18

On a cold day the horses' breaths would pulse like a steam engine. Enveloped in a cloud, the horses grunted with effort, harness leather creaked, small roots snapped as they were ripped apart, the metal scraped on stone and sea gulls screamed as they dived for worms. Sometimes the upturned sod would fall over onto a sea gull, trapping it. There was no time to stop for it, as the horses' goal was to keep going until their next break, when they could drink, eat and rest their aching muscles.

At the end of the day, tired from their exertions and having eaten, the horses joined Tosser and Scrote and talked together quietly, as friends do when they share concerns and want to help each other's understanding. Tosser was a large and formidable horned bull, Scrote a confrontational Dorset Horn ram, with a coil on each side of his head and a thick fleece. They were prominent leaders of the workers. Scrote was 2IC, under Tosser. He envied Tosser his large size and sharp horns. He could usually get his own way with Tosser by skilful argument, which he planned carefully.

'The pigs are going from bad to worse,' said Scrote. 'They don't understand how to run a farm.'

'They have never worked themselves and they don't respect us for the work we do,' Horace grumbled. 'I don't like it that they have taken over. They are cruel, lazy and dishonest.'

'Animals don't work on other farms,' Titani said. 'We have worked hard to keep our farm going, but the pigs have spent what we have earned on themselves.'

'They aren't interested in improving our lives,' said Tosser.

'They claim to be protecting us,' said Scrote.

'How?'

'They have dealt with the government, which could have taken over or helped Jones to get back.'

'They have kept us away from the rest of Caruba: I want to find out more about the outside world,' Tosser said.

The pigs supplied the animals with a news sheet they compiled: Farm Events. It was their propaganda. The analytical quality and investigative content of the articles was nil and the tone was dictatorial.

'It's faked news,' said Tosser, 'designed to keep us in fear.'

At the next farm community meeting, in his address to the animals, Nikos elaborated on the imperial ambitions of the DU in the west and of the vast Republic of Ceramica resurging as an economic power in the east.

'We pigs, as your leaders, are making progress with new projects that require your hard work to succeed,' said Lord Nikos. 'I know your wants are not all being met yet, but you must be patient. Comrades, do not be deceived by the Social Republican Government propaganda about conserving the natural environment. They have exaggerated our problems, for example land degradation. Sure, we could have done more to stop it; but we can fix the damage.

'A bigger problem is that humans want to end our occupation of this farm, grab the land for themselves and send us to the abattoir. They will eat us if they can and we must not give them the opportunity. The Caruban Government must build a wall right around Animal Farm.'

'A wall would keep us in,' said Mokey the donkey.

'Quiet. You'll get us both killed,' said Tosser. 'Humans fear the spread of Animalism. But so do the pigs.'

'Why do the pigs fear Animalism spreading?' said Wizard the goat, on the other side.

'It could fail in the outside world, lose traction here and then they would lose their privileges,' Mokey said.

'Do you mean the pigs lack confidence?' asked Titani.

'That's what I think,' said Mokey. 'Animal workers might not stay unless they are compelled to by a wall. Many of us would leave and take our chances with humans if we could. The pigs want a wall to keep us in, pretending it would defend against human attack by other Carubans or by the DU. The DU do not have territorial ambitions for the Farm, but will use it to demonstrate to their own people that Animalists have to be contained.'

20

'Do you mean a wall would stop our philosophy spreading?' said Wizard. 'Would human supremacists want a wall to deter animal liberation from reaching the DU and other countries?'

'Yes, that's right,' said Tosser. 'Both sides want a wall, either to exclude or constrain us.'

'Development of humans and animals would be kept separate,' said Mokey.

'The pigs don't want animals to be liberated.'

'Humans want to use animals for menial and dangerous tasks, like the SR sent up that dog Laika in a satellite,' said Tosser.

'The dog had nothing to do,' said Mokey.

'Laika illustrated the unimportance of astronauts,' said Tosser. 'Rocket scientists prefer unmanned space flights because humans are difficult to keep alive and make more mistakes than robots. They sent the dog up for the human interest, so their people would allow public money to be spent on robot adventures in space.'

'The pigs regard us as robots too,' said Wizard. 'They want us to work hard behind a wall.'

'The pigs' only interest in our liberation is to lord it over us. A wall will help them do it.'

A group of animal workers inspected the partly completed wall.

'What do you suppose is Nikos's purpose?' asked Milk Bar. 'Is it simply to rule over us?'

'Lord Nikos says the wall is to keep out enemies, but it conceals us inside and hides our bad conditions, away from the view of those who would want to see Farmer Jones reinstated,' said Tosser. 'There are plenty of humans who would like to see Farmer Jones running Manor Farm again.'

'Don't be so pompous,' said Milk Bar to him. It was true. The bull was wrapped up in controlling the situation, telling the others what to think.

'What do you think,' he asked them.

'Building a wall is risky,' said Scrote. 'Treating us badly could be Lord Nikos' downfall.'

'If they want the whole world ruled by pigs,' said Sharon, his favourite ewe, 'this is not the way to do it.'

A high wall was completed right around the Farm, topped with barbed wire.

The superpowers were embroiled in a Cold War, a contest for global supremacy. The SR and DU governments were more interested in military expansion than in space exploration. The arms race created uncertainty in Caruba.

'The DU might attack at any time,' warned Lord Nikos. 'To pay for our defences and the wall, you are required to increase farm output.'

The animals had to work harder, without either improvement of working conditions or better nutrition.

'What can we do?' asked Sharon. She jealously guarded her position as Scrote's favourite ewe, driving away other ewes inclined to linger with him. Sharon was box-shaped, like him, but without horns. The pair were respected for their unobtrusive oversight of the smooth running of the Farm. She attended meetings and took part in discussions with other animals and was the worldly-wise matriarch of the ewe flock.

'Nothing now,' said Tosser. 'We will watch and wait.'

'The pigs are a menace,' said Scrote.

'It's better than being ruled by humans, don't you think?' Sharon said.

'Under Animalism we're no better off than we would have been under Farmer Jones,' said Tosser.

He was about the same maturity as Scrote, middle-aged, but cattle often lived twice as long as sheep and had seniority. Most of the cattle were Tosser's offspring. With Milk Bar he had fathered Rondo, Cynthia and Myrtle. She had borne calves regularly, until the pigs had castrated his son Hugo, nicknamed Steroid and started taking calves to the slaughterhouse. Then they had refrained from mating.

They longed for liberation.

'Perhaps when Lord Nikos goes things will improve,' said ewe Sharon.

22

Sharon had a Suffolk mother and was fathered by a Border Leicester ram. She had a speckled face with a Roman nose and long loose wool. Most of her flock had a Suffolk black face and close thick fleece. She had borne twin lambs for three past seasons, all of them to Scrote.

Scrote ran with the Farm's flock of 50 ewes in Autumn for Spring lambing, with a sheep's gestation taking 150 days. He could manage 3 or 4 ewes per day, but by the time all 50 were served he was exhausted. When the ewes had all been impregnated, he was separated to rest in the orchard with a barren ewe, a wether and younger rams, who mounted each other endlessly, in alternation, until the next tupping season.

In summer, Scrote indulged his interest in science, studying, researching and teaching the other animals. Compared with the other species, sheep were determined and would repeat experiments until satisfied. Scrote enjoyed helping younger sheep to test their ideas and obtain useful results. Besides meteorology, he had students investigating genetics and horticultural practices.

Sharon's udder had two teats, suitable for twin lambs. She dreaded having a triplet, for she wouldn't be able to feed them properly and the pigs would take one away and transfer it to a ewe having a singleton. Getting the lamb accepted by the unrelated ewe required experience. The pigs would tie a sheepdog in the surrogate's pen when they introduced the strange lamb, causing her great fear, triggering her kin protection instinct, with a usual result of strong bonding between ewe and lamb. She would join the other ewes, bumbling around each with two lambs in tow, as pretty as violets in Spring.

CHAPTER 4 FARMWORK

Lord Nikos's regime was oppressive and vicious. Animals were forbidden to talk about the Farm's policies. They conducted lightning raids to catch any animals fraternising and searched the sheds and stalls regularly for weapons.

The workers wanted to oppose the pigs but did not dare to recruit, train or arm insurgents. The pigs had a network of spies, coercing animals to reveal potential treachery, with threats to their offspring, or to relatives. Animals found out were torn apart by Nikos's dogs and their friends killed. The animals went in fear of their lives, even when doing wholly innocent tasks. They were too exhausted from their work to organize a rebellion.

'We're prisoners,' Tosser whispered to Mokey as they worked side by side in a field. They had worked together for many years and enjoyed each other's company. 'Even if we get over the wall, we cannot escape because there is nowhere we can go outside the Animal Farm bloc, except to another farm.'

'Humans won't give us refuge,' said Mokey who had a mournful outlook. 'Escaped livestock don't get asylum. We would be returned and punished.'

'More likely killed,' said Tosser mildly. He was normally optimistic but their situation was dire.

'Our rebellion didn't liberate us,' said Mokey sadly. 'The pigs make us work harder than Farmer Jones did. Animals may never be free. It says in the Bible that on the fifth day God said unto them: *'Man shall have dominion over every living thing that moveth upon the earth'*. God has given humans a superordinate right over other animals.'

24

'The Bible is horseshit,' said Tosser. 'I'm not going back to the old days under Farmer Jones.'

'Conditions are getting worse,' said Mokey.

'You miserable old bugger,' said Tosser. 'This is a beautiful place. Look at those heifers over there! Aren't they a picture?'

'Beauty lies in the eye of the beholder.'

'There's more to it than that,' said Tosser. 'Did you ever wonder how the tail on Farmer Jones' peacock could have evolved?'

'Yes, amazing,' Mokey said. 'I suppose peahens have always wanted extravagant patterned tails on their cocks. The males simply show willing to display and serve the hens who most like their tail. The best tails get most of the matings and the worst tails fewest. Having a territory or nest doesn't seem to come into it. Females take their chances with all of them going for the same peacock tail pattern.'

'You admire heifers for having what it takes, don't you?'

'Of course.'

'Do cows decide which one the bull goes to?'

'It's hard to say. Perhaps having a certain characteristic does it,' said Tosser.

'Or they might all seem irresistible.'

'It's a pity you don't have a jenny,' said Tosser. 'But I've seen you with Titani haven't I?'

'She's a bit tall, but when we lie down, it does it for me,' said Mokey.

'Go for it Dude!'

Later that year Titani bore Muffin from Mokey, a large, strong and docile mule. With his ears flopping, lumpy awkward body and knobbly knees he was everyone's friend. He worked long hours plodding around the mill turntable. Although he possessed lusty instincts and engaged with Lucy, no progeny resulted, probably due to the chromosomal difference that made mules infertile.

Lord Nikos liked to take visitors on a tour of the farm. In a field, they saw four animals lying belly down on a buckrake behind a tractor, spanning rows of crop plants. As they passed over the plants,

25

the workers reached down and pulled out weeds from the rows with their mouths.

'Productivity has doubled since we animals took over,' Lord Nikos said.

A few days later Cynthia, a heifer parented by Tosser and Milk Bar, slim, pretty and sassy, her neat udder not yet milk-producing, had refused to go with the others to weed turnips from the buckrake.

'I can't do anymore weeding,' she said. 'My tongue is raw from pulling weeds and my back hurts. I won't go.'

Lord Nikos turned his dogs on her. They tore out her throat and she bled to death. Many of the animals were present. It was sudden and they were shocked. They were too frightened to do anything except continue with their work, grieving. They lacked the unity needed to oppose the pigs.

Tosser tried to hold back the negative thought that he would be allowed to live only as long as he worked in with the pigs.

'The killing of Cynthia was very wrong, especially as it was done by animals,' said Mokey.

'Child labour enforced by murder!' said Tosser. 'There is no limit to the pigs' brutality. Cynthia's unwillingness should have been dealt with by our elders, as a problem for the community. We won't put up with her life being cruelly terminated. We will strike back when the time is right.'

'What can we do?' asked Milk Bar.

'We can rise up and overthrow them,' said Tosser.

'You'll get us killed.'

'If we plan carefully, we can overcome them. We must start collecting weapons.'

Keep Me, the collie, took Tosser aside. 'I overheard the pigs talking. They're going to raid the stables this evening.'

'What are they looking for?' asked Tosser.

'A hand axe has disappeared from the tool shed.'

'Thank you, Keep Me.'

Keep Me wagged her tail. 'You won't let them put it back in the shed before the raid, will you?' she asked.

'Why not?' Tosser said.

26

'The pigs might suspect I tipped you off. There shouldn't be any workers hanging around the stables, either.'

'No,' said Tosser. 'But I'm not sure how much your information is going to be worth, if we can't act on it. You're a double agent and have to stay one step ahead of both of us. Be careful, won't you?'

When Keep Me had gone, Tosser asked around to find out who had taken it.

'Why would a worker animal want a hand axe?' asked Milk Bar.

'For self-defence,' he said. 'Many of us have stolen or made a weapon and hidden it. Without our weapons we could be slaughtered in a pogrom, as has happened in the SR.'

'Humans have guns in the DU,' Milk Bar said. 'They haven't had pogroms there.'

'We can't get guns,' said Tosser. 'But we need weapons to guarantee our freedom from a regime that is tyrannical and becoming more abusive.'

Tosser warned the others of the coming raid. 'Pretend to be surprised,' he said.

That evening the pigs searched the stables.

'At least Keep Me has shown us some loyalty,' Tosser thought. *'The next step for her is to feed our misinformation to the pigs.'*

Tosser exaggerated how animal workers' ill health made them unable to perform their duties and Keep Me told it to the pigs. The pigs' allowed other workers to do their work. After that, Tosser used Keep Me several times to mislead the pigs.

Animals were rostered to harvest apples from the orchard into storage in the apple barn, or to sell in the town. The pigs had purchased Horace after the legendary Boxer had foundered. Horace moved along the rows of fruit trees as a mobile platform, with animal pickers standing on his back. Other animals used ladders to reach the fruit.

Human visitors talked with animal workers and were impressed by their language skills.

'Amazing,' they said. 'Animals think like we do.'

It didn't seem to occur to them that the animals regarded their meat eating as offensive.

The pigs obtained a Government loan to pay a contractor to construct a tourist resort where Farm land abutted the coast, using the animal workers' labour. The new resort was fabulous. The Caruba Government and the animal workers expected human tourists to bring prosperity, but the pigs occupied the guest rooms, enjoying swimming pools, saunas, jacuzzis, sports facilities, a restaurant, tropical gardens and burlesque entertainment. A 'geisha gilt' service met pig demands for erotica.

The pigs kept the animals hard at work, growing crops to pay for their recreations. When there was a break in their toil, the animals threw themselves down on the grass exhausted, but not without hope. Despite their exhaustion, it was their own farm, a republic, no matter that the pigs held the title deeds. It belonged to them and always would. They enjoyed the fresh, sharp, tangy taste of apples filched from their own trees. When they could, they strolled up to Lookout Point and gazed out over the island, admiring the view. They belonged here and momentarily felt safe and happy.

They trusted each other and solidarity emerged.

'United, united, we will never be defeated,' they chanted quietly together as they returned to the fields and stooped to their work. Sometimes liberation seemed close.

CHAPTER 5 ANIMAL LEARNING

The Animal Farm revolution was widely known on Caruba. It had ignited the hopes of enslaved livestock animals that they would soon be liberated but years had passed without the hoped-for liberation eventuating.

Farm animals everywhere had dreamed of freedom ever since they were taken from the wild and domesticated by humans. With the passing of time, the dream had receded but not disappeared. Capitulation to humans and slavery was a Faustian bargain that bought protection from enemies, food and shelter, at the cost of an eventual abattoir death, arguably kinder.

The certainty of being taken to the slaughterhouse detracted from animals' happy living. A belief of Animalism was that a saviour would come one day and liberate them, but no-one had come and few still believed it.

Most workers still followed the egalitarian precepts of Animalism begun by Old Major, who had predicted a worldwide movement of animals along a path to freedom. The seizing and holding of Animal Farm was a triumph. Freedom had been short-lived because control had passed from humans to pigs. Through bluster and bullying, the pigs elevated themselves to controlling the activities of the workers, replacing the human bourgeoisie as a higher caste.

The revolution had stimulated the animals to question their subservience and consider possible alternatives. Domestication by humans had atrophied the innate reasoning and problem-solving abilities they had depended on to survive in the wild. When the pigs ascended to power, it had been surreptitious, taking advantage of workers bewildered by the complexity of pig skills and languages.

The animals had lost ability to act independently and became workers. Wild kangaroos had been employed and adapted to kitchen work by the pigs, in a domestic animal role.

The farm animals respected the few wild animals that lived in the vicinity of Animal Farm: badgers, foxes, rabbits and birds. Their freedom was a constant reminder to the animals not to accept their captivity as final.

On assuming power, the pigs began daily language lessons, led by a human linguist from the University of Salton. Afterwards, there were classes for the animals. The pigs allowed the workers to learn English and Science. They seized this opportunity, imagining it could lead to independence and freedom from captivity.

A teacher came from the university for lessons twice weekly. All the animals adapted their grunts, snorts, bellows, bleats, cackles and hisses into Pidgin English, with elements of piggish.

The Pidgin English vocabulary was small and easy to relate to English speakers and texts, in the following examples.

How you dey? – How are you doing today?
Wetin dey happen? – What's happening?
Make you no vex me! — Don't upset me!
I go land you slap – I will slap you!
I wan chop – I am hungry
Make we comot — Let us go out

At first, Mokey didn't takeup the offer to learn Pidgin English..

'Can't you see this is how we can get equality with humans?' Scrote said.

'You're dreaming,' said the donkey. 'Learn English if you want, but leave me out.'

'It won't succeed unless we all learn it,' Scrote said. 'You can't quit on us, you useless piece of shit.'

Mokey was offended and tried to kick Scrote, who butted him, knocking him over.

30

Scrote was on a short fuse because sheep's lives were brief and they lived in the shadow of the abattoir.

When Tosser arrived with Milk Bar, they heard what had been happening.

Tosser was indignant. Mokey was hiding behind his lack of language, wise but morose. 'Mokey, you will come to the language class, even if I have to stick my horn up your skinny arse,' he said. 'How dare you try and skive off!'

The donkey attended, becoming one of the better students.

The workers went to the language classes for reasons that varied.

'I want to insult the pig bastards in a language they understand,' said Rondo. 'They killed my sister Cynthia.'

Animals adapted their own languages, quickly learning passable Pidgin English and adding expressions from their own languages that they all learned to use. They learned to read English too, reciting passages from their books and discussing the meanings. Conversation challenged them but they enjoyed it as a relief from the aching loneliness of their servitude.

'Pigs and workers need to practice with each other,' said the teacher.

They all learned to read, speak, listen and write in Pidgin English and Science. At first, the pigs refused to speak the languages of the other animals and this inhibited their learning. At their own peril, the animals had to learn to interpret the pigs' guttural tones. Conversely, the pigs benefited by learning animals' renditions of piggish. The language that developed had sounds that were the least common denominator of speaking and listening ease. The workers found learning scientific concepts easier than informal topics because the terms were defined, organised in sentences and composed into logical arguments.

Animal Farm became a place where development of language skills was an integral part of everyday life, for solving problems, dealing with each other and recreating. The new language was aided by signing. Primates sometimes use their digits for signing, but the animals made signs using a common code of movements of: eye, leg, head, shoulder and body movements. These conveyed messages, for a shrug could sometimes be used when words could not.

The teacher addressed the worker animals after class.

'It may take you some time to talk well. We will see if you pick up the language as quickly as the pigs have. There could be differences between species.

'Washoe, a chimpanzee in the DU, has set the bar at 350 words of sign language, using them spontaneously and appropriately for 14 consecutive days,' the tutor said. 'We will find out if you Farm animals can do as well.'

'Hain't no chimp gonna beat me,' said Rondo. 'What signs and sounds should I learn?'

'Leaving out your bull-dust would be a good start,' said Steroid. He often joshed with his brother, not letting his emasculation come between them.

Animals could see the benefits of communicating in English. They helped each other learn English and most of them readily picked up a vocabulary of 300 words, while Rondo achieved 1000. He knew enough to understand the pigs' instructions for farm work.

'You animals are amazing,' said the teacher. 'You learn quicker than the pigs!'

'We're smarter!'

'I can see that now. How come they're in charge of the farm?'

'They're pushy.'

'I hope you'll be able to talk with them into letting you have a say.'

'We're working on it.'

The animals began to use English for communication amongst themselves. Some of the animals learned slowly and had to be helped. Lucy the pony helped Titani the giant carthorse mare, who seldom spoke. Horses' discourse was generally protracted but it was not known whether this was because their processes were more exacting, or because their ability was limited. Horace was unable to lead a group discussion, although his memory was good. They considered his aversion for talk to be wisdom.

"I can get a lot of the heavy work done,' he said. 'The others can help me with fine work that I'm not so good at. Together we can keep the Farm going. I'm not a talker. I believe most things will happen anyway, so I have nothing to say.'

Their teacher told them human children at about age three years suddenly open brain 'windows', with rapid gains in vocabulary and grammar. This learning phenomenon was explained as maturational 'brain plasticity'. Liberation opened a window too and they made rapid gains.

Humans had supposed that animals' intelligences would be insufficient to learn English and Science, but it was discovered that the livestock animals possessed innate skills that domestication had repressed. Intelligence had been measured under unfavourable conditions and neither wild animals', nor livestock animals', skills had been recognised. The animals were capable of abstract problem solving. Denied opportunity, their abilities had atrophied. They had not been able to learn and when the opportunity presented, they took it up with alacrity.

The workers' egalitarian ideals had been repressed by Napoleon's and subsequent regimes, but they had not been extinguished. Resentment of pig tyranny simmered.

A factor mitigating the pigs' arrogance was their fondness for Science. They wanted to replace the customs, myths and country lore, that had prevailed in earlier human management of the Farm, with empirical know-how and established theories. In short, they wanted success that exceeded that of the human farmers in their neighbourhood.

Lord Nikos's ambitions were expanding and for his takeover he needed compliant and willing workers able to operate autonomously at neighbouring farms. He sent workers who could solve problems. Lord Nikos and the other pigs continued to dominate and terrorise, but there was gradual improvement in the workers' living and working conditions. They were keen to learn, enjoying learning that brought more food and better living.

Despite their interest in science, the pigs were lazy and indolent students. They did not follow normal rules of discourse and their

33

utterances lacked courtesy, logic and reason. They used unscientific terms like *truth, prove, disprove* and *fact* that the animals' abhorred.

'The pigs' hubris will be their undoing,' said Tosser. He was impatient that the pigs' learning was so slow. 'History has recorded evil empires of the complacent, with greedy and self-indulgent humans being undermined and overthrown by their former slaves. Learning is freedom.'

The teacher from the University of Salton developed linguistic concepts enabling oral and written communication in Pidgin English between all the domestic species. Wild animals declined to learn. Because the pigs were keen to adopt latest farming techniques, researchers from the university's farm came to instruct the worker animals. The agricultural college enrolled some animals as students and Animal Farm conducted crop and machinery trials.

With their Pidgin English vocabulary and grammar, the animal workers learned discourse, argument and debate. The pigs were less adept because their arrogance and stubbornness prevented lively discourse. The animals learned most from each other but when pig Ivan, Nikos' deputy, tutored them and helped them understand subject matter from the internet, they learned to investigate whatever interested them.

Ivan guided the animal learning leaders, Scrote and Noddy and they passed their learning to the other workers. They learned to reject remnant beliefs of monarchism, religion and Stalinism, which had inhibited their understanding.

The animals varied in their ability to acquire human skills. Writing challenged cloven feet, requiring mouth-held tools for keying. English diction was difficult for ungulates accustomed to emitting long and low sounds. Whereas animals were disadvantaged in some skills, they had advantages in some others. For example, cattle had excellent memories and sheep were good at group work.

Ravens boasted they had spiritual abilities and could communicate with a supernatural being. The pigs rejected this claim, until the Ravens declared they had found supernatural qualities in the pigs' leadership. The Ravens adapted their religion to supporting the pigs with moral guidance ideas they could impose on the worker

34

animals, such as exposing non-compliance in their colleagues. The Ravens' influence on the worker animals waned as they gained scientific understanding.

Discussion amongst the workers had initially been discouraged as counter-revolutionary but as their knowledge and interest increased, they talked amongst themselves when the pigs weren't around. Their perennial favourite topic was liberation from their servitude. The topic was forbidden but secretly amongst themselves their criticisms of the pigs multiplied. With a language in common the animals could pool their information and understand events in the outside world.

'It's not fair,' said Noddy to Scrote as they watched fat lambs being loaded into a trailer to go to the slaughterhouse. 'Why are our best young offspring being killed?'

'Humans like to eat them and the pigs like to make money,' said Scrote, 'There's nothing we can do to stop it. What would you do about it?'

'Even if humans won't change their diets, the pigs should recognise that supplying human greed does not justify killing. Pigs are being slaughtered on other farms. Don't our pigs have consciences?'

The pigs regarded the worker animals as inferior. They dismissed the animals' concerns without hearing them. The animals regarded the pigs fearfully, as hostile, stupid, remorseless and dangerous.

'Could we change their minds about sending the lambs?'

'It will be difficult, but I won't give up hope. It's our most serious problem. We're getting smarter and with affluence the pigs are getting dumber.'

They never doubted that one day animals would be liberated.

CHAPTER 6 INAUGURATION

The animals were gathered in the barnyard, to hear Caruba's President Felix, a bearded man, standing on the platform with Milk Bar and Scrote. Behind them in a row were Lord Nikos with his henchpigs. The animal workers were in a packed audience, spruced up for the occasion, jostling to find space near friends and jesting with each other. In front of them was a group of young animals, playing at chasing. When Nikos's deputy Ivan stood in front of them, they scurried to sit down and attend.

'Animals: our President of Caruba, Felix Younucko will now speak.'

There was applause.

Good afternoon, animal workers. Today we have gathered to inaugurate a development in education by my government and Salton University. We are following the SR's lead in replacing religion with science within our system of communism. We on Caruba depend on the SR for security, defence, finance, investment and trade. Our best hope for peaceful co-existence on Earth is education.

Animal Farm now has a new education office. It will provide teachers and materials for classes in English and Science, to equip animal workers with skills for modern farming. I want to acknowledge the work of your voluntary instructors who have been conducting classes here for many years. Lord Nikos has told me animal workers have already learned basic English, basic science and are solving farming problems. These are great achievements and my heartfelt congratulations to all of you.

The new education office will continue your learning, with more advanced subjects, such as nutrition and meteorology. I hope you will enjoy your studies and they will bring you closer to your goal of liberation.'

There was applause.

'Animal Farm is well known to our parliament in Salton. One day soon a representative from your Farm will attend parliament as an observer. This could lead to more participation in Caruban society by farm animals. I look forward to that day. Thank you.'

The audience clapped dutifully.

Ivan announced: *'Next is your Convenor, Milk Bar.'*

The cow on the stage sauntered forward. She was large and white, with black patches and a wedge-shaped body that widened from her muzzle back to a voluminous rear end, with a huge udder. Her shape had first been imagined and then created by humans applying artificial selection to cattle breeding over centuries. To display her magnificent proportions, she stood in profile, her wise head turned sideways to speak to them, her voice mellow and placid.

'Good morning animals. Good morning President Younucko!

'Thank you for coming to open our new education office. It is an important development, made possible by the support of your government and the university. Our classes have had volunteer instructors in temporary rooms, but today the arrangement becomes permanent, with classrooms and the opening of an office to organise our studies.

'I want to say a few words about some animals without whose hard work this facility would not be possible.

'We thank Horace the horse, our hardest working student of English, for learning to sign. The sign language has been taken up by all the species. We have reached a stage where every animal can communicate basic needs and if necessary call upon others to help in interpretation. Isn't it marvellous that an animal as large as Horace can use a flick of an ear to convey his meaning to others!

37

'Scrote, our leader of the sheep, has led us to learn science, teaching us vocabulary and theories we can use to discuss farming problems with the pigs and others.'

The pigs behind her shifted uncomfortably. Milk Bar, as the dominant worker animal, required their attention, but they were not accustomed to being spoken to by a worker for so long and began to talk together.

'You have been learning other skills, such as behaviour and courtesies,' said Milk Bar. 'Good manners are so important. Some individuals are more courteous than others.'

Milk Bar paused and gave the pigs a meaningful look. Her confrontation was sensed and attention switched to her.

'Finally, we animals have come together from time to time to advise the pigs of our wants. We have been fortunate to have my partner Tosser to help us agree what we most want. Hopefully our wants will have increasing attention.
'I hope you will continue to support learning and attend classes. Thank you.'

Applause was enthusiastic, for Milk Bar was respected. This placid, modest and wise matriarch was a strong voice in the community calling for better conditions.

'Our last speaker is Scrote.'

Scrote the ram stepped up haughtily, with his massive curling horns. Tosser had urged him to talk.

'You have to speak to us,' he said. 'You are our chief educator.'

He was dignified and grandiose, with an iron will, contemptuous of sentiment and self-congratulation. He had the determination of a military campaigner. He would transform the livestock, weak and uncertain, into a knowledgeable workforce by his example of diligent study.

'Animals! We are on an exciting adventure,' Scrote began. *'Since the Revolution when we took over, we have sustained life and learned farming skills, using English and science. The next step is to learn alternatives for animals to increase their responsibilities and rights and gain the liberation we urgently want.*

'To achieve our place as equal citizens, we need to develop our knowledge of Animal Farm in relation to Caruba and the World. We animals have gained representation in Caruba's Parliament, where our special circumstances are known and respected.

'You are fortunate to have able teachers. Tosser will lead us in citizenship studies and towards liberation. Patriarch the Raven will lead us in our study of international relations, to find out Caruba's alternatives in relation to the DU and SR. Finally, Caruba has recently suffered extreme weather events and our climate could be changing. We need to prepare for change and I will begin a class on meteorology.

There are enough different areas of study that no animal should lack interest or feel left out.

'I look forward to seeing all of you in the classes.

'Thank you.'

Scrote finished and stepped down to applause.

After that the meeting became social. President Younucko and the pig leaders went down from the platform and mingled with the worker animals. Milk Bar introduced President Felix to the others and he stayed talking with Lord Nikos and Deputy Ivan at the front. Rondo, her son, joined them.

The new education office, where animals would enrol in classes, was situated in the tack shed where the pigs had a shelf with books on English, science, maths, agriculture and other topics. The animals referred to it as their Library.

Scrote had found a book on weather prediction and studied it. He had obtained other science books from visitors. He had enough information for his meteorology class. The animals would study weather by practical observation, measuring conditions and analysing the data, applying the findings to their farm.

In the first class, later that week, about 30 animals turned up.

'We will begin with temperature,' Scrote said. 'Is that reasonable?'

'Why not the Sun? That causes weather.'

'True,' said Scrote. 'Temperature is the Sun's main effect. We can infer from it what the Sun does.'

The others remained silent.

'Is temperature important?' asked Noddy, trying to help his father get a discussion going.

'We need to know and understand temperature to improve our farming,' Scrote said. 'It affects seed germination, plant growth and animal nutrition.'

'We can't do anything about temperature, can we?' Noddy asked. 'So what's the point of studying it?'

'Accurate weather forecasts are important for good farming,' Scrote said. 'To forecast the future you need to measure the present. I have found a book that tells how to measure air temperature.'

'To measure air temperature, you need a thermometer, not a book,' said Noddy.

It was impertinent, but he wanted the others to get more involved in the discussion.

'A book can help us measure,' Scrote said. 'There are different ways to take thermometer readings, at different places and different times.'

'You can stick a medical thermometer in your mouth, under your arm or up your arse,' Noddy said.

The others laughed.

'Arses don't come into it,' said Scrote. 'For air temperature, the thermometer is put in the shade, never in full sun.'

'You need a special kind of thermometer to measure the weather,' said Tosser, sitting at the back. 'There's a weather station at Caruba airport. They publish their measurements. Could we ask to see their data?'

'Good idea,' said Scrote. 'Tosser would you get in touch with them.'

He agreed.

The lesson continued with a discussion of local weather conditions and how these varied throughout the year.

A week later, they had heard back from the airport weather office, that they wouldn't have time to share their temperature data.

'If you measure temperature daily and send us your temperatures at 3-monthly intervals, we'll comment on them,' they said.

Tosser persuaded the pigs to buy a weather station kit for the farm. When it came, Scrote studied the instructions and supervised installation of the louvered box on the farmhouse lawn. Noddy helped him dig a hole for the post. They fixed the box in position 1.5 metres above ground level.

When they had finished, Tosser, Keep Me and Asshole came and inspected it.

'What's the interest in measuring temperature?' asked Asshole. 'It never stays the same very long.'

'To find out if there's another ice age coming.'

'How would we know that?' asked Noddy.

'There would be cooling.'

'What if we're still warming from the last ice age?'

'Warming could be a problem in hot countries like Australia.'

'Eskimos might not mind a bit of warming,' Noddy said.

'Not when the ice gets too thin for ice fishing,' said Tosser.

'They could go fishing in a boat.'

'That would mean changing their lifestyle,' Tosser said. 'People don't like change.'

'I do,' said Noddy, giving a jump and a buck. He was a tearaway.

'That's because you're young,' said Tosser. 'You'll get over it.'

They had nicknamed Scrote and Sharon's son Noddy because he was a naive and agreeable sheep. He seemed to them boyish and they expected with time he would grow out of it. Quite naturally he became absorbed in his father's passion, science. Scrote conducted evening classes in science and meteorology and Noddy began to help

41

him. From his mother, ewe Sharon, he learned how to join with others and be a friend. He was popular on the Farm, helping anyone in need and always a positive contributor in groups. Like his father, he enjoyed teaching others.

Noddy was patient and persistent in trying to steer a group's reasoning to be objective. Usually this meant he could influence perceptions, rather than affect judgements directly. He was the inventive one, wanting to test limits, taking on challenges, enthusing and enjoying arguing on both sides in a discussion.

He did not have much common sense and the others often had to rein Noddy in from pursuing some hare-brained idea, through lack of understanding of their feelings. It wasn't that he was thoughtless; it was rather that his emotional range was limited and he was naive in many situations.

Cookie was the title of a live-in position in the farmhouse, preparing food for the pigs meals three times daily. The job, which was well paid, involved peeling, cutting, baking, washing up, use of electrical appliances and supervision of sheep who helped in the kitchen. The incumbent had for several years been a female kangaroo, anatomically predisposed to do kitchen bench work, with prehensile marsupial forepaws able to grasp and rotate materials, tools and utensils. She had attended language and science classes regularly.

One of her helpers was Sharon, who visited her friend after work sometimes.

One day, Cookie was in the kitchen and came out to chat with her, wiping her paws on a towel. She offered Sharon a piece of bread, which she took and nibbled.

'What's the buzz?' Cookie asked, friendly.

'They've opened an office to organise our evening classes.'

'That seems pretty good.'

'You can come. The classes are for all animals.'

'I understand as much as I want to.'

'The classes will help you to have a say, don't you think?'

'Hmm. I would like to be more respected. Maybe I'll give it a try.'.

CHAPTER 7 MAXIMIN

The animals learned science theories in Scrote's classes and applied them in experiments devised by Noddy. He showed them the melting of floating ice cubes would not raise the water level in a jar.

'It is explained by Archimedes' Principle,' Scrote told them. 'Floating objects will displace their own weight of water.'

'It is counter-intuitive,' Tosser said, 'because we expect ice to melt to the same volume. But it shrinks when it melts.'

'Does melting of Arctic ice raise sea level?' asked Noddy, enjoying questioning their understanding.

'No,' said Pamela. 'The ice has to be grounded and it isn't.'

'That's correct,' Noddy said. 'Melting of ice has been wrongly attributed to causing sea level rise, which only happens when it runs down from on land.'

'With ice and sea level, we have a definite theory of what to look for. When we measure air temperature, what to expect is less certain. People may imagine they have observed warming.'

'They should expect any change, up or down,' Noddy said.

'When I was your age I liked change,' Scrote said. 'Everything seemed to be fixed by adults for adults. I wanted to overthrow it and start again.'

'That's still true,' said Noddy. 'We younger animals don't get a say in anything.'

'We older animals want our lifetime's experience taken into account,' said Tosser, 'even though conditions have changed and most of our knowledge is irrelevant.'

'Carl Popper wrote a book called the Poverty of Historicism,' said Scrote. 'He said nothing can be learned from history because events never repeat. Popper wanted theories to be able to be falsified, with evidence amassing until there was a clear result, for or against.'

'It doesn't sound at all practical, ' said Pamela. 'How did they get anything done?'

'They would look at the weight of evidence and know when the risk was too much.'

'You mean they would only bet on a sure thing.'

'It's the same in government,' said Noddy. 'Our leaders are unprincipled and slippery.'

'Flexible puts a better spin on it,' said Tosser. 'They won't do anything about global warming until they have to.'

'If farm earnings were threatened by climate change, the pigs would be interested,' said Tosser.

'Is that possible?' asked Noddy. 'How could climate affect our farming?'

'Hay-making could be affected.'

'Weather for hay-making needs a combination of temperature and humidity,' said Noddy.

'Change in moisture would have more effect than temperature,' said Milk Bar.

Keep Me said she could tell when rain was likely, by observing sheep lying down in their pastures and birds searching for food.

Asshole said the weather was too complicated to be understood by anyone. The others were used to his pessimism. He kept his own council and disdained everything.

'We need to explore practical problems,' said Noddy. 'Global warming is said to be occurring and they say it has to be stopped.'

'Is something new happening?' asked Scrote.

'Yes, the Greenhouse Effect has been enhanced by pollution,' said Noddy. 'Until recently we thought Earth's temperature averaged between hot and cold, with the atmosphere smoothing the days' highs with night time lows. The atmosphere was envisaged as a layer of insulating gases more than 100 kilometres thick, moderating temperatures into a warm range that people have adapted to live in.'

'Do you believe that?' asked Pamela.

45

'Yes, I do,' Noddy said. 'It's the next part that I don't get. They likened warming of the atmosphere to a greenhouse effect, keeping the Earth warm, with the gases acting like they're glass. This greenhouse idea was supposed to explain differences between temperatures on the Earth, Moon, Mars and Venus. But glass is a physical barrier and there was nothing like that trapping heat on the planets. Their explanation was absorption of infrared by CO_2.'

Noddy pulled something out of an invisible top hat, like a conjuror.

'Hey presto! CO_2 must be like glass,' he said. 'Global warming magic!'

'You don't believe it?' asked Pamela.

'No, I don't,' he said. 'CO_2 has captured attention because its concentration is increasing dramatically, seven times faster than global temperature, but its role in warming is insignificant. The possibility of warming by combustion heat, or some other warming effect, is overlooked. A complex mechanism detailing the role of CO_2 was invented and named an Enhanced Greenhouse Effect (EGHE). It was an extension of the greenhouse effect, which had been regarded as benign, with additional CO_2 transforming it into a problem of major global significance.'

'So CO_2 was benign but when it increased it became a pollutant?' asked Pamela.

'Yes. Strange, don't you think?' asked Noddy.

'You are going against the conventional wisdom,' she said. 'Perhaps you have misunderstood.'

'It seems perfectly logical to me. If I am wrong, I would like to know.'

'Perhaps it became a pollutant when the amount increased?' Pamela said.

'How did an innocuous process suddenly turn bad?'

'Like a cumulative poison?'

'CO_2 in the atmosphere is not thermally toxic, at any concentration.'

'How do you know?'

'It has never been demonstrated in a controlled experiment.'

46

'Is that possible?'

'Yes. I have an idea how to do such a test. I'll tell you about it after class.'

'Why don't you start an applied science study group?' Tosser said to Noddy. 'You're our best investigator. You could take a group in the evening in the cowshed.'

'I would like that,' said Noddy, flattered. 'Hey Keep Me, would you ask Lord Nikos if I can hold an applied science study class?'

'What would be in it for him?'

'Increased farm output.'

'He'll like that. Who could be in the class?'

'Anyone interested,' said Noddy.

'Including pigs?' asked Tosser.

'Their presence would honour us.' Noddy's smile was rueful.

Tosser rolled his eyes without Keep Me seeing him. Noddy did not want any pigs in his class, as their presence would inhibit open discussion, but he daren't say so. They weren't sure whether Keep Me supported the pigs or the worker animals. Hopefully no pig would want to attend.

Keep Me brought Lord Nikos's answer a few days later.

'Yes, Lord Nikos will allow an applied science group,' Keep Me said to Noddy. 'He wants a better educated and more efficient workforce. He will only allow topics relevant to The Farm. Your studies must be in your own time and will not distract you from your farm work.'

Classes commenced in the cowshed one evening, with about 20 worker animals sprawled on straw bales. Horace and the larger animals stood at the back, with Noddy raised on some bales at the front, an intrepid gleam in his mottled green and blue eyes.

'Today we will find out how to take air temperatures with this,' Noddy said. He held up a plastic instrument case about the size of a small book.

'This is a '*maximin*' thermometer,' he said. 'It's placed inside a screened weather station and air passes over these two bulbs. The liquid in this bulb expands when heated and pushes a marker to the maximum for the day. As the day cools, the marker stays put, so the

47

maximum can be read later. The liquid in the other bulb does the opposite. It controls a marker which is pulled down as the temperature drops to its lowest for the day. The marker stays there marking the minimum temperature.'

'Did you say it was called a *'maximin'* thermometer?' someone asked.

'Yes. It is an abbreviation for *'maximum and minimum'*,' Noddy said. 'We read the values daily.'

'At what time?'

'Good question. The best time to read the high and the low, at the same time, would be late afternoon, away from the day's high at noon and before the low around midnight. Would anyone here like to help with daily reading?'

The animals wrote down their names on a roster.

In the weeks following they were diligent in maintaining the record of temperatures.

When Horace inspected the maximin instrument, he peered out from under his forelock and said: 'I can read that. The maximum is 28.6 and the minimum is above 15.4 and below 15.6.'

'Call it 15.5,' said Noddy.

'It's not exactly halfway.'

'15.5 is where the closest division would be.'

'Where do I write it down?' asked Horace.

'In this table. If you have difficulty using a pen, Nestle here will write it for you.'

'You'll have to speak clearly,' said Nestle the hen. 'Your voices are deep and at the bottom of my hearing range.'

Horace recited the temperatures and Nestle dipped her beak in ink and wrote the numbers in the table. Horace thanked her. She and Solo the rooster kept the animals up to the mark with temperature measurement. He crowed to remind the volunteers when it was time to take measurements and Nestle recorded their readings.

The animal workers applied themselves diligently to their studies. The animals varied in ability as students. Cattle liked to chew over discussion topics; horses liked to meditate; sheep preferred reciting anything by rote; and poultry learned most from photo images

48

projected on the cowshed wall. The classes were well-attended and a highlight of the animals' day. Noddy varied activities with listening, discussing in groups and performing experiments.

They lacked news of developments in the world outside the farm. The news brought by the Ravens had stopped when Nikos banned them. All the animals could study were the books provided by the pigs. Noddy stole from the farmhouse a crystal radio. It had been built by one of the pigs but discarded when they purchased a battery radio. It had few parts and ran without electricity, relying on high ear sensitivity to very faint sounds. The pigs hadn't missed it.

Noddy and Scrote listened to radio newscasts and science programmes. The two worked together and as Scrote reached middle age it was evident that Noddy might eventually take over his meteorology teaching.

When the SR triumphed in putting a man into Earth orbit, the popularity of science was boosted. The DU responded they intended to land a man on the Moon. These events were of great interest to the animal workers, who were awestruck that humans had control over the physical world. The radio helped their reading of books and they were able to pass on their learning of science in weekly lessons that proceeded steadily year after year with growing understanding.

Evening classes were a bright light in lives that in every other respect were drudgery, with their participation harshly administered. They believed their studies would bring liberation closer.

'How are your evening classes going?' Cookie asked Sharon.
'We have been studying temperature measurement,' she said.
'Temperature of what?'
'Air.'
'Oh, is that what that white box on the lawn is for?'
'Yes.'
'Why are you animals interested in the temperature of the lawn?'
'The box measures temperature of air. It's the same everywhere. There is a global warming problem. We want to understand it.'
'Who says there's a problem?'

49

'The Government. They say hot countries could be badly affected.'

'What do you think?'

'We haven't seen any evidence so far. If it isn't a problem for us, why worry?'

'What if it gets worse?'

'People in hot countries will have to put up with it or move to somewhere cooler.'

CHAPTER 8 ROW CROP TERROR

Lord Nikos and the pigs lived luxuriously, with farm and farmhouse tasks done by hard-working animal slaves who could be brutalized or killed at any moment. Young sheep attended to food preparation, fetching and cleaning in the farmhouse. The oppression day after day, year after year, made the workers uncertain, reactive, hesitant, and solicitous of pig approval. The pigs dominated and exploited them ruthlessly.

The worker animals slaved in the fields all day and studied English and Science in the evenings, hoping it would bring them freedom.

'They exhaust us and crush us with fieldwork,' said Tosser. 'It ensures our compliance, for we are too exhausted and oppressed to revolt. The pigs have seduced some workers to betray unrest in our ranks with bribes of easy work and time off. Hopefully they will have more sense.

The animal workers' daily tasks include planting and tending the rows of plants in fields. Turnips were grown from seeds after planting with a disc drill. The seedlings grew in bunches and required thinning into single plants spaced far enough apart that each plant could develop into a large turnip.

Two young horses, Gloria and Lucy, were assigned to thinning the seedlings. Gloria was a hybrid carthorse with greater size and more strength than either of Titani and Tiny, her parents. She was huge. Lucy was a Shetland, a small pony. Different in size, their abilities were complementary. Gloria removed the largest weeds while Lucy did the final separation leaving a single seedling. They grasped the seedlings to be removed with their teeth and pulled them out of the ground, their mouths filling with dirt unpleasantly. It was tiring, continuing throughout daylight hours, for weeks on end.

The way the pigs regulated the work was demeaning, humiliating and depressing. They issued detailed instructions that were difficult to follow. Having no experience of doing field work themselves, they didn't anticipate or understand workers' needs. The pigs were always dissatisfied and they frequently criticised the workers for not following their instructions. It was oppressive and the workers were angry and unhappy.

Archie, a bossy pig, came stomping along between rows to where Gloria and Lucy were thinning seedlings. 'You're leaving bunches. You've left some doubles and threes. They'll grow stunted. It is not good enough.'

'But . . .' began Gloria.

'No buts,' snarled Archie. He beckoned to another pig, who came striding over in support. 'It must be done properly,' Archie squealed angrily. 'Go back and redo all the rows, leaving singles only. Or else.'

When they had gone, Lucy wept.

'I'm frightened of those pigs,' she told Gloria. 'I don't think I can do this type of work anymore.'

'I too hate working for the pigs,' said Gloria. 'But we have to, or they'll send us to the abattoir. Don't let them stress you; what they want is dumb obedience. If we can avoid seeming disobedient, we'll get through this.'

Gloria and Lucy complied but when Archie inspected the work he wasn't satisfied.

'You've left some twos.'

Their errors were negligible. The horses were exhausted and they only cared about getting finished.

'We tried to do it right,' Gloria said.

'You didn't try hard enough, so you'll be punished,' Archie said. He gashed Gloria with his tusk. Blood ran down her flank.

'I have grown up on the Farm with parents Horace and Titani and a brother Tiny,' thought Gloria. 'The other animals have

52

respected me and been kind. I know I don't deserve to be treated like this.'

Lucy whinnied in fear.

'You'll be next,' Archie said to her. 'Do it again properly this evening in your own time. If it isn't done correctly, you'll be whipped.'

Later, Tosser tried to intercede on behalf of Gloria and Lucy.

'The horses were doing their best,' Tosser protested.

'That's not for you to say,' Archie said: 'Wait here.'

He returned bringing the Rottweilers and four large guard pigs. They forced Tosser into the chute of a stock crate and clamped his head. He was held immobile in the hot sun for three days without food. Gloria and Lucy took a bucket of water to him secretly, but he wasn't able to reach it or drink it.

'Do you agree not to question our treatment of animal workers?' Archie asked Tosser, who was almost unconscious.

'I agree,' said Tosser.

He was freed, dehydrated and barely able to walk.

In the meantime, Gloria and Lucy had corrected their row crop work but Archie whipped them anyway. Afterwards, they could hardly stand. They ate their meagre rations and collapsed on the straw in their stalls.

Gloria lay on straw in a loose box, her back hurting from the whipping. It was bruised, with weeping lacerations and pain as if pierced by something sharp. Her surroundings were run down and filthy. The humiliating conditions made life almost unbearable.

Some of her friends had visited earlier, their sympathy and support helping her endure. They were frightened by how cruelly she had been treated, for they could be next. There was no glimmer of escape.

Gloria would rather remain invalided than go back to work. She lay with her eyes closed, disconsolate. She didn't care if she got better. Animal Farm was a concentration camp. The pigs were genocidal.

It was difficult for her to accept that the pigs could be so evil. Her life so far had been mostly good. Now she knew that to them she was simply a tool, to be thrown away when she ceased to be useful.

'I'm quitting this life,' she said when Gloria visited. She had no intention of moving ever again.

Lucy wept. She was only a small Shetland pony but her feelings were full size. Lucy imagined herself as the inheritor of a Shetland pit pony tradition in which her ancestors had been alternately beaten and starved by humans, for years. Now, with the pigs, it was more of the same but it did not deter her, only hardening her resolve. She wanted to help Gloria because she knew Gloria would do the same for her. She valued Gloria, wanted her to live and to be together with her again.

'C'mon Gloria,' said Lucy. 'You have to try and get better, for the rest of us. We are in a hell of a predicament but together we will find a way out. If you quit, it will pull the others down. Some of them have been beaten up too, maybe worse than you. Please try to keep going, for them and for all of us.'

'I know you don't feel like it, Gloria,' she said, 'but I want you to get better for me. If you care about me, you have to put your pain aside, make yourself as comfortable as you can and rest, without thinking about the future. You are going to get better.'

The next day, their work in the turnip rows continued and it seemed they would never be finished.

'The pigs' oppression is cruel and evil,' Gloria said. 'The fear on this farm is unbearable.'

'I hate the pigs more than I fear them,' Lucy said. 'I hope we find out how to end this hell soon.'

'Assassinating Lord Nikos would result in another pig leader who might be as bad,' said Gloria. 'There must be a way to escape. Shall we get away together?'

'I'd love to,' said Lucy.

'Lone animals have tried to get away but they have either failed to get over the wall or been hunted down by the pigs' dogs,' Gloria said.

'A mass exodus has never been tried because animals have doubted finding any refuge,' said Lucy. 'The most successful escapees have been goats, individually and in small groups. They have stayed in the vicinity of Animal Farm and come back when persecution reduced.'

'Muffin hopes to win the lottery and bribe his way to freedom,' said Gloria. 'It's a good plan, except for having to get the money needed.'

'There must be a place where we could live free of human captivity,' said Lucy

'A neighbour told me that ponies live wild on High Moor, upland hill country a week away from here,' Gloria said. The country is wild, open grassland with bracken and gorse bushes. The only other animals are sheep. Humans go there to herd the sheep each year and muster the horses for a horse fair, where they take youngsters into captivity for riding. The older horses return to the moor to live alone and breed, without doing farm work for humans, free of hunting. It isn't exactly a return to the wild, but it would be a good life.'

'It sounds ideal,' said Lucy.

'Let's make a plan in detail,' said Gloria.

The two continued their row crop work, with hope.

CHAPTER 9 CONFIDENT OF UNCERTAINTY

Not all the animals studied meteorology.

'Weather is decided by the gods,' Mokey said dolefully. 'Studying it is a waste of time.'

The Ravens, under Patriarch, believed the weather was a mystery to be revealed by meditation on God's teachings within Paradoxy.

Lucy lacked interest in meteorology. 'I don't see how it would improve my appearance,' Lucy said. Her work was to take Lord Nikos' family for rides in a trap, a two-wheeled open-topped carriage. She was vain, prettying herself with plaits and ribbons, at a time when the excesses of the previous aristocracy were denigrated.

Lucy attended the meteorology class because she enjoyed company and most of the animals would go.

It was the first meteorology class of a new year. Noddy was pleased to see Hannah sitting in the front row, alert and cute, as always.

'We are starting a new topic: statistical uncertainty. When anything can happen, but some things are more likely than others, there is uncertainty. Weather at a location can be explained with single measurements, but to understand climate you need to understand statistics. Two years ago, you learned to take daily readings at our weather station. I have analysed the data you recorded. There has been a small amount of warming with periods of cooling.

'Interpreting observations made by others is a big responsibility,' he said. 'Early scientists made observations personally. Today, scientists often rely on measurements made by people they have never met. They count on scrupulous accuracy and honesty in their colleagues' work. They want to be confident of their findings, because their methods could be questioned, as we will see later.'

'Can they ever be completely confident?' asked Hannah, with a smile. She was a llama arrived on Animal Farm as an asylum seeker, escaped from a zoo.

'They need as much confidence as possible,' said Noddy. 'Certainty is when they know it all.'

'Or think they do, as you would know,' said Hannah, smirking playfully. She was fun and the ewes accepted her readily, although she lacked their sociality. At the zoo she had lived in a small group where individuality counted but for the sheep unanimity and conformance was everything. Hannah found it restrictive.

'Scientists always want more measurements for their confidence,' said Tosser. 'But it takes time and is expensive. If there really is a temperature change, wouldn't a few measurements be enough to tell the tale?'

'Good question,' said Noddy. He turned to Milk Bar. 'Can you tell us how many temperature measurements would be enough?'

'It depends,' she said. 'If you measure several and they are different, you have to do more measurements. When they are close, then that's enough.'

'What if when you measure more, there isn't a pattern?' he said

'There has to be a pattern. Or you could take an average.'

'Do changes in the average show that conditions have changed?' said Hannah.

'She's a smart llama,' Noddy thought, *'and fun to be with. We might do a lot more than science together.'*

'No, not always,' he said. 'Averages of samples taken from the same population can vary widely. We achieve confidence by taking many samples. They sample temperatures from 6,300 meteorological stations worldwide,' said Scrote. 'Australia uses records from 112 weather stations.'

'Do they average them?'

'Not normally. They mostly look at trends at one station.'

'Do they compare it with many other stations?' asked Hannah.

'It's a matter of being confident that the measured trend is not merely local. When other locations are considered, there can be confidence in a range of possible outcomes.'

'A range doesn't help much,' said Hannah. 'People want certainty.'

'When you have a barrel of apples of varying ripeness, checking for bad apples requires you examine enough apples for the certainty you need,' said Noddy.

'If you take out too few, and they are bad, you might falsely declare the barrel is unacceptable making a Type 1 error of commission. Alternatively, if few are bad, you might declare falsely that the barrel is acceptable, making a Type 2 omission error.

'Why do I need to know about rotten apples?' asked Gloria. She had planned her escape and was negative about long term projects like understanding statistics.

'Temperature sampling has to have enough measurements not to declare a false trend by commission or omission,' Noddy said. 'Picking a trend is like taking a chance on an apple barrel being good or bad.'

'When there is a trend, the confidence level should be declared. If it is below 50% it will be wrong more than 50% of the time,' he said.

'I hate it when people guess over-confidently,' said Eugenia. She was a good-looking Suffolk ewe the pigs had bought to diversify the sheep gene pool. Noddy was attracted to her but his favourite was llama Hannah.

'People with insufficient measurements tend to be overconfident,' said Noddy. 'They make mistakes. Woodworkers measure twice and cut once.

'When a climate problem is unclear, a solution should not be attempted. Historical temperature data must be analysed omitting bias. People's memories can be unreliable, causing them to catastrophize. Correct understanding requires many accurate measurements.'

'Unfortunately people these days accept subjective impressions of climate and have little confidence,' said Hannah. 'It's pathetic.'

Hannah never lacked confidence and some of the sheep ridiculed her because she was prepared to be different.

'Some sheep aren't smart.' she said.

'You're right,' Noddy said. 'Opinions change with the weather. When it is cold, they will say the climate is cooling. When it is hot, they forget about cold times. Humans spend a lot of time talking about weather when they don't have reliable data.'

'Are people idiots?' asked Eugenia.

'Many humans certainly are,' said Noddy. 'Some animals are smart.' He looked at Hannah.

'Some animals are dumb,' said Hannah, looking at Eugenia.

'According to Plato, individuals are not deliberately bad,' said Sharon. 'They mean well but make mistakes.'

'Governments can't wait for certainty before acting,' said Old Scrote. 'Inaction is seen as weakness. Citizens demand action. Mistakes are covered up.'

'By the time individuals have learned to recognise foolishness in the larger patterns of life, they are often too old to influence change and are sidelined.'

Old Scrote didn't complain but his views were reactionary and ignored.

'What have you been learning about today?' asked Cookie handing Sharon an apple. She couldn't come to every class because she had to work and used her chats with Sharon to keep up.

'We found out about air temperature and how changes in temperature are detected.'

'What about it?'

'To see if there's change, scientists need measurements at weather stations all over the World.'

'What if some places are warming and others are cooling?'

'That's normal.'

'But they want warming to be everywhere.'

'That's when they get into doctoring the statistics.'

'How are we affected here on the Farm?'

'The effect of warming could be small but they speculate it will continue and after a century could become a problem.'

'Like what?'

'Living things could be affected or the sea-level could rise.'

'It sounds like scientists are into generating bad news.'

'It is a reflex they have.'

CHAPTER 10 STAND OFF

Lord Nikos announced that weapons researchers in the Social Republic had developed intercontinental ballistic missiles (Icbms) each with 10 times more explosive power than any nation had ever used in a nuclear attack.

'Our friends in the SR are sending ICBMs to Caruba,' he said. 'It's an escalation of the Cold War. They will defend us against attack by the DU. But there is work to be done to prepare our defences and, from now on, you'll work an extra hour every day.'

The animal workers were fearful that Caruba had become the epicentre of a conflict between the SR and DU superpowers.

'What is the SR government playing at?' Tosser said to Scrote. 'Don't they have better things to do than antagonise the DU, by setting up a missile arsenal on their doorstep?'

Two months later Lord Nikos made another announcement.

'A DU fleet is off Caruba Island. The DU commander has objected to the SR deploying its missiles here. They have demanded that construction of missile bases on Caruba cease and the missiles be disarmed.'

'Bloody hell,' Tosser whispered. 'We're in the middle of a nuclear confrontation.'

'Could the DU nuke us?' asked Eugenia.

'Definitely,' said Tosser. 'They would too.'

'What can President Younucko do?'

'Wait for them to attack, or back down.'

'How will President Felix be able to save face? Right now he's looking pretty foolish.'

'A missile from Caruba can reach any part of the DU in under 20 minutes,' Lord Nikos said. 'If the DU attacks, President Younucko can retaliate.'

'I don't like our chances,' said Tosser. 'Anyway, the word is out that Felix is haute-bourgeois and would want to make peace with the DU.'

'It will be the SR that calls the shots, not Felix, whatever his social class.'

After an agonising wait, the SR backed down. Work on the missile system halted. The missile delivery ship returned to the SR. The DU fleet moved away. But missiles previously installed could possibly be retained on Caruba.

'While we have missiles aimed at the DU, they won't want to be friends with us,' Eugenia said.

'It's good the SR have withdrawn, but Caruba is still being used as a pawn,' said Tosser. 'We could be sacrificed in a pre-emptive strike by either side at any time.'

'Thanks to my leadership, we have defeated the DU,' President Felix Younucko announced.

'Is it possible that the de-escalation was agreed?' Tosser asked Noddy.

'You mean a conspiracy?'

'Very likely. The SR and DU negotiators did a lot of talking.'

'Is the Cold War over?'

'Not likely. It might go on for many years. The War is needed to get the leaders re-elected.'

'The DU is planning to put a man on the Moon next,' he said. 'That will get more kudos with developing countries than by attacking the SR.'

Lord Nikos's term in office was ending.

'The Social Republic could be losing the space race with the DU,' said Tosser.

'What if the SR put a pig on the Moon,' said Noddy.

'A pig would be a better astronaut; humans are too curious and erratic.'

'I really don't care,' said Pamela. 'So long as they don't drag us into it.'

'A space race is better than a nuke race,' said Tosser.

'Conquering the Moon won't do us any good,' Pamela said.

'Space exploration is kick-arse,' said Tosser. 'I prefer space hype to getting caught in the crossfire between the psychopathic leaders of two superpowers. It's a sick World that allows these bullies to swagger around brandishing nukes.'

On Caruba Island, President Felix Younucko planned to retire. He supported election of Natalia Alphancourt to be the new president. It would be the first free election of a leader on Caruba. The DU dropped propaganda leaflets from planes to influence the voters of Caruba to oppose her. The DU attributed malevolence to Caruba's alignment with their arch enemy the SR. They blockaded SR tankers trying to deliver diesel fuel to the island, cutting supply to 30%.

Caruba's economy reverted from internal combustion power to human and animal power. The Farm's tractor was now useless and cultivation of the land had to be done manually. Without a backhoe, the ditches filled up with sediment and water pooled in low lying areas killing off the grass and crops. Without mechanical hedge cutters, saplings grew up and brambles spread out from the hedgerows.

The island population was hungry and grew food by cultivating the land using horses, oxen and hand tools. People responded with home-grown horticulture methods. The soil was rebuilt by permaculture. Companion plantings replaced pesticides. Wastes were processed to make fertilizers, or used to fuel an old steam engine that milled, sawed and threshed.

Manual labour in the fields brought animals and humans closer to nature than mechanization had allowed. There were treed hedgerows and copses where birds lived and flew out to control crop pests. There were elm, cedar, beech and horse chestnut. Trees had been cut down to allow farming machinery to be used, but with the machinery stopped, they began to grow back.

The animals walked in a line, carrying their tools, across pastures, along headlands of arable fields, to their fieldwork. Rabbits bolted to their burrows in hedgerows. Only the blur of rapid movement and flashes of white tails were visible. The grassland was eaten close, with worn pathways and depressions where rabbits crouched to nibble. Surprised by the walkers, a rabbit would thump with a rear leg and dash to safety in the hedgerow.

Science was beginning to investigate farming practices. When Rachel Carson's book *Silent Spring* was published, the SR Government banned DDT and other pesticides. Export of them to Caruba ceased.

'The SR Government is concerned about conserving the natural environment,' said Tosser. 'But without pesticides we won't be able to control mosquitoes or insect infestation of crops. Carubans are going to be dying from malaria and starving for lack of vegetables. Ticks, fleas and flies have become a nuisance.'

'Why did they ban DDT?' asked Asshole the cat.

'Hawks' reproduction was endangered,' said Tosser. 'DDT causes eggshells to go soft.'

'I haven't seen any hawks around for years,' said Asshole. 'Their disappearance is probably due to something else.'

'There were scientific studies,' Tosser said. 'You shouldn't be so sceptical.'

'If the SR Government is promoting the DDT story, it is probably false,' said Asshole. 'Mismanagement of the environment is part of their hegemony.'

Asshole was getting old and critical of everything. His contribution on the farm was catching mice and he was slowing down. Unless he kept mice under control, the pigs would club him and throw his body into the blacksmith's forge. He was followed around by a young cat, Ammo, who was taking over his duties.

'Why are you so pessimistic?' Keep Me asked Asshole.

'I am better off being negative, because I find out what I have to avoid,' said Asshole. 'When they contradict my pessimism, it is reassuring. If they corroborate it, it shows that something bad is really happening.'

'Doesn't it get you down?'

'No. I'm happy enough, probably the same as you. It's just a face I put on.'

'A sour face?'

'Why not?'

'You're a sourpuss then!'

Asshole's mousing ability declined with advancing age and a year later he disappeared. Ammo, took his place.

Despite the SR ban, Animal Farm continued to use DDT. Carubans imported large quantities of fertilizers, herbicides and pesticides from the DU.

'What happens on Animal Farm is no-one's business but our own,' said Lord Leonard.

'We'll see,' said Tosser. 'There are activists who would not agree. Caring for the environment is a everyone's responsibility.'

Farm dogs were blamed when things went wrong and they tried to protect themselves by adopting a posture of fawning sycophancy, obedience and happy optimism. When the pigs bought a Border Collie pup they called Molly, they asked Keep Me to train her. It meant Keep Me didn't have long to live. They might allow her an extra year or two, but she could expect to be killed as soon as she made a serious mistake and would end up on the blacksmith's hearth like Asshole. As always, she displayed her trademark optimism and trained Molly with care. Border Collies were an elite breed of working dog, able to herd sheep and cattle, obeying the whistles and shouts of the herdsman.

Then one day Keep Me disappeared and they didn't find her. They missed her happy manner and ached dully with the realisation that their own lives were precarious. Their only hope was for liberation, but that was a distant prospect.

65

CHAPTER 11 LEONARD

Under Lord Nikos' rule, Animal Farm had increased productivity and the pigs had become affluent. After he had served the maximum of two terms, there was an election to find his successor. All the candidates were pigs and a boar named Leonard was elected. The worker animals hoped he would relax the conditions of their servitude.

Lord Leonard was a Large Black, with a long, deep-body, bred by humans for foraging. Under Lord Nikos, he had been the farm's construction engineer, managing civil works such as the dam. His planning was bureaucratic. He informed the community what they should want, without consideration for others. He had no interest in the worker animals. He ordered their food like a person feeding goldfish he has inherited and doesn't want to live, allowing them to slowly starve, distancing himself so as not to appear cruel.

He ushered in an age of autocratic efficiency in the running of the Farm, allocating resources carefully and assigning every animal a specific task.

'Your main concern is to do the work assigned to you in the time required,' he said. 'When you have done it, you will be eligible to receive food and shelter.'

Although they didn't like their assignments, they gave the worker animals purpose.

'I have become a mobile milk factory,' said Milk Bar. 'I have to eat continually.'

'You should be so lucky,' said Tosser, her partner. 'I am bloody starving.'

'If a hen fails to lay an egg daily, the pigs give it the chop,' said Nestle. She was a gentle creature, speckled and cautious, moving quietly around the farm buildings, foraging and hiding away her eggs. She had never dared to give an opinion.

Like all the worker animals, Milk Bar's lifestyle had tedium. She had more variety than most animals. She ate, digested, was milked and bore calves.

Even so, Milk Bar perceived a bleak future.

'My milk is declining. I haven't many years left,' she said.

'We will all be eaten eventually,' said Mokey the donkey, mournfully. He was needed to pull puts. Donkeys ate little and had stamina to load and pull heavy loads of hay, grain sheaves, turnips and potatoes. Mokey was overloaded and complained a lot. Pathos was his forte, with a dismal outlook on events but intuitive intelligence.

The Farm customarily had only one donkey and Mokey's existence was lonely but pivotal. When the other animals heard Mokey bray, it reassured them that all was well, punctuating their lives that otherwise would have seemed empty.

Although the Farm kept only one donkey jack and Mokey lacked a donkey jenny, he was not discouraged from mating with the carthorse mares, if he was able. Through athletic persistence, these unions produced a steady supply of mules, strong and steady animals, suitable for ploughing and cultivation.

When the abattoir truck came to take Scrote and Sharon away later that week, the workers detected a new desperate note in Mokey's sonorous braying and came running. They were shocked and sad. The two had been cornerstones of their lives on the Farm. They were consoled to have Noddy, their son, still with them.

'My father wanted us to be independent thinkers and we have come a long way,' Noddy said. 'We must continue developing the skills he taught us, earning respect that will gain our liberation.'

Mokey reached old age. A lorry brought Oscar, a younger donkey jack, taking away a couple of sheep and Mellie the goat in exchange. Old Mokey enjoyed Oscar's company for a few more months, until the abattoir truck took him away. He knew where he was going, but told the younger animals he was going to a retirement farm.

'I'm looking forward to this,' he said.

The older animals were sad.

'We have to hope that they allow him dignity,' Tosser said. 'He was an important part of Animal Farm.'

The Farm was a commercial success and the pigs held Open Days each year to show it off. Visitors saw how wind power was used to mill grain and how efficiently the labour of animal workers could be utilised. Oscar, a donkey jack and a mule, Big Ears, were harnessed side by side, towing a turntable around driving the mill when there was no wind. Big Ears was tall, like his mother Titani and he walked the longer outer circle, staying abreast of Oscar, with his shorter legs on the inside.

Tosser was past middle age and in splendid condition. He and Milk Bar had birthed a series of calves but only Rondo, Steroid and Myrtle were left to them. Milk Bar's milk was beginning to dry up and Tosser had lost his drive. He knew that it wouldn't be long before the pigs would send him to the abattoir and Rondo would take over from him. He had taken to questioning his ideas. Leadership of the cattle was a constant challenge, with younger animals always disagreeing and challenging.

'I try to have some fun,' thought Rondo. 'Our lives would be drab otherwise. I was lucky the pigs kept me when they sold off my siblings. Being chief bull to a herd of cattle has its rewards but I try not to let it go to my head. My first was Buttercup but she is small, a Jersey and I have grown too heavy for her now. I am leader of all the animals in dealing with the pigs on farming matters. The pigs are unreliable and dishonest, difficult to deal with.'

Matings between relatives were inevitable in the closed community of the Farm. Dysfunctional characteristics from inbreeding seldom occurred. Because Rondo's incestuous mating with his cousins could inbreed recessive defects, such as albinism, the pigs bought Earl, a Charolais bull calf, large and pale straw coloured, a fast grower.

The pigs had castrated Steroid, a step brother, with Burdizzo pinchers, severing his epididymides. Although he could not perform all a bull's duties, he was gentle and an excellent group leader, in intimate relations with both males and females.

68

Pamela could be mated now and take over from Milk Bar. She was sassy and inclined to be flighty, sharing her company with several young bulls. Buttercup, a Jersey, was a small cow and needed a lighter bull to avoid injuring her. Perhaps if Rondo served her before he was fully grown he would not be too heavy for her to bear.

Lord Leonard was less autocratic than Lord Nikos with a committee of high-ranking pigs advising him. It was a rigid bureaucracy, merciless in its exploitation of worker animals.

Molly skulked around the perimeter of the home paddock, waiting for strays, before racing in and driving the sheep into a tight mob where they stood facing her, stamping their feet. The sheep would stay together in a flock where they felt protected. They disliked isolation or being the centre of attention and preferred to go along with their leader's view. Noddy had attempted to charge Molly down but she was too quick for him and they eyed each other warily, as he stamped his foot.

'Molly can't stop herself from herding sheep,' said Noddy.

She loved to round up and drive mobs of unruly animals from pasture to pasture, bailing them up and waiting for someone to separate some out. With cattle she was circumspect because they could injure or kill her with a kick or a charge.

Molly lived with the pigs at the farmhouse. Sometimes, she came sneaking down to the farmyard, in her sheepdog way, to find out what the animals were doing.

'We can suppose Molly lets the pigs know what we are talking about,' said Hannah.

'She helps keep us on the same page as the pigs,' said Tosser. 'It could be worse.'

He had inducted Molly into her predecessor Keep Me's double agent role.

'It would be good if she could get the pigs to respect us.'

'She is helping our communication with them,' Tosser said. 'Without her, there would be more cruelty and violence.'

'D'you think so?' said Noddy. 'If it gets any worse we will revolt and kill the bastards.'

'Maybe Molly has passed that view to the pigs.'

69

'Their view is that unless we comply, we will be sent to the abattoir.'

'She mediates between us and without her things would probably be worse.'

'I suppose we should be grateful for her.'

'I wonder what she wants?'

'Hmm. What does she get?'

'A dog's life. She gets the blame.'

'I'm going to be nicer to her.'

Molly either didn't know, or pretended to be unaware, of the sheep's dancing. They met secretly at night to spin like whirling dervishes under the Moon, transported by their motion together, whirling and twirling, trying to outdo each other in speed and grace of movements.

Sometimes when Molly had discussed ideas with the animal workers, she would pass them to Giraud. He was a scientific pig, an idealist who advised Lord Leonard. A Gascon boar, an ancient French breed, he was a hardy type with black skin covered in thick wiry black hair, a pointed face and heavy lop ears. He kept his books in the harness room and allowed the animals to use them. He advised Lord Leonard on horticulture, veterinary treatments, meteorology, energy supply technology and atmospheric physics.

'Giraud's good value,' Noddy said to Harvey, a growing lamb mothered by Noddy's sister Eugenia. 'He's friendly, knows a lot and answers my questions. He might be interested in animal rights.'

The animals' wider interest was in bettering their conditions.

'When are the pigs going to liberate us?' Gloria asked Molly. 'We have rights.'

Gloria was young and excitable, a tall draft horse. She cantered past Tosser and Milk Bar every morning as they took their walk. She had not revealed her plan to escape with Lucy to anyone. They couldn't go until they could get past the wall. There was a rumour it would be opened up.

'I want to keep in shape,' she said. 'The work we do is physical and my back gets plenty to do, but I have other muscles that are seldom used, unless I go for a run.'

'Gloria is in good shape,' said Tosser.

'Hmph,' Milk Bar said. 'She's an attractive filly. She turns a few heads I've noticed. I wonder if she has any other reason for getting fit.'

Education was the way to freedom for Noddy and many of the animals. They studied in the harness room after finishing work in the fields and domestic chores. Noddy taught applied science on days alternating with the meteorology class he had also taken over from his father. He led wide-ranging discussions, careful to avoid criticism of the pigs. Science lessons were usually hands-on experiments for the animal students to do. The language teacher brought equipment borrowed from the university for experiments. The animals also studied the library books privately, asking Giraud questions and discussing news about energy policy that Keep Me brought from the pigs, or gleaned from television broadcasts, or they heard from neighbouring farm animals. Environmental concerns were effluents, liquid and solid wastes, smoky fires, waste heat, trees, forests and wetlands. The worker animals came to understand the pigs' policies on the environment, pollution and energy, but they were not allowed to ask questions.

Lord Leonard's bureaucracy planned and managed the Farm's production of fruit, vegetables, grains, legumes, roots, hay and livestock. Molly had good access to Lord Leonard. She tried to persuade the other animals to accept the pigs' harsh leadership was necessary and their luxuries were reasonable.

'Our pigs have to decide difficult matters,' said Molly. 'In order to concentrate, they need superior conditions. They would prefer to have a simple life and live down here in the farm buildings with you, but living in the farmhouse is a sacrifice they are willing to make for everyone.'

The animals didn't believe her and resented pig privileges. Pigs lazed in the farmhouse and when they came out, barged around with

71

their heads down, ill-mannered and quarrelsome, looking under stones for worms, snails and slugs. They were unfriendly with the other animals, perceiving themselves as more worthy.

The animals were suspicious of Molly and some of them wanted to exclude her but Tosser always took her side.

The animals' conformance was ensured by pig police, who terrorised them, luring dissidents from hiding and punishing them savagely. The pigs' ethos was that their leader had an ambitious and splendid vision, to be achieved by the other animals' hard work, which it was their duty to enforce. Part of their ideology was that goats were conspiring to lead the other animals astray. They locked up Coral in solitary confinement for a week.

'She hasn't done anything wrong,' Noddy told Molly.

'The pigs say they caught her just in time,' said Molly.

'I hardly think she was any threat. This was prejudiced persecution.'

Electricity from an old wood-fired steam generator was reticulated to homes and businesses throughout the island. But even at full capacity, there was not enough power to meet demand. The animals had rebuilt the windmill twice during Napoleon's time, once after Farmer Jones' attack and again after a storm. Lord Leonard had the windmill converted to drive an electrical generator and the electricity was used in brewing beer. When a paddock was ploughed up, and potatoes planted for fermenting vodka, the electricity was available for barn machinery and the farmhouse. There wasn't enough to reticulate to the animal workers' quarters and they were without light and warmth.

Growing potatoes required a lot of work. First the ground had to be ploughed and harrowed. Horace poured his huge energy into cultivation from daylight to dusk. He and Titani pulled a single furrow mole-board plough and Tiny followed with drag harrows. He was another Clydesdale stallion but younger, who would one day replace Horace. He had made advances to Gloria but had been warned off by her parents because she was not yet sufficiently mature to work and raise a foal. They heaped up the soil in ridges, placing seed potatoes along the troughs and turning the soil back

72

over them. They pumped water from the dam to flow between the ridges and start the sets growing. When greenery emerged on the ridges, they heaped the soil up around the plants with the plough.

Four months later, when the plants had fully grown, they used the plough to unearth clusters of white new potatoes, which sheep picked into baskets to take to the store in a clamp beside the buildings. The potatoes were heaped together and covered with dirt to keep them moist but cool to prevent sprouting.

Most of the potatoes went for vodka-making. They were a favourite of the pigs, who boiled them in an old laundry tub.

'Will we get to eat any of the potatoes?' asked Harvey.

Potatoes were a preferred food of most of the animals.

'No. Potatoes are bad for ordinary animals,' said Molly, trotting to and fro anxiously in the sheepdog manner. 'Leonard says they could poison us. Fortunately, pigs are not affected. So there's nothing to worry about.' She wagged her tail winningly.

The animals' food supply remained confined to mouldy hay and turnips that sometimes were rotten.

The windmill generated little electricity.

'In summer the cyclonic winds are too strong.' Molly said. 'When they feather the turbine blades to prevent damage, no electricity is generated. In winter anticyclones bring cold air and there is too little wind to turn them. Neither in winter nor summer can the wind generator be relied on to supply electricity.'

Lord Leonard cancelled other wind turbines he had ordered.

When winter came, the animals were kept warm by the thick coats they had grown and by huddling together for warmth in the draughty buildings. Frosts froze the dam and horses had to stamp on the ice to break it so the animals could drink. The liberation they hoped for would have food, shelter, warmth and be free of pigs.

73

CHAPTER 12 SUCCESSION

After a Science class on the topic of reproduction, several animals stayed afterwards and stood around discussing how the pigs decided when an animal would be sent to the abattoir. The pigs looked for successors for horses and cattle when incumbents were in middle age. With working dogs, it took a year to whelp and train a pup. Molly took over the work done by her mother Keep Me. Asshole was shadowed by a young tom, Ammo, bought from a neighbouring farm. After Noddy's parents, Scrote and Sharon, had been taken away, he took up the arduous duties of chief ram.

It would have been lonely being the only ram with the flock for most of the year. He tried to participate in the social lives of the ewes but his life experiences were limited and they excluded him from their conversation.

One evening after work, Tosser, Milk Bar, Molly, Noddy and Hannah stood together in the shade of a tree, talking.

'Would you ask Lord Leonard if we animals can retire when we get old?' Noddy asked Tosser. 'My parents had many good years left in them. It was wrong to send them to the slaughterhouse.'

'It is better if an old animal has trained a successor, like your father did you,' said Milk Bar. 'They do it with dogs, so why not with all animals as they near old age?'

'I don't think Lord Leonard has considered it,' Molly said.

'It is fulfilling for the retiree and transitions the replacement process,' said Tosser. 'Would you ask him?'

'It would be better coming from you,' she said, acknowledging Tosser's preeminent position.

Tosser spoke to Lord Leonard about it later that week, when he inspected the farm.

74

'He wants worker animals to participate more in running the Farm, to do their work more cleverly,' Tosser told the others. 'After that, he says liberation might be possible.'

'Wow! There is hope!' said Noddy. 'What do we have to do?'

'Lord Leonard said we workers need to understand agricultural science. We need to learn how things grow. The effects of the environment are important. We must study the books in the harness room.'

'It's not exactly liberating us, is it?' said Noddy. 'He's delaying. They will never liberate us, the swine.'

'I agree,' said Hannah, his partner, loyally. 'They are exploiting us and won't stop.'

The pigs wanted to breed her with a sheep to test hybrid wool production. Serene and spiritual, Hannah was popular for her thoughtfulness and courtesy. Her personality balanced Noddy's; he lacked emotional intelligence and was rather impulsive but made up for it with his practical skills.

'You're right,' said Tosser. 'Studying might allow us to take some responsibility. It won't do us any harm though. It's a start towards being respected. It could take us towards where we want to go.'

'Noddy is unlikely to settle for a quiet life here on Animal Farm,' Milk Bar said to Hannah, her son's partner. 'He has a revolutionary outlook and would be one of those who will sooner or later confront the pigs.'

'Fucking right,' said Noddy.

'I have thought about how to keep him out of trouble,' said Hannah. 'Would starting a family make him less idealistic?'

'He will be more responsible as a parent, more calculating and more circumspect,' said Milk Bar. 'His rebelliousness could sublimate into a long term plan to overthrow the pigs. Until then, he has to be compliant.'

'Compliance is not his strong suit,' said Hannah.

'You're telling me!' said his aunt Eugenia. 'When he was young he was a tearaway. He tried out all the rules and found every possible way to make trouble. But Noddy has quietened down since you arrived, Hannah.'

Noddy planned to have a 'cia' (pronounced kri:.ə) offspring with Hannah, who was a llama. It wasn't yet known who would take over from Noddy: the cia, if it was male, or Harvey his sister's son. This would depend on how many rams the pigs wanted to keep. Both Noddy and Hannah had inherited llama characteristics and cross breeding could pass on to the flock the llama characteristics of long slender legs and neck, thick white fleece, erect forward pointing ears and short tail.

'Why have a cia?' Noddy asked.

'It will be fulfilling,' she said.

'It would be something joyful we can share,' he said.

'We have to get permission from the pigs,' said Hannah.

'How ridiculous,' Noddy said.

'It's a formality.'

'Not really. If we go ahead without permission, they might kill it.'

'If we ask, they might knock us back,' Hannah said.

But they did ask.

'Lord Miguel has given you special permission to breed,' Penny the new dog informed them. 'He said a hybrid 'cia' would be an asset to the Farm for fieldwork. The wool would be finer than a llama's and its body would be larger than a sheep's, able to carry panniers.'

'Perhaps a male cia wouldn't go to the abattoir,' Noddy said.

'I will pray we have a ewe cia,' Hannah said. 'You don't believe in prayer, do you?'

'A ram lamb would be as good as a ewe lamb, wouldn't it?' he said, avoiding the question because Hannah followed Paradoxy. 'I want to call him Stanley.'

'It would grow wool too, but we don't need another ram yet. The pigs would probably take a ram lamb to the abattoir.'

'We would be taking a chance.'

For a decade Lord Leonard kept the animal workers toiling in the fields. Farming operations went on day in and day out, year after year. The pigs allowed some animals to mate. The offspring could be sold or kept to replace worker animals when they aged. When

76

they could no longer do the work required, the pigs arranged for the abattoir lorry to take them away.

Not all animals taken to the abattoir were old. There was a steady stream of young succulent animals, lambs and calves. Different species aged and declined at different rates. Workloads were not reduced with age. Replacement was traumatic for everyone, except for the pigs, who did nothing to relieve it. Overlap between an incumbent and the successor was avoided because the scene could turn ugly, with fighting. When a father was to be replaced by his son, there could be a contest of loyalties.

Sheep lives were short and a ram had only a few years on top. Noddy's prowess declined as Harvey matured. As a cia he showed exceptional ability at studying science and joined in adult discussions. There was succession too in the female lines and Sharon was expected to go to the abattoir soon, with Hannah taking over. Male and female lines of succession had little place on the Farm now and could be varied but males generally competed more vigorously and lost position more abruptly.

The excitement of sexual relations was dampened by the dismal prospects for offspring. Some of the animals had adopted celibacy voluntarily. Most couplings were ordered.

Polygamous love in nature is usual for cattle, horses, sheep and other species. On Animal Farm there were fewer males than females, but harems were smaller than in the wild. Many of the animals engaged in a core coupling with a favourite, seeming to gain contentment from the stability this brought despite mating duties.

A new sheepdog, Penny, replaced Molly and Ammo was replaced by Chester, a prodigious mouser. A new rooster, Gregory, launched the daily cycle at day-break, tip-toeing around the farmyard, rounding up his favourite hen Mabel and the others. The flock of hens had the run of the farm yard, but usually stayed around the farmhouse where the pigs threw out waste food or around the corn stacks where there were grain screenings. They declined to use the laying boxes when they had a nest secreted away in stinging nettles, where it was likely to remain undiscovered and they could hatch

77

chicks. The pigs sold eggs and live poultry from the farm. When they found a nest, they would sell the eggs and the hen too, as a deterrent to any other free-laying hens. Hens who had laid eggs in nest boxes cackled jubilantly, whereas their peers came under suspicion when they were silent.

The cockerel's role was to sound his alarm call, during the day or night, whenever a fox or wild cat or snake came skulking around his hens. At other times if a rooster overdid his cacophany it could put his life in peril. The pigs were late sleepers and would take revenge on a rooster who woke them up early.

Gregory had replaced his father, Solo, who had been shot by Lord Leonard in a fit of pique, when he found the rooster's shit in his hat, after he roasted his favourite hen.

'I didn't know pigs are carnivorous,' said Hannah.

'Our pigs don't usually eat meat. Perhaps Napoleon banned meat because it was inconsistent with the Animalism he was preaching.'

'That was sensible. Let's hope he doesn't do it again.'

CHAPTER 13 FOSSIL FIND

A pig rooting for worms discovered an outcrop of coal on Animal Farm. Lord Leonard obtained a licence to mine the seam and sell coal to the islanders. Animals removed the overburden and coal with wheelbarrows and horse-drawn carts.

Every animal contributed to mining except the pigs, who languished in the farmhouse. Sheep scooped up the topsoil, holding bucket handles in their mouths. Horses pulled ploughs and loosened up the overburden. Other sheep uncovered the coal.

The animals' labour in the mines was gruelling. Cows with boards mounted across their horns pushed the broken rock into spoil piles. Sheep filled skips with lumps of coal, for horses to drag and lift into a put drawn by Dynamo, the donkey who had taken over from Oscar. Poultry and geese completed the mining, scratching small coal lumps and fines into piles for the sheep to bucket away.

The only worker animal who did not mine coal was Lucy. She was a Shetland pony, small, fat, hairy and frisky.

'Mining is too dusty for me,' she said, flicking her long tail. Her forebearse had never laboured like the rest of them. Jones had kept her to give rides to his children and the pigs had continued to keep a pony for children visitors to ride. Lucy had learned dressage, could do tricks, entertained and wheedled attention from the pigs who admired her and fed her sugar lumps. She was allowed to shirk, staying at the stables, caring for any animal too sick to work. She was narcissistic and gazed at her reflection in the horse trough, while pigeons braided her mane.

'Lucy is a disgrace to animaldom,' said Rondo.

'No! Through having Lucy as their pet,' said Tosser, 'pigs can recall they once coexisted amiably with other domestic species and perhaps they will be kinder to the rest of us.'

'Pigs' ass,' said Noddy. 'They are never kind.'

Coal was hauled to the city for heating, or to the harbour to be shipped overseas. With the revenue, the pigs purchased adjacent property which they integrated with Animal Farm. The animals' accommodation remained basic and mean. They slept on damp concrete in sheds. When they obtained straw bedding, the pigs made them remove it, reducing comfort, privacy and individuality.

'Why do the pigs want us to be uncomfortable?' asked Gloria.

'To keep us mindful of their power,' said Tosser. 'They want us to be fearful of them.'

'I'm not likely to forget,' she said.

The animals worked hard but they were allowed little food.

'An animal's need for food depends on adaptation, not size,' said Scottie, a Shetland who would replace Lucy when she retired. 'We Shetland ponies have evolved for dragging coal wagons through small underground tunnels with low roofs. We were starved and when they brought us up to the surface in a near skeletal state at intervals months apart, we were rested in pastures, where we gorged all day and all night, to put on weight quickly. Unless we were fat, when we went underground again, we would perish. I have fattening in my genes. If I don't eat when I can, I get hunger pangs. I should get more food than other animals, more than larger horses.'

After that, when they had food to spare, they offered some to Scottie. But it wasn't often.

Horace was near the end of his working life and would soon be replaced by his son Tiny. Gloria their daughter would take over from Titani, who did the heaviest work.

Tiny and Gloria worked in a pair but had not mated because they were siblings. Tiny was a huge, loose-limbed and awkward horse with hairy legs that feathered down to large feet.

He was kept in a paddock with several other animals for company. He had a phobia of cattle, as had his father Horace.

'They're mindless,' he said.

His one indulgence was sheep - he loved a ewe, Cosette. He would stand for hours with his nose buried in her fleece, snuffling and savouring her rancourous odour of sweat and shit. Sometimes they danced, with Cosette intertwining Tiny's legs. He said little and dreamed of freedom but the two shared intimacy that was real and no-one thought anything of it. Cross species friendships were common but not always sexual.

He was mildly depressed and didn't join in the others' pranks, such as lying down, feet up, pretending to be dead. He stood immobile by the gate and you couldn't tell if he was worried. Although he could crush any other animal, his behaviour was always exemplary and reliable, but everyone expected that one day he would break out.

When a cow came near and he was smooching with Cosette, he would abuse it.

'F**k off you stupid b******', he said, with venom.

Tiny had learned Pidgin English, like all of them, by talking with the other animals. He had a vocabulary of 40 words, which was all he needed.

His talk was slow, even slower than his thinking. He tried to ignore the bellowing of the cows. Cosette's bleating was faster than anyone could understand, including Cosette.

'Tiny must have good intuition to understand that sheep,' the others said.

It could have been that Cosette's ideas were obvious, usually about food.

'What will happen to you, Cosette?' Tiny asked his beloved.

'When I go back to my field, they will have moved the fence to some fresh turnips. Then I will have a wonderful feed and sleep soundly after.'

'And tomorrow?'

Cosette thought.

'No. Sleeping all night is enough for me.'

'No, I mean what do you think will happen tomorrow?'

She thought for a while. 'I give up. I don't want to think about tomorrow. If I expected something good and it didn't happen, I

81

would be disappointed. If I expected something bad, there is nothing I could do about it anyway. I think it's best not to think about tomorrow. What about you, Tiny? Do you believe something is going to happen to you tomorrow?'

'I might run away.'

'Is that good or bad?'

'If I get lost, it will be bad.'

'Where would you try to go?'

'I'll push open the gate and follow the road. Gloria has told me the road goes to some hills, with good grazing, where horses live, without any humans. I could live there, free, like my ancestors.'

'Before the cave men killed them?'

'Earlier than that...'

'When there were just wolves?'

'Stop it. I'm getting muddled. Back when there were only horses.'

'I see. There would be SOMETHING scary. I would rather be sleeping with my flock. Wouldn't you miss us here?'

'I wouldn't miss the cows. It would be tough getting by without you, Cosette,' he said. 'Maybe I won't go.'

'You'll be disappointed if you don't.'

'Not really. It's not too bad here.'

'That's nice. I would miss you.'

'How about a dance?'

When they were having lunch by the dam, the animals sometimes ate in silence but more often they kicked around some topic of current interest.

'I heard the Government is going to give a subsidy for clearing hedges and trees, to allow bigger machines,' said Rondo.

'Well that's a turnabout,' said Tosser. 'They gave us a subsidy to plant those trees over there, that had been cleared with an earlier subsidy. They called it Re-greening and we sowed native seeds. It was only 5 years ago. I suppose they've changed their minds and want the land put back into production?'

'Yes, they now want us to grow grain,' Rondo said.

'Have the replanted trees grown?' asked Pamela.

82

'It's a wilderness,' Rondo said. 'The critters love it.'

'Is the timber big enough to sell?' Pamela asked.

'Not for construction,' said Rondo. 'It can be used for woodchips. We won't get much for it.'

'Is the subsidy enough to pay for our work?' asked Hannah.

'No. They say we will make money from being more efficient.'

'Is that true?'

'Not for us,' said Rondo. 'We can't afford bigger machines.'

'Must we take out the rest of the hedges and trees?' asked Hannah. 'They're not in the way. Animals will be homeless.'

'We might omit to do the clearing.'

'They'll find some way to put us under pressure,' said Tosser.

'Funnily enough, in other places they are wanting trees planted to mop up carbon dioxide and hedges as homes for birds and varmints,' said Hannah. 'Denuding the countryside is a bad thing, I think.'

'Maybe it's a sign they are accepting carbon dioxide is okay,' said Noddy. 'They have given up on protecting trees.'

'Maybe they're clearing trees to be able to plant more trees,' said Rondo. 'Is it necessary that one government reverses what the previous one has done?'

'It's called progress,' said Tosser. 'They say it keeps people employed.'

'Albert Einstein said that doing the same thing over and over, like our clearing and replanting, when it expects different results, is insanity.'

'It fits.'

The animals' feelings about having this new source of energy on their doorstep were mixed.

'Lord Leonard wants to construct a power station on the farm,' said Tosser. ''Year after year we have slaved to feed the pigs and ourselves, with little left over to exchange for goods and services from outside,' he said. 'Mining the coal for a power generation would earn money to improve our living conditions.'

'Mining is shit work,' Rondo said quietly to Pamela his partner. 'They would have to pay us well.'

83

'Fat chance,' Pamela said. 'They aren't about to liberate us, even a little.'

'It would be good to trade with the outside world,' said Noddy. 'Electricity users would value our work and could pay us well.'

'Why?'

'They would depend on us for their supply of electricity,' said Rondo.

'Couldn't they get it someplace else?' asked Pamela.

'No. There is no bulk supply nearby and electricity can't be stored,' said Noddy.

'How badly do you think humans need electricity?' asked old Tosser.

'A lot, like we do,' said Pamela.

'Do we really have to have electricity?' said old Tosser.

'Don't you want us to join in the electrical age?' Noddy said.

'Would our lives be better?' said Pamela.

'I doubt it,' said Tosser. 'The pigs will keep us needy.'

'Couldn't we have small-scale energy, like biogas generators fuelled with dung?' asked Rondo, the prankster of the cattle family. He was always up for fun.

'Good idea,' said his brother Steroid, a pleasant steer, placid and companionable. 'Shitting in a tank is better than mining coal.'

'We don't do enough shit,' said Tosser.

'That's bullshit,' said Pamela, laughing. 'We have more than enough.'

'If they fed us better, we would shit more,' said Rondo.

'I've heard gas heats things more quickly,' said Pamela.

'Burning coal would be less smelly,' said old Tosser.

'The coal discovery is wonderful. It can provide electricity, export and employment. It is the biggest event ever, hereabouts.'

'Try telling the greenies that!'

CHAPTER 14 POWERHOUSE

President Natalia Alphancourt opposed Lord Leonard's powerhouse proposal.

'The SR won't allow the pollution and mining hazards from coal,' she said. 'They want a nuclear plant because it would affect the environment less.'

'There could be a nuclear disaster and then coal would seem more attractive.'

Lord Leonard received a bid from a company in the DU to construct a coal-fired generating plant. President Alphancourt delayed plans but there wasn't sufficient evidence to prevent the powerhouse.

'The design will minimise pollution,' Harvey said. 'It is a great opportunity for us animals to contribute to the island community.'

'Coal mining seems more like slavery,' said Trudy, Harvey's favourite ewe.

'They will depend on us and that could get us our freedom,' Harvey said. 'It's how human slaves became emancipated, by valuation of their work.'

'No-one will know what you're doing in the mine,' she said.

'They'll become aware of us,' said Harvey. 'We would be helping pioneer Caruba's largest enterprise. A power station will be Caruba's most intricate technology and will create jobs and skills for humans and animals. When they have seen we can do the mining, they could want us to help construct and run the thing.'

Construction was delayed when President Alphancourt applied environmental control standards from the SR that added to costs. Dispute with the developer about protecting the environment delayed approval. Caruba suffered economic depression. Desperate for development, President Alphancourt approved a private powerhouse to be constructed with money from investors in the DU. Skilled workers were brought from the DU. The project was the largest in the island's history and brought needed infrastructure and housing development. Electricity supply brought a development boom.

The powerhouse was constructed. It had been operating for several years when President Natalia Alphancourt contacted Lord Leonard.

'The SR wants us to shut down the power house.'

'Oh no, not this again!' he thought.

'That would crash the island's economy,' he said to her, annoyed.

He would wait to see what she would do next.

A few days later, he received a telegram from the DUs foreign office.

'We have been approached by a DU corporation with a proposal to construct an aluminium smelter on Caruba,' Lord Leonard said to President Natalia. 'They want electricity from the powerhouse for a smelter. We thought you would be interested in the employment and infrastructure possibilities.'

'Too right we would be,' said President Natalia Alphancourt. 'It could save our bacon. But the SR are opposed to the effects on the environment.'

'Our mine would be a showcase of environment control,' he said.

He wrote a letter to President Natalia thanking her for her interest in the welfare of his employees and in protecting the environment. He said he had instigated a programme of mine safety, dust suppression and noxious gas reduction. Until there was alternative employment for his workers he could not accept a breach of their coal supply contract. Investors could be expected to take legal action if they shut down the powerhouse and the outcome could be expensive for the Caruba government.

'We have a carrot and a stick,' he said to Giraud. 'Shutting down Caruba's most efficient power supply would seem to be a criminal offense. The coal mine, power station and smelter are the largest developments ever on Caruba. Shutting them down without

86

replacement would cause extreme hardship. We ask that the powerhouse is allowed to continue to avoid animals employed in mining coal going to the abattoir.'

Under Lord Leonard's leadership, totalitarian government of the farm begun by Napoleon 60 years earlier became ideological and bureaucratic. The animal workers were treated badly but knowledge of the pigs' cruelty was kept from the Caruban public and government. When the farm and mine were opened for public inspection, the pigs released the animal workers for the day from their bonds, hobbles, yokes, tethers, cages and pens. Visitors didn't see the cruelty and assumed that the animals were being well cared for. As soon as guests exited through the farm gate, the animals' imprisonment was reinstated.

The two horses maintained their escape plan and exercised to develop their strength and endurance.

'They might take down the wall,' said Gloria.

'What can be taking so long?' Lucy asked impatiently.

'Removing the wall is a big step for them. It changes the way Animal Farm relates to the world outside.'

'It is going to change everything for us.'

Pamela hadn't talked to her friend Cookie for a while and found her in the scullery by the kitchen peeling potatoes. Pamela stayed at the door as she didn't dare enter.

'Knock. Knock,' she said.

'Hello, Pamela,' said Cookie. 'What have you been up to lately.'

Noticing Pamela's emaciated state, she gave her a potato, which she started eating.

'I've been mining coal,' she said, 'working long hours doing backbreaking labour, carrying buckets with my mouth. It's very hard work.'

'It must be worth it to someone,' said Cookie. 'They get electricity from it, don't they?'

'Yeah. They burn it.'

'What do you get?'

87

'Shelter and food, that's all.'

'How is it different from farm work?'

'It is harder and more tedious.'

'It seems as though the people who get the electricity should be paying you more. What if you don't go to work?'

'Someone else will do the work and I won't have any money for food.'

'Could you all demand more money and stop work if they won't pay it?'

'They would punish the leaders.'

'Who is your leader?'

Pamela hesitated. Cookie could pass a name on to the pigs who would try to crush the movement.

'Is it that stroppy ram, what's his name: 'Noddy?''

Pamela denied it but Cookie could read from Pamela her guess was right.

Perhaps Cookie passed Noddy's dissatisfaction to the pigs, for the abattoir truck came and took him away, leaving Hannah distraught.

'Is a powerhouse really such a good thing?' asked Harvey, who had been helping Noddy with the science classes. He was now chief ram. 'Coal mining employment isn't healthy. There's also noxious flue gas from the powerhouse to contend with.'

'Sulphur and nitrogen oxides don't smell,' said Rondo.

'They might not smell, but they're toxic,' Harvey said.

'They can put up tall chimney stacks to disperse the gases,' said Rondo.

'Wouldn't the toxic gas diffuse down to the ground?' asked Harvey

'Yes, but it would be further away and diluted, so it won't be a problem,' said old Tosser. 'It won't affect us.'

'What about effects on strangers?' said Pamela. 'We wouldn't want to pollute their air.'

'They will be too far away to worry about.'

'That's right,' said old Tosser. 'If they don't like it, they can move away.'

'Is it fair to dump toxic gases we don't like on other people?' said Pamela.

'Yes. absolutely,' said old Tosser. 'By Kant's Categorical Imperative, we can do to others what they could do to us. Because we aren't protected, we don't have to protect others. It's a tradition that goes back hundreds of years.'

'Is it the same as the Christian Bible's requirement to do as you would be done by?' asked Pamela.

'Not exactly. We can dump waste in each other's space,' said old Tosser. 'The way things are today, the air, space, waterways, oceans and the deep underground are anybody's to dump waste in. We don't have to be concerned about other people.'

'Working conditions are regulated to protect our people. We don't have to be concerned about others further away,' said Harvey.

'I think it's changing,' said Pamela. 'Polluters will be prosecuted.'

'Not often,' old Tosser replied. 'A plaintiff would have to demonstrate that the shit was coming from somewhere specific. That would be difficult. It's the victims' responsibility to protect themselves. It's been that way since the first agriculturalists had to fence out nomadic herders' animals, to stop them straying into their crops. There was no onus on herders to keep their animals from straying on to the common. Allowing stock to stray is ethical and everyone has rights to access common land.

'It's the same with wastes. Since the Industrial Revolution started, industrialists have been able to release pollutants from their factories, leaving responsibility with private property owners to protect themselves from all kinds of incursions: pollution; restricted access; blocked outlook; and loss of customers. Existing occupants do not normally get compensated.'

'Humans are selfish and inconsiderate!' said Pamela.

'They are kind to dogs,' said Penny. 'Sometimes.'

'Humans are always selfish,' said Rondo. 'Can they dump any kind of waste into the environment?'

'Basically, yes,' said old Tosser. 'There are some regulations, demanding separation and recycling of plastics and storage of radioactive wastes. Industrial plants are required to dispose of waste heat, ashes, dust and flue gases in acceptable ways. Raising the temperature of air, rivers and oceans is allowed, up to limits.'

'When a polluter doesn't comply, is he made to shut down?' asked Pamela.

'Rarely; not if the only alternative is more expensive for him,' old Tosser said.

'Would it be better to do without electricity?' said Pamela. 'I'd rather have clean air and cool water.'

'Really?' said Harvey. 'Everyone expects electricity to bring deliverance. It's like a cargo cult mentality. It brings everything they want: jobs, money, goods, convenience, community and growth.'

'We animals don't want any of those, do we?' asked Pamela. She had her calf with her. It was playing, running away a short distance, turning and scurrying back.

'Doesn't having a job mean anything to you?,' said Milk Bar. 'More work opportunities could provide an animal with self-satisfaction as well as a living.'

'No, a job is only a source of money. More leisure would be better.'

'Animals can benefit from material prosperity and better conditions, just like humans do,' said Harvey.

'I'd rather keep my independence and go without,' said old Milk Bar.

'I don't think we're going to have a say in it,' said old Tosser.

A few days later the abattoir truck came and took away old Tosser and Milk Bar. It had been expected as they had been kept on at the farm into retirement. When all the animals were at work in the fields and they had been given light duties near the farmyard, the truck came, loaded them quickly and drove away. The animals came running but they were too late. They grieved for these elders, who had been their leaders and they held a memorial service for them beside the dam where they had held forth with their quiet wisdom for so many years.

Since the revolution, totalitarianism had taken over the Farm. Individuality had been extinguished. Lord Leonard's dictatorial rule controlled every aspect of their lives. Worker animals had no political say and differences between species were not respected. They had learned to distrust the pigs for their arbitrary cruelty and they had begun to distrust each other.

The farm work was unpleasant and endless, enforced ruthlessly by guard pigs with whips.

The workers were assigned to work groups, without fair opportunities for betterment, except by informing on co-workers. Even passive resistance was dangerous because their quarters and public spaces were under surveillance. In retribution for dissent, workers were taken to the abattoir. Everyone's continued existence was precarious.

Lord Leonard's totalitarian ideology and terror had reduced the worker animals to a fearful disorganised mass. It was a revival of the terror of the years under Napoleon's rule.

Tosser was at heart a democrat who valued a diversity of opinion and open government. Lord Leonard's bureaucracy was anathema.

'We can't oppose the pigs' control verbally,' said Tosser, 'but we are unlikely to do our best work.'

The animals' productivity declined. Worker animals covertly sabotaged farm machinery. Animal Farm stagnated under Lord Leonard's grasping rule until he died. It was the only liberation they could get.

CHAPTER 15 MIGUEL

The workers strove year after year to meet Lord Leonard's ambitious production targets. When he died, Lord Miguel was elected to succeed him shortly after a nuclear reactor explosion in the SR, with effects hidden by the government. The animals wanted a president who would be open with them and elected Miguel in an election restricted to pig candidates. He was a Belarus Black Pied boar whose body was deep, wide, straight and white with black spots. His head was angular, his face lines radiating out from the snout, with ears hanging over his eyes.

Lord Miguel was self-educated by internet correspondence courses, in psychology, sociology and political economy. Such humanity was unknown in any previous pig president but his compassion for his subservient animals was token. He kindled the workers' hopes of liberation but did little to reduce their slavery. He brought a current of change to the stagnating farm he inherited. He proposed a cultural revolution, as Ceramica had done, sending bourgeois pigs to work in the fields. His plan was that by sharing in the hard work, his pigs would better understand the other animals. But the pig oligarchy opposed it. The animals were disappointed.

'They won't change now,' Noddy said. 'Bourgeois pigs have never worked. They have differentiated their lives of privilege from ours as workers.'

A few young pigs began to help with the farm work.

Although Lord Miguel had little interest in the views of the animal workers, he liked to discuss farm policy. He was inventive, testing the limits of possibility, arguing both sides and injecting brinkmanship into proceedings that would have been dull. The animals found it difficult to follow what he wanted but he persisted until objection was quashed.

'He may be educated, but he treats us the same as the others did, like slaves,' said young Stanley, the hybrid offspring of Harvey and Trudy. He was taking over the chief ram role from Harvey. The previous tupping season had been Harvey's last.

The Farm ran one ram with 50 ewes normally and a second ram wasn't needed. One day the abattoir lorry took Harvey away. The animals were too shocked to protest.

'I wanted Harvey to withdraw gradually,' Stanley said. 'It is tough on everyone when animals are unplugged like disposable units. But Lord Miguel wanted Harvey gone.'

'Lord Miguel recognises our feelings but ignores them,' said Trudy, Stanley's mother, in despair. She connected well with the other animals and always knew what their preferences would be.

'That makes his disregard worse,' said Stanley. 'We must demand rights to fair treatment. If we can get Lord Miguel's attention we might revive the workers' democracy that Napoleon's oligarchy derailed.'

Lord Miguel recognised that many workers wanted to practice a religion. He allowed Ravens back on the Farm. They resumed their self-appointed role of inculcating animals in the dogma of the Paradox church. They would inform the pigs of any goat resistance, deflecting attention from their own parasitism.

Lord Miguel approved the animals' request to commemorate the revolution 70 years earlier. He gave them the day off work and provided materials and labour to spruce up the Farm.

He reduced working hours and improved the animals' accommodation and food. Animals were allowed to work together in groups in the fields and freely discuss events.

Giraud, now very old, continued in his former role as technical adviser, with Monty, a gilt, helping him. She had been born on the farm to Lord Leonard and Hyacinth, inheriting her father's black coloration with her mother's white patches. She had studied climate science. When they were not busy in the farmhouse, Monty and

Giraud spent time with the worker animals, answering their questions and teaching them meteorology, ecology and energy technology.

One evening Monty was lying on the farmhouse lawn, on her back, with Giraud and the rest of the science class as she talked them through a tour of the night sky. They viewed the constellations: Aries, Taurus, Porcus, Pegasus, Capricornis, Canis Major and Felis.

'Humans saw these animal shapes in the night sky long ago,' said Monty. 'They must have respected the animals. You should be proud that your animal type is so grandly commemorated by a constellation.'

Afterwards, they thanked her. 'It was a pleasure,' she said. 'Lord Miguel is pleased that you're interested in the history and future of Animal Farm. A tenet of Animalism is *'Participative democracy by education of workers.'* You have embraced it tonight.'

Lord Miguel visited work groups and explained his 'new openness'. He wanted increased transparency in the Farm's management processes. He discussed Farm energy policy with the animals and listened to their ideas.

Lord Miguel improved working conditions. The animals were overjoyed when he announced they would be paid wages for their mining work. Slavery would end. They had never had money before and were able to supplement their rations with favourite foods and small things they had not been able to obtain before.

'We'll be able to buy stuff,' said Trudy. 'We've waited a long time for this.'

'There is nothing I want to buy,' said Dynamo. 'Why should I work for nothing?'

'Because you are a slave,' she said. 'Get a life.'

'They may be paying us wages for mining but they are expecting us to work harder,' said Dynamo. 'We have become wage slaves. There is no improvement.'

When Giraud died, Lord Miguel buried him in the pig graveyard in the orchard. Monty was energy adviser and prominent in technical discussions in the farmhouse.

Later, Dynamo the donkey complained to Rondo: 'Monty is wanting to allow the SR Government more influence here than they deserve. They know nothing about our climate.'

'Why is Lord Miguel kowtowing to the SR?' Rondo asked Monty.

'They're on his back with their environment policy.'

'He doesn't have to do what they say,' said Rondo.

'They want us to follow their principles.'

'What if we don't?' he asked.

'They have others,' Monty laughed.

'The SR are bullying us on environment,' Monty told Dynamo, 'because they are bullies and they can.'

The pigs had improved the animals' accommodation and infrastructure but there were few amenities and the worker animals' quality of life remained squalid, exploited by the pigs. The wages they received for mining were enough to improve their living conditions but low.

Lord Miguel promised worker animals a small plot of land each, where they could grow food for themselves, as had feudal serfs in the Middle Ages in Europe.

'We can grow our own food of we lose our jobs when he adopts the SR's environmental policy,' said Gloria.

'It lowers their provision for us,' said Dynamo. 'The principle in the SR used to be that workers had employment and received food.'

'On this Farm, workers are ruled by pigs,' said Chester. 'The SR and DU have different ideas of the Caruban government's role.'

'Both the SR and the DU are promising liberation,' said Rondo.

'SR liberation is not the same as DU liberation,' said Rondo. 'But neither has come good with any liberation yet.'

'The DU is offering more freedom,' said Rondo.

'It's difficult to know which side would be better for us,' said Stanley. 'To the SR we are labour units; to the DU we are consumption units. It's not much of a choice.'

95

'Any side is better than sitting on the fence,' said Ruby the cattle dog, who had replaced Penny when she became slow. 'We're getting the worst of both worlds now: bad SR labouring conditions and DU freedom to starve.'

'Like Schrodinger's cat we have a choice between the SR and DU. Which world do you choose, Chester?' asked Stanley.

'The DU. The SR's conditions are tougher for a cat. DU people have meat with every meal. It's a no brainer.'

'What do you prefer, beef, mutton, chicken?' Rondo snorted angrily. 'I suppose so long as you get your meat, it's all the same to you? You're a disgrace to animal-dom.'

Chester looked around and realised he was the only carnivore present.

'Maybe having meat isn't so important,' he said.

'Damn right it isn't, you selfish flea-bag,' said Rondo. 'The SR's vegan diet is healthiest and most economical, but the DU wants citizens to have meat at every meal. Here on Caruba we're caught in the middle of a superpower food war.'

'We're the meat in the sandwich, so to speak,' said Tiny, who had taken over from Horace. 'We're being subjugated and exploited. What can we do about it?'

'The pigs' are keeping their options open,' said Rondo. 'Their position is derived from pandering to the SR and DU, so we have to be ready to flex.'

Rondo peeked through a window into the farmhouse one evening during a pig party. He reported to the other animals: 'Pigs and humans are having a great time together.'

'Who are the humans?'

'Natalia Alphancourt's people and some SR and DU officials.'

'What are they doing?

'Mixing like old friends,' said Rondo.

'Not quarrelling?'

'No. They are joking about the possible causes of global warming, such as man-made thermal pollution, solar change and geothermal change.'

'What were they saying?'

'They were laughing, as if global warming was faked.'

'A conspiracy?'

'I suppose.'

'By whom?'

'Between the SR and DU.'

'If the climate change conflict is a conspiracy,' said Stanley the ram, 'that leaves us in a bad place.'

'The lowest common denominator of the two sides is pretended confrontation, like the Cold War. Living standards on both sides have been mired for the past 40 years.'

'The War seems to have a binary outcome. The reality probably lies in between.'

'Our pigs have a trotter in both camps,' said Penny, the young sheepdog bred from Molly. 'They are clever. If they can't get help from one side, they seek it from the other. Lord Miguel may seem to be taking a hard line against the DU but he wants peaceful co-existence. It's simply a quarrel in which the Farm is playing piggy in the middle. Nor do we want to go against the Greens.'

'Is it an advantage to be indecisive?'

'Lord Miguel says its safest sitting on the fence,' said Penny, with a disarming smile.

'Safest for him maybe,' said old Rondo. 'Without the burden of work and hardship to keep us oppressed, he knows we workers would rebel. The Cold War has gone on for too long. It seems contrived to prevent liberation of workers.'

'Lord Miguel seems aware of that. If we are patient, he may find a solution.'

97

CHAPTER 16 OPENNESS

The Farm produced an excess of coal and electricity. Overhead transmission lines marched away from the new powerhouse to the city and the island's industrial area at Salton. The road from the Farm carried wagon trains of coal to the port.

Electricity was kept for the farm and farmhouse. The pigs purchased a hot water system, an electric oven, a dishwasher, a stereo, a sauna, a jacuzzi and other electrical appliances. Lord Miguel bought a television set for himself and his favourites.

Penny told the animals: 'The pigs need a television to keep up with developments in the outside world, so they can update us on everything we need to know.'

The pigs seldom left the farmhouse, except to give instructions and punish errant animals.

One evening, Stanley and several of the worker animals crept up to the farmhouse and peered in through a front window, to see what the 'television thing' did. They saw a box with dolls performing miniature lifelike dramas inside and were puzzled.

'I don't see what the pigs see in these simulations,' Stanley said. 'We have real situations with real problems needing attention. If all they do is watch television, the problems will worsen.'

'At least they're off our backs!'

'Good thought. Maybe they'll spend less time fornicating and there will be fewer piglets.'

'It couldn't get better than that.'

'Would you ask them to install lights in the buildings so we can study?' Rondo said. 'Study will make us contented and loyal, benefitting them.'

Lord Miguel had electric lighting wired to the animals' sheds, stalls and pens. For the first time, they were able to study at night. It was 'democratization' that increased the openness and transparency of his regime. Worker animals had a say in how the Farm was run for the first time. They could participate in resolving economic and social issues.

'I am in foal to Tiny,' Gloria said to Lucy.

Lucy declined to comment that he was her brother. Sibling matings were were quite common.

She thought for a moment.

'Will you still want to go?'

'Yes, more than ever,' said Gloria. The two had carefully planned their escape. 'This is no place to raise a youngster. He can come with us, when the wall comes down.'

'Will he be up to travelling?'

'Absolutely. Foals have evolved to tag along.'

'What about Tiny? Will he come with us?'

'No. He thinks we will be better off without him. The hill farmers won't accept a Shire stallion breeding with their mares. It's sad but I will be able to manage without him.'

The workers' employment in the coal mine was uncertain, with too much demand rather than too little. A smelter would be built to use electricity from the powerhouse. A reliable supply of electricity was wanted to attract investors to commit funds.

'An electricity supply failure to the smelter would be disastrous, with the melt solidifying and cracking the pots,' Monty said sombrely. 'Compliance with electricity production goals is compulsory. Any slacking off at the mine would be punishable by death.'

'I can't see the workers causing any difficulty,' Penny said, trotting to and fro. 'Electricity production benefits everyone. Workers value having steady employment.'

Wanting to guarantee electricity supply to the smelter, the pigs obtained consent from the SR Government for a uranium-fuelled powerhouse.

When Monty came with Gloria and Stanley on an inspection of the mine, Gloria wanted to know the difference between nuclear and coal stations.

Gloria's foal was with her, born the previous day, wobbling uncertainly on spindly legs.

'Will there be any environmental effects?' Gloria asked.

'Such as what?' Monty asked.

'Radioactive pollution, for one.'

'There is no problem,' Monty said. 'We will dump the drums of spent uranium in the ocean.'

'That may have to stop,' said Stanley. 'Any pollution is an offence. The SR Government is coming here to measure our emissions.'

'They will want us to plant trees,' said Monty.

'The island doesn't need any more trees,' Stanley said. 'They've banned logging and chipping. Forest vegetation loads have increased and bushfires are more frequent, more intense and longer lasting.'

'A balance has to be found between conserving forests and limiting air pollution,' said Monty. 'It's the same with thermal pollution. Unless we cool the turbines by warming up the sea or the air, we won't be able to generate electricity efficiently.'

'Creating waste heat to get efficiency seems like a contradiction,' Gloria said.

'A turbine generates most electricity if steam going in is cooled at the outlet making a vacuum,' said Monty.

'That totally sucks,' said Gloria.

Then Caruba's nuclear reactor sprang a leak, it contaminated a part of the island with radioactive material. Fortunately, the evacuation exclusion zone did not include any of Animal Farm. The reactor was shut down for investigation of the accident and the island's energy supply was thrown into chaos. The residents grumbled about black-outs until the coal station was upgraded to make good the shortage in supply. The SR sent money to the island's research institute to consider energy alternatives.

'Antis are calling for the coal powered station to be shut down too, to reduce emissions,' said Stanley.

'When emissions are invisible, people get hysterical,' said Tiny.

'Scientists are alarmed about atmospheric warming,' said Monty. 'Ultra violet radiation is coming through the atmosphere and causing skin cancer, so sunbathing isn't safe anymore. They're blaming it on industrial pollution.'

'Of course they are,' said Stanley. 'It's self-serving for their careers to create alarm by exaggerating all types of pollution: refrigerants, mercury, pesticides, heavy metals, acid gases, chemical carcinogens, radioactive fallout and electromagnetic radiation.'

One day Monty told them a new concern.

'UV has been getting in through a hole in the ozone layer.'

'What is the cause of the hole?' asked Stanley.

'No-one knows,' said Monty. 'Maybe it doesn't have a cause.'

'That's ridiculous,' Stanley said. 'It must have a cause. Scientists will guess one.'

'Peaceniks after the Cold War ended in the SR have restyled themselves as 'antis' and operate at the national level conserving forests, planting trees, recycling resources and opposing environmental damage,' said Stanley.

Later, Monty informed them again.

'They say the hole in the ozone layer is caused by certain gases. A conference of 20 nations in Montreal decided unanimously to limit the use of chlorofluorocarbon gases in refrigerators.

'They prevented the chemical pollution and now the Ozone Hole has closed over.'

'It shows what can be done when everyone works together,' said Penny, Molly's daughter. Sheepdogs liked consensus.

'It would have closed over anyway,' said Chester, Ammo's disagreeable son. 'The so-called hole may never ever have existed except as a temporary thinning.'

'The SR claimed credit for instigating the Montreal Protocol,' said Monty. 'We should respect that.'

101

'They are using the ozone hole success as the method for fixing all the bad stuff, like pollution, waste, resources depletion, environmental degradation, and so on, all to be tackled by international collaboration.

'They believe they stopped the Cold War by international activism and won't take No for an answer,' said Monty. 'They style themselves as 'antis': anti-class, anti-capitalism, anti-profit, anti-auto, anti-industry, anti-materialism and anti-pollution. All these movements are united by a 'green' agenda' and potential militancy.'

'Are you sure there isn't an animal liberation movement?' asked Tiny.

'No. There's anti-vivisection. But the main thrust is anti-industry.'

'Will we have to go 'green'? asked Gloria.

'What does going green involve?' asked Tiny. 'What would we have to do?'

'Plant trees; recycle wastes; reduce resources use; conserve environments; develop sustainably,' said Monty. 'Climb onto the Green bandwagon and make a lot of noise.'

'The DU won't like us going green,' said Gloria. 'It reduces business opportunities.'

'Too bad,' said Monty. 'Other countries are going green. The DU are the odd ones out.'

'The pigs are between the green SR devil and the deep blue DU sea,' said Tiny.

'Regulations are coming and will transform the technologies we use. Hopefully the changes will be gradual,' Stanley said.

CHAPTER 17 CALF TERROR

The Farm's pig population burgeoned but worker animals were often reluctant to reproduce because their offspring were sent by the pigs to the abattoir.

Pamela was carrying a calf that she and Rondo hoped would be a female, able to supply milk and live a long life. Bull calves were taken to the abattoir after one year, to supply the ravening human demand for veal.

Pamela gave a low moan.

'It's trying to come,' she told Rondo.

She was in a loose box in the cowshed for the birth, remaining standing as pushing started and became more urgent. In between bouts of pushing, she lay down.

After six hours with little progress, she stood up and pushed with all her remaining strength, roaring with the effort.

'Here it comes,' said Rondo.

The calf slid out in a rush and he broke its fall.

'It's a bull,' he said, joyfully.

The calf stood up shakily and tried to suck a teat, but was unable to grasp it in its little mouth, until Rondo helped. He and Pamela watched their offspring, marvelling as it moved around and explored.

The next day, when the animals trooped in after working all day in the fields, Pamela rushed around the farmyard, looking frantically in the sheds and pens, bellowing.

'My calf . . . it's gone!' she cried.

She was still weak from her labour. The calf had suckled only once and milk was squirting from her swollen udder and teats. The calf was due to feed again, but it was nowhere to be found.

'I know what's happened,' said Rondo.

'What?' she said.

'Think,' he said kindly. 'Where could it be?'

'Maybe it has run into the fields,' she said.

'It's unlikely. What happened to our last calf?'

Pamela dimly remembered. 'It disappeared. We never found it.'

'No, but the pigs had a party that night. Where do you think the money came from for their booze?'

'They could have saved up.'

'Not them. They must have sold something.'

'What?'

'What could they have sold?'

Pamela paused, thinking.

'Our calf!' she said with a sob. 'But they told me they had arranged for it to be reared in the calf lot on the farm next door. They would bring it back in a few months' time.'

'That was a year ago.'

'They could still bring it back.'

'They are not going to bring it back, Pamela,' he said sadly. 'We will never see either of our calves again.'

Pamela wept.

'I will never have another calf,' she said.

'Are you sure?'

'I know what caused it!'

'What?'

'You, you horny bastard.'

'That's not the real problem, is it?' he said. 'I'm sorry about our calf too. The pigs have treated us with contempt.'

In separating offspring from their parents, the pigs never hesitated.

'The pigs don't value parenting of the new-born,' said Pamela. 'They don't even want them to stay long enough to feed on the colostrum, for their immunity.'

104

'Perhaps connection with the mother is overrated. In some species, like brush turkeys and turtles, separation is immediate. The young hatch unaided and depart the nest alone to find food independently.'

'I suppose they inherit the instincts they need. In humans, offspring stay with parents for up to 20 or 30 years. The immediate weening of our calves is obviously traumatic and almost certainly dysfunctional.'

Gloria's foal raced around, kicking and jumping. Pamela sadly recalled that her calf should have been playing with him.

She and Rondo would have no more calves. After a couple of years, old Rondo lost interest in the Farm and ceased fathering. Pamela's milk dried up.

When Sophie heard about the missing calf, she was distraught.

'If the pigs are going to sell our young, I won't breed,' she said to Stanley.

'They might not sell them. They might keep ewe lambs on the farm to replace old ewes,' he said.

'It's not much of a life for them, is it? Is it worth the risk?'

But she realised that it was not her choice. The pigs controlled mating. Resistance risked you being loaded into the abattoir truck and could not be ignored.

Earl took over from old Rondo. He was a different type, in looks and a more intellectual thinker. The cows weren't used to discussing matters with a bull, except Dolly, who was an import too. She and Earl got on famously. She replaced old Pamela as the leading cow.

The pigs sent Rondo and Pamela to the abattoir.

At the end of Earl's first year as chief bull, his favourite Dolly bore them Henry. Her Friesian was in the calf, as mostly white, with black patches. A year later she bore Simone, almost black. Dolly diligently fed and cared for her calves. She went with Earl to the meteorology classes. He was a keen student of environmental science and occasionally presented a topic to the group. He took over from Rondo and was the spokesperson for all the animals with Lord Leonard and after with Lord Miguel.

Dolly encouraged Henry to follow in his father's footsteps and become involved in farm policy-making with the males.

She involved Simone with the females, helping to raise their youngsters.

'Why can't I get involved in policy meetings?' asked Simone.

'You can if you want, but you would find those meetings deadly boring,' Dolly said. 'I used to go but they spend their time puffing themselves up and trying to deflate each other. You wouldn't like it at all.'

Although couples mated under pig control, they sometimes enjoyed intimacy. Stanley and Sophie lay together in the grass at night and gazed up at the majesty of the Milky Way.

'This sky humbles me,' said Stanley. 'I feel very small.'

He remembered then Harvey and Trudy, his parents, missing them for their goodness and kindness to him, that had guided him to become the person he was. He hoped that his example was helping younger animals to realize what they wanted and to commit to the travails of getting it.

'There are other couples doing this,' said Sophie, caressing a horn. 'But not like us.'

Sophie was taller than him. They had practiced mating and found that lying together was best.

'Are we special?' he asked, pressing his nose into her long neck. 'In all the universe are we the only couple like us?'

'Probably,' Sophie said. 'Is that good?'

'Our uniqueness confers importance,' he said. 'It's better than being replaceable.'

'What's so good about being unique?'

'Being the same would mean being predictable,' said Stanley. 'We would be typecast, without recognition of our individuality and with few rights.'

'Things have reached a pretty pass,' said Earl. 'We won our revolution against human oppression, but under Lord Napoleon we were too demoralized to claim rights to life, to a home, to liberty, to pursue happiness, to have equality before the law, to have an

106

opinion, to reproduce, to express ourselves publicly, to have political freedom and to have government protection.

'We have no rights and the pigs have been our undoing. They have presumed genetic superiority and claimed precedence over other animal species. They have taken control of our lives without consultation, exploiting us as beasts of burden, stealing our potential, using us for animal power and for demeaning fieldwork.'

'Coral is worst off,' said Dolly. 'Goats are at the bottom of the ladder, with no rights at all.'

'Others have problems too,' said Upstart. He had taken over from Gregory and with his partner Bessie scratched up small stones in the mine helped by their pullets. They had proudly led a stream of poults out into the world that week, only to have the pigs seize them to sell.

The pigs had tried to exterminate the goats and they hid away, or blended in with the sheep whenever the pigs started a pogrom, or escaped to adjacent property. Goats habitually dissented, despite the punishment this brought them. The pigs had animal workers build pens where goats were starved, as a deterrent to troublemakers.

Goats were valued by the worker animals for their wisdom and fearless criticism of the pigs. Refugees from their homeland, lacking rights to justice and representation, the pigs expelled them individually from Animal Farm, for faked misdemeanours. In despair, goats sought refuge in wasteland areas around Animal Farm. When the pigs enmity had dissipated, they would return, starving, to the farm.

There was usually at least one goat running with the sheep on Animal Farm, either a billy or a nanny, sometimes with a kid. Alone, goats had to leave the Farm to mate. It was easy for them to get over hedges and walls, with their strong climbing ability.

'We would help you if there was a way,' Earl said to Coral.

'You do help,' she said. 'One day the persecution of goats will end and you give us hope that it will be soon.'

'Animal Farm is rotten at the core with pig self-interest,' said Earl. 'Their management of livestock reproduction and selling animals to the abattoir is arbitrary and cruel. We must prepare to end their hegemony. In the meantime, we can try to prevent matters getting any worse by passive resistance.'

'You mean a go-slow?'

'No. There would be reprisals. Our passive resistance will be subtle and they won't be aware we are white-anting them until the farm disintegrates.'

Central planning on Animal Farm foundered when other farms in their economic bloc lost confidence and sought independence. There was a feeling that Animal Farm was in trouble. The pigs were losing control. Fearing their worker animals would rebel, the pigs sold off the farms they had acquired and concentrated on domestic problems making increased demands on the worker animals. Prospects for animal liberation receded.

CHAPTER 18 SENTIENCE

Farm animals were without rights or legal protection. They were unprotected by animal welfare legislation, which dealt with isolated acts of cruelty committed against domestic pets. It didn't take account of the isolation, confinement in cages, crowding in sheds, lack of access to a natural environment, inhumane transport, violent handling, castration, docking, dehorning and slaughter of farm animals, all without pain relief or anaesthesia.

The pigs on Animal Farm had different standards for their own species. They made known to pigs throughout the whole island, the philosophy of Animalism. They pretended to be instigating uprisings to overthrow humans on other farms but their interest was to liberate pigs from castration and slaughterhouse death.

'It has been obvious from the start,' said Earl, 'our pigs only care about themselves.'

When the animal liberationist Phil Sopher visited Caruba, Lord Miguel invited him to speak at the Farm about the rights of sentient animals. It was arranged that he would come with President Natalia Alphancourt to speak to all the animal workers.

Lord Miguel stood with the President, Sopher and Monty to address a packed gathering in the farmyard.

'Good afternoon, animals. We are honoured to have with us President Alphancourt and from the DU Professor Phil Sopher, a philosopher and animal rights activist.'

Sopher began speaking.

'This afternoon I want to talk about sentience because animals in other places have been using it to obtain their rights and you may want to claim yours. Sentience *is the capacity to be aware of feelings and sensations.*

'The law classifies farm animals as property and fails to recognise their sentience. Sentient animals have complex social lives involving communication, organised groups and family bonds. Farm animals feel pleasure, sadness, excitement, resentment, depression, fear and pain. They are aware and more intelligent than is generally supposed, having been bred as domestic slaves. But they are individual beings in their own right and deserve our respect. Despite the growing body of scientific evidence, some people remain sceptical of animal sentience. This uncertainty should not justify the reckless treatment of animals. If all available evidence suggests that animals are sentient, they ought to be treated as such. It is morally incumbent upon us to give the animals the benefit of the doubt and to protect them so far as is possible from conditions that may be reasonably supposed to cause suffering, even if it cannot be proved.'

Sopher gave examples of situations where animals' sentience was, or was not, observed by humans.

When he had finished speaking, the animals applauded enthusiastically.

In question time, President Alphancourt announced: 'Lord Miguel, your Monty already attends our parliament as an observer. In the future, representative animals may be able to speak and vote.'

'Could a representative of the farm's worker animals attend?' asked Earl.

'Eventually yes,' said President Natalia diplomatically. 'We are starting with Monty and it could develop from there. Your English is very good, Mr Bull. Yes, a worker animal should certainly be able to attend in future.'

'I don't see how humans can possibly doubt that we are as sentient as they are,' said Dolly afterwards. 'When I see a human looking at me, I can guess their feelings from their eyes, from the appearance of their face and body posture.'

'Me too,' said Earl. 'What feelings do you see?'

'A few humans genuinely respect me, a few fear me, but most see me as an automaton incapable of pleasure or pain.'

'They don't see our suffering?'

'I think they could, but they don't want to recognise it, because they are ashamed of how they treat us.'

'If they could admit to understanding our feelings, maybe they would treat us better,' said Dolly.

'They do care about their pet animals.'

'I have heard it called compartmentalisation, or lack of transitivity.'

'Stupidity and cruelty are better words.'

Lord Miguel's presidency had brought a new level of openness and the animals' productivity soared. Recognition of animals' sentience was improving livestock management practices worldwide. Lord Miguel began a programme of reform of the animals' working and living conditions, which they perceived as first steps towards personal rights.

Farm activities went on into Spring and it was soon time to shear the sheep again. A fleece would eventually fall off, but the wool would have inclusions, such as sticks and burrs, that would reduce its value.

The pigs had relented and purchased electric shearing machines. They hired itinerant shearers because holding them required dexterity beyond any of the animals' skills. Sale of the wool would more than cover the cost.

Conditions on Animal Farm were usually dry and sheep's pellets dropped away cleanly. But in wet weather, stools could be loose and foul the area around the anus, allowing blowfly strike to occur. The pigs made the ewes dock their lambs' tails using rubber rings to reduce the problem. Farmer Jones had also shortened the fleece near the anus to prevent wet excrement accumulating, treating maggot

111

infections with insecticides and disinfectant, but the animals lacked the skills to apply more than superficial treatments. The sheep endeavoured to keep their rear ends clean and the pigs gave the sheep disinfectant to treat any infections. Sometimes the eggs hatched, the larvae ate the excrement, then the wool and then the flesh of the sheep, eventually killing it if unattended. When discovered in time, they immersed the sheep in an insecticide bath and it would make a complete recovery.

The pigs continued to send animals to the abattoir.

They began dismantling the wall, at long last. Gloria told Lucy it was time to put into action their escape plan.

'My foal is old enough to keep up with us. I want him to grow up in freedom.

'Will we be able to find our way?'

'Tiny will get us a map.'

'Could you read a map?'

'He will explain it. Also we will be able to ask animals on the way.'

Tiny had been excited by Sopher's talks and was prepared to fight for liberation. He downloaded a map for them from the internet. To protect from incrimination, his connivance was the only confidence in other animals they made until they left.

'Escape has never been tried by three horses before,' Gloria said. 'My large size is unusual. We will be conspicuous, but people who see us will assume we are getting away from a local farm and leave it to the farmer to find us and take us back. The pigs won't bother to search far afield. We will travel by backroads, keeping away from places with humans. We will walk at night and lie up in daytime.'

Gloria and Lucy finalised their preparations by eating as much as possible, because they might have to go without food.

CHAPTER 19 BORAT

Lord Miguel imported a boar, Borat, from the DU to diversify the pigs' gene pool. He was a Tamworth, a UK breed, ginger in colour. His body was large, deep sided, with a strong arch of back, a muscular top and a long rump. His head was elongated with a straight snout and erect ears. Lord Miguel made him Farm construction manager because he could get things done.

Lord Miguel had opened the floodgates of the animals' pent up demand for goods, the Farm accounts were in chaos and Lord Miguel was forced by demonstrators to resign. The trading bloc of farms was dissolved. Lord Borat was elected to the Farm presidency with 59 percent of the vote. His closest competitor was a sow, Hyacinth, with 18 percent.

Lord Borat continued the change to openness begun by Lord Miguel. He wanted the animal workers to become more independent, starting businesses that would operate independently, within his guidelines.

'I'll pay you to plough, an amount per acre,' he said to the horses.

The animals' wages were lower than for human workers in treadmill-like occupations. Caruban employers were for the first time able to set their wages as in the SR. They had difficulty. The communes looked inward for direction and when there was none, they tended to disintegrate. Workers were unable to buy goods available in other countries and attributed their low standard of living to state communism. Animal Farm was independent but lacked market access for farm products and security of supply of inputs, until new relationships were developed.

'We lack buyers for some of our vegetable crops,' Lord Borat said. 'My priority is to find customers.'

Lord Borat tried to graft capitalism onto the SR's central planning rootstock, while continuing the totalitarian tradition of arbitrary terror, exploiting the worker animals. The intended transition to a more open western style economy failed.

The Farm had stagnated for most of the 70 years since the revolution but now the oligarchs led a development boom. Lord Borat's experience in development and construction enabled the emergence of Animal Farm as an investment province attractive to global capital.

'With a new barn, we can raise more feedlot beef,' he said.

'Factory farming is cruel and it would be better to expand our horticulture,' said Earl.

'Horticulture is less profitable and you would have to work harder,' Lord Borat said.

Lord Borat traded the Farm's products worldwide for foreign currencies, food and equipment. Animal Farm eventually entered into a new era of prosperity, doing away with outdated methods, providing further luxuries for the pigs and continuing the workers' slavery.

He expanded the freedoms begun by Lord Miguel, allowing the animals to discuss Farm policy matters, but they could never question the pigs' control.

With few goods in the shops, some of the animals bought lottery tickets.

'Winning the lottery is the only chance I have of getting what I want,' Big Ears the mule said.

'What is it that you want, Big Ears?' asked Dolly.

'I want to run wild and live with hill ponies,' he said.

'That takes guts, not money.'

'I need money to bribe my way to freedom.'

The animal workers were eating by the pond when Ruby the collie sidled up. She had taken over when Penny was put down. Earl thought she might be there to eavesdrop.

'Hey, Ruby,' said Earl. 'What is Lord Borat up to these days?'

114

'He's booking an air-plane ticket to a climate conference in Kyoto.'

Earl was astonished. 'When pigs can fly,' he said.

'Next month,' said Ruby.

Before Lord Borat went to the conference with President Natalia Alphancourt, she refused to close down the power station and allowed export of coal to continue.

'If coal mining is stopped,' she said, in a meeting at the Farm with the animal workers, 'lifestyles and development will languish on Caruba. Environmentalists want us to stop supplying coal to developing countries and impose on them environmental values they cannot afford. In those countries people often go without electricity and live in poverty. Their women scrub clothes by hand on rocky river beaches. It is wrong to deny them coal to generate electricity for washing machines. It would be wrong to put our need to prevent pollution above theirs to access electricity. We must continue to meet their demand for coal.'

'Then our coal-fired power station will continue?' asked Earl. 'Coal is the most efficient supply because it wastes least heat. Besides, we have a large investment in coal technology. It will cost least to keep it going.'

'You have a blind spot to keep that power station going,' said President Alphancourt to Earl. 'What is so wonderful about coal?'

'It warms the environment least.'

'That's your theory,' said President Natalia. 'I don't believe it.'

'I can explain,' Earl said.

'It's not me you have to convince,' she said. 'Scientists won't accept it.'

She struggled to say this in Pidgin English.

'I had heard that you make up your own mind,' Earl said.

'I have made up my own mind that islanders want the power station replaced, not shut down,' she said crossly in Englsh. 'Our coal-fired steam turbine is 20th century technology, inefficient and polluting. Better methods of electricity production are available. Coal has too many problems. I have asked the SR to fund installation of renewable energy technology.'

'The problems you speak of are the propaganda of the renewables advocates, who would profit by installing new technology,' Earl said. He had taken a risk in speaking out when his Pidgin English could be misconstrued. 'It is a scam.'

'I disagree,' she said shrilly. 'Could it be that you favour coal because it is your main source of income on this Farm? Switching to renewable energy would be an improvement for all Caruba. I am considering reducing the output of the power station to zero.

'I can assure you, I will be doing the best I can for all Carubans in Kyoto.'

After she was gone, the workers talked together in a group in the farmyard..

'Natalia is right,' said Sophie to Dolly. 'Carubans have no right to impose values on developing countries.'

'The antis think people in less developed countries don't know what's bad for them,' Dolly said. 'They think they are saving them.'

'The SR has hotheads and some of them are here on Caruba,' Sophie said. 'Will Natalia be able to oppose them?'

'The environmental lobby will try to replace her if she allows the power station and mine to continue producing,' said Earl.

'Carubans would be without cheap electricity and would oppose a shutdown,' Dolly said, chewing a mouthful of hay.

'It would conserve energy,' Sophie said, rubbing her bottom against the fence. 'Everyone wastes electricity.'

'Remind me to give you a worm powder,' said Dolly.

When Lord Borat returned from Kyoto, he spoke to Earl and a couple of the other worker animals.

'I have grave news. There is a consensus of scientists that global warming is occurring and that it is caused by emissions.'

'Thermal emissions?'

'No. Emissions of greenhouse gases are growing seven times faster. 153 nations have united to lower greenhouse gas emissions, 5.2 per cent below 1990 levels by between 2008 and 2012. They

116

want coal combustion to be stopped or greatly reduced. Output of our power station, coal exports and smelting will have to be reduced.

'I have talked with President Natalia about this change and there will be less work mining coal and fewer animals will be required to do it. This will put some of you out of work but sacrifices have to be made and can be overcome by sharing with others. We will make the cutbacks fairly, but I ask you all to cooperate in overcoming the climate menace.'

'I am in favour of liberating worker animals from death in the abattoir, but this is being blocked by the pigs' Central Committee,' he said.

Lord Borat went off to the farmhouse.

'Well, it sounds as though Lord Borat is going to shut down our mining, electricity, coal exports and metal production,' said Ruby.

The worker animals were indignant.

'That will cause massive unemployment and hunger,' said Stanley. 'Lord Borat's cutbacks are shit.'

'Lord Borat is using global warming to dominate and terrorise us,' said Earl. 'It is a straw-man fallacy, declaring a catastrophe and then taking the credit for saving us from it when nothing eventuates.'

'It is President Natalia who will decide.'

'Let's hope she uses common sense.'

'What can they have been talking about in Kyoto?'

'I have heard the SR short circuited debate by plumping for the enhanced greenhouse theory,' Earl said.

'In the DU individuals are free to choose from alternative viewpoints,' said Dolly. 'They let the market decide. Mistakes are paid for by the investors who made those mistakes, whereas in the SR the government makes everyone pay.'

'Few people in either superpower are able to make an informed decision,' said Stanley. 'Who stands to benefit most from the Kyoto emissions reduction?'

'It is supposed everyone will be saved from the effects of climate change,' Earl said.

'Won't emissions continue at existing levels in the other half of the World not represented at Kyoto?' said Dolly.

'Yes, but reducing growth in half the world is better than doing nothing,' said Earl.

'Lord Borat says there is a scientific consensus and the debate is over.'

'There hasn't been a debate,' Earl said. 'There has been a debacle. The philosopher John Dewey wanted public policies to be advised by experts, with everyone having a say. What we have is experts generating alarm. Instead of debate, a post-truth mentality has taken over, with declarations carried by appeal to emotion.'

'What emotion?'

'Naturalism, as if the industrial revolution can be reversed.

Caruba ratified the Kyoto Protocol and President Natalia gave one year's notice of shutdown of the power station. Without electricity, lifestyles would be hit and Caruban industry was shocked. She established a committee of businessmen and finaciers to establish Caruba's new market economy without central control.

'Populations are in fear from the heightened publicity being given to extreme weather events and disasters,' said Earl. 'They are the new terror.'

'What is the reason for that?' asked Stanley.

'Governments want fearful populations who will re-elect leaders who appear to have control of the climate,' said Earl. 'Leaders want to have a finger in the global pie to avoid the stigma they would get as non-participants.'

'Worker animals can vote for our candidate in elections but we will have no say in anything else,' said President Natalia. 'We will rebuild industry and Lord Borat will find other work for the coal miners.

'Lord Borat said he he supports our liberation.'

'A likely story,' said Earl. 'Lord Borat is hiding behind the Central Committee. They won't liberate us. He wants to retain the abattoir as a tool for his totalitarian terror. As long as the pigs retain control, we worker animals will be no better off than we were under

Farmer Jones before the revolution. The pigs are our new bourgeoisie and we worker animals are the proletariat for exploitation. Marxist revolution was our beginning but our struggle for equality has brought us full circle from human tyranny to equal pig tyranny. It will take another revolution to liberate animals from the work system that has captured us.'

'Is it possible?'

'Yes,' said Earl. 'We have a formed a nucleus and our cause will grow. We're just getting started.'

CHAPTER 20 RAVENOUS

Under Lord Napoleon's atheistic rule, religion had been expunged from Animal Farm. He had made a determined attempt to eradicate faiths, replacing them with education in science. Believers opposed loss of their religious freedom by dissent, extremism and martyrdom. The pigs dispersed congregations, banned services, destroyed churches and tortured clergy. Religious activity went underground.

The pigs' misbehaviours included prejudice, ignorance, repression, oppression, persecution, destruction, illegality, greed, corruption and murder. Most martyrs had been killed, or died in old age. In an underground group who maintained Paradox worship, Dolly the cow carried the torch for her faith.

'It's the evil in the pigs that makes religious virtue necessary,' said Dolly. 'I will never give up my faith.'

Paradoxy, as espoused by the Ravens, elaborated the animals' beliefs, requiring obedience to its rituals, catechism and dogma, supplying justice. Not all animals followed the Ravens' teaching.

'If we had to invent a religion that would support its clergy, Paradoxy would fulfil it nicely. The Ravens are entirely self-serving,' said Artemis the goat.

The Ravens' attempts to lead the worker animals have brought them into conflict with the pigs who banned Paradoxy from Animal Farm

'The pigs think they can excise religion like a tumour, but it has already metastasized,' said Dolly to Earl. 'It has grown too widespread and it is too late to cut out now.'

'Religion is not like cancer,' he said. 'It doesn't kill you.'

'On the contrary, for many people religion lies at the heart of their well-being,' said Dolly. 'Without belief many are condemned to a partial existence or even to die.'

'If you have a religion, the pigs certainly give you a hard time,' said Earl.

'Living on our farm is difficult, with or without religion,' Dolly said.

The pigs' experiment with atheism was heartless, and it ultimately failed. In the late Lord Leonard years, the Paradox religion was reinstated. Raven descendants of Patriarch, who had stayed away during Lord Napoleon's and Lord Nikos's dictatorships, now returned in a flock to the Farm. Now Lord Borat welcomed the Ravens to provide community leadership, because Caruba was in chaos. Soon the Paradox religion was providing people with certainty their political leaders could not provide.

Lord Nikos expected to drive the Ravens away forever, but they had hidden. Lord Leonard allowed them back to hold services. Later, Lord Miguel permitted them to reopen churches and conduct religious ceremonies. The faith of the worker animals was that their suffering was ordained by the pigs' evil and if they lived virtuously would be overcome by final liberation. The state of nature lacked government and civility and their lives were, according to Thomas Hobbes: 'solitary, poore, nasty, brutish, and short.' They awaited a messiah who would lead them to freedom.

Ravens flew to the outside world and brought news and views which the animals eagerly absorbed. Their preaching glorified the worker animals' suffering. The Ravens were accepted by the pigs for amplifying their catechism of mindless subservience and leaving thinking to the leaders.

The Ravens did no work and fed by scavenging. The pigs rewarded them for opposing other faiths. Miguel allowed Ravens back onto Animal Farm on condition they would report any animal learnings that challenged the pigs' authority. For many years the Ravens had exclusive religious incumbency. While disseminating ideas about tolerance, religious pluralism, and ecumenism, they repressed, with alacrity and malice, missionaries from evangelical churches who came into the Farm, to spread their ideas among the animals.

A missionary for the Jehovah's Witnesses had attracted a small congregation of sheep and was holding services before the Ravens found out and reported it to the pigs, who ejected the intruder from the Farm.

'What about religious freedom?' Sophie asked Ruby. 'I thought there was tolerance.'

'There is tolerance — to worship Paradoxy with the Ravens,' she said.

'The end of the world is nigh,' said the missionary. 'Witnesses will be saved from eternal damnation and relieved from suffering the execution of Jehovah's righteous judgements.'

The missionary was silenced and ejected from the Farm. The followers appeared to disperse but continued to meet secretly and worship using the books left by the missionary.

'Our church is the only religion allowed on Animal Farm,' the Ravens told congregants. 'Our God knows how hard it has been for you. Hard work and your loyalty to the pigs will be rewarded.'

The Ravens' church attracted worker-animal parishioners who were able to influence Lord Miguel's policies. However, the resurgence of religion seemed to confirm the animals' slavery rather than offer them hope of liberation from their suffering.

Dolly read from the bible.

'On the fifth day, God said unto them: 'Man shall have dominion over every living thing that moveth upon the Earth,'(12).

Perhaps God wants humans to be superior.'

'The Bible is horseshit,' said Earl. 'I'm not going back to the old days under Farmer Jones.'

'Science isn't enough for me,' said Dolly. 'It doesn't tell me how to live a good life.'

'A good life is a matter for experiment, not belief,' said Earl.

'Experimenting takes courage,' Dolly said. 'Many animal workers prefer to be told what to do.'

122

'By whom? God?'

'No, by leaders, advised by Science. Marx was an economist and he knew what we had to do to put food on the table.'

'There were famines.'

'The hunger would have been worse without science.'

'The pigs don't understand the importance of religion,' said Earl. 'They want the animals to obey them, not god.'

'Atheism has failed in the SR because they misconceived that faiths could be suppressed,' Earl thought. *'Their anti-religion experiment could not succeed because individual humans' rights to their religions were too deeply engraved on their psyches. The atheists attempted to amputate a rich part of human culture, not just religious worship, but also their art, idealism, critical thinking and interest in social reform. The same thing will happen with Animalism. Without regeneration from within, Animalism must fail.'*

Eventually, Caruba's legislation for freedom of religion allowed in missionaries from the DU and elsewhere. They raised the animals' awareness of conditions outside. The Wall had been an obstacle to developing community and culture, at a time when the animals rejected captivity and wanted to develop closer relationships with neighbouring farms and make visitors welcome.

Other religions started up on the Farm, with confession, prostration, sacraments and genuflection. When the Ravens found this out, they reported it to the pigs who expelled the leaders, punished the perpetrators, banned access to premises, confiscated bibles and other paraphernalia.

Pig guards at the wall stopped workers from escaping to the outside world. Any animal caught was punished with solitary confinement or killed. The animals daren't protest but they held secret forums to demonstrate their opposition and made contact with rescuers outside. Differences between the two sides in rights and economic circumstances aggravated the separation. Religions sought to integrate their followers. Eventually these movements combined and dismantled the Wall from both sides.

'This wall has prevented us from joining with others,' said Goliath, pausing as he pushed over a section of wall .

123

'Foreigners will find out the conditions we have been suffering,' said Dongle. 'They will demand the pigs treat us better.'

Many animals escaped and were welcomed at neighbouring farms but the pigs did not merge Animal Farm with humanised farms outside, who did not recognise pigs' status above other livestock animals.

'If we try to spread Animalism, we could find ourselves back in the pigsties again,' a pig said.

Without the wall to keep outsiders out, vandals trespassed on the Farm in increasing numbers. Animal Farm was known on Caruba as an experiment in animal liberation. The farm and its occupants were a magnet for curious islanders and teenage troublemakers. They invaded at night, coming right up to the buildings where the pigs and timid animals cowered. They painted graffiti, damaged property, stole tools and took fruit, until large animals chased them away.

'We must deter the raiders somehow,' said Earl. 'The island police won't protect us.'

Earl was always in the forefront of defensive action but was never violent and would not condone others to use violence.

'Could we lie in wait and ambush them?' asked Dolly.

'We need to scare them away without hurting them,' Earl said. 'We could threaten or capture them.'

'Could we set a trap?' said Tiny, joining in their planning.

'What if we capture one of them and frighten him,' said Steroid. 'How would we do that?'

'We could seem to be going to hang him, but let him get away.'

'Could we use a rope that snaps?' said Tiny.

'Good idea,' said Earl. 'An old rope from a hay dray would do it.'

At the next weekend, the animals intercepted and chased a gang of half a dozen youths. Tiny galloped up to them, knocked one over and stood with a massive foot holding him down. He was abusive until Tiny put weight on his foot, when he screamed. Stanley wrapped a rope around him, holding his arms by his sides. They lifted him into a put drawn by Lucy and took him to the barn where they put a rope over a high beam and then around his neck. Tiny hauled him aloft. A string prevented the noose tightening. There he

124

hung dripping, his anal sphincter open. Hours later, at dawn, Stanley pulled on the string, the noose opened and he dropped to the floor, where he soon wriggled free and fled, with animals chasing after him. He crawled under the thorn hedge at the farm boundary and got away.

After that, there were no more night intruders on Animal Farm.

'What's it like without humans?' asked animal neighbours across the fence.

'We have pigs lording over us,' said Pamela.

'Do they beat you with sticks?'

'Whips.'

'Do they have dogs?'

'Yes, savage ones.'

'Is it better with pigs than with humans?' the neighbour asked Pamela.

'The farm belongs to all of us and we have a say in what happens.'

'D'you have proper meetings then?'

'We do have meetings,' said Pamela. 'I won't say they're proper though.'

'D'you have to do work?'

'Yes, a lot. I get milked twice a day and have to do fieldwork too.'

'Is there enough food?'

'Usually not.'

'We could let you have some food.'

'Thank you.'

'We will leave it here by the fence for you.'

'That will be great,' said Pamela.

'Oh. Here's one of your pigs coming. Bye for now.'

'Bye.'

The divide between Animal Farm and neighbours was maintained by speciesism. Human neighbours felt too threatened by the animals' education and control to communicate with them and stayed away.

One evening at dusk, Gloria, her foal and Lucy walked across the border where the farm wall had stood. Only their closest friends knew they were going. Discovery would have brought certain death.

Tiny was there.

'I wish I was going with you,' he said to his sister..

'You can come.'

'They wouldn't let me stay. I will come and find you one day, when I can get free from this place. Perhaps we can make it good enough for you to come back.'

'You'll have to find a way to get rid of the pigs.'

'We won't put up with them much longer.'

'I'll miss you. Goodbye.'

They travelled all that night and at dawn crept into a thicket away from curious eyes.

Their luck held and a week later they were thrilled to reach the lowlands leading up to High Moor. They had never been in the wild before and exulted at the space and feeling of security they gained without humans or pigs threatening in the distance.

They were made welcome by the herd of hill ponies and began a new life.

CHAPTER 21 CHANGE IS RELATIVE

On a rare day of holiday, all the animals had gathered to listen to Earl the bull, who stood on a dray parked in the farmyard with other leading animals. Monty was there and Earl knew any criticism he made of the pigs would be reported to Lord Borat and he would be punished.

He was thinking: *'I will have to watch my step. I want to object to the excesses of environmental control being applied to our farm by governments, preventing efficient farming and threatening operation of our powerhouse. I will be careful.'*

Earl spoke as follows.

'Good morning.,

'Fellow farm animals, today June 5th is the anniversary of our revolution when Animal Farm began. We are gathered today to celebrate, to reflect on our past and future.

'70 years ago, on Revolution Day, Old Major inspired Napoleon to lead the animals of Manor Farm in revolt and Farmer Jones fled. Since then, pigs have taken over the farm which rightfully belongs to all the animals. We workers have kept this farm going through thick and thin. Recently, outsiders in the Caruban Government have started telling us what we can and can't do and we need to unite in response.

'In the SR far away, the army returned as victors and overthrew their monarchy, commencing a communist state. A movement began for less profligate use of resources, with respect for flora, fauna and the physical environment.

*'The Vietnam war brought the hippy movement and opposition to:
industry, pollution, resources extraction, forestry, animal feedlots,
circuses, zoos, corporations, consumerism, profits, investment and
development. Generations X and Y grew up wanting an end to big
technology and reduction in economic growth.*

*'These concerns have affected us here in Caruba. The SR is
urging our Government to close down our only coal-fired power
station. The antis are imposing their values on Carubans in a big
way and affecting what we do on the Farm. We don't have to follow
what they want and if we unite we can make a stand.*

*'Are there any questions or comments so far? When I continue it
will be to review what we want for Animal Farm.'*

Stanley stood up. 'The pigs want to shut down our power station
because of global warming,' he said. 'Is the temperature increase a
problem? I would like to know what evidence of that there is?'

'A good question,' said Earl. *'Temperature increase is not a
problem for us, is it? Grass will grow better at higher temperatures
and there could even be an improvement in our living and feeding
conditions.*

*'The Caruba Government wants us to play our part with other
countries in stopping warming in other parts of the globe where
warming is a problem. For example, Australia is a hot dry country,
where climate warming is fiercely opposed.*

'Why should we care about them?' asked Earl. *'Our government's
responsibility is to the people of Caruba, not to the whole world.'*

'Thank you for your answer,' said Stanley. 'Carubans could also
be adversely affected by warming. Working in hot conditions could
be less comfortable and the cows might go off their milk.
Temperature increase could be accompanied by a change in rainfall
and storms could be more frequent. These effects are not known with
certainty. But Carubans want to join the other countries to stop
warming. When pollution made a hole in the ozone layer, we joined
with the other nations in stopping it.'

128

'Your view is that warming is a concern,' said Earl. *'I'm not convinced that the amount of global warming is a severe problem,'* said Earl. *'Earth's temperature changes continually. The global daily average swung 78 times between 25°C and 10°C in the last 4,500 years. The total increase over the last century was only 1 or 2 degrees. We are going to have to look at how temperature change is measured and whether it is significant. We shouldn't have to go without electricity because Australians settled in a hot place.'*

Earl paused, quaffed a bucket of water and continued his speech.

'When the SR disintegrated, the 'anti' movements emerged as environmentalists,' said Earl. *'The antis didn't have a real solution. Their ambitions were dreams. The peaceniks in the superpower nations turned from anti-war protests in the Cold War to environmental alarmism. They were anti-development, anti-capital, anti-industry, anti-material, anti-auto, anti-government, anti-authority and anti-expert. Hippies aspired to pastoral collective living, reversing the industrial revolution and migrating to rural communes where they would subsist growing food crops with a minimum of technology, improving it by trial and error. The lifestyle they aspired to was building a cabin on an acreage, planting trees, eating home grown vegetables, playing musical instruments and meditating.*
'Hippiedom spread into every aspect of life. Their ethos included critical attitudes as consumers, employees and citizens.'

'Tree huggers,' someone called out.

''Make love not war,' was their mantra,' Earl continued. *'The hippies' dreams went largely unfulfilled.'*

'Hippy wankers,' jeered the same voice, to laughter.

129

'They campaigned as activists,' said Earl.'They were opposed to dams, logging, mining, oil exploration, rejecting almost everything technological. Some trained in environmental science and worked for governments. Corporations for self-defence had their own environmental scientists

'The SR's air quality standards remained below DU and EU norms but have caught up. Power plants were aging and lacked equipment for pollution control, resulting in toxic emissions and wastes that endanger flora and fauna in lakes, rivers and countryside. Motor vehicles had minimum regulation and lead in petrol, exhausts with carbon and nitrogen gases caused air pollution. Replacement of older vehicles, with new having catalytic converters, mitigated the problem somewhat.

'Industries have come under the scrutiny of environmentalists, requiring safer employment and cessation of pollution.

'Conservationists have promoted preservation of nature and avoided locking horns with the establishment. The organisation has limited itself to holding educational forums about conservation, keeping track of endangered species and assisting government agencies responsible for maintaining nature preserves. Patrols hide out in forests to identify and bring poachers to justice.

'For many, environmentalism is the new religion,' said Earl.

'Recently Raven clergy have restored Paradoxy on our farm. This does not mean there is a relaxation of pig control. Old Major told us: 'Religion is the opium of the people.' Religion will not bring our liberation.'

'Here is the main question: Are we Carubans bound to follow in the footsteps of the SR and DU? Or are we able to decide our future independently? These questions are on our agenda. We will answer them slowly and try to persuade the pigs of our view.

'Today, Animal Day, I want you to appreciate that we are determined to continue, whatever the future may hold.

'I will stop there. I leave you to draw your own conclusions about where environmentalism could take us and discuss them with our leader group. I hope we can talk about it again soon.'

130

CHAPTER 22 HONEST BIASES

A group of animals was gathered in the cowshed for a class on 'temperature'. For three decades the workers had operated a weather station at the farmhouse and attended evening classes on science topics related to weather. Today it was raining, dripping down into the open doorway, falling into a gutter and flowing away into a brook that ran through the farm.

Stanley the ram was there first, with his partner Sophie. He had taken over the class from Harvey, his father. He liked being with Sophie, beautiful and knowledgeable, with whom even routines became adventures. They were lying on straw in the front row to be near their cia, Norman, who was playing with several youngsters. Sheep were packed quietly in the front rows chewing the cud, with cattle and horses behind.

Science classes were a highpoint in the animals' week, with news of public issues, exposition by Stanley, lively discussion and controversies in which their opinions would be sought.

The cowshed had stalls where the cows were milked by the pigs, using an electric milking machine. Teat cup clusters and milk pails were stored hanging from hooks on the wall. Pigs carried the milk to the farmhouse for their mash. At one end there was a box where calves were kept away while their mothers were milked.

Cattle were second in number to sheep. Despite their hard lives, they indulged in fun when they could. Late at night, they would gather in a meadow, with lookouts in position and on a signal of all clear they would rise erect on their back legs, in pairs, holding each other, sashaying, waltzing, wheeling and gliding in ballroom dances,

131

to a plaintive melody played by a goat on a homemade clarinet, with a thumping rhythm beaten out by a wild badger on a hollow log and intoned by a cow bawling into a length of plastic drainage pipe, like a didgeridoo. They would dance for hours, stepping, whirling, in graceful partnerships, the whole company undulating in synchrony. The pigs were oblivious and Penny didn't give the game away.

Dolly and several other cows and heifers now stood together in the cowshed chewing the cud with Earl the bull. Towering over them were the carthorses, Goliath and Fiona, with their filly Blondie. She was impatient to begin the class, fretting and fidgeting, nuzzling her friend, young donkey Dongle. Glock the cockerel strutted around self-importantly.

'This rain could make it too wet for fieldwork tomorrow,' said Dolly to Fiona.

'It will be muddy,' said Blondie, spunky and wild. 'The pigs like mud. If we balk at crossing the brook, maybe they'll give us the day off?'

Horses were unwilling to take risks with their footing and often spooked when they had to walk through water and couldn't see the bottom. An injured leg and inability to keep up with the others could, in the wild, mean death from predators.

'Balking would work with the horses but not with us,' said Dolly. 'The pigs would know we were faking it. If it is pouring, they'll find us work to do inside, mucking out, changing straw bedding, sharpening tools and oiling harnesses.'

'The pigs like wet weather and they will be in a good mood,' said Dolly. 'We ought to ask them about our rights.' She turned to Stanley. 'Will you ask Lord Miguel?'

He nodded unenthusiastically.

Earl the bull bustled in and shook himself vigorously, showering them.

'Earl! Do you mind?' said Stanley indignantly.

'Sorry,' said Earl, not seeming at all contrite. 'I shook myself without thinking.'

'I'm soaked,' said Stanley the ram. 'You must have been sodden, you old sod.'

132

He called out officiously. 'Let's make a start.'

The hubbub faded. When the animals were attending to him, Stanley addressed them, referring to a page of notes. His voice was confident and relished each syllable, without pomp. He was their best speaker. He was middle aged and it was expected he would soon hand over to Norman, his son and offsider, his horns not yet fully grown, who was watching him closely, learning as much science as he could, ready to help his father.

'I want to continue from where Earl left off the other day, in his talk about environmental change,' Stanley said. 'My concern is that measurement should be true and agree with others' measurements.

'Weather science begins with measuring physical conditions and reporting findings. The skill is in using the instruments correctly, recording readings and summarising. So far in your science studies you have weighed objects, measured lengths and used thermometers to find the temperature of liquids. Now you will measure the temperature of air and make instruments to find humidity and wind speed.

'We are fortunate on this farm to be able to study towards our liberation. Our masters, the pigs, have allowed us to measure the weather and for the past 33 years you and your predecessors have kept a continuous record of temperatures. Some of you will remember Horace the horse, who was in the first group. Those who began the measurements are no longer with us but their descendants, equally committed to the cause, have taken it up voluntarily and continued with diligence and accuracy.'

'What do you do with the measurements?' asked young Dongle. He had the knack of asking questions that everyone wanted answers to.

'We use the readings to calculate an average temperature for each day, for each month and then for a year,' said Stanley.

'How will that bring liberation?'

'When we know about our environment, we will be closer to having control over it. If we can predict future temperatures, we can plant suitable crops and trees.'

'How is a global average calculated?' asked Sophie. She and Stanley explored science together and she was a keen participant in all his classes.

'We have held refresher classes every few years on how to read the maximum-minimum thermometer. First, we calculate the daily average of the two maximin values and then an annual average. That is for one station and it is averaged with some or all of the other 6300 stations.'

'Why are only the maximum and minimum values used?' asked Dongle.

'For practical convenience,' said Stanley. 'Only two readings per day are needed and can be taken at any time of day, because the instrument stores the values.

He displayed a page from a bundle of papers with tabulated measurements.

'When you read the temperature, you record the division closest to the top of the mercury. What should you do if the mercury is halfway between two divisions?'

'Choose the closest.'

'And when it is exactly halfway?' asked Stanley, not getting an answer. 'Then you can go down or up, at random.'

'Does it matter?'

'If you always go up, or always go down, it could affect the average,' Stanley said. 'You should vary at random. I have compared your maximin readings with my own. My average was slightly lower because I rounded lower more often than you did. Perhaps subconsciously you wanted to verify warming and rounded up?'

'Are you saying we have been biased?' asked Dolly, indignantly.

'Perhaps you were expecting a higher temperature,' said Stanley. 'Measurements by one person can potentially have their bias. At least one other observer is needed to verify every reading. In trials of medical treatments, observer bias is eliminated by paired tests, with a 'blinded' observer who does not know which treatments are

134

placebos. The possibility of observer bias at weather stations cannot be ignored when measuring small changes, unless there is validation, training or active supervision.'

'Hah!' said Dongle. 'Couldn't the differences be errors?'

'Yes,' Stanley said. 'No-one is being blamed. Individuals can have subconscious biases.'

'You are splitting hairs!' said Dolly impatiently. 'It is too small to matter.'

'Small climate differences are taken seriously,' said Stanley. 'When temperatures are read wrongly, averaging won't correct it. Errors are recorded permanently.

'There were only a few differences between your readings and mine, mainly mistakes and slip ups in transposing values. There was not a significant confirmatory bias for global warming. Well done everyone.'

'It seems a little odd to me to be so concerned with small temperature differences, when we lack food and are brutally oppressed,' said Earl.

'Making observations scientifically is exciting,' said Norman, contradicting him.

'I agree we have more pressing problems but people throughout the world are worried about their climates,' said Stanley. 'We need to play our part in the world community by measuring temperature accurately.'

'So what? How will measuring the temperature make any difference?' asked Dolly, Earl's favourite. She had little interest in science and her interest in the class was mainly social.

'People want to look for small changes in climate,' said Stanley.

'Why do they matter?' asked Earl, following up Dolly's question.

'No-one wants their climate to change,' said Stanley. 'It's called the Goldilocks Effect. The existing climate is just right, for everyone.'

'Climate activists want to change industrial emissions to control the climate,' said Earl.

'Where?'

135

'Everywhere,' said Earl. 'The whole World is connected by its atmosphere.'

'Is it possible to control the World's climate?' asked Dolly.

'It might be possible, if everyone adopts a new technology,' said Stanley.

Young Norman listened raptly to Stanley's words. They were a revelation to him. Scientific measurement was so much better than anything else on the Farm, for pigs did not control the outcomes with their biases, as they did for everything else.

'Future classes will consider how much temperature has changed, allowing for biased measurements, theories and forecasts.'

'In today's class we have simply looked into the evidence for temperature change,' said Stanley. 'Later we will relate it to what the pigs are doing about climate change and advise them, if they will listen.'

'They won't listen,' said Earl.

'Mind you don't get stuck in the mud, Earl,' said Stanley.

'The only stick in the mud round here is you,' Earl said. 'Just kidding.'

'Science could be the best hope we have for liberation,' said Stanley. 'But I fear the pigs are deaf to our wants.'

CHAPTER 23 STAB IN THE DARK

The worker animals were waiting in the farmyard for Stanley to arrive for his next class. Today they were sitting or lying on the cobblestones facing the raised platform used for loading grain from the granary into wagons. It was a sunny day and some animals stood in the shade from the hay barn behind them. Sheep chewed the cud quietly as they waited but the cattle were in a huddle, milling around slowly, gently pushing against each other, enjoying the social contact as they discussed events.

Overhead, swallows flew into and around the barn to their nests in wall corners, where their eggs were inaccessible to rats and snakes. The nests were cups of mud, facing upwards, lined with down and soft dried grasses. For a couple of weeks every year, pairs shared egg sitting, until the young hatched. Feeding took all their time and the young birds grew quickly. Three weeks after hatching, the cup lip was adorned by a row of 4 orange gapes. Days later these small metallic blue-black birds, with a distinctive rust red forehead, breast, and throat, would take to the wing as aerial feeders, nature's pest controllers, chasing mosquitoes, midges, moths, and flies. Seldom alighting they would skim through the air, dart and manoeuver aerobatically with their forked tails.

In autumn they would line up on overhead cables, before migrating up to 6000 kms, flying low and covering 320 kms per day. Small and inoffensive, the birds were favourites with the animals.

Stanley the ram arrived with a clipboard and a large chart for an outdoor class.

He eyed the milling cattle. 'What's the matter with that lot?' he said to Sophie.

'The usual. They are arguing about extreme climate events, temperature change and sea level rise.'

'Good for them,' Stanley said. He raised his voice as he always did to animals larger than himself. 'Today's topic is forecasting and there's plenty to discuss. It is empowering to make our own predictions for something as large as atmospheric temperature, instead of relying on forecasts by strangers faraway.

'Your views about the future might differ from one another and who is wrong or right will not be known until the future has become the present. Good and bad forecasts are eventually found out, but the forecaster is seldom held to account. Climate forecasting is more of an art than a science. It is a topic that has been in the news lately. When there is temperature change, as discussed in our last class, the obvious question is How much will the change be? This can be answered by denying any change, by guessing it, or by relating it to past temperatures. They are all valid ways of forecasting.'

He held up a clipboard where they could see displayed tables with temperature measurements they had made over the past year.

'Let's suppose we want to forecast the temperature here next year. How should we go about it? Anyone?'

'Draw a graph,' said Jolene.

'I thought you would say that,' he said. 'I have here my graph of the daily averages for the past year.'

It was an erratic line, from January 1st on the left, to December 31st on the right. The measurements were points on a continuous jagged line with days marked along the scale below and varying between about 10°C and 25°C.

'How can this be used to get a forecast?' asked Stanley.

'Find the trend and continue it on,' said Jolene.

'Would you be able to find a straight line?'

'Maybe.'

'If so, would the forecast for next year be a continuation of that line?'

'It could be, but this year the temperature cycled down in winter and then up again,' said Henry. 'Wouldn't it be more accurate to assume every day next year will have the same temperature as it did this year.'

'Why should it be the same?' said Stanley.

'Why not?' asked Henry.

'Because the weather could differ. You can't assume it would be the same.'

'You could draw a trend line,' said Jolene, 'even a flat one. You would need data from several past years.'

'I agree,' said Stanley. 'A rule of thumb is to have three years of back data for each year of forward forecast. We put our trust in trends. Every trend assumes a catechism of constants. Forecasting is more like a religion than a science.'

Stanley put down the graph.

'It takes measurements to reveal trends. Accuracy of temperature forecasts was improved after 1714 when Fahrenheit invented his thermometer. Not all forecasts use measurements. Deaths from famine and disease in Ancient Rome and the Middle Ages were forecast by haruspicy, which is inspection of entrails of animals, especially the livers of sacrificed sheep and poultry.'

'Yuck,' said Fiona the mare, Goliath's partner, an imported part-thoroughbred who had mothered a string of foals.

'How else can we forecast?' asked Stanley.

'The pigs ask my opinion sometimes,' said Ruby. 'Dogs know things other animals don't.'

'Do you have magical powers, Ruby?' said Fiona, condescending.

'Not exactly magical ...'

'What then?'

'We collies have common sense,' she said. 'We're good at making predictions. We look for signs. For example, when sheep are lying down it can indicate rain is imminent.'

'It's the converse of the situation where a person walks across a basketball game in a gorilla suit and no-one sees it, because people are watching the game,' said Stanley. 'With climate, everyone is watching for the gorilla of bad news, such as global warming and they don't see that the game is proceeding normally. They see the sheep lying down but nothing else. A forecast has to take in the full picture. It's a myth that the gaze of science is unbiased. Forecasting is seldom reliable.'

'Trying to forecast a climate is doomed to failure,' said Sophie. She was eating a weed she had brought. 'It is too extensive and change is too slow.'

'Sophie, are you at all concerned that the climate could be changing?' asked Stanley.

'Llamas will survive,' she said, munching on her weed. 'We can live where cattle and sheep would starve. It does concern me, but only a bit.'

'Unusual weather happens all the time,' said Stanley. 'A place can experience a weird weather event, without it being a universal change in climate.'

'There is definitely a global warming trend,' said Chester. 'Birds are relocating south.'

'How do you know that?'

'I have seen them flying over,' said Chester. 'Migratory species used to stop by here every year, but they haven't dropped in lately.'

'It might not be temperature. Their food sources may have changed due to agriculture and urbanisation.'

'Maybe the birds have changed to a different route,' said Stanley. 'When conditions change, animals adapt.'

'Hold on,' said Stanley. 'We are getting ahead of ourselves. We need to find out how much temperature increase would be a problem and then find out how soon that could occur. Some scientists seem sure we have to act immediately.'

'Warming is not bad for all species in all places,' said Henry. 'There can be advantages. They say that photosynthesis speeds up at higher temperatures and we get higher yielding crops and greening of deserts. Are they not a good thing?'

'Humans who live in hot climates could want to oppose the discomfort of warming,' said Chester. 'In cold countries they could want to maintain ice and snow, for recreation and tourism.'

'Temperature effects are two sided,' said Stanley. 'There can be changes both warmer and cooler. Environmentalists oppose change

- both ways. They want climates that don't change either way, for food supply from nature and for production from domestic species, for human shelter and living, for clothing and for recreation.'

'Humans have put up with weather abnormalities, causing droughts, bushfires and extreme events, since forever,' said Sophie. 'Why can't they now put up with occasional climate change?'

'Humans have ridden roughshod over environments,' said Stanley. 'Climate change is gradual, accumulates and can have insidious results. Many people want a response that is better than ignoring it. They want something sophisticated.'

'Like stopping change altogether,' said Henry.

'Fat chance,' said Fiona. 'Humans have survived change in the past and will again.'

'Many people think climate change has to be opposed,' said Stanley. 'They want governments to act.'

'It would seem niggardly to not contribute to the worldwide cause if we could,' said Stanley, 'but the Caruba Government won't question the forecasts or consider whether there are grounds for local concern.'

'We need unbiased observations of temperature, glaciers, sea levels and extreme events, to be collected for many years,' said Stanley. 'Consequences of effects for people and indicators of any potential causes should also be recorded. When that information is available, analysis will be possible and actions can be considered.'

'Even if we have good historical data and find a pattern, the events may not happen again.' said Chester.

'What we should NOT have is people doing the forecasting with low confidence and justifying a course of action that cannot possibly succeed,' Stanley said.

He paused.

'This evening we have heard how climate forecasting is intrinsically uncertain, like betting on a race, with favourites and outsiders. The choice can create alarm or be disbelieved.

'It is often assumed that climate change can be opposed as if there is a common cause worldwide, but it can threaten different places differently. Warming, sea-level rise and extreme weather all have

141

local effects. Consequently, a unified global response is probably unobtainable.'

'We have assumed countries have only a selfish interest to consider,' Henry said. 'But they want to cooperate. Would they not act for the good of all?'

'I agree they should do, but history records that help given by governments to overcome situations of famine, conflict, invasion, diseases and natural disaster have been little, made for their own advantage and taken place too late,' said Stanley. 'Their excuse can be difficulty in forecasting. People don't want their governments to take disaster relief gambles.'

'If there is confidence that global warming would have a significant effect, trying to stop it could be reasonable,' said Henry.

'It would be reasonable if they were confident they could have technology to stop it. How to be confident about the future is a skill in science that we'll come to later,' said Stanley. 'Henry is correct, we need to know if warming could be a problem here and how to stop it by a method better than being bullied. That's all for today. Good evening everyone.'

'I would be more interested in the future if it included liberation of our animals,' said Henry.

'Our employment is our only freedom and it's more like slavery,' said Stanley to Sophie. 'But it is something. I don't think there is a case for shutting down the power station.'

'Well, it's going to happen,' she said. 'President Alphancourt wants it and you may have to wear it.'

CHAPTER 24 TRAPPING HEAT

It was lunch time at the halcyon picnic spot and the animals were sitting around on logs and stumps, basking in the sun overlooking the farm dam. They had brought their lunches - a turnip apiece.

The dam was beside a shady grove where wild animals once had lived. When Farmer Jones had operated Animal Farm, several copses had been left wild for nature to harbour creatures whose presence made country life worthwhile. These reserves were treed, brambled and so dense humans could not penetrate. Animals moved freely in and out along pathways through the scrub. Deer and foxes took refuge there from hunters on horseback. When horse-back hunting was banned, shooters killed them. No deer came now and few foxes. There were a few harried badgers, rabbits, hares, polecats, stoats, otters and other varmints. Hunters sicced gun dogs onto living targets but the dogs found penetrating the undergrowth difficult, emerging with thorns stuck in their muzzles. Overhead there were buzzards nests and a squirrels' dray. At dusk Indian pheasants ascended noisily to their roosts, their wingbeats whirring.

Goliath was stretched out lying on his side beside Fiona. Their half-grown foal Domino was playing with Myrtle, Henry and Claudia's sister. They were talking with Stanley and Sophie. About thirty cattle and sheep were spread out, enjoying the company, drowsing, several pairs were amorously engaged and one or two individuals slept. Dongle the young donkey, the goat Coral, a pair of geese and several hens were searching the ground for hazel nuts and chestnuts, eating them.

Earl watched Myrtle. His youngest gave him immense pleasure. He could see himself in her conformation and colouring. Her body was softer and with more rounded muscle in her legs, from his Charolais inheritance, unlike her mother's bony Friesian body. His love for Myrtle was of a different kind to Dolly, unconditional. She was bright and outgoing, her inquisitiveness matching his. They talked together, about her young life and what she wanted. It saddened him that he couldn't do more for her but he was thankful for his family and friends providing islands of joy in the midst of the austerity they were all suffering.

'Have you heard from Gloria and Lucy?' Earl asked Tiny.

He shook his head. There had been no message. He missed Gloria, Lucy and the foal.

'It could be a while before you hear,' said Earl. 'They're a long way away.'

Old Goliath the carthorse, was grumbling.

'Why are humans so concerned that climates are changing?' he asked.

'A theory is that a small change to existing weather systems does not add more of the same but tips them over, into instability,' said Stanley. 'They want to prevent it.'

'Can air temperature be controlled?' Henry asked Stanley.

'According to the Gaia Hypothesis, it is being controlled now, ' said Stanley. 'Earth self-regulates to keep conditions for life constant.'

'How can it do that?' asked Fiona the mare.

'Solar radiation is reradiated in equilibrium with the Sun, keeping Earth temperatures the same overall. The atmosphere acts like a blanket holding temperatures within the ranges we are used to.'

'That's reasonable. Can it be falsified?' asked Fiona.

'Since it predicts constancy, any major change would falsify it, but there hasn't been one.'

'Do you believe it's true?' she asked.

'I don't disbelieve it,' Stanley said.

'If there is no evidence against it, could that verify it?'

144

'No,' Stanley said. 'It could be false: we haven't seen everything yet. The climate system is physically too big for me to observe and judge it.'

'No theory can always be true,' she said.

'You're right,' he said. 'There has to be the possibility of refuting it and that's why I don't accept Gaia. I don't want to go into it here but could we talk about it with the others in my class this evening?'

'Sure. Let's enjoy the beautiful weather and let the climate do its thing.'

'I am more concerned about the EGHE. It is a widely accepted theory of global warming. 'The EGHE was first described in the 1990s, with radiation from the Sun being converted into infrared and trapped by increased trace gases, causing global warming. Do you believe it?'

'No. It was a hypothesis, an educated guess.' Fiona said.

'Is it pseudoscience because there is no falsification experiment proposed?'

'I think so.' she said. 'But not everyone defines science by Popper's requirement for falsifiability.'

'Because ice was melting and bad weather events were said to be worsening, many people believed it vehemently,' Sophie said. 'People are not sensible. Why can't the matter of warming be decided once and for all? I'm fed up with hearing about theories.'

'A theory could be wishful thinking?' Stanley said. 'Having a warming theory mitigates the discomfort of living in a hot climate, as a sort of thermal cringe. The part of the EGHE theory I want to test is that global warming is caused by increasing CO_2 content of the atmosphere. How can I do such a test?'

'Could you check whether the warming process proposed can be explained?' said Henry.

'I can use logic,' said Stanley. 'The increase is under 2 ppm of CO_2 per year, or 1 molecule of CO_2 per 500,000 of the other gases, which are N_2, O_2 and H_2O. Could such a relatively small change warm up something as large as the Earth with its 5.11×10^{15} tonnes of atmosphere and 1.46×10^{15} tonnes of water? It doesn't seem

145

likely. CO_2 molecules are 57% heavier than the other gases and can absorb more vibrational energy, but this would not make such a dramatic change to the atmosphere's heat insulating properties. Logic refutes the EGHE hypothesis.

'Perhaps the small amount of pollution has a disproportionally large effect on the temperature of the atmosphere,' said Henry.

'There is a belief that global warming can be stopped by reducing certain trace gases, as was done with the ozone hole and refrigerator gases leaking into the atmosphere,' Stanley said. 'CO_2 could not possibly have their chemical catalytic effect. A small quantity of those had a very large effect, breaking down the ozone molecules, without ever being used up. To cast CO_2 in such a role is fantasy.'

'So fixing the ozone is not relevant experience of a pollution effect?' said Henry.

'No, I don't think so,' said Stanley. 'Ozone was polluted with trace quantities of a catalyst. CO_2 is not a catalyst and traces of it could not cause warming.'

'Perhaps CO_2 has some other effect that we don't know about yet?' asked Sophie.

'Some people believe in the Tooth Fairy but that doesn't affect the electricity supply,' said Stanley.

'Some of us believe in animal liberation,' said Sophie, 'but carbon dioxide pollution attracts more interest from humans.'

'Killing animals doesn't affect the electricity supply.'

CHAPTER 25 AN HYPOTHESIS

It was a week later when the science class met again.

Stanley wrote 'EGHE' on the board. 'Our topic this evening will be the Enhanced Greenhouse Effect theory.'

The 30 class members became silent and sat down where they could hear and watch Stanley.

'Do you believe the EGHE is false, Stanley?' asked Sophie, his favourite ewe. She knew his views but the others didn't and she was helping him to get the class started.

'I haven't seen evidence falsifying it,' he said. 'But I haven't seen evidence confirming it either. Before I believe something is true, I need to have seen positive test results.'

'What do you want tested?' she asked.

'That warming has been caused by increase in CO_2.'

'Are there tests showing it is *not* caused by CO2, but by something else?'

'Science isn't able to dismiss a theory,' said Stanley. 'It remains possible, always, even without any verifying evidence. Many respectable scientific theories such as: natural selection, relativity and plate tectonics, have been accepted even without falsification tests. These theories have been accepted by scientists and by the public because the results were accompanied by convincing thought experiments.'

'What would it take to make the EGHE scientific?' asked Henry.

'I will tell you about another popular theory that was found to be unscientific. The theory of *phlogiston* was postulated between 1766-1791 by Priestley and others, who proposed the existence of a fire-

147

like element called *phlogiston,* pronounced *flojiston,* contained within combustible bodies and released during combustion. There was intense speculation by many scientists who believed all or part of the new theory.'

Stanley wrote *'phlogiston'* on the board.

'The more phlogiston a substance contained, the better and more completely it burned. The theory was elaborated to explain phenomena, experiments and according to Stahl *phlogiston* was a constituent of *'sulphur, bitumens, asphalte, oils, all parts of vegetables and animals, charcoal, nitric acid, vinegar, tartar, volatile alkalis, metals, and all substances coloured or opaque'.*

'In short, phlogiston was supposed to be in almost everything,' Stanley said. 'A Frenchman, Antoine Lavoisier, opposed the *phlogiston* theory. His accurate weighing of combustion reactants and products discovered combustion did not release mass, but gained it. He recognized and named oxygen (1778) and hydrogen (1783). His explanation of combustion with oxygen replaced the *phlogiston* theory, which had been accepted by many scientists of the day but was totally wrong.'

'The EGHE can possibly be rejected in the same way that *phlogiston* was rejected, by having an explanation better than the existing theory. The EGHE is supposed to be validated by explaining hot temperatures on Venus as a greenhouse effect, whatever that is, because it has an atmosphere of CO_2, but other explanations are possible, not requiring CO_2.'

'What theory does explain global warming?'

'Combustion heat.'

'Could the EGHE be tested by an empirical measurement?'

'It's possible,' said Stanley. 'I can't make an increase to the world's CO_2, but I might be able to see if there's any effect on a scaled-down model of the world.'

'Wasn't that done by Tyndall and Arrhenius in the 1800s?' said Sophie.

'Not conclusively,' said Stanley. 'It had been assumed based on small-scale experiments in the 19th Century that only CO_2 and CH_4 absorb infrared. The Raman spectroscope was invented in 1928 and

148

showed that the other atmospheric gases N_2, O_2 and water vapour, which make up about 99% of the atmosphere, absorb infrared too. CO_2, is only a small part.

"But recent measurements indicate that none of the gases warm the atmosphere very much directly and N_2, O_2 and H_2O, molecule by molecule, warm like CO_2 and CH_4 and there is 2000 times more of them. It appears CO_2 hardly causes any warming.

'The absorption process is contentious but it appears that the warming of the atmosphere is from the Earth's surface where the radiation is absorbed, rather than from being heated by contact with vibrating gas molecules. An infrared space heater warms air by convection from surfaces, leaving the air penetrated cool. Small changes in the composition of the air could have no significant effect on atmospheric warming.'

'That isn't evidence: it's surmise,' said Earl.

'The process of heat transfer from the Sun to the Earth and out into space has complex theories without clear scientific agreement,' said Stanley. 'Salton university physics researchers have not tested the EGHE theory. An empirical test is needed. If we have two identical containers of gas and hypothesise they will be warmed equally by solar radiation, then if gas composition in one container is the only change and there is no difference in warming, could we conclude that the change in gas composition had no effect?' asked Stanley.

'Yes,' said Henry. 'That could be deduced reasonably, there being no other changes.'

'I want to tell you about the experiment Norman and I are conducting to test the EGHE theory,' said Stanley. 'We are going to measure the amount of atmospheric warming by CO_2 compared with the other gases. We think this will help clarify whether burning coal causes global warming.

'Accurate measurement would also be difficult because the fractional change in the independent variable, CO_2 concentration, is under 0.0002% per annum and response of the dependent variable, warming, only about 0.04% per year. This would be such a minute and slow change, it would be difficult to detect in an experiment.'

149

'The Earth and atmosphere are too large to collect as a sample. But a scaled-down model of the Earth's atmosphere could be made to measure and compare heat absorbed by the Earth and its atmosphere with enhanced CO_2 concentration.

'So you want to compare evidence of heating both without and with CO_2?' said Fiona.

'Exactly,' said Stanley. 'The EGHE theory can be falsified in a fair test. We will heat the gas in two grain silos, one with air the other with CO_2, both having equal exposure to infrared. The test should simulate the absorption of radiation by, and heating of the gases, at the surface of the Earth. If CO_2 traps more radiation, as is claimed, the CO_2 silo will become warmer than the one containing air. The test should simulate the absorption of radiation by, and heating of the gases, at the surface of the Earth. The one with CO_2 would warm more.'

'It would agree with the EGHE theory,' said Sophie.

'If the CO_2 does not warm more, the EGHE theory would not be verified,' said Stanley. 'A large number of results in agreement would reject the EGHE.'

'But climate scientists claim there are observations that reject combustion heat as cause,' she said.

'You mean they have claimed to have measured the Earth's solar heat flux in and out,' Stanley said. 'We cannot rely on their results because however well-intentioned they are, the tests are poorly controlled and experimenters might be suspected to have a confirmatory bias. If a difference was measured on one day, it might no longer exist the next day.

'Before the EGHE can be rejected as unscientific, other tests would be needed to falsify it too.'

'How soon will you have your results?' she said.

'We should have enough CO_2 to fill the silo by the end of the week.'

'It's exciting to create new knowledge.'

'I agree, it is liberating because it could unshackle us from the past,' Stanley said.

150

CHAPTER 26 A TEST

Clouds scudded and blotches of shadow passed overhead, as the science discussion group met on the grass by the dam. It was a favourite place, for they were proud of building it across the brook several years previously. The farmhouse was on one side and the pig residents could look across the water, past ducks and a pair of swans, to animal sheds and pens on the far side.

Run-off varied and the lake held insufficient water for horticulture or for irrigation of crops.

'Here's some news from the farmhouse,' said Ruby. 'Our neighbouring farmer downstream has complained to the pigs that his water supply has been cut off by this dam. He says it is illegal. He complained he is unable to grow cotton.'

'What if we want to grow cotton?' asked Earl.

'Other farms further up the creek have taken most of the water,' said Pamela.

'We should be able to get compensation,' said Earl.

'For what?'

'Not being able to grow cotton,' he said.

'Good idea,' said Pamela, grinning. 'There's a heap of other things we can put in for too, like not being able to grow rice or hydroponic lettuces.'

'What about sugar cane?'

'That too.'

'They will only consider compensation if others have limited our taking up water rights.'

'The government will say we have to release an amount of water downstream.'

151

'We don't have sufficient to release any into the spillway,' Lord Borat told him. He said: 'Get fucked.'

'Really?'

'Yes. The pigs ignored his complaint,' said Ruby. 'He took it to the Government and they sent a water engineer here. His conclusion was that the spillway had remained dry because evaporation from the dam had exceeded the meagre inflow. To conserve the water supply they should introduce *salvinia,* a water plant, into the dam. It would spread across the surface and reduce evaporation. The pigs have imported some weed and the geese are going to plant it.'

'Will it start the spillway flowing, d'you think?' asked Earl.

'The theory's okay,' said Stanley. 'It will in the wet.'

'It would've anyway,' said Norman.

'That's the problem with science theories, you often can't do a controlled test.'

'If it flows, the pigs will claim it,' Earl said.

One fine day, the animal workers were in a group having lunch by the lake when Ruby arrived, with a colourful towel and wearing sunglasses. She spreadeagled on the towel. It was a beautiful place to recreate.

'This is the life,' she said. 'I have earned it, don't you think?'

They were used to her indolence and no-one contradicted her. They suspected she was spying for the pigs.

'What's with the sunglasses, Ruby?' said Earl. 'Is there too much sun for you?'

'They cut out glare.'

'Maybe giant sunglasses could shield the Earth and prevent it warming?' said Sophie. 'How do they absorb glare?'

'These have vertical slits called polaroids,' said Norman, passing Ruby's glasses to Sophie for her to look through. 'Vertical waves of sunlight are absorbed by the water surface. The remaining waves are horizontal. They are reflected off the water as glare and stopped by the vertical slits. Here, look at the water over there.'

'Oh yes,' said Sophie, liking Norman's attention. 'The glare has gone. It's dark. Are the horizontal waves being stopped by the vertical grill?''

'Yes. Now rotate the glasses 90°. What do you see?'

'The glare comes back. Is that because the horizontal waves are getting through the grill now it's horizontal?'

'Yes.'

'That's amazing,' said Sophie. 'I knew you could split light up into colours, but not into different wave directions.'

'Norman, your silo experiment tests radiation absorption by gases, doesn't it?' said Goliath.

Norman was pleased to be asked, because Stanley his father was there. Norman had slowly taken the lead from him with their experiment.

'Yes. I'm comparing absorption by different gases, by air and by CO_2.'

'What have you found?'

'There might not be any difference in the amount of heating by infrared, because it penetrates equally and is absorbed by solid surfaces with equal convection.'

'So CO_2 may not cause heating of the atmosphere?'

'No; it doesn't,' said Norman.

'Would shutting down our power station reduce warming?'

'No. That would be a mistake.'

'CO_2 entrapment is being publicised by Algy worldwide,' said Norman.

'Humans are gullible.'

'Wow. Algy isn't going to like your finding, Norman.'

'He can provide his own test result,' said Stanley. 'I'll show you our experiment. Let's meet at the grain silos at dusk on Friday. That will give us results from a couple of days more.'

Cookie talked with Pamela on the back lawn.

'What is the talk about now?' she asked.

'Today we talked about the greenhouse effect.

'What is the ram saying now?'

153

'That he looked for evidence of warming by CO_2 but didn't find any.'

'Of course it exists. That's why greenhouses get warm and Venus is hot.'

'That's a different type of greenhouse with a different warming process.'

'Why is Venus hot and Mars cold? They both have mainly CO_2.'

'Venus stays warm like Earth, because of its atmosphere. Mars has very little atmosphere to hold heat in.'

'Hmm. I hope you check it out because scientists have been saying CO_2 causes warming, bigtime.'

'I will.'

The water weed spread rapidly, but the water level didn't rise.

'Rainfall has continued low and you must wait until conditions return to normal,' Lord Borat told the neighbour. 'The lack of outflow is not due to our dam: it results from drought. You must be patient.'

Without rain, the Government eventually paid the pigs to release water downstream, charging the neighbour for the volume he took. The pigs wanted payment from him too.

'It is only fair that we should be reimbursed for harvesting water for you to use,' said Lord Borat, when the neighbour complained. 'You are fortunate to be able to buy it from us. We are under no obligation to supply you.'

The matter remained in dispute.

When they swam in the dam, the animals got tangled in the weed. It built up into a thick matte that died, rotted and sucked oxygen out of the water, killing the fish and pond creatures. When the water became tainted, the pigs ordered the animals to drag out the weed, but there were tonnes of it and it grew back immediately.

'Not all problems have solutions,' Lord Borat told the neighbour. 'Your farm is in the wrong place to grow cotton.'

'Bulldust,' said the neighbour. 'What is wrong is that you pigs think you are free to do what you want.'

154

'You were at liberty to build a dam before us,' Lord Borat said. 'The early bird catches the worm. Liberty doesn't come on a plate. You have to seize it.'

CHAPTER 27 BENIGN EMISSION

The animals, except the pigs, gathered beside two tall grain silos where Stanley and Norman were testing infrared absorption by gases of the atmosphere.

'Let's go inside,' Norman said.

He went in through a door and the others followed in a line. Goliath and Fiona had to stoop and squeeze through the opening. It was empty and dark inside, with a radiant heater glowing in the centre of the floor, aimed upwards. They stood around it, feeling its heat on their faces and on their skin.

'I borrowed the IR lamp from a pig farrowing pen,' Norman said, his voice echoing in the cavernous silence. 'Pregnant sows live in the old piggery and give birth in farrowing pens, where IR lamps warm the piglets.'

'Why does the heater have to be IR?' asked Pamela his partner.

'Because atmospheric warming is said to be mainly by IR from the Sun,' said Norman. 'The lamp glows red but it emits invisible radiation of longer wavelength than red or other heaters. It passes through air and heats up solid surfaces.'

'Does the radiation heat the air?'

'Only a little directly. At outdoor restaurants in winter they use infrared heaters to warm the customers but the air stays cold. Heat is absorbed by the surfaces of the metal walls, which touch the air and heat circulates in convection currents. This model has a metal wall absorbing IR instead of the Earth's surfaces. The emissivity of the thin metal would be quite different to vegetated land or ocean water.

156

But it would be the same as in the other silo which is all we need to test the theory.'

'It doesn't seem likely that a little CO_2 in the air would make any difference.'

'That's what we figure. This silo is the control experiment, with air, which is supposed to heat up less. I have taken the air temperature in here several times every day.'

'Has the air warmed much?'

'About 10°C. Now, let's go next door and see the rise with pure CO_2.'

They went outside and to the next silo.

Sophie hesitated to go in.

'Can we breathe pure CO_2?'

'I have let air in and the CO_2 has gone. It has cooled down too.'

They went inside.

'This silo is identical. We started piping in CO_2 through a duct pipe from the vodka plant a week ago, produced by fermentation. It flowed in here for a week and flushed out most of the air. When I brought a candle inside, it went out.'

'Why did you go for pure CO_2? Air has only 0.041%?' said Pamela, Norman's partner. She was Trudy's daughter, with enough llama to look like a leggy sheep.

'Scientists would want to do the test with a range of concentrations. I figured it would be easiest to see a difference with 100% CO_2 and we can scale the results proportionally back to 0.041%. Scientists are used to scaling up and scaling down effects.'

'Do you expect a greater effect with 100%?'

'Hell yes. If there is any warming effect, we should have it in a big way. About 2400 times greater than with air having only 0.041%.

'Did you get more warming in here than in the other silo?'

'The temperature increased 25% more, about 12.5°C, but the increase in heat after adjusting for 20% lower heat capacity was the same as with air, 10°C.

'But shouldn't CO_2's lower heat capacity make it warm up less?'

157

'No. The same amount of heat would cause it to warm up more. We were comparing amounts of heat absorbed by equal gas volumes, with equal numbers of molecules, from equal amounts of infrared.

'Does your test reject the EGHE theory?'

'No. This first measurement was very approximate. The test has to be done more precisely. Even if the observations were made by impartial judges, you would still have to repeat it many times.'

'What if they found a small temperature increase with CO_2?'

'When divided by 2200 to scale it back to the concentration in air, it would not be significant for the climate.'

'Does this test refute the hypothesis that there is a difference?'

'No. This is only one piece of evidence corroborating refutation. Results by others could reinstate the EGHE theory.'

'Has anyone else done this kind of test?'

'Yes, at laboratory scale. A coke bottle filled with CO_2 is reported to have warmed up more than a bottle filled with air, but after adjusting the temperature down for CO_2's lower specific heat capacity, heating in the CO_2 bottle was approximately the same (8). It was evidence that CO_2 did not cause more heating than the other gases.

'There is up to 100 times more H_2O than CO_2 in air and it resides for about the same time,' said Henry. 'H_2O stays in the atmosphere long enough to add to the atmospheric blanket and it deserves much more attention than CO_2.

'Our thought experiment indicates that CO_2 does not trap more heat than N_2 and O_2,' said Norman. 'They have consigned water vapour to obscurity and levered the tiny amount of CO_2 into undeserved prominence, perhaps because it is more easily measured globally and can be labelled 'pollution'.

'Are you sure CO_2 is benign? Does this thought experiment provide enough evidence that it doesn't cause warming?'

'The hypothesis has been thoroughly tested with refuting results. Is it fair to conclude that it is false?'

'Our thought experiment is not an exact simulation of atmospheric absorption of solar radiation. No-one seems to have done such a simulation yet. Our finding refutes the EGHE theory and

158

although it does not conclusively falsify it, it adds weight to that cause. Complete rejection may never be possible.

'No reason can be given for preferring a corroborated theory over a non-corroborated unfalsified one. The adventurous element Popper allowed, which the logical positivists would not have allowed, is that provided the theory can be tested, it need not have corroborating data and that is what the proponents of the EGHE have counted on.

'For a theory to be determined as 'scientific', Popper has set the bar high. Quine wanted holistic testing, including related variables and assumptions. Perhaps our test can tell no more than what was done.'

Old Stanley joined his son Norman in a science class that reviewed the results of their experiment.

'The claim that human emissions of CO_2 are leading to catastrophic global warming is a pseudo-scientific hypothesis, because it cannot be tested experimentally and there is no way to potentially falsify it,' said Stanley. 'It is not scientific.'

'Is it true that CO_2 is benign, Norman?' asked Fiona.

'The EGHE hypothesis is not acceptable without corroborating evidence,' said Stanley. 'It cannot be rejected until more falsification testing has been carried out.

'Our thought experiment rejects the EGHE hypothesis and calls attention to alternative theories of warming, caused by the other products of combustion and respiration, heat energy and water vapour. These would be preferred by a test of simplicity, as recommended by Occam's Razor.

'I saw you all down by the silos just now,' Cookie said to Sophie. What's happening?'

'A ram has done an experiment to find out if coal is causing the World to warm up.'

'Is it? Do you believe it is really warming up?'

'Yes, but it is only a very small amount.'

'So who cares?'

159

'If it continues for hundreds of years, we'll be in trouble, they say.'

'So what has your ram found out?'

'Coal isn't the problem,' said Sophie. 'It causes warming like other heating.'

'That's good news. They were saying we would have to stop farting.'

'Go on!'

'Now we can fart freely and we can even use coal again,' Sophie said.

'Well, that's a relief,' Cookie said. 'Are you going to ask President Natalia Alphancourt to restart the power station?'

'Stanley told Lord Borat what he had discovered,' said Sophie. 'But Lord Borat tried to minimise the local implications. Stanley hoped he'd want to get back to mining coal. But when Algy returned and heard about the experiment, shit hit the fan. Stanley was warned to stay away from the carbon dioxide topic.'

'It's not up to Lord Borat,' said Cookie. 'It's science. We have to seek truth. The workers will be pleased to be earning again.'

CHAPTER 28 HAY MAKING

Dimitri was selected by the pigs as their candidate for President. He had been head of the secret police, which conducted surveillance and clandestine operations. His reputation was for strength and order. He was an American Landrace boar, long, lean and white, his back flat, his head, long and narrow, his ears large and heavy, hanging forwards close to his snout. He was an imposing figure of porcine virility: impassive, aquiline, self-controlled, understated, unemotional and brooding.

Henry was twice Dimitri's weight, but he was a peaceful bull and had never fought the boar or even threatened him.

'I would love to gore the boar,' Henry said. 'He's a nasty little bastard.'

'It wouldn't do you any good,' Dolly said. 'He would have you slaughtered.'

'We would be better off with a less aggressive president. Another species would be better.'

'If pigs could fly,' Dolly said. 'The pigs aren't going to let that happen,'

The election was decided by pig-only voting and Lord Dimitri won unopposed. The worker animals, familiar with his cruelty, secretly opposed his appointment but they didn't dare criticise him in public. Their new President had the farm under central control, the livestock population atomised and voiceless, living under surveillance in terror of his police. His management was efficient, with an iron fist. He created a pig oligarchy and controlled it for his own purposes.

'Dimitri does not obey the will of the people,' said Artemis the goat. 'His regime is totalitarian and ruthlessly crushes criticism and opposition, like Napoleon did after the revolution.'

'Shh,' said the Raven Patriarch. 'With talk like that you'll get us all killed.'

A pig leader had to have physical prowess. He was strong with a good figure and walked with a swagger. Lord Dimitri pitted his strength daily in friendly wrestling with his colleague pigs. They would try to push each other out of the ring, until they fell or were pinned down. Lord Dimitri's large size enabled him to win. In conversation he was often silent and watchful. When he spoke it was in a monologue, ponderous and forceful. He was intolerant of wordiness and bluster, becoming short tempered.

The animal workers were too tired from hay-making for much discussion of Stanley's and Norman's experimental results. Their work was back breaking from dawn to dusk, seven days, for a month. Most of them were ruminants and hay was an important food for their several stomachs and fermentation ability, whereas pigs were monogastrics with one stomach that used enzymes to digest roots and grain.

All the worker animals joined in making hay to store until winter. They followed a time-honoured sequence of activities. In the spring they blocked rabbit burrows with dirt and rested pastures from livestock grazing until summer. The grass grew tall and thick, with a profusion of flowering plants that would enhance the flavour of the hay. Farmer Jones had seeded the pasture with a mixture of Rye grass, Triticale, Meadow Fescue, Kikuyu and white clover and it had yielded hay steadily over the past 40 years. Other grasses and edible plants had established: Timothy, Common Couch, Barnyard Grass, Kangaroo Grass, Cocksfoot, Barley Grass. These had added to the flavours. But weeds had also spread: Bull Thistle, Dandelion, Nutgrass, Yellow Foxtail and Oxalis. Bull Thistles were removed, by cutting them off close to the ground, to prevent them growing back.

By late Spring the grass was tall and luxuriant, rolling in waves with the wind. Many of the animals helped with hay-making, enjoying the rich green odour of the cut grass and the sweet spicy smell of the dried hay. Butterflies and mayflies flew around in profusion. The only hazards were the savage bites of horse flies.

Goliath and Norman mowed the grass. An ancient hay-making machine, a mower and a swather. All were towed and ground-propelled.

With Goliath harnessed to the mower and Norman the ram riding on the seat at the back, they cut the fields back and forth in swathes. Norman raised the cutter bar with a lever to pass over stones that could damage the blades, lifting the bed up to loop around at ends and corners.

'Your cutting is too slow,' said Hyacinth, Lord Leonard's favourite sow, standing legs astride, whip in hand. 'More effort, Goliath!'

Goliath's strength wasn't what it had been. Several cutting blades were missing and the rest were blunt, requiring more pull. They had told the pigs, but nothing had been done to repair them. Repairs were difficult and neglected.

'I'm going as fast as I can,' said Goliath, his sides heaving. 'This grass is old, tough and dry and the blades won't cut it.'

'That's bullshit. You're too slow, you big lug,' Hyacinth said. 'It'll be the abattoir for you!' She bit Goliath's fetlock viciously. He whinnied in pain. Domino, his son, would soon join him at the plough, relieving Fiona. Norman, too, was past his prime and had more difficulty lifting the heavy bed than last year.

'You two have to pull your weight,' Hyacinth said. 'This farm has carried you for long enough. You need to go faster. If you don't finish this field this afternoon, you'll have to continue after dark.'

The criticism was undeserved and spiteful, for Goliath did more work than any single animal on the Farm.

Norman spoke up in his defence. 'We could damage the mower if we hit rocks in the dark.'

'I didn't ask you, sheep face!' said Hyacinth. 'If you break the equipment, *you* will have to mend it and do the mowing too. You had better get finished while you're still able to see.'

Hyacinth's threats and whip made the task intolerable. Their efforts were never good enough for her.

'It's not fair that we do so much work and are treated so badly,' said Norman.

'I'm not sure I can keep going,' said Goliath. 'I am exhausted and the pigs won't allow me to take a break. They seem to enjoy being cruel. It seems hopeless.'

'Don't give in,' said Norman. 'It will get better.'

'If I had more food, I could work harder,' Goliath said.

'I'll give you some of mine,' said Norman.

The next day many animals were hay-making in the same field. Fiona, Titani's granddaughter, pulled a swather, which turned up the grass into rows to dry. Others raked it up and when it had dried they carried it in puts drawn by the Shetlands to stack in hay-cocks in the field. When the hay was green and had overheated one year, it had ignited and burned down the hay barn. They had almost starved that winter. Now they were very careful to leave hay in the field until it had dried. Then they loaded it onto drays and took it to the hay barn for storage.

None of the animals liked entering the cavernous haybarn, domain of a large and ghostly barn owl. Shaped like a figure 8, with a large round head that swivelled robotically, the owl roosted high up on the beams under the barn roof, a dark and secluded place. When it flew through the barn, it spooked the sheep and they rushed outside bleating in fear. In the evenings, it glided sedately through the barn and outside to hunt, exiting through a window opening and causing the animals in the farmyard to cower down. The animals thought this mysterious bird had magical powers, although its worst offence was to discard pellets of mice bones.

Lord Dimitri had announced he would show Algy's speech in Kyoto to the animals.

164

'He's been going around the countries wanting them to reduce emissions.'

'What emissions?'

'Greenhouse gases.'

'Mostly CO_2.'

'Algy's obsession with CO_2 is a worry,' said Goliath. 'I have heard he wants us to stop farting.'

'My farts are more CH_4 than CO_2,' said Henry.

'How do you know?'

'I've lit them.'

Henry surveyed Goliath's long body.

'You must have had help?'

'Domino wanted to. He collected jars full. We tested how much of them would burn.'

'I would never have guessed so much CH_4. CH_4 is said to be a greenhouse gas too.'

'Anyway, he can't tell me to stop farting. He doesn't have legal jurisdiction. I am liberty to fart when I want.'

'That wouldn't deter Algy. But Norman's results will, because he has shown the so-called greenhouse gases are benign.'

'I wish we could be sure,' said Goliath. 'Stanley's was a preliminary experiment. It could falsify the EGHE but more data is needed. If we are going to put our farts on the line, we need more facts.'

'CO_2 has been benign for things living on Earth in the past,' said Henry. 'That's a fact. It hasn't been a problem.'

'There has been a steady decline in CO_2 over the past 170 million years. The recent level of 410 ppm recently is relatively low. Both CO_2 and temperature have varied but animals and plants have thrived.'

165

CHAPTER 29 WHEN EFFECT IS THE CAUSE

On a screen in the farmyard, the animals watched Algy spruiking at a climate conference in Kyoto. His movie 'A Calculated Doom' had been popular and when Monty retired, Algy had replaced him as Lord Borat's energy adviser. Monty's expertise was missed, because Algy did not have a scientific background. He could not answer their questions and was often overseas at climate talks and conferences.

Lord Dimitri had set up a TV screen for the workers to hear Algy speak.

'Algy is a respected international expert on climate change,' he said to the animal workers. 'He has advised me to shut down our coal operations. He is advising other countries to do the same.'

Algy spoke with passion that stirred the emotions of the audience.

'Proper scientific objectivity has gone out the window,' Norman said to Henry.

When Algy finished his speech, Lord Dimitri turned off the screen.

'Many nations have not yet fulfilled their Kyoto obligations and the rest of us think there is a possibility that they are freeloading,' said Lord Dimitri. 'If you have leaders who take their climate obligations seriously you are fortunate.'

'Shutting down fossil-fuelled generators is emblematic and ridiculous,' Henry said quietly to Norman. 'The inconvenience to electrical consumers would be much larger than the benefits that would be accrued by hypothetical glacier huggers and sea fringe dwellers on the other side of the globe. It would transform our society without evidence of the soundness of Algy's ideas.'

166

'We know they are unsound,' said Henry. 'We have evidence that CO_2 is just another gas of the air. There is no need to prevent fossil fuels.'

'Dissent will be severely punished,' Algy warned the workers when he returned to the Farm several weeks later. 'Some of you could be out of work, but sacrifices have to be made and can be overcome by sharing with others.

'We must have animals' full support or humans could try to retake the Farm,' said Lord Dimitri. 'You are not permitted to state a personal opinion about any Animal Farm policy, nor to research, or discuss, or think about climate matters at anytime, anywhere. To do so would be a thought-crime, punishable by death. You must report anyone who does. Is that clear? This is the only warning I will give.'

'Thought-crime, bloody hell,' Henry whispered to Dolly. 'Who does Algy think he is? I am free to think what I want.'

'Not any more. If you are suspected of opposing him, the police will keep you under surveillance, arrest you and torture you until you confess and change your mind or are eliminated.'

'He must have Lord Dimitri around his little finger,' she said.

'I've heard he has the DU president bamboozled too,' he said.

Later, Ruby came skipping down to where the animals had gathered in a subdued group by the dam. They became silent in case she would report their talk as dissent.

'Algy has our interests at heart, comrades,' said Ruby. 'He has his eyes on future generations who could have their environments polluted, heated and flooded. That is why he is committed to stopping global warming.'

They said nothing and after a while Ruby went away.

Later, Goliath spoke to Henry, as they pulled a cultivator in tandem.

'Fuck thought-crime,' said Henry.

Lord Dimitri assigned Andrea, a gilt pig who had studied science, to liaise with the workers. She was slightly built and vulpine in manner, trotting around lightly, interested in everything, with

167

cunning and craftiness. Lord Dimitri relied on her understanding of the thinking of the animal workers. She befriended the animals and they respected her for her empathy, talking freely with her, letting her help with their studies, although they knew her interest was self-centred rather than kind.

Most evenings the workers gathered around the computer. The university provided digital access technology, for example, the animals had mouth-held tools to assist their keying. Henry held a keying tool in his mouth. They also used voice enhancement software. When the pigs installed internet terminals in the farmhouse, Ruby brought several old keyboards with enlarged keys down to the tack shed, for the animals to use. They were able to consider more difficult questions online.

The animals had been forbidden to investigate climate science but under Lord Borat this had been relaxed. As a precaution when searching banned source material, if a pig patrol came by, with a single keystroke an article about the high intelligence of pigs could be screened.

'So why is there so much fuss about CO_2?' asked Henry, sitting at the computer, mumbling with a keying tool in his mouth.

'Napoleon used to say: 'Give them something to fear and they will be less revolting,'' said Dongle.

'There is nothing fearful about CO_2,' said Henry. 'It does us good. CO_2 grows plants. Gardeners have promoted plant growth by injecting CO_2 into greenhouses. An increase in CO_2 is no cause for alarm; it is to be welcomed.'

'Last year's increase from 0.040 to 0.041 percent could account for the vegetation being lusher,' said Norman. 'CO_2 would feed plant growth and animals in the food chain.'

'Does CO_2 ever cause warming?'

'No. Warming causes CO_2, not the other way round,' said Norman.

'Wow! How could warming cause CO_2?'

'Warming of the oceans increases CO_2 in the atmosphere by dissolution from ocean water. Oceans contain 95% of the Earth's CO_2. Warming by only a degree or two can cause CO_2 to bubble out, like lemonade fizzes when it warms. People have been led to believe that the increase in CO_2 in the atmosphere has been put there by industry. Probably more than a half comes from non-industrial heating from natural sources, such as bushfires, volcanoes, bacterial decomposition, farts, fermentation and body respiration. Almost all CO_2 dissolves in oceans. About a half the CO_2 in the air is released by ocean warming, but I don't know how reliable that estimate is.'

'The CO_2 concentration has increased because of, not caused by, global warming. CO_2 is the effect of warming.'

'Wow,' said the donkey Dongle. 'That's a backflip and a half.'

'The true picture is CO_2 is not the beginning of global warming, but dissolves in the oceans, until ocean warming returns it to the atmosphere.'

'Could scientists really have got it back to front?'

'Yes, CO_2 spikes in the atmosphere match spikes in ocean warming, such as ENSO events, allowing time for ocean mixing to warm the deep water and release the gas.'

'What a mistaka to maka!'

'Global warming has many possible causes, but CO_2 is not one of them,' said Norman.

'Why have we been so misled?' asked Dongle.

'Many research jobs and grants have an *a priori* assumption that an EGHE exists. To get hired and retain their positions they have to assume the EGHE.'

'Powerful interests could want to hold on to their sales of energy and their energy-using technologies, like automobiles. CO_2 is their red herring and coal is their fall guy.'

'That sounds like a political evaluation.'

'Climate change is being tackled as a political problem.'

'With circular reasoning.'

Algy's movie mobilized the antis. Most governments swung behind his campaign to prevent emissions by shutting down power stations.

After delaying it for a year at half capacity, President Natalia Alphancourt ordered Caruba's coal-fired power station completely shut down, promising funding for renewable energy installation when it could be afforded.

'I shut it down before,' said President Alphancourt. 'I was persuaded to try it at half-capacity. Algy has persuaded me that he can get funding for renewable energy. I have decided to shut down the power station.'

Coal operations on Caruba ceased and the animals lost their jobs and coal mining incomes. They began to starve.

Dinah found Cookie peeling potatoes at the kitchen sink and chatted with her through the window.

'What have you been doing today?' Cookie asked.

'We solved the puzzle of where the CO_2 building up in the air has been coming from. It had been thought it was building from human activity.'

'That's reasonable isn't it?'

'No. When oceans warm they undissolve it, explaining the increase in the air.

'How does that change anything?'

'Now we know CO_2 is caused by warming, not the other way around and it has no effect on the climate. CO_2 is one thing we don't need to worry about. CO_2 in the air is beneficial. They should restart the power station and we'll have mining work.'

'Let's hope Andrea can get the pigs to accept your findings,' said Cookie.

She gave Dinah a bag of potato peelings.

CHAPTER 30 THERMAL POLLUTION

At the science class a week later, Norman started the discussion.

'Climate scientists have modelled the balance between solar radiation going into the Earth with radiation coming out,' he said. 'They have deduced slightly more goes in than goes out, calling this 'solar forcing'.'

'What evidence do they have?'

'They measured by pyrometers on satellites (15) solar energy incoming at 341 Watts per square metre and outgoing at 340.1,' he said. 'The difference, or *'forcing'*, is a net influx of 0.9 W/m². That is an instantaneous rate, presumably a 24 hour average for a point on the Earth's surface that varies between day, night and varying oblique angles continuously throughout a year.'

'I wonder how reliable is that figure of 0.9 W/m² ?' asked Henry.

'Not reliable at all and the number of decimal places is confusing. It seems to be a measurement so highly qualified that it is virtually an assumption. I imagine they assumed an amount of warming and claimed to have measured it.'

'It's not a compelling case for shutting down the coal industry.'

'The pigs won't know who to believe.'

'They will see it as an area for research.'

'This evening we will consider if global warming is not caused by CO_2, as we found out last week, then what could possibly cause it?' he asked. 'Causation of warming is a complex question. Andrea will tell us what she has found.'

'Thank you, Norman,' said Andrea. 'Good afternoon everyone. The most plausible causes of planet warming are industrial

171

combustion, urban heating, solar activity, geothermal activity, nuclear reactions in Earth's interior, magnetic terrestrial orbit change, bushfires, volcanoes, biological life, bacteriological decomposition and biochemical warming. Others that could cause warming are heat entrapment by gases, heat from condensation of water vapour lofted by agriculture and from rotting of vegetation.'

'Fucking hell,' said Norman. 'We'll never know which of that lot is to blame.'

'Which cause is the most likely?' asked Simone, Earl and Dolly's other daughter, Henry's sister. Attractive and curious, she asked questions to draw the bulls' attention to herself.

'The cause must be anthropogenic,' said Andrea, 'because human industry has grown quickly causing rapid warming.'

'The industrial revolution was a time of rapid change,' said Norman. 'CO_2 increased after about 1760. Combustion also released heat and this could have caused most of the global warming from then on.

'Anthropogenic heat pollution seems most likely, but there could be other possibilities,' Norman said. 'The warming observed could be measurement error, or from Sun activity, Earth orbit, or cyclical change in the Earth's interior.'

'I agree,' said Andrea.

'Could the Earth have wobbled closer to the Sun?'

'Yes.'

'The Sun could have changed,' Fiona said to Andrea. 'Earth is being pulled closer to the Sun by gravity, heightening Spring tides. It is only 180 million kilometres away and orbit decay is fast enough for a rise in temperature of a few degrees. The Sun's surface is at 5500°C and global warming can be expected when solar flares throw material out into space. Earth is being warmed. In a few billion years we'll all melt.'

Fiona's wisdom was respected. Horses were renowned for synthesising understanding. While the others debated, Fiona had quietly amassed the elements of a persuasive analysis. Now her words were conclusive and the others adopted her perspective and elaborated it.

172

'Orbit decay is very slow, because friction between Earth and solar particles is small. It will be billions of years before Earth falls into the Sun,' said Andrea. Her information was respected because she helped the animals learn, unlike the other pigs.

'The Sun varies too,' said Norman. 'Daily global solar exposure at Brisbane varied from 16.3 to 20.0 last year.'

'16.3 what?'

'Maybe cumulative radiation units. The units don't matter. The point is, it varied.

'Temperature could be changing within a cycle involving changes in either planetary movement, or it could be solar radioactivity, planetary movement, or both. But most of the warming could be local heating on Earth.'

'Humans cause enough energy release to cause it,' said Norman. 'I've done the calculations. The enthalpy, or energy, that humans release Worldwide by combustion, is sufficient to cause the amount of global warming reported several times over. Waste and spent heat as thermal pollution is a simpler explanation of warming than the EGHE. By Occam's Razor, we should give it more credence. Urban heat islands are evidence of thermal pollution occurring wherever humans live.'

'The EGHE is a complex theory, unneeded and wrong,' said Norman.

'That settles it, for the moment,' said Henry. 'It has taken all of us, contributing in our own ways, to figure it out.'

'Dismissing the EGHE will be hard for some people after investing their time and interest in it for so long. It is an inconvenient untruth and it will take a paradigm shift to oust the obsession with carbon and realise that our civilisation is up to its ears in waste heat which has to be managed away. Some may die believing CO_2 causes warming. The inconvenient truth is that it doesn't and humans probably warm the environment with their heat emissions. Humans will have to take a close look at their lifestyles. Turn off your computer while I'm talking to you!' Norman's tone startled them. He smiled. 'Just testing. We are so used to having energy, we don't think about using it, when we should.'

173

No-one spoke for a while, as they listened to the hum of bees and the ducks squabbling on the lake outside. A sheep ran past in pursuit of a turnip rolling down the slope but it went into the dam. A duck brought the turnip to the side, where the sheep gratefully carried it away.

'How much of the fossil fuel energy humans use is lost into space?' asked Norman.

'All of it, eventually,' said Andrea. 'I calculate the average residence time of heat as 140 years. That is how long combustion heat is held on Earth, on average, before it dissipates into space.'

'How can heat be building up and warming Earth if the Sun and Earth are in equilibrium?' asked Norman.

'There could be a slight imbalance,' said Andrea. 'It could be attributable to anthropomorphic heat pollution but there are other possibilities, as we have discussed.'

'To stop global warming humans would have to release less energy,' said Henry. 'Attention has wrongly been on an imagined CO_2 trapping mechanism, when it would have been better to stop the heat being produced in the first place. We have to reduce combustion.'

'Isn't that what's happened? Power stations have shut down. What would you do differently?'

'I would allow low cost electricity suppliers to continue,' said Henry. 'I would restart the coal power station.'

'It is difficult to reverse a shutdown,' said Norman. 'It's not like turning on a light switch. It can take a week to restart a power station, even when the shutdown has anticipated restarting. The systems have to be started up with coal, water, ash and steam, until they reach full capacity. '

'First things first,' said Henry. 'Can we be sure that thermal pollution is the problem?'

'No. We aren't sure there's a significant warming problem here, are we?' asked Dolly.

'It isn't agreed,' said Norman. 'Shutting down fossil fuels, vilifying CO_2, was spectacularly wrong.'

174

'Reducing CO$_2$ emission does reduce heat emission, which is what we want,' said Andrea.

She had told Norman the pigs had rejected the results of the animals' test.

'The animals are too dumb to be doing science experiments,' Lord Dimitri had said. 'I don't believe their findings.'

Andrea had persuaded the pigs to accept that warming might be caused by something other than CO$_2$, probably thermal pollution.

Now Andrea tried to get a compromise with the animals' view.

'Reducing CO$_2$ is a step in the right direction then,' said Andrea. 'It has a precautionary effect.'

'We need to reduce all types of energy growth, not just fossil fuel combustion,' said Norman. 'The problem is we are using too much of all types of energy.'

'We should oppose wasting capital on more expensive and less efficient technologies, like renewable energy,' said Henry.

There was silence.

'That's an issue for another day,' said Henry.

Norman said: 'I propose we ask the pigs to use energy frugally until the sun's heating of the earth has been investigated and we can deduce whether global warming could be caused by thermal pollution.'

'That hedges our bets nicely,' said Henry. 'We are agreed then. The power station has to stay shut down until we have more information. The new President will probably impose his point of view.'

Cookie had carried outside a bucket of food scraps and was scattering them for the poultry to pick over. She retrieved half a loaf of bread and gave it to Dinah.

'What has been the topic of your studies this week?' she asked as Dinah munched.

'We have been looking for the cause of global warming. After rejecting carbon dioxide, there were many possibilities, but the culprit is most likely thermal pollution.'

175

'Heat?' said Cookie. 'Warming is caused by heat! That's pretty obvious. Would anyone think otherwise?'

'Many, unfortunately. We need to know where the heat has come from,' said Dinah. 'Heat released by humans' combustion is enough. The CO_2 they release at the same time is benign.'

'Do you really think humans could generate enough heat to warm up the planet?' asked Cookie.

'Yes, I do,' Dinah said. 'Heat is released extracting energy, converting it, transporting it and using it. Humans do a lot of heating one way or another.'

'That change seems simpler than having heat trapped by a tiny amount of CO_2,' Cookie said.

'Well, that narrows it down nicely, although it may be inconvenient for those banking on an EGHE,' Cookie said.

'Tell it to Lord Dimitri!' Dinah said. 'He is counting on getting funded to replace coal with renewable energy. If he doesn't get that, he'll have to find another source of money.'

'We should go back to coal. There's plenty to be going on with and we will have time to come up with a replacement before it runs out.'

CHAPTER 31
TOTALITARIANISM

Henry wanted to guide the newly elected and inexperienced farm President Dimitri on climate policy matters. He felt that the animals' conclusion that CO_2 did not cause warming was a time bomb that could explode and endanger them. It had to be acted on as early as possible to prevent global warming accelerating when less efficient technologies than fossil fuels were adopted. He called a meeting of the animals to discuss how to respond to Algy's campaign to keep the power station shut down.

The worker animals met for lunch and gathered around a put brought by Lucy, with a tea urn. The workers discussed the implications of the climate falsity they were living with.

'CO_2 may not be a problem, as you say,' Ruby said in a dogged way, 'but fossil fuels have to be stopped anyway, because they are running out.'

'They are running out in some places, but there is enough coal to supply the world for at least 1000 years, taking only the shallow coal.,' said Henry. 'There's vastly more deep coal.'

'We must leave some coal for future generations,' said Ruby.

'No problems. Humans have always found substitutes in the past when resources such as forests, whales and gas were running out,' said Norman.

'Why not let the oil, coal and uranium run out then?' Henry said.

'Don't you agree we should keep some?' asked Jolene.

'I do agree,' said Ruby. 'We should hang on to enough for a smooth transition. There are other technologies available now, but conversion efficiencies are low. Engineers are frantically re-running new combinations of energy sources, extraction technologies, converters and heat sinks, applying latest materials and control devices, but thermodynamics has rigid limits on what is possible and there hasn't been much progress for some time. So we need to conserve with optimism.'

'Ruby's right,' said Norman. 'We are using fossil fuels too quickly and heating the environment. That's reason enough to reduce consumption.'

'It may be impossible to stop,' said Henry. 'I don't think humans will allow resources to be locked away. People take as much energy as they want up to the limit of what they can afford, for example, for air travel. When coal eventually runs out, many years in the future, the main hope is for a brand new energy resource, as happened when petroleum and uranium were discovered in time to prevent western civilisation from collapsing or being taken over.'

'Resources are being depleted,' said Norman. 'Energy resources are being used up and there may be none left for future generations.'

'The great hope is renewable energy.'

'Renewable energy can help but it heats the environment,' said Norman. 'It needs to be reconsidered, even hydro.'

'Does hydro really cause warming?' asked Ruby.

'Hydro heats the environment the same as if the water fell down naturally and heated the river rocks with friction,' said Norman. 'Energy would also be used evaporating water to become rain and refill the dam. The energy would be replaced by the Sun, but not more than before the dam was built. Hydro is a contributor of energy to the environment, but not a major one.'

'Alarm about depletion of fuels can be overstated,' said Henry. 'It's the way of the world. Whatever resources humans use, the population grows and depletes them until supplies crash, as happened with timber on Easter Island and with whale oil.'

'Growing populations are the problem for sure,' said Ruby. 'Land and water resources can't be replaced. Malthus in 1798 proposed populations were controlled by hunger, disease and war. Recently we have added birth control, euthanasia and conservation of

178

resources, but depletion is still occurring. Locking away resources merely puts a Band-Aid on a wound that can never heal.'

'There are no revolutionary new energy supplies waiting in the wings,' Norman said. 'Few people now believe in perpetual motion or fusion energy. Science seems to have few new answers and many we have relied on are worn out. When petroleum has all gone, planes won't be able to fly.'

'Hooray,' said Chester.

'That's a long way off,' Ruby said. 'Oil consumption is continuing to grow. The date of peak oil has receded from around 2000 to 2025 or later.'

'Petroleum resources are finite,' said Henry. 'Allowing consumption to grow is criminal. There has to be a peak soon.'

'Exploration and extraction methods may continue to improve,' said Ruby.

'It's the same with coal,' said Henry. 'Although some coal has been mined out in developed countries, there are still vast resources in seams deep underground. Coal mining has barely scratched the surface.

'Many people figure technology causes problems and is hopeless.' said Andrea. 'Some want to throw in the towel. Accelerationists want fossil fuels to be depleted.

'Who are accelerationists?' asked Henry.

'They are young and idealistic humans who want to hasten the economic collapse predicted by Karl Marx,' she said. 'They think it is inevitable and should be brought on sooner rather than later by intensifying capitalism. To end current conditions they want to undermine the pillars of capitalism: private property; capital accumulation; wage labour; voluntary exchange; the price system; and competitive markets. They welcome growth in energy use to bring on collapse.'

'Their behaviour is unreasonable and immoral,' said Henry. 'Neither the ends nor the means is justified. Collapsing capitalist economies is possible, but not by increasing consumption. Profligate wasting of energy resources can never be reversed and would be harmful overall.'

179

'It is a short-sighted, cruel and unnecessary strategy,' said Norman. 'In an economic collapse, ordinary people would suffer. Do the accelerationists have a model for a new society?'

'They are vague about this. They would possibly want a variant of socialism.'

'Old Major's revolution was socialism. Unfortunately he set up the pigs as a ruling class. The best way to achieve socialism would be to get rid of the pigs. But we are ruled too by SR and DU charlatans and now by accelerationists too. They have hijacked climate science for profit.'

'Other revolutionaries want to overthrow technological industries,' said Andrea. 'They imagine humankind can return to the pastoral bliss idolised by the Romantic era poets and the hippie movement. It is not practical because they will be unable to turn down energy consumption far enough. But they need to make a start by reducing it to stop environments deteriorating.'

'Thank you, Andrea,' said Henry. 'I can see we all agree with you.'

The animal workers went back to their work.

Henry and Norman were talking one evening after the climate class when they started a new thread.

'Have you noticed that conditions round here have worsened since we've had Dimitri as President?' said Norman.

'You mean he's taken back the control that Lord Miguel gave us?' Henry said.

'Yes, that and the pigs have become demanding and more ruthless, there has been more work to do and they won't listen to our complaints at all.'

Norman had voiced something that Henry had noticed but never discussed.

'There is a worldwide trend of totalitarianism,' said Henry. 'The Caruban Government has become dominating and tyrannical.'

Henry the bull was talking down to the ram. Although he was older, he wanted to share his views rather than impose them.

180

'They follow the SR government, who have become more totalitarian,' Norman said. 'The pendulum has swung from State control under Stalin, to personal control under Miguel's openness policy and now is swinging back to totalitarianism again. Individual freedom is disappearing.

'Individual freedom gets more respect in the DU than in the SR.'

Henry was a dyed-in-the-wool libertarian and hoped his view wouldn't clash with the ram's, inclined towards socialism like most sheep.

'That is a misconception,' said Norman. 'There isn't much freedom anywhere. Humans are more able to voice dissent in the DU if they are wealthy. Corporations control private individuals and public life. They monopolize markets and collude with supposed competitors, holding customers in contempt. The masses are controlled to consume. There is a ruling ideology, central control and mass terror. The DU is as totalitarian as the SR and Ceramica.'

'Ceramicans may have less freedom,' said Henry.

He was taken aback to have the DU lumped in with Ceramica.

'Perhaps they don't care as much about freedom in the DU?' Norman said.

'Do you mean socialism limits its people with social control?' said Henry.

'Not necessarily,' said Norman. 'Perhaps socialism extends welfare to them and removes the so-called 'freedom of the jungle' which is an oxymoron for true freedom.'

'Scaling down for Ceramica's larger population, an individual's say could be as good as a citizen's in the DU,' said Henry. 'The DU is less authoritarian but there is more dissent and hot air. Their system is not less totalitarian, having citizens who are atomised, isolated and fearful like theirs.'

Henry was surprised to find he was talking down the DU whom he had often championed. He realised that ordinary lives in all three superpowers were the same beneath different veneers of materialism.

'Neither the SR, the DU or Ceramica include animal liberation in their concerns. I'm not likely to side with any of them until they

181

recognise our needs,' said Henry. 'The leaders of all three superpowers are ambiguous and opaque in policy announcements, especially in their dealing with each other. Vagueness and secrecy are hallmarks of totalitarian ideologies. I am not sure whether ambiguity exists first in a leader's heart or in his words. It seems to me they are in a conspiracy to maintain their leaderships. Their ideologies are in the garb of ambition to dominate. We animals have had enough of that.'

CHAPTER 32 GLOBAL EFFECTS

Dinah was giving birth in a corner of the home paddock. Norman was with her, keeping away scavenging crows. They perched in trees surrounding Dinah, cawing aggressively, creating a wall of jeering sound to exclude irresolute competitors, such as foxes. They were waiting for a chance to peck out the eyes of the lamb and feed on the afterbirth, even during delivery.

Dinah alternately stood and lay down, to ease the pain. Eventually the cria came in a rush. It had Dorset Horn sheep characteristics but had its great grandmother's long neck, long legs and long wool.

'It's a ewe,' said Norman.

'Good,' Dinah said.

She licked it, cleaning away the slime and stimulating it. It stood up and lurched to suck its first external meal.

It was their first offspring and they were joyful.

They led it to a straw bale shelter nearby. The straw would protect a young lamb while it was vulnerable to wet and cold, until its wool had grown a little.

They named the cria Larissa.

Climate warming was predicted to bring discomfort to humans, but heat waves on the farm were difficult to enumerate in retrospect, when memories had faded. Extreme sea level rise events were sometimes difficult to distinguish from spring tides and storm surges.

Animal Farm was situated on fertile land at the coast. Fields next to the beach were below the high tide level and protected by an artificial pebble bank several kilometres long. The bund was maintained by a bulldozer, with costs shared between the farmers whose land was protected. Water from the land drained through channels having sea doors that shut automatically at high tide, preventing backflow. On several occasions, the pebble bank was breached in a storm and the land was flooded with salt water, destroying crops and killing pastures. It was said to be due to climate change, but controlled measurements were not available and there was little to distinguish the flooding from other breaches that had occurred regularly for centuries.

Natalia Alphancourt visited the Farm and asked Lord Dimitri if she could address the worker animals.

'Unfortunately, the news is dire,' she said when they were all assembled. 'Sea level rise will flood low-lying coastal land and inundate our capital, Salton. The low-lying part of Animal Farm will go under when tides are highest. We are not sure when this will happen. We can't do anything to stop it directly but we must play our part in reducing flooding disasters from climate change worldwide.'

'She's lying,' Jolene whispered to Henry. 'Changes in sea level have been measured and found to be insignificant in other places. It's a false alarm. Algy's levees are a waste of time and effort.'

'Sea level change is a local effect, not a worldwide disaster,' Dongle the donkey said to Jolene.

He stood up to ask a question.

'Yes, I will take a question,' said Natalia. 'Go ahead, Mr Donkey.'

'Could it be that the tectonic plate Caruba is on is sinking, causing the sea level to rise by displacing water?' Dongle asked. 'If sea level is rising now, it may fall again. The geological record shows that in the past sea level has in places oscillated up and down over a wide range of height. According to Professor Ian Plimer (6), that process is continuing today.'

'You must be aware low-lying islands are being inundated,' said President Natalia Alphancourt irritably. 'Inhabitants want to evacuate.'

184

'When people have the misfortune of living in the wrong place, it is not usual to compensate them until after the predicted disaster has occurred,' Dongle said.

'That is selfish, cynical and disrespectful,' said Alphancourt. 'Sea level really is rising. Trust me. We have commenced to construct, along both sides of the River Salt, earth embankments 10 metres above the current high tide level, to prevent the sea flooding the city of Salton.'

'How much sea level rise has been observed?' asked Norman, backing up Dongle.

'That's all you need to know for now,' said President Natalia Alphancourt crossly. 'I won't be taking any more questions from you animals. You lack experience to respect evidence. We are acting to prevent the effects on everyone of sea level rise. Does anyone else have a question?'

'According to the Gaia Hypothesis, the Earth is an organism with natural changes that balance out,' said Dongle. 'Variations in climate have happened before and the living and non-living systems adjust and are eventually restored.'

'How can non-living systems adjust?' Lord Dimitri snorted derisively.

'For example, coal seams are formed in sandstone and shale, compressed under the weight of growing vegetation,' said Dongle. 'Vegetation layers sink down in swamps under sand and mud sediments deposited during floods. Their adjustment is to compress and bend, until they are uplifted.'

'I get it,' said Lord Dimitri, covering his embarrassment at Dongle' correction. 'Rocks get eroded, sedimented, compressed, cemented and uplifted, in a cycle.'

'That's the Gaia theory,' said Dongle. 'Climate change is part of a self-restoring cycle. Like a thermostat can turn off a heater when the water becomes hot, so there are mechanisms that switch off global warming when it gets too warm. Recent warming is relatively small and could be a temporary aberration. Either the Sun and the Earth could have wobbled on its axis, with its molten interior varying unpredictably. The current variations may not be a problem.'

185

'It's a theory, an unlikely one and we can't afford to wait,' said President Alphancourt. 'My government has acted to prevent flooding. Closure of the power station will reduce CO_2 emissions and the flooding it causes.'

Henry looked at Norman and rolled up his eyes in despair.

President Alphancourt prepared to leave.

'Thank you, Lord Dimitri and animals. We are facing climate problems together and my government will keep them to a minimum.'

At the next meteorology class, Norman said to Dongle: 'I congratulate you on your questioning of the President. It was brave of you. Have you had any repercussions?'

'No,' said old Dongle. 'Not yet. But there could be.'

'Maybe they'll overlook it,' said Norman. 'There is little evidence of sea level rise. Sensational photography and alarming news dominate. It is the same with ice and snow. Few people observe conditions throughout the seasons. Polar and mountain ice get most visitors in warmer weather when ice is melting. An objective viewpoint is wanted.'

'Could they measure the lengths of glaciers,' said Dinah.

'With glaciers retreating, that's a no brainer.'

'Not really. Glaciers get shorter in summer.'

'A drought of snow in the catchment area can be the cause of a glacier retreating,' said Henry.

'Not every summer has equal warming,' said Jolene. 'Reports exaggerate climate change. Neither retreat of a glacier, nor calving of an iceberg, necessarily signifies universal global warming.'

'There isn't evidence of significant global warming,' said Norman. 'I don't know what all the fuss is about. It is ludicrous seizing on the disappearance of polar ice and glaciers as evidence of climate change.

'The ice caps on Mars have disappeared in the last few years, but not from atmospheric warming. Mars doesn't have an atmosphere. They think direct radiation from the Sun heated the ice.'

'Solar radiation could be melting polar ice on Earth,' said Jolene.

186

'Certainly. After all, the Sun is implicated in large warming cycles in Earth's history.'

'Photographs of destruction of the Great Barrier Reef are concerning,' said Ruby.

'Perhaps natural cycles of coral death are sensationalized in some camera reports.'

'Heatwaves and extreme weather can wreak havoc with flora and fauna,' said Ruby. 'Coral can suffer and die if the sea heats up even a little.'

'I doubt it,' Norman said. 'Coral evolved in the Palaeozoic Era. Since then Earth has heated up and cooled many times, in a range of about 10 to 30°C, but corals are still with us today. How can you be sure corals would suffer and die from a tiny increase of 0.6°C total over 130 years, as the International Policy Committee for Climates(IPCC) found? Wouldn't the coral adapt, as it does to seasonal changes? The onus is on alarmists to demonstrate that ocean temperature change is persisting and is perilous to coral.'

'If people are told there is a gorilla coming, they will imagine it and look for it.'

'Are you sure that confirmation bias in science observation is significant?'

'Not more than in other parts of life. Wanting scientists to be honest and trusting them is like believing all children will behave well at all times. When they think they can get away with something, a few may try it on. Some children steal until they are caught and a few scientists will cheat and skew results their way, possibly unconsciously, until they are found out. Trusting them blindly is foolish.

'Today I have oriented you with a balanced overview of effects often presented as evidence of warming,' said Norman. 'The evidence is sometimes questionable, meaning that causes are not definitely known. Without definite evidence, we should be sceptical of effects. Our next class will quantify effects and their implications.'

'There seems to be a desire to wrap up local environmental effects into a single package of 'climate change' that is happening at the same time everywhere, that can be talked about as a single problem, which is easier to sensationalize, because it is more dramatic and has less detail,' said Henry. 'It is the kind of thinking that opposes animal liberation as a general principle, trying to suppress local developments where animals are becoming more liberated. We need to present Animal Liberation as a series of practical steps rather than a new philosophy.'

CHAPTER 33 ARE ANIMAL SPECIES EQUAL

The prospect of ending their lives in an abattoir was always present for the Farm's worker animals. Fear stunted their emotional growth. They yearned for the idyllic free living of their ancestors who lived in the wild until humans domesticated them into slavery.

'I am beginning to lose hope of ever being liberated,' said Norman to Henry.

'What do you want most?'

'Freedom, happiness and democracy.'

'After they were domesticated, farm animals have never had those,' said Henry.

'When Lord Miguel was president, conditions seemed to improve. Since then our rights have been cut back.'

'Do you think we should revolt?' Henry said.

Norman thought for a moment.

'Yes, definitely. There's everything to gain and not enough to lose.'

The human owners of Manor Farm had used artificial selection to breed utility into their livestock. Jolene's adaptations for milk production, grazing pastures, calf-bearing and meat growth were unsuited to living independently in the wild. Flight from predators would be impossible for her with her large udder. Her kind calved, was milked and taken to the abattoir.

Despite being bred as domestic slaves, like animals on other Caruba farms, the animals on Animal Farm had learned to speak Pidgin English English and apply scientific methods to problems.

They were more aware and more intelligent than humans imagined. They wanted respect for their individual minds and feelings, for their ability to reason. They wanted to be liberated from the psychological bondage of their slavery. The worst excesses of factory farming were being stopped, but progress was slow, with no end in sight to killing for meat.

The animals knew that some humans were vegetarian or vegan and hoped for news that it was becoming commonplace. But change was very slow. Humans could not revert to conditions before agriculture and before herding, when nomads hunted animals.

"Meat is a sine qua non of human eating,' Henry said, reading from a screen. 'What does that mean?'

'They won't or can't go without meat,' said Jolene. 'But the habit may not be inherited. Have you heard the Pink Floyd song where a school teacher shouts: 'If you won't eat your meat, how can you have any pudding?' It suggests meat eating doesn't come naturally to humans and to get them to eat meat, they must be bribed or threatened.'

'It could also suggest they are indoctrinated that meat is a superior food,' said Hunter the cat who had replaced Chester.

'Hmm,' said Henry. 'There's not much liberty for us in that!'

The animal workers imagined that they were gaining control over their lives by learning a language and science.

Kant's categorical imperative requiring actions to have universal application could be applied to all animals, including humans and pigs. Human Christians aspired to treat others as they wanted to be treated themselves, but they didn't apply it across species boundaries. They discriminated against livestock animals with wholesale slaughter that was murder. The pigs on Animal Farm were no better than humans and they had no compunction in sending harmless worker animals to their deaths.

Animals were unable to live the way they wanted. Endlessly they explored ways to avoid being sent to the abattoir, to be exempted from farm work and allowed to leave the Farm. But the pigs' authority was ruthless and their freedom was fiercely denied, without compromise.

190

When they heard about the attack on the DU's World Trade Centre, the animals realised that human civilisation had venomous rifts between races, worse than between any species they knew of.

Some species, like humans and pigs, claimed they had superior skills, awarding themselves positions of leadership. The worker animals believed, by contrast, all animals were of equal value to the community, without domination by species having better language abilities, like humans and pigs. They wanted their leaders to be scrupulously honest and fair to others. Being able to work with other leaders was also essential. They had been able to vote in only one election, when they had preferred Borat to Hyacinth. They had not been able to vote in the recent election when Dimitri had seized power.

Pigs saw themselves as progressive but limited by idealistic animal workers who were unable to adapt to realities. In their own view, the animal workers were worse off than the people of India, who also lacked electricity but had freedom to move to elsewhere in the country if they could afford it. They had a choice of not working, whereas the Farm animals had no choice: they had to work.

It seemed to Jolene she would always have a life of servitude to pigs, or humans, or to some other exploitative species. She asked herself: '*What are the limits on moral treatment of a domestic farm animal? How much respect should a farm animal get?*'

She wanted not to be used harmfully, but despaired that the entire canon of western thought on religion, morality and philosophy was constructed on the notion that only humans have a right to consideration; animals may be used or abused by their owners, with a few restrictions on treatment of pet animals and limits to factory farming.

'Are you as intelligent as Borat?' Norman the ram asked Ruby the collie.

'I wouldn't know,' she said. 'How could anyone find out?'

'Dogs' intelligence is said to be exceeded only by humans, primates and dolphins.'

'Pigs are about equal to dogs,' said Jolene.

'Who says so?' asked Ruby.

191

'Humans and me,' said Norman. 'I'll bet you're as smart as Borat.'

'That's crap,' said Ruby. 'We dogs are *smarter* than pigs. We're more human-like. We seek out human company. Humans like dogs more than pigs. Dogs understand them. Humans don't let pigs into their lives the way they do dogs.'

'Humans like pig best when it comes with crackling,' said Henry, smirking.

'Humans don't eat their pets,' said Ruby.

'As a pet of the pigs, do you feel safe Ruby?'

'Pigs like dogs and if I behave well, they'll keep me. When I gaze into their eyes, they think I like them for their kindness and they would never harm me.'

'You are an optimist.'

'What could go wrong?' said Ruby.

'They could think you have betrayed their secrets.'

'I keep secrets.'

'We sheep bleat,' said Dinah, Norman's partner.

'That's because you don't know the words,' said Sophie.

There was laughter.

'Anyway, what secrets do you have Ruby?' asked Norman. 'C'mon. Tell.'

'I have to go and bring in the cows for milking now,' said Ruby, getting up. 'Sorry folks. Bye.'

The abattoir lorry came and the pigs nominated Stanley and Sophie.

'They're not old,' protested Norman.

'You seem to be doing a good job, Norman,' said Lord Borat. 'We can't afford to run two rams. Stanley's had a good innings. I am aware of his climate teaching work from Monty, who has told me all the animals have benefitted. Andrea says you have taken over his class.

'That's right. What about Sophie? Why is she being taken?'

'She's had a good few lambs and it's time to give younger ewes a go.'

192

Stanley and Sophie had expected they would be despatched sooner or later. They had spent several evenings with Norman and Dinah so they would know how to keep their investigations and classes running.

'This was Algy's retribution for our experiment,' Norman said to Dinah. 'I had better be careful.'

'Don't take any unnecessary risks, but continue the fight for our liberation with urgency. Finding out the lies about that gas will help us win. We're just getting started and your work with your father has given us hope.'

The animal workers' Pidgin English and science had improved steadily. Their diction was rather different from Oxford English but they could talk with each other and with human visitors to the farm. Keeping a conversation going had become easy, whereas once they would have laboured to establish terms and arguments. After years of practice, they could decipher research findings and dispute conclusions.

For Norman's next meeting, he wanted the animals to consider their rights relative to pigs and humans. As they trudged to the barnyard for the meeting, Pearl, the filly of Goliath and Fiona, startled and stamped her foot.

On the path ahead a large carpet python was coiled. Although it was non-venomous, they gave it a wide berth, the horses snorting. It had a large bulge in the middle of its body. Randy the cockerel rushed off to check his hens and sure enough one was missing.

'Stomp on the horrible thing, Goliath,' said Randy when he came back.

'No,' said Jolene. 'This is its home. It has a right to live here and hunt here. Its kind were here long before there was a farm.'

'It gives me the creeps,' said Pearl.

'It's harmless to large animals,' said Jolene. 'Perhaps we can get it to live in the farmhouse roof, to feed on rats and mice?'

'It could dine on piglet.'

'That would be good.'

193

'Moving it there is a task for Randy. He can offer himself as a dainty morsel and lure it into the farmhouse.'

'How can it get into the roof?'

'It'll find a way in. There are all sorts of cracks and holes where it can enter.'

A week later, a tradesman employed to mend leaks in the farmhouse roof was descending his ladder when he stepped on the snake and fell. When he recovered he accused Archie who had instructed him on the task.

'You didn't tell me about that fucking snake. I was going up the ladder; it was coming down. Frightened the shit out of me.'

'Sorry about that,' said Archie. 'We weren't sure it was up there. You're okay aren't you?'

'A bit sore.'

At the rights meeting they considered the question of animals' ability to claim rights.

'Since Lord Dimitri took over as President, our position has deteriorated,' said Dinah. 'He is turning his dogs on us regularly.'

'We have to assert our rights.'

'What rights do we have?'

'We can try to get rights they allow other animals, like dogs and cats.'

'I can't see sheep taking up barking or meowing.'

'Nor would cattle be able to sleep all day, like a cat,' said Norman.

'Charles Darwin distinguished between species but recognised humans had some features in common with other species,' Jolene said. 'There is no fundamental difference between man and the higher mammals in their mental faculties. He attributed to animals the power of reason, decision making, memory, sympathy, and imagination.'

'At the beginning of Animal Farm, the slogan was *'All animals are equal'* but the words *'some are more equal than others'* were added,' said Norman. 'Nevertheless, we have had threads of equality binding most of the livestock community together, excepting the

194

pigs. Now, as we consider liberation, similarities and differences between species assume new importance.'

Henry said: 'Darwin's purpose was to explain evolution of different physical forms. If he had studied evolution of diets, predation and cannibalism, he would have found that refraining from eating members of another species confers on both certain obligations. That is a long way short of establishing their legal rights, property rights, fiscal responsibility and civic equality. We animals are far from being accepted as equals. Until the rights of animals equal those of humans has a long way to go. Religion has taught for too long that animals are ruled by humans.'

'We need to do something about the pigs.'

'Not all humans have full rights and nor do pigs,' said Jolene. 'Humans draw the line at physical deficiencies, arbitrarily excluding the disabled. Humans exclude from responsibility individuals who are mentally disabled, mentally ill, undeveloped, children or senile. They are without the ethical protection accorded others of their species. Pigs have provided us with no protection from humans. Animal workers have even fewer rights than pigs.'

'Henry is right,' said Norman. 'Our position is weak. When it has suited the pigs, they have acknowledged animal abilities but they have not granted animals the ethical consideration they give each other. It would be contradictory and aberrant to have civil relations with pigs who could send us to be killed by humans, or keep us as hostages to be sacrificed for their group to survive.

'Freedom for our pigs prevents other species freedom and is invalidly taken. Pig leadership is failing because, in pursuing their freedom, they are reducing ours. They are attempting totalitarianism and their leadership opposes our liberty.

'Ethical difficulties such as these differentiate the animals on Animal Farm,' said Henry. 'In the world outside the Farm, vegetarians and vegans are redrawing the human diet map. The sale of animals from Animal Farm is demanded by the pigs' appetites for luxurious living and material self-indulgence. If their consumption was more modest, the Farm could produce enough provender for all the animals, including the pigs, to live and die naturally. As it is, the

195

greed of the pigs is causing our compatriots to be slaughtered.'

'We have to reduce meat eating as a matter of urgency,' Jolene said. 'Meat eating by humans is indefensible. Belief that meat eating confers a nutritional advantage can be countered by re-education. The use of meat as a convenience food is inexcusable and requires a legislated penalty to prevent infringement of others' rights.

'Besides meat, we animals are valued for farm work, coal mining, animal power, farm defence and animal products. We must diminish their desire to eat us by increasing our value alive in these roles and decreasing our value as meat.'

'Perhaps we could spread endemic livestock diseases such as BSE that can transfer to humans and make us less palatable?'

'They might slaughter all of us.'

'Not if outbreaks are mild. The pigs are not meat eaters and for them it is simply a matter of revenue. They need us for our farm work. We must make sure we are worth more to the pigs alive than dead.'

'How?'

'Our work and our individuality must be valued and every death vigorously protested.'

'The best strategy for our liberation is to foster alternatives to eating our meat, while using our labour and skills. It's a narrow path to tread.'

'Could we have a delegation take our concerns to Lord Dimitri?' asked Jolene.

'He won't like it if we come on strong,' said Henry. 'It might be more effective if one of us talks with him.'

'You should do it Henry,' said Jolene. 'You have dealt with Lord Dimitri before and he knows you.'

'Okay. But don't expect miracles. He's heartless. He might throw me out.'

CHAPTER 34 HOW MUCH WARMING IS TOO MUCH?

The next class on weather met in the stables because two cows were calving in the cowshed. There were looseboxes and stalls, with a chest containing hand tools for grooming horses, hoof care and shoeing. Saddle and bridle racks protruded from the walls, but the riding equipment had been sold by the pigs long ago. The stable accommodated the working horses and there were stands for their collars and pegs for hanging up the harnesses.

The animals had low interest in acquiring goods, materials, property and wealth. Most things on the farm, like machinery and buildings, were antiquated. The exception was the farmhouse, where the pigs indulged themselves with the latest appliances they had bought. There was a doorway to the library in the old tack room, where the animals studied in the evenings, using books for research assignments and an old computer brought from the farmhouse.

Norman had for some time been presenting evening classes with scientific and meteorological topics.

'We have studied: temperature, temperature change and forecasting,' he said. 'Now we will study global warming. I hope you are not too tired from your work today, because this evening we need to do some thinking.

'40 years ago they installed our weather station and started recording temperatures,' he said. 'Since then, our predecessors in this class have from time to time looked at the data collected.' He held up a thick folder. 'They have looked for trends. It takes a lot of work to reach a conclusion about temperature trends. Sometimes they have found trends of cooling, at other times warming, but mostly without distinct patterns emerging. Our data is on file and can be analysed. So far the data is consistent with there being a small continuous increase in temperature like that reported in the First Assessment Report of the International Policy Committee for Climates(IPCC), in 1990. They said in the Overview:

'Our judgement is that: global mean surface air temperature has increased by 0.3 to 0.6°C over the last 100 years...;

'Could the increase have resulted from a change in the temperature measurement technique?' asked Jolene.

'It could, possibly, but the increase is erratic, as if many factors could be involved.'

'Alarmists say it is extreme conditions that are worsening: floods, hurricanes and bushfires,' said Muriel, Dongle's partner.

'If you mean that there have been trends in extremes, while the average has been steady all along, that is possible too,' said Norman. 'It is difficult to measure extremes on absolute scales because weather events are not reproducible. There is no easy way to generalise extreme weather variations.'

'If we are going to be able to change the climate, don't we have to be able to describe weather events?' asked Jolene.

'Ideally yes,' said Norman. 'Not everyone needs such certainty. There are persons in responsible positions who would happily spend billions of dollars of public money to counter events lacking an agreed description.'

'Greed is seldom agreed,' said Jolene.

'Controlling a climate is a new idea,' said Dinah. 'Quite ridiculous in fact! In the past humans have been able to adapt.'

'Doing nothing is not politically acceptable today,' Jolene said.

'Is that true for all variations?' said Norman. 'Can you give me an example of something that wouldn't cope with the IPCC's increases of 0.006°C per year.'

'A teensy-weensy increase could eventually lead to catastrophe,' said Dolly despondently.

'Would anyone notice?' asked Dinah.

'They should,' Jolene said.

'Wouldn't it depend where you are? There are small variations all the time and no-one takes any notice,' Norman said. 'Possibly they do in extreme climates like Australia?'

'You might notice if you were a delicate coral,' said Domino.

'What amount of increase would be a catastrophe for livestock and humans?' asked Norman.

'20°C above average, every day,' said Henry.

'Why would that be a catastrophe?' asked Norman.

'We would be sweating and heat exhausted,' said Henry. 'It would get too hot to go outdoors and the warble fly would stampede us.'

An earlier science class had learned how cattle hide under bushes from the warble fly, which lays its eggs on them, hatching into larvae centimetres long and migrating through their bodies to live under the skin on their backs, irritating them. In hot weather, fly attacks upset them and they stampeded and injured themselves. In the days of Farmer Jones, egg-laying was prevented with sprays and by brushing insecticide lotion onto animals' warbled backs. The pigs didn't bother and the cattle had to suffer the depredations of warble flies. The the pigs' one concession was to allow cattle to seek shelter in bushes and have time off from work when the flies were biting them.

'Cattle would have to live in a cooler place than Caruba,' said Henry.

'Would an increase of 19 degrees concern you, Henry?'

'Yes,' he said. 'A disaster.'

'How about 10 degrees?'

'Torrid,' he said.

'5 degrees?'

'Sweltering. Maybe okay in the shade and indoors,' said Henry.

'On an Australian summer day, almost any voluntary increase in ambient temperature would be rejected as unacceptable. Heat tolerance varies between individuals, of course, but extreme conditions can bring panic and fear of climate change.'

'The situation doesn't have to be so dire,' said Artemis. He was in hiding from the pigs. The workers valued his input, which was visionary. 'Whinging about the weather is a pastime in many places but in others people just get on with it. For example, goats feed at the ends of the day to avoid the heat.'

'Temperature variation at a particular location is complex. Maximin thermometers do not indicate discomfort when the peaks are hidden by averaging. Days would be difficult to compare.'

'Why don't we compare the temperature on July 14th with the same day last year, and likewise for every other day on the calendar?' asked Henry. 'The day-for-day change would give a better comparison.'

'Would you compare everywhere with everywhere else?'

'A sample of places.'

'At what time of day, exactly?'

'At a sample of times.'

'With electronic weather stations, it could be hourly,' said Norman. 'We don't have that capability for all stations yet.'

'It would be a good investment,' said Henry.

'We might not be able to see the wood for the trees,' said Jolene.

'Climate change is a hot potato,' said Norman. 'Politicians everywhere overlook that the climate changes slowly and because field research is slow, their response is to give money to get quick answers by desktop research. Such answers would simplify the problem. The number of meteorological stations in some areas has decreased. Stations powered by solar or nuclear are needed, to measure independently, frequently and accurately. I would like to find out exactly what global warming is occurring.'

'It is a complex problem,' old Andrea said. 'There are various opinions of how much warming there is. People are not all the same. Some are more concerned about climate change than others. There is verbal conflict between believers, deniers and sceptics.

'Believers state, with emotion, that climate change is definite,' said Jolene. 'They cite instances of adverse effects, such as ice melting, bushfires and sea level rise,' said Jolene. 'Their evidence is second-hand and may be obtained using special effects and arbitrarily sampling of images to dramatize effects, such as with time lapse photography. They are sure the cause is anthropomorphic, resulting from CO_2 pollution by the greenhouse effect, as publicised in Algy's movie. They associate images of change with supposed causes. They do not consider alternative explanations or the possibility of faked science and biased reporting. They want governments to take action, especially by preventing fossil fuel combustion, except in vehicles.'

Jolene paused and sipped from a drinking tank.

'Believers want their majorities to rule over everyone by the consensual decrees of international forums,' she said, continuing. 'They don't require definitive investigation because they are sufficiently mobilised by their beliefs. The edicts of their leaders contradict and overrule scientific and democratic freedoms, by autocratic rulings, or even by hegemonic tyranny. For example, the temperature record may be altered to match theory (22).'

'You sound like a denier,' said Dinah.

'Believers label as deniers the 'heretics' who challenge their monotheism with arguments they are unable to counter with reason,' said Jolene. 'With deniers, believers' defence fails miserably. Compromise between believers and deniers is difficult to negotiate when there is little evidence and beliefs are fragile. They claim deniers heresies to be self-evidently false, dishonest, illogical and too stupid to be considered. Denying is often claimed to have motives corrupted by greed, ignorance and self-interest. Believers sometimes call angrily for reprisals against deniers.

'Sceptics,' said Jolene, 'simply don't know. Their indecision is less acceptable to believers than deniers, because scepticism is a moving target of doubt, rather than an alternative reality presented by a denier which can easily be dismissed. Sceptics are unconvinced that climate change is significant but they do not usually have an accepted standard for what would be significant. Their concern is that processes are transparent. They want a credible process of climate change to be verified before launching into remedial action. They want evidence that there is a greenhouse effect and that CO_2 traps more infrared, molecule for molecule, than N_2 and O_2, rather than quoting physics theories. They point out that climate data can be biased and is presented by believers to mislead. Most of us worker animals on this Farm would be sceptics.'

201

'I am sceptical about the closure of the power station,' said old Andrea. 'I want to know effects on global warming on what we do on the Farm and in the coal mine. Coal mining and the power station could restart one day.'

'I agree, but it might not occur until human civilisation based on fossil fuels is rebuilt,' said Artemis. 'The antis are intent on destroying it. Thermodynamics dictates they cannot succeed. It was forecast that canals would takeover transportation in Europe, but road vehicles displaced barges because they were more efficient. There is no more efficient supplier of large quantities of energy than fossil fuels, but believers do not accept it.'

'It could take a long time to convince them,' said old Andrea. 'I don't think it will be in my time.'

A few weeks later, Andrea retired. She came to some of the discussions but no longer took part.

CHAPTER 35 ANIMALS HAVE RIGHTS

Worker animals knew by reputation the bearded man, philosopher Phil Sopher, standing before them with Lord Dimitri and President Alphancourt. Goliath and Fiona had heard him speak when he visited the Farm 15 years earlier and presented his ideas about the sentience of all animals. Since then he had been active in the DU, progressing animals' rights.

'Good afternoon President Alphancourt, Lord Dimitri and animals,' he said. 'My name is Phil Sopher and I represent the Animal Rights Action Group in the DU. Henry asked me here today with the agreement of President Natalia Alphancourt and your Lord Dimitri.

The Ceramican and SR governments have been oppressing you by requiring your conformance to their climate policies, which are totalitarian. The DU's policies are more respectful of individual rights, including animals' rights. You haven't achieved liberty yet, but the DU could help you to get it.'

The animals hadn't heard their rights acknowledged before and listened rapt.

'We in the DU support animal rights,' said Sopher, *'whereas the SR opposes them. We want individual self-determination to be respected for all animals. We want an end to killing of animals for food. My diet has gone to vegetarianism and then to veganism - foregoing dairy products and the wearing of wool or leather. A moral question is: does the killing of animals reduce human suffering and increase human happiness? The answer is no. Humans*

203

have regarded eating of animals as a 'means to our ends' even when there were other more nutritional ways. No more. In the DU, humans are eating fewer animals and relinquishing their subjugation and speciesism. Meat-eating is on the way out. Abattoirs are closing down. I expect the human population on Caruba to become vegan, with animals growing vegetables everywhere. Oppression of animals as slaves is wrong,' Sopher said. *'Human killing of animals for food was an assumed condition of their domestication that animals are now keen to revoke peacefully.'*

President Alphancourt spoke next and disagreed with him, her views reflecting those of her constituents, who included livestock farmers and abattoir workers.

'Animals on farms will continue to be eaten by humans. Although there could be a reduction in meat eating, meat is an essential part of the SR and Caruban diet. Animal Farm will continue to supply it. It is unlikely that veganism will become popular on Caruba soon.'

Henry wanted to boo, but restrained himself to shaking is huge head vigorously.

The speakers talked about the way forward for livestock animals in detail and the assembly broke up.

The animals dispersed into the night, talking about what had been said. Sopher's words gave the animals new hope that here was human interest in vegan diets and animal liberation. But Alphancourt's view was discouraging and some workers on Animal Farm despaired.

'Cows will always be milked,' said Jolene. 'Hens' eggs will always be eaten and fish will always be caught.'

'Milk, eggs and fish would decrease with veganism,' said Henry. 'Jolene, I agree we have to draw a line and unless the pigs join our side, they are our enemy. They oversee our deaths. According to Phil Sopher, the true moral boundary for the equal consideration of animals' interests is not in our being rational, but in our having the capacity to suffer physically or emotionally. Ultimately, it is a matter of them treating us with consideration, to prevent suffering and allowing us our own natures and freedom from exploitation.'

'Natalia derailed the issue of pig exploitation by going on about the SR diet, which has nothing to do with it,' said Henry.

Jolene whispered to Henry: 'I don't trust the SR. To get freedom we animals will have to fight. They won't liberate us.'

'What do we need to fight for?' asked Henry.

'We can prepare for veganism by researching attitudes on Caruba and how humans could adjust their diets,' said Jolene. 'Humans need to be more familiar with buying, preparing and eating large quantities of vegetables.'

In the following months, the worker animals waited for the pigs to acknowledge their rights, treat them with respect and save them from the abattoir but there was little change. Lord Borat consulted them to get their cooperation, even allowing them to express opinions about his policies. But opposing his proposals was not permitted and dissidents were punished.

Bulls were polyamorous with freedom to mate with all the cows as often as they liked and this declined with age. One day Henry stood with his aging father Earl, overlooking their neighbour's field where a herd of comely heifers was grazing.

'If I pushed that gate over, we could run in there and have us one apiece,' Henry said.

''Not so fast,' said Earl, speaking with the wisdom of his years. 'Why don't we walk over and have us the lot?'

The morals of livestock mating had been under human control for so long that farm animals don't make love with the deliberation and absence of haste of wild animals of their species. Livestock matings lacked partner choice, were hurried and brief. By contrast the pigs passed many hours in copulation, sometimes locked in engagements continuing for days.

Pigs declined to assist in cultivating the land, claiming their role was supervision, despite being better at rooting than any other species. In the few hours free from labour, the worker animals sought

205

to supplement their meagre diets by scouring the hedgerows, fields and forests for berries, nuts and fungi. They traded these when they could.

'I have a quart of wicked blueberries,' said Simone. 'Does anyone have blackberries they want to swap?'

They snared rabbits and took wild duck eggs from nests. The animal workers went berrying in a group, finding hazel nuts, chestnuts and crab apples. The provender was doubly delicious because it was obtained as their right and obligation free. The horses and cattle enjoyed visiting pastures on common land where there were herbs and delicious plants that supplemented their meagre rations.

The farm buildings were hundreds of years old. The floor under the granary was planks supported on wooden beams. Tunnels from outside passed under the grain, keeping it aerated and cool.

Barrow ducks landed at Animal Farm on their way to and from the Arctic. The birds were exhausted when they arrived. They rested and grazed in the paddock before resuming their long journey. A pair nested in an air duct beneath the granary floor.

The duck and drake led out a long line of ducklings on a sortie from under the floorboards. Within a few days the young were flying. More than a month had passed since their parents had descended from a migrating echelon and now they relaunched to join the migratory flight, alone at first but converging at altitude with other families who had stopped to nest.

The farm's hedges were laden with bunches of luscious blackberries and the animals ate them off the brambles, taking care not to get hooked.

The pigs required the animals to deliver to the farmhouse most of the fruit they picked. The fruit grew in positions difficult to reach and they attached knives to poles to cut bunches free.

'This is my favourite taste,' said Claudia, dripping mauve juice from her mouth. 'It is sweet and a little tart.'

'Like you,' said Simone.

Claudia poked her with her pole. The sisters often engaged in friendly banter.

206

The pigs kept for themselves the right of pannage: gathering acorns, their favourite food, from the forest floor. Poultry collected nuts for the pigs, encouraged by a reduced egg quota.

After rain, the horses' paddock was sprinkled with field mushrooms. Squirrels, chipmunks, rabbits and wild pigs came to eat them. As the night sky turned grey, the paddock was dotted with stooped figures gathering fungi. Sheep didn't eat them but went out at first light to collect and take them to the pigs to be boiled in milk, their favourite food.

When the abattoir truck pulled up in the farmyard, the animals slunk away, for they knew when it left it would be carrying one of them to a certain death. It was a cattle truck, with a rear door that hinged down to become a loading ramp, complete with siding rails to prevent escape. It could carry many animals. They never knew who was going until a pig told the driver: 'Take that one.' The animals had tried protesting to save a friend, to no avail. The pigs used the abattoir to dispose of troublemakers, whingers, the lazy, the greedy, the old, the sick, the disabled, the superfluous and leaders in non-compliance. The pigs were smaller than some of the other animals and they ganged up to help the driver load the abattoir truck. Old Dongle had spoken against President Natalia about sea-level rise and the truck had come for him.

Alarmed, the animal workers raced to the farmyard and pigeons flew with the news out to workers in the fields.

Biscuit called out to the driver: 'Please don't take our old friend away from us!'

'I am just doing my job,' the man said.

The animals crowded around as several pigs forced Dongle up the tailboard ramp with the Rottweilers barking.

'He's going to a retirement farm,' a pig said. 'He will have a lovely time.'

But the doors of the lorry carried the word 'Knacker'.

'They're taking him to his death,' said Muriel the donkey his partner, trying to stop them raising the tailgate. If a worker threatened a pig it would incur certain death. The driver bolted it shut.

Dongle had fathered the mule Biscuit with Fiona. It was the end of the donkey's line because mules could not reproduce.

'Goodbye everyone,' Dongle brayed from inside the truck. 'Don't let the bastards get you down.'

'He may not have been able to do much work recently,' said Henry, 'but he was smart and asked good questions. He should not be killed. The pigs have gone too far this time!'

'We must all come to death eventually,' said Henry, kindly, 'but it should be a way of our own choosing. Pigs simply dispose of animals they no longer have a use for, as if they have a right to do that. In the DU, they used to lynch human slaves on trumped up pretexts. We must oppose the pigs use of the abattoir to control us.'

Muriel was overcome by grief. She demanded to see Lord Dimitri but they told her he was in a meeting.

The Farm was a place of death but also renewal. Eventually Muriel had a mule foal with the stallion Brandy. They called it Dougal.

'Life is hard,' Muriel taught Dougal, 'but liberation will come. Never forget that.'

CHAPTER 36 CONVERGENCE ALARM

Dimitri's energy minister at-large was Algy. Previously he had been in this role with Lord Borat. He was a huge American Yorkshire boar, with an elongated body and a straight back. His ears were erect, his snout long, his body covered with fine white hair.

Algy had represented energy interests of the Caruba government and was an international figure. It was rumoured his vision was to join the SR and DU in a duopoly able to compete with the Republic of Ceramica. Lord Dimitri sent him overseas to attract investment for development of the Farm. Foreign investors scrambled to invest in developments run by Caruban oligarchs. He toured in the SR, DU, Ceramica and developed nations, campaigning about environmental effects of pollution and depletion of finite mineral resources.

Despite the EGHE having little corroboration, Algy campaigned with religious fervour to stop carbon emissions worldwide. In the SR the antis followed his leadership in energy policy and in the DU he led a cult of antis in climate alarmism.

Algy's quasi-political party was hidden behind government and science establishments who declared a climate crisis. Algy operated like an oligarch, the Farm as his fiefdom. Animal Farm had ceased to be a workers' collective. He had swashbuckling geopolitical ambitions, curbed by Lord Dimitri.

'Animal Farm is free to seize a new future,' Algy said.

'The Farm does not exist for our oligarchs' cupidity,' Lord Dimitri said on television. 'Our growth has to make Animal Farm great, for all of us.'

Algy spent most of his time overseas on his yacht, sailing to conferences to speak on climate change. He was an international celebrity. On his return, Lord Dimitri used him to attract funds for the Farm and to win votes for his regime.

All the animals had gathered to hear Algy, as he stood tall on two legs, beside President Natalia Alphancourt, President of Caruba. He wore a tan velvet morning coat, his muscular fore-limbs filling the sleeves and his thick neck bulging from the unbuttoned collar of a white shirt. Four Rottweilers, their tongues lolling, slavered at his feet.

In a silence born of fear, the animals watched his movie: 'A Calculated Doom'. It showed concocted evidence for climate change. There were time-lapsed images of ice melting, drought, storms and low-lying land inundated by the sea. Pretending to be a commercial movie and neutral, it tried to persuade viewers that climate change was universal, real and to be feared, blaming industrial pollution and demonizing carbon, despite carbon being a common element essential for all living things. He mobilized supporters to mount campaigns anti-industry and anti-coal. The movie showed him entertaining business executives, politicians and academics seeking funds for their research and receiving donations from industries that produced renewable energy technology, batteries, pumped storage dams, electric cars and substitutes for carbon.

'This is propaganda,' said Hagar, the young ram who replaced old Norman. 'Algy's description of climate change has a strong confirmation bias.'

Algy was a politician, not a climate scientist. The thesis of his university research was that when individuals were swayed by emotions, their prejudices overrode scientific objectivity. His campaigns mobilised people using emotion to overcome reason.

'To be successful, a lie must be enormous,' Algy said, in words Hitler had used.

He faked climate change as a means to keep citizens fearful and subservient to rule by the oligarchy. Algy's climate ideology was

210

implemented with totalitarian contempt for reality and factuality. Standards for truth and falsity no longer existed on Animal Farm. The movie was demagoguery, appealing emotionally to the desires and prejudices of workers, rather than to knowledge or reason. His Enhanced Greenhouse Effect Theory was a political construct, not empirical science.

'When people are swayed by Algy, is it an Algyithm?' asked Hagar, joking with wordplay.

Algy's movie preached: 'Life on Earth, as we know it, is under threat. The government must provide money for science to solve climate change. Our way of life is being destroyed by those who pour harmful gases into our pure air, warming oceans and climates. Plants and corals that have grown here for all eternity are running out of time. We will not let the selfishness of a few members of the community destroy our precious world.

'Climate change is the greatest threat our civilisation has encountered. Extreme weather events are causing natural disasters with increasing frequency and they will get worse. Chronic changes associated with climate are: deforestation, desertification, erosion, land degradation, eutrophication of waterways, environment destruction, harmful agriculture, fauna decline, loss in fauna reproduction, fauna extinction, river pollution, ocean pollution and accumulation of toxic wastes and plastics, to name but a few.'

'We must fight to prevent and mitigate these effects while we still have the resources to do so, before we are pulled down by climate change. All of you must be ready to take part bravely in our opposition against the insidious climate enemy, being ready to give your all, if necessary.

'The land and forests have been destroyed, the air has been polluted by gases that have changed the climate, humans have multiplied, lifestyles have become technological. Lacking human kindness, wild animals are being slaughtered in growing numbers. It is time to restore the Earth to the way it was before the industrial revolution.'

211

The emotive movie was without evidence and promoted a solution: it said that climate was changing due to air pollution. Wind turbines and solar panels did not cause pollution and could replace coal. Coal was dangerous to mine, dirty to burn and would soon be used up in many countries.

'Carbon gases stay in the atmosphere for 1000 years. Polluters will have their activities stopped by law and they will be punished.'

'Carbon dioxide is replaced every 60 years, not 1000,' whispered Hagar.

'Is that less or more of a problem?' Henry asked him.

'It isn't a problem at all, but anyway it disperses more quickly and accumulates more slowly than he said.'

But most of the audience were fearful and were aroused to listen as the movie enumerated actions. When it finished, Algy spoke to them about what they must do on the Farm.

'Fostering release of carbon is criminal,' he said. 'Excessive carbon ingestion and inhalation will be severely punished. Farm wastes must be ploughed into the ground to sequester carbon for a time, however short.

'We must prevent CO_2 emissions by reducing production and sequester it underground. Coal-fired power stations must be closed down and destroyed.'

It was an emotional appeal and a line of Ravens, perched on the roof ridge of the cowshed, cawed noisily, drowning out talk and opposition.

After the movie, the animals discussed it.

'Do you believe the situation is as dire as the movies says?' asked Larissa.

'No,' said Hagar. 'The movie had many untruths. Calling for destruction of serviceable power stations that have shutdown is foolish. The boar is reckless.'

'His intention is to rabble rouse,' said Henry. 'Algy has adopted 'Post Truth' as his philosophy. He declares what he wants and then carries it by emotion and lies, like the EGHE. It is post-modern and lacks theory or reason or coherence supported by evidence. It is not possible to reverse the way we live back to before the industrial revolution.'

'We have to stop Algy worsening our working conditions on The Farm.'

'Algy's excesses include his own travel, his car and yacht,' said Hagar quietly to Henry. 'He is a hypocrite. His doctrine is pseudo-science. It lacks agreeable facts and he makes his appeal to the emotions. He should not be influencing public policy.'

'Algy is our Minister for Energy,' said Henry. 'His strategy aims to kill two birds with one stone: it is called 'convergence'.

'He has brought two problems together with the solution of shutting down of the fossil fuels industry. By stopping fossil fuel use, in one action it tackles global warming and depletion of resources.

'He has assumed changing from fossil fuels will stop global warming. Vilifying of the carbonaceous fuels is false,' said Hagar. 'A better way to prevent global warming would be to reduce all types of energy use. That would have convergence too, reducing global warming and energy resources depletion.'

'That would be more logical,' said Henry. 'Reducing energy use won't be acceptable to the government because it would not be PC, threatening their mantra of growth. Algy has painted governments into a corner, where they can't have growth and stop CO_2 production.'

'A steady state economy is the solution,' Hagar said. 'CO_2 is of no consequence.'

When the animals gathered later for a secret meeting, they discussed Algy's passionate campaign and his alarming movie.

'He has hijacked climate science to make false predictions and generated chaos, by sensationalizing weather events, mongering fear, creating false alarm, inducing panic and preventing rational response,' Henry said. 'He is using climate change to dominate us.'

Henry's words were overheard by Lady, Ruby's replacement, who was standing beside them. If she reported him to the pigs, he could be punished.

213

'You didn't hear me just then, did you Lady?' Henry said to her. 'Don't make trouble for me, please. If you look after me, I'll look after you.'

Lady smiled and sidled away.

Afterwards, Henry laughed. 'Algy's passionate campaign will not lead us to freedom on this Farm. Existential freedom requires a more thoughtful and deliberate approach, considerate of others' freedoms.'

'What if they won't give us freedom?'

'Before we can liberate ourselves from meat-eating humans, we have to liberate ourselves from a boar pig who wants us to sacrifice our present for his vision of a future which is a delusion of lies. He has created a huge lie in the belief that the consternation will overcome reason and line his pockets.'

'We will have to take it for ourselves. Violence may be necessary, but not as an end. Algy's tyranny consumes our freedom.'

'Is violence ever justifiable?' asked Hannah.

'The outrage of violence is excused by its utility,' Norman said. 'Winners are better off.'

'Our freedom would be enough to win,' said Henry.

'What freedom is that?' asked Pickle, the donkey who had replaced Dongle.

'We have the right to live freed from slavery,' Henry said. 'The Farm is our territory too.'

CHAPTER 37 ENDING LIVES

A week after Dongle had been taken away, there was a commotion at the dam. The body of one of the Rottweilers was floating with its neck broken.

Lord Dimitri demanded to know by noon who the killer was, or he would execute the yearling Myrtle, Henry's sister. She was a happy, sassy animal, a favourite with everyone. Half grown, she ran everywhere and was much-loved.

Henry seemed preoccupied.

'Henry most likely did it,' thought Jolene, *'in retaliation for them taking Dongle. He is under pressure now to own up to save his sister Myrtle. If he does they will kill him.'*

'Henry must not confess,' said Myrtle to Jolene, Henry's partner. 'You need him to lead you against the pigs. It is better that I am the one who they kill.'

At noon, when no killer had come forward, the three surviving Rottweilers surrounded Myrtle where she stood with her family. She screamed. Pigs kept back the animals and there was a struggle.

Lady stood by barking: 'Confess! Confess!'

Henry threw himself at the dogs, but his son Jack pulled him back. Myrtle was smothered under a heap of pig bodies. When they got up, she was dead.

'We should have stopped them,' said Jolene, wailing.

'No, that would have taken too many lives,' Henry was grief stricken. 'I didn't think they would do it, I wanted to confess but it was too late.'

'They set the price of our freedom as high as they could,' said Goliath. 'Myrtle was an innocent yearling with her whole life before her.

'We have lost brave, loyal Myrtle,' said Henry. 'The pigs chose our most precious animal, to test our resolve. By killing her, they have made a mistake.'

He wanted to kill Lord Dimitri, but his friends stopped him.

'He is expecting it and has a guard,' they said. 'You will only succeed in getting yourself killed.'

Henry and Jolene were left with their grief. He was alone without his parents, old Earl and Dolly, who had been sent to the abattoir. Jolene comforted him but he was inconsolable. He had not confessed and Myrtle had died. He had thought the pigs were bluffing and only realised they would kill her when the Rottweilers attacked her. Then it was too late to save her.

They had killed Myrtle in retribution for his killing of a paltry dog,' he told himself. *'I should have confessed. I have failed to live up to the standards of Earl, my father and Dolly, my mother. I have let everyone down. My defiance of the pigs only served to help myself. I failed to protect poor innocent Myrtle.'*

Henry was devastated and he became despondent.

Henry was responsible for his other sisters Simone, who was in-calf and Claudia, a heifer, who would bear a calf soon by AI. He couldn't face them.

The pigs controlled animal matings, to get progeny as replacement workers and as meat for the abattoir. When they needed another draft animal to haul loads of hay and vegetables, they wanted to breed a mule to replace Biscuit. Believing that Muriel was pregnant with old Dongle's donkey foal, they put Domino and Muriel in a paddock to rest up together. When Muriel discovered she was not pregnant, Domino did a job on her and they called their hinney Jasper. The Farm went without a mule and Jasper was no substitute.

Hinneys are uncommon for a good reason: they are notoriously cantankerous and reluctant to work. Nor could Jasper be relied on to keep their insurrection plans secret. He was unpopular. His father, Domino, kept him out of trouble, but they left him out when they met to plan their revolt.

One morning Henry's body was floating in the dam.

'This was payback for the dog in the dam,' said Jolene, grief stricken. 'They may have guessed it was him when he had opposed the dogs' attack on Myrtle. He died for seeking justice.'

Lord Dimitri was nonchalant: 'The bull picked a fight with my dogs. He lost. Too bad.'

They dragged out his body and buried it in a corner of the farmyard under a walnut tree, next to his sister Myrtle. The others' grief was relieved by Jack's oration, from his new position as chief bull.

'Henry was our leader and friend. We have benefitted from better conditions he obtained for us. It is a tragedy that he has met a violent death. We aren't sure who was responsible but hope that justice will be served soon. We must try to carry on without him, as he would have wished.'

The pall of evil gradually cleared as they bent to cultivating the honest soil, nurturing the plants that grew hopefully, harvesting the wholesome foods and resting from their hard labour. Liberation came, little by little, with gains almost imperceptible, but all they had.

Years came and went on Animal Farm, following the same routines, more or less. Each individual knew their place and their work. At harvest, grain was bound into sheaves with a binder and stacked beside the barn. Months later, it had dried and was fed into a stationary threshing machine, belt driven by a tractor.

Everyone pitched in, joining in teamwork as the hungry thresher drum thundered, spewing dust over the barnyard. They bagged off the grain and disposed of the straw. The rick had become home to a profusion of rats and mice evicted from their hiding places. Hunter the cat held rodents under each paw and several in his mouth.

'Threshing is my favourite activity,' Pearl confided. 'It has a satisfying finality, the end of a year-long cycle of ploughing, planting, growing and harvesting.'

It was the end of the farming year. A makeshift altar was adorned with sheaves, fruits and vegetables, symbols of the harvest. It was an

217

important annual event and many of the animals attended. Patriarch held a church service to thank God for his bounty and the strength that had overcome difficulties and produced the provender and seeds they would carry forward to a better future.

After the harvest festival was over, the annual farming cycle started again, with ploughing. The animals worked all day, every day, from dawn to dusk. They sometimes took the opportunity for a few moments respite.

'I don't feel safe here since they sent Dongle to the abattoir,' said Dinah, Norman's favourite ewe.

'Why not?'

'It was murder,' said Dinah, 'retaliation for asking questions.'

'Questioning of Algy's policies was forbidden,' Lady said. 'The pigs have a fixed view about sea level rise.'

'Why shouldn't he be able to disagree?'

'He would have had to die soon, anyway,' Lady said, flanked by her pups who she was teaching to drive sheep and cattle. The young dogs stayed glued to her side. 'He was old. We don't want old animals hanging around, waiting to die.'

Dinah confronted her. 'Why not? Speak for yourself. He was a friend of mine.'

'Would you have taken care of him?' Lady said, countering.

'Sometimes I would.'

'And at other times?'

'He could have looked after himself for many years, with the community helping him to be independent,' said Dinah.

'That's a theory,' said Lady. ''In reality, not many would help old animals. People have their own difficulties.'

'Looking after each other, they could do it,' said Simone.

'It would have happened if we wanted it. We are responsible for ourselves, with not much time for caring left over.'

That ended the discussion.

The lives of animal workers were hard. When they were no longer useful and had some weight on, they could expect to be trailered away to the abattoir.

218

'Only pigs die naturally,' said Lady. 'The destiny of animal workers is the slaughterhouse.'

'It doesn't happen in India.'

'Cows are sacred there,' said Pickle. 'It seems unlikely that our pigs would develop a spiritual reverence for our workers.'

'We should revere Horace,' said Jolene. 'He has worked tirelessly year after year. He will be the next to go. It is ungrateful to put him down. '

'That's how it goes for livestock animals, everywhere,' said Lady. 'Farmer Jones sent all his old animals to the knackers.'

'We are a farm owned and run by animals,' Jolene said. 'We ought to be able to take care of Horace.'

'Caring is a burden no-one wants,' Lady said. 'Being eaten is efficient and useful. It's better than waiting to die in pain and discomfort.'

'Being slaughtered isn't dignified,' said Horace. 'I'd prefer to die in my sleep and be cremated. A tidy exit like that wouldn't inconvenience anyone.'

'Burying a friend can be a positive experience, they say.'

'A wake?'

'Yes, a renewal, with singing and dancing.'

But Horace was troubled by his privilege.

'I don't want to be a burden,' he said.

'Equal provision for all can be a problem,' said Jack. 'Voluntary assistance need not be a burden.'

The workers petitioned Lord Dimitri and he allowed Horace to stay on the farm, in the orchard. Lord Dimitri presented him with a Medal of Meritorious Service which he wore proudly around his neck. After several years in retirement, he died and the worker animals buried him by the dam, where he had enjoyed brief periods of respite from his herculean service. The worker animals held a wake for him that lasted two days, as they consumed copious quantities of vodka, with most of them falling into the dam.

After the funeral, Lord Dimitri allowed the Ravens to hold religious services in the barn on Sundays, to console the workers for the hardship and misery of their lives.

219

Animal workers spent their wages on food and comforts. They heard from neighbouring farms that humans were eating less meat. But the flow of old animals to the abattoir continued unabated. There was no prospect of natural death except by accident or ill health. An exception was Goliath who had retired to the orchard with Fiona. Brandy took over at the plough in tandem with his son, Domino.

Domino had told President Alphancourt about the pigs' cruelty but there was little she could do. The animals were work units, without rights or legal redress for wrongs. She legislated for farms to treat animals humanely and Lord Dimitri had to get rid of his Rottweilers, ending torture and executions.

The animals' lot was to be without rights and work in slavery, but they desperately wanted equality and freedom. They had a deep hatred of coal mining under the pigs' authoritarian management, with its demeaning conditions and ill health effects. Algy's anti-industrial campaign sought to restore preindustrial living with pastoral and agrarian lifestyles for humans and animals, but the workers were sceptical.

'The antis seem to imagine we can all return to a pastoral lifestyle,' said Larissa. 'They want to reverse civilisation, going without tools, metals and technology. They want us to live off the land, taking refuge in caves or trees.'

'There are too many of us for that,' said Jack. 'There aren't enough trees.'

'Nor enough land, nor caves.'

'We have never received the allotments Lord Miguel promised.'

Denied the pastoral idyll, but wanting a good life, the animals consulted the writing of J S Mill 'On Liberty'.

The only freedom which deserves the name, is that of pursuing our own good in our own way, without depriving others of theirs.

Their goal would be to live on the Farm with individual responsibility for the common good, with the pigs' roles reduced to be equal.

In the meantime, Hagar and Larissa had crias Barry and Juliet.

CHAPTER 38 HOCKEY STICK FRAUD

At one end of the cowshed the animals were gathered for Jack's meteorology class. Jolene's youngest calf lay with its legs folded up under it, gazing intently at a spider weaving a web between two bales. Releasing thread, it dropped down and was blown across in a draught, erecting a mainstay, then connected other threads at a centre, with radii at equal intervals. It circled around from the middle, linking chords. The calf watched in fascination, never having seen such deliberation and precision.

'Today I would like us to consider methods used to prepare plans to counter climate change,' said Jack.

'Do they have methods?' said Jolene to Jack and the class. 'It seems haphazard to me. Compared with that spider's planning, human planning seems shoddy.'

'The spider has a routine,' said Jack. 'Our problems are less familiar to us. Climate affects everyone and agreement has to consider wide views. Climate effects are difficult to discern. With passing of time, connections between events can be made and reveal a larger pattern. The stakes in spending public funds are high. Self-interest, biased data and false science are common in publicity about climate change. I'm going to tell you about one bad case of bias at the highest level, the United Nations. There have been others and I want you to be sceptical about reports and find out what they truly show.'

He told them in 1999 the United Nations had published a 'hockey stick' graph of temperature prepared by a Dr Michael Mann, of Pennsylvania State University. Temperature had increased gradually

221

for 900+ years (the shaft of the hockey stick), and then increased dramatically, from the early 20th century (the blade of the stick).

'The graph was published by the International Policy Committee for Climates(IPCC) with a doom-saying narrative. TV news sensationalised the graph with pictures of weather disasters. Many people were swayed by the graph to believe that there was significant climate change and clamoured for urgent action.'

The graph was prominent in Algy's movie 'A Calculated Doom.' Dr Tim Ball from the University of Winnipeg alleged Mann was a liar and had presented measurements falsely.

'The climate record does not warrant alarmism,' he said.

Mann claimed he had been defamed, but refused to produce, when requested by the court, his 'working out' of the graph that had taken pride of place in the United Nations report.

"We have 25 or so years invested in the work,' Dr Mann told the court, when asked to substantiate his claims. *'Why should I make the data available to you, when your aim is to try and find something wrong with it?'*

Jack paused.

'Do you see how that opposes the openness at the heart of science?'

'Scientists are supposed to share their data,' said Jolene.

'The court case proceeded for 5 years in Oregon, concluding when the judge finally dismissed the case, because Ball and Mann were now 70-80 years old and it was difficult for them to participate,' said Jack. 'Significantly, costs were awarded against the plaintiff, as if Ball was correct in calling Mann a liar.

'The IPCC is the United Nations body for assessing the science related to climate change,' said Jack. 'It was created **to** provide policymakers with regular scientific assessments on climate change, its implications and potential future risks, as well as to put forward adaptation and mitigation options. This case shows we cannot rely on the IPCC to present unbiased information. They did not reveal their method nor amend their flawed graph.'

'A majority of climate commentators are truthful and they report genuine climate change. Exaggeration by a few others has resulted in sensationalism and unnecessary alarm.'

'Mann's secrecy was peculiar,' said Jolene. 'Peer review is widely agreed to be a necessary part of science reporting.'

'It is not usual to hide scientific data,' said Jack. 'There was probably something badly wrong with it.'

'Maybe it was a mistake,' said Hagar.

'No,' said Jack. 'Some scientists have been systematically rorting data for years. The 'climate-gate' incident at the University of East Anglia in the UK revealed extensive manipulation of data by scientists to falsely claim man-made global warming. In Australia, systematic official misrepresentation of temperature data was exposed by Marohasy (22).

'What should have happened?' said Jolene.

'Practicality of reversing a trend must be carefully considered before public funds are committed to remedial action. If they had admitted their dishonesty and straightened out their uptick on the temperature graph, there wouldn't be climate change requiring urgent response,' said Norman. 'Hundreds of power stations were shut down by Algy's campaign, including our Caruban powerhouse, incurring high costs to electricity users. It was shutdown by fraud and is being kept shutdown by fraud. President Natalia was correct not to have our powerhouse dismantled because it needs to be restarted.'

'I have not seen evidence convincing me that climate change is as rapid as the IPCC has claimed.,' said Jack. 'Claims that the climate was changing, like the hockey stick, have been of dubious authenticity. Most of the media had long since ceased investigative reporting and become mouthpieces for self-interested groups with a climate agenda. The conditions for a debate were not present. Data was unsourced, analyses were superficial and sensationalism was rife. It was left to a few brave individuals to use reasoned arguments to confront what had become near-hysteria.'

Jack communicated his concerns to President Natalia and she replied: 'Keeping the power station shut down might not have beneficial effects. We will keep the situation under review.'

The next day, she ordered the power station to restart at half capacity.

'I planned this when I shut it down,' she said, trying to save face. 'I had orders to follow. They wanted me to destroy it.'

It was never easy to turn back and after the falsity of the hockey stick was revealed, it was difficult for her as it could mean losing face. The animals despaired that their liberation would depend on human competence.

CHAPTER 39 MODELLING

A TV anchor, Jessica Devine, hosted The Science Show on Caruba Television. She knew of Animal Farm and the animal workers' interest in science. When Jack contacted her asking about the other side of the climate debate from Algy's movie, she told him she had done an interview with a climate scientist, Dr Don Simmer.

'I'll send you a copy to see if your animals would understand it. It is for people interested in, but not expert in, climate matters,' Devine said. 'Dr Simmer is a modelling expert and can put into perspective the wild rumours that started after Algy's movie. He is a cautious scientist and sceptical about some of the climate predictions made in the movie. Simmer fills in between Algy's dots with real data.'

'Algy won't approve,' Jack said.

'I have heard he is away for several weeks. What is Lord Dimitri's position on climate?'

'He usually supports Algy but accepts that his views are controversial.'

'Simmer is a reputable scientist. Lord Dimitri should be glad to have his input.'

'Okay. Please send us a copy.'

Jack checked it and it was suitable and asked Lord Dimitri, who agreed to show it to the workers.

'He wants to show the interview but he won't allow the animals to discuss it afterwards,' Jack said to Devine.

'Too bad,' she said. 'Perhaps they could discuss it together later.'

Jack arranged for a large TV screen to be set up in the farmyard. Watching TV was a treat for the animals. They hadn't watched anything since Algy's movie.'

Jolene addressed the assembled animals.

'This movie has Jessica Devine in an interview with Dr Don Simmer on an important topic: climate modelling. A model is what we use to investigate something that is inaccessible otherwise, like the climate being too large. Dr Simmer uses a model of the World.'

Jolene unpaused the recording. They saw the Science Show host in a studio interview.

'Good evening, viewers. I am Jessica Devine. My guest this evening is Dr Don Simmer. He uses a model to make climate predictions for the International Policy Committee for Climates(IPCC).'

Dr Don: 'Good evening.'

Jess: 'The IPCC in 2007 forecast that global temperatures in 2100 could probably increase with a likely range of 2.4 to 6.4 °C. Is that correct?'

Dr Don: 'Yes.'

Jess: 'It's a wide range?'

Dr Don: 'The process of change is not certain.'

Jess: 'Would you explain to viewers how this prediction was made?'

Dr Don: 'Our model calculates how heat and air would move around the entire world.'

Jess: 'Would it calculate the Sun's effect on temperatures and winds?'

Dr Don: 'Yes. The whole Earth has 12000 blocks of land, ocean or atmosphere, each 300 kilometres long, by 300 wide, in two layers each 100 kilometres deep. 170 of these blocks represent Australia. The model calculates climate conditions for all these blocks from heat and air movements. Temperature and wind were measured around the world at 6300 meteorological stations. Some blocks do not have a weather station and others have several, so we joined the dots to complete fine details needed for calculations. Measurements at a single station were applied to large parts of the Pacific Ocean and to the atmosphere extending 200 kilometres vertically.'

Jess: 'How many meteorological stations are there in the Pacific Ocean?'

226

Dr Don: 'Not many. Not enough for predictions to be confident. Conditions are also measured by satellites, from moored and floating buoys and from weather ships. Conditions often have to be guessed.'

Jess: 'How do you allow for heating by the Sun?'

Dr Don: 'Solar UV flux is reradiated from the Earth's surface as infrared and warms the blocks of air vertically and laterally, by conduction and convection. We can calculate the changing heat flows and temperatures hourly.'

'Is there global warming?'

'That is what we are trying to calculate. We have solar forcing, assuming radiation from the sun.'

Jess: 'Did you run the model forward, hour after hour, to the year 2100?'

Dr Don: 'Yes. First we went back and made the calculated conditions match the climate record. Then we calculated changes forward for thousands of hours of real time. The calculation took several days.'

Jess: 'Did you tweak the model so temperature calculated would match temperatures observed?'

Dr Don: 'Yes. At some of the blocks we had to guess conditions.'

Jess: 'How reliable is it to guesstimate like that?'

Dr Don: 'We were not shooting in the dark. We looked at adjacent weather stations too.'

Jess: 'How far back did you go?'

Dr Don: '1950. Before that there were too few weather stations to model global conditions.'

Jess: 'Then you had sufficient data to calculate the changing picture?'

Dr Don: 'Yes, for short term predictions. We calculated air movement and temperatures over the whole world, every hour.'

Jess: 'Were your predictions accurate?'

Dr Don: 'Time will tell. Confidence is low because there are so many degrees of freedom and predicted temperatures are in a wide range.

Jess: 'How does many degrees of freedom cause low confidence?'

227

Dr Don: 'When a model is excessively complex there are many more explanatory variables than observations and overfitting results. If you make up enough variables and data you can match any history. When you have two explanatory equations, each with two variables, you can solve them precisely. When you have divided the atmosphere into thousands of blocks each with its equations in hundreds of variables but only have observations from a few widely spaced weather stations, you can have only low confidence in predictions.

Jess: 'How did you find a solution?'

Dr Don: 'We 'nudged' the calculations to reach a credible solution. Sceptics call this 'cultural climate physics'.'

Jess: 'What does that mean?'

Dr Don: 'We tweaked the physics to give the answers people wanted. For example, global temperatures have been erratic, with warming and cooling periods. Our model smooths results to give continuous warming, because that is what people expect.'

Jess: 'You mean you stop when you get to the number you first thought of. Like you had assumed a certain solar forcing and so you obtained the global warming you wanted?'

Dr Don: 'Something like that. Predictions are expected within a range.'

Jess: 'Then you know how much climate change to expect?'

Dr Don: 'More or less; within a range.'

Jess: 'Would you agree that your predictions have a confirmation bias. Your modelling seeks, interprets and recalls information to support what you already believe?'

Dr Don: 'We can't publish everything we calculate.'

Jess: 'Why not?'

Dr Don: 'It has to be broadly acceptable.'

Jess: 'How confident are you that your predictions will eventuate?'

Dr Don: 'We are reasonably confident.'

Jess: 'How confident is that?'

Dr Don: 'Our model is logical and matches the record but its ability to predict the future may not be good at all. Climate models

228

are only as good as their thousands of assumptions. People have unrealistic expectations about climate forecasting and what modelling can achieve.'

Jess: 'Can they be improved?'

Dr Don: 'A little. Our grid size of 300 kilometres omits the fine grain of weather, such as clouds, fronts and cyclones. A smaller grid size would require a more powerful computer.'

Jess 'What is the value of these predictions?'

Dr Don, hesitating, thinking. 'They are better than nothing.'

Jess: 'What if the climate does not change as you have predicted?'

Dr Don: 'We readjust the model to match observations. With experience, our predictions are improving.'

Jess: 'The IPCC has said: *We are dealing with a coupled non-linear chaotic system, and therefore the long-term prediction of future climate states is not possible.* ' Do you agree?'

Dr Don: 'Climate is chaotic because of many random unpredictable events. Prediction can never be completely confident.'

Jess: 'Is it confident enough now or should we wait?'

Dr Don: 'We could have to wait decades or even centuries. Science takes time. Science has investigated complex systems before. Look at what happened to our understanding of how plants grow. In 1637, a Dutch scientist, Van Helmont, believed that plant growth came from the soil. He obtained a small willow tree, removed soil from the roots and weighed it.

'It was about 5 kilograms. He planted it in a pot with a weighed quantity of soil. He watered it every day, recording the weight of water added. After 5 years, he took it out of the pot, removed, dried and weighed the soil. The tree was now 100 kilograms but the weight of soil had not changed. The weight of water used far exceeded the 95 kilograms of growth. His conclusion was that the tree had not grown from soil, but possibly from part of the water and possibly also from something invisible. Over the following three centuries, the chemicals water, carbon dioxide, oxygen, sunlight energy and the photosynthetic pigment chlorophyll were discovered and their roles demonstrated in experiments. By the 1930s, a precise photo biochemical reaction, photosynthesis was finally revealed, able to be

229

represented by a chemical equation, involving three reactants, two products, light, heat and a catalyst in exact stoichiometric ratios.

'Understanding of climate change has begun but is only partly completed. It is even more difficult to investigate than photosynthesis, because the scale is too large to do experiments. To reach understanding could also take 300 years.'

Jess: 'We don't have that much time. Animals are becoming extinct; forests are burning; people's homes are flooding.'

Dr Don: 'They didn't like having to wait to find out about plant growth either. In 1637 there was famine and starvation, but they waited 5 years for the tree to grow.'

Jess: 'Now people want answers by tomorrow.'

Dr Don: 'Modellers have represented the climate as a black box and deduced notional quantities, such as 'solar forcing'. The weakness of this approach is that the model's purpose of understanding has been short-circuited by *a priori* assumptions, it is low in confidence and may be false. Unless effects of changes to the system can be tested, the method is unreliable.'

Jess: 'Is what you are saying that we must expect delays for decades or more, because errors of understanding will occur?'

Dr Don: 'That's right. Everyone must be patient and wait for measurements to be made. Lack of understanding is not a deficiency of scientific effort. Investigation takes time and taking short-cuts is risky. The climate system is complex and unlike a Rubix Cube, the solution won't appear more quickly by manipulating the model faster. Correct understanding of the patterns can only emerge from many repeated observations. Pre-emptive over-reaction would be counter-productive.'

Jess: 'There you have it viewers: the inside story on climate prediction. Thank you for your frankness Don. I think we have realised climate predictions are less certain than we are sometimes led to believe. Good night everyone.'

Dr Don: 'Thank you for having me, Jessica. Good night.'

Jack switched off the screen and addressed the animals assembled.

'I hope you understand why models like Dr Simmer's are used. An unfamiliar situation can be dealt with better using a model that combines all the important facets of complexity for testing a solution. The goodness of the model can be ascertained from its ability to reproduce past events with accuracy and make confident predictions for the future.'

The stallion Domino raised his head to ask a question.

'Sorry, Domino. Lord Dimitri won't allow questions or discussion. Thank you everyone for your interest. I hope you found that enlightening. You may leave.'

The animals got to their feet and shuffled away towards the farm buildings.

'Bloody hell,' said Hagar. 'More negativity and uncertainty.'

'Trying to fill the gaps in knowledge with a model is a big waste of time and money,' said Barry.

'That isn't its purpose.'

'What is?'

'They want to bamboozle us into believing we have a climate problem and even before the diagnosis and prognosis have been tested, they are going to start a treatment that will benefit the leaders,' Hagar said.

'Having an imminent global catastrophe keeps us workers working and them in bigger jobs,' said Barry.

'There is reason to doubt the competence of climate modelling but there is one thing we can be sure of,' Hagar said. 'It will be followed by chaos as they strive to understand a task that is too difficult for that method.'

'That will be good for us,' said Barry. 'While the future is uncertain, we can hope for liberation, whereas there is little hope when like now it is stuffed with falsity, all sewn up.'

231

CHAPTER 40
REGENERATION

Lord Dimitri had watched the interview with Dr Simmer. He told President Natalia Alphancourt that Dr Simmer's climate forecasts were unreliable.

'The situation is worse than Dr Simmer indicated,' said Lord Dimitri. 'He is a typical over-cautious scientist who prefers calculation to judgement. The confidence he seeks is a luxury we leaders never have but must pretend to have to keep our people docile. By the time he predicts climate conditions with confidence, the predictions will be wrong and there will be new trends. We would have to backflip and our followers would lose faith.

I am going to ignore Simmer's forecasts of gloom and doom. My information is that global warming is almost certainly caused by thermal pollution. We must proceed to stop it without delay. I am preparing a comprehensive plan. I will tell you about it shortly.'

'The SR has demanded we shut down our coal power station,' said President Alphancourt in a media interview. 'Because of the uncertainty, I have decided to maintain output at half capacity.'

Lord Dimitri phoned her. 'Isn't reducing electricity generation rather drastic?'

'Not half as drastic as the predicted rise in sea levels and depletion of fossil fuels,' she said. "The SR has promised funding for installation of renewable energy. Our powerhouse is 30 years old and due for retirement. It would most benefit the public good, by fewer emissions, protection of health, more sustainability. We will change to solar panels and wind turbines when funds for these become available. Algy is backing my decision.'

On Animal Farm the animals were sceptical about the desirability of renewable energy.

'Shutting down the power station will increase electricity costs and reduce reliability of supply,' said Jack. 'The coal power is irreplaceable. The government says renewable energy will be available but solar panels and wind turbines have problems: funding, inefficiency, environmental warming, unreliability, pollution.

'Is President Natalia aware of the high cost of renewable energy?' Barry asked Jack.

'Lord Dimitri won't tell her,' he said. 'His goal is to stay in office for as long as possible and he wants her support.'

'His ideology is megalomania, framed as totalitarianism and repression,' said Barry who had replaced Hagar as ram. 'He is probably embezzling our Farm's funds.'

'Where will Natalia get the funds she needs?'

Jack shrugged.

'Exactly,' said Barry. 'Nowhere.'

Lord Dimitri ran in the next presidential election, swapping places with Algy who became Prime Minister. Voting had been rigged, but the workers could do nothing about it. The ruling cliques continued despite impassioned opposition. The few protesters were silenced by his secret police and dogs.

'This election has put democracy on Animal Farm in reverse,' said Barry.

Lord Dimitri won resoundingly. Back as President, he cultivated popular support, restored family values, religion and national traditions. He wanted to turn back the clock to when there was faith in leadership synonymous with religious belief. He relaunched Animal Farm in a new economic bloc with neighbouring farms.

'Animal Farm will be great again,' Lord Dimitri said. 'This is a new era. We are a true democracy of the people

But Lord Dimitri's rule became even more despotic.

He was keen to present a favourable image. A reporter asked him: 'How is your rule different from Lord Napoleon's, when animals first took over the Farm?'

'Lord Napoleon was an idealist,' said Lord Dimitri. 'My leadership is practical, for the benefit of all the animals and for Carubans.'

He reasserted the planned change to renewable energy.

'The substitution of renewables would be harmful and most of the animal workers would be without employment or any income.'

'You'll have to convince President Natalia that climate change isn't real.'

'Why does this farm have incessant wrangling about climate change and the power station?' asked Clarabelle.

'The power station is the meat in a sandwich, with the SR on one side and the DU on the other. The SR want President Natalia to develop the socialist way, by government command and the DU want to prevent that and develop the capitalist way, with private investment. The DU have funded the power station but the SR are trying to shut it down. Algy wants it shut down. Pressident Natalia has compromised and turned it down to half-capacity.'

'Algy's reasons don't make sense,' said Henry. 'A coal powered station doesn't cause global warming. Whenever there's combustion there are four outputs: energy, waste heat, carbon dioxide and water vapour. Carbon dioxide from coal has been falsely blamed for pollution caused by the other three.'

'We need the power station at full capacity.'

'Coal mining is our employment,' said Barry. 'Without it we could starve. We must persuade Lord Dimitri to persuade President Natalia to turn it up to full capacity.'

Barry organised a strike to protest loss of employment, low wages, bad working conditions and the high cost of food. The strike had brought farm production almost to a halt and when they ran out of food they had to call it off.

Lord Dimitri, took sides with President Alphancourt against the workers.

234

'You can protest loss of employment, or low wages, or bad working conditions, but not all at the same time,' he said when Barry served him with a log of claims. 'Which one do you want most?'

'Employment,' said Barry. 'Having a job is important to most people. It earns money for sustenance and provides participation in the community that reduces status anxiety. It's not true the powerhouse is worn out. It has many years' life left and there is nothing to replace it. It is wrong to restrict it to half capacity and would be disastrous to shut it down completely.'

Barry chatted with Lord Dimitri, an unprecedented occurrence. Afterwards, Barry told the others about their talk.

'I said we animals wanted our rights. We wanted equal opportunities and unambiguous freedoms. We wanted to have a worker candidate in the coming election of Farm president, with scrutiny of the voting by workers.

'He listened but conceded nothing. He is a totalitarian who knows what he wants, with nothing for us. Dealing with him is difficult.'

'He has changed,' said Clarabelle, a Guernsey cow acquired to raise fat content of milk for the pigs' mash. She was orange brown with white patches, larger than Buttercup her predecessor, a Jersey. 'He used to be more principled, imbued with Marxist-Leninist idealism. Now his only principle is self-advancement.'

'It would be better if he treated us animals with respect,' Rose said. She was a gentle animal and devoted to militant Jack.

One day the pigs brought their TV from the farmhouse to the barn, so the animals could watch Algy speaking to a world climate conference in Paris. The nations were there to negotiate a new agreement. The old Kyoto plan had failed and many countries had not fulfilled their obligations to reduce emissions by 5.2%.

Algy stood at the lectern using sanguine invective to shame other nations into joining in with Caruba.

'We on Caruba have reduced our CO_2 emissions as we agreed at Kyoto. It has not been easy for us but everyone of you is benefitting.'

235

Algy paused for embarrassment to sting the nations who had not yet committed.

'He hasn't sacrificed anything but we have,' whispered Clarabelle to Barry.

There was an awkward silence as Algy glared out over the rows of delegates.

'We need a new treaty which lowers emissions levels.'

A series of speakers accepted that they would make more effort in the years ahead with nationally determined contributions.

U.N. climate chief Christiana Figueres declared:

'The true aim of a treaty is to change the capitalist economic development model that has been reigning for at least 150 years, since the Industrial Revolution.'

At this juncture the DU delegate stood up and walked out.

'The DU is fond of capitalistic development,' said Barry. 'Algy has put a spanner in their works.'

'What's the problem?' asked Eeyore.

'The DU wants energy supply left to corporations in competition.'

'What would be the difference for us?'

'Caruba would have several power stations to meet demand and an economic boom.'

'How would other countries supply it?'

'They would have slower development under government control.'

'Like our power station,' said Eeyore. 'On again, off again.'

The next day the DU delegate returned and stated as follows.

'Global economic development by private investment must continue. State enterprise won't work.'

'DU private investors won't accept government emission controls,' said Barry. 'They want it left to corporations.'

236

Barry explained to the animals the background to the Paris Agreement and the DU's withdrawal.

'In defiance of the DU, there has been general agreement on emissions reduction. The assembly will sign a treaty with a triumphant feeling of self-worth and empowerment. Consequently, the nations of the world agreed to reduce CO_2 emissions and even agreed to declaration of universal brotherhood, named the Paris Agreement. The DU refused to sign it.

'Under the Paris Agreement, nations 'volunteered' to limit greenhouse gas emission levels, which would virtually limit energy consumption to supply by non-carbonaceous fuels. A small number of nations emitted most of the emissions and these high emitters would observe the same growth limits as low emitters. Nations causing most warming would have the same proportional restriction as those causing least.

'The burden of emissions reduction would fall on developed nations with the highest per capita electricity consumption, Canada, USA and Australia, with self-indulgent demand such as for air conditioning, whereas poor nations might possibly have no electricity connected and need the growth desperately. In developed countries, most energy was consumed as electricity and petrol.'

Barry paused and sipped from a water bucket.

'In a developed country, the restriction of emissions growth could conceivably limit the use of a third family car, whereas in an undeveloped country, a carless family could have use of its washing machine limited and more manual labour would be needed,' Barry said. 'The difference is not equitable.'

'There is no precedent for the limitation by The Paris Agreement on emissions, in order to make a contribution to reducing universal external costs of climate change,' said Jack. 'Energy consumption has sometimes been rationed in wartime, but usually it is regulated by supply and demand. Never before by emission limits.'

'The rich are advantaged but my concern is for the poor nations who would be disadvantaged,' Barry said. 'Emissions limitation is an unprecedented restriction on energy growth with disproportionate effect on developing countries. At best, it is a bold attempt to rein in

237

emissions growth but it is heavily weighted against low energy users who need growth to develop.

'Energy consumption is liberation for people in developing countries,' Jack said. 'They must be helped to freedom with energy they can afford, by the reticence of the greediest peoples.

'Do people have a limitless right to consume limitless energy, as they would for using oxygen from the air?' Barry said. 'I say No.'

'I agree that energy emissions should be elevated to be anti-societal,' said Jack. 'My answer is that people do not have a right to consume energy without limit, except in the nations with little per capita consumption. Conversely, the highest per capita consumers must be cutback severely.

'This emissions control agreement won't hold it down let alone reduce global warming. The Paris Agreement has serious problems,' said Barry. 'The DU has said they are withdrawing. Algy will be back soon and he's sure to tell us what is going on, but it won't be the concerns we have from the television broadcast.'

On Animal Farm the animals' studies had revealed that global warming was small and emissions control was absurd because carbon dioxide did not cause warming. President Natalia Alphancourt didn't have a good reason to keep the power station turned down to half capacity.

CHAPTER 41 RENEWABLE ENERGY DEAL

Algy returned from Paris as vaingloriously as he went, exulting that a new treaty had been agreed. When the DU realised they would be shouldering the largest part of emissions reduction, they had withdrawn from the treaty. Algy was furious.

'The DU is hiding its head in the sand from climate change. Here on Animal Farm, we are going to respect the Paris Agreement,' said Algy. 'The time has come to act. We can't stand back from this climate emergency any longer.'

Algy expanded his role from being the Farm's energy minister to Caruba's international energy envoy. He was attempting to cobble the DU and SR together into a duopoly able to balance the might of Ceramica. The three superpowers had relaxed their military confrontation and were now contesting trade.

Algy's sponsors sent him on another world tour.

'To be in time to fix the climate, we have to do it now,' Algy said in his talks to international forums. 'We won't tolerate nervous nellies sitting on the fence.'

Back on Animal Farm, Algy addressed the worker animals sombrely.

'Market forces are too weak to hold the climate constant. Superpower governments are interceding and Caruba has to adjust to the new economic order.

'The DU plans to scrap coal-fired power stations by 10 years' time, decarbonising all emissions and installing wind power and solar panels to supply all electricity. Fossil fuel civilization will collapse within 10 years. Renewable energy will enable converting

239

the car fleet to electricity and increasing efficiency of building services such as air conditioning. The cost of the changeover would be high and paid for by energy users. Caruba is on track to reducing emissions as required by the Renewable Energy Deal (RED).'

Some pigs clapped and sheep joined in.

'The RED will not improve climates and will badly affect citizens and national economies,' said Jack.

Algy showed no concern for the animals' difficult lives nor for the effect on Carubans.

'The Caruban economy may collapse,' said Barry. 'The Renewable Energy Deal (RED) is just another plan to perpetuate economic growth through consumerism, except it will be greenwashed growth.'

'It is an expensive dream no-one can afford,' said Barry. 'It will never happen.'

'More than half of the animal workers would be unemployed,' said Judy. 'Without revenue from coal they would be without wages to buy food and would have to beg or steal.'

'It's too bad for us that Algy's theory of climate change is wrong,' said Barry. 'His restructuring of economies is being driven by those who stand to gain most. Energy consumers have a choice of paying escalating energy costs or reducing their energy consumption.'

The animal workers were less sceptical.

'But energy reduction is what we want, isn't it!' asked Judy. She was Barry's favourite, an imported Suffolk ewe.

'There isn't enough warming to justify taking out the base load supply that Carubans rely on,' said Barry.

'The RED is founded on nonsense,' Judy said. 'Our power station uses a substantial public asset and our mineral wealth to benefit the population at relatively low cost. To stop it seems immoral.'

'It is supposed to start a huge new industry: renewable energy,' said Barry.

'We workers would be worse off,' said Judy.

'As usual,' said Eeyore.

'Guess what the RED wants next?' asked Barry. 'They want to reduce ruminants' methane gas emissions.'

'I used to enjoy beans,' said Barry.

'Beans contain sugars and fibre that our bodies have a hard time digesting. It's better to eat soups.'

'Swallowing air in hay is farty.'

'A fart is a natural part of life,' said old Fiona. 'Bugger the effect on the climate.'

'As you know, children visiting the farm feed Lucy lumps of sugar, which she loves,' said Judy. 'The pigs have ordered 'Lucy must not eat sugar' and Lucy's response is classic: 'What about carbon free sugar?' There were a few laughs and Barry explained sugar was a hydrocarbon chemical with carbon integral to each molecule. Replacing carbon in most industrial products was impossible.

The pigs said Lucy was decadent and if she continued to eat sugar they would send her to the abattoir.

The antis went on a rampage, tracing carbon use throughout industry and demanding shutdowns. When it was revealed by an anti that the smelters' pots were lined with carbon and released carbon dioxide, President Alphancourt switched off the smelter, throwing hundreds out of work. She redeployed the nuclear power station to the island grid, keeping the power station at half capacity.

'Algy wants to decarbonize the economy. How ridiculous!' said Barry.

'It's crazy!' said Barry. He had replaced his father, Hagar, following in the tradition of sheep excellence in science. 'Carbon is benign and carbon dioxide is beneficial. Algy and President Natalia Alphancourt are using this carbon nonsense and the RED ideology to terrorise us and other Carubans.

The RED carbon fiasco proliferated.

Blondie was a Shire heavy working horse, a descendent of Horace and Titani. She was black when young but had gradually lightened to grey. The science and climate evening classes had been a main interest of hers. She overheard a radio news broadcast telling that in

241

the Republic of Ceramica, India and many other countries, coal was still being combusted.

'Algy should have checked that CO_2 really does cause global warming, before destroying Caruba's economy,' said Blondie.

'He wouldn't care; his aim is to keep his boss Lord Dimitri in power,' said her partner Domino.

'There is a movement called Instinctive Rebellion,' she said. 'They are people who feel threatened with the way things are going. They believe nothing should stand in the way of conserving the species and environment. Their stated aim is using nonviolent civil disobedience to compel government action to avoid tipping points in the climate system, loss of biodiversity and avoid social and ecological collapse.'

'How can people be so opposed to reason?' asked Domino.

'Green activists assume they have the moral high ground.,' said Blondie. 'Their understanding is often merely myths, prejudices and false theories propagated by pretended scientists. The extremists' actions are not a solution: they have become the problem.'

'Be careful not to let the pigs hear your views,' said Domino. 'They wouldn't think twice about sending you to the abattoir.'

The worker animals were without electricity for many hours daily and at night there was only darkness. After a party at the farmhouse given by the pigs for Caruba government people and neighbouring farmers, a string of party lights was left up, decorating the house and gardens. Trees were lit by twinkling strings of fairy lights and the farm had a festive air.

'It's not fair,' said Claudia. 'Our quarters have no light at all.'

'They probably don't realise how offensive it is to us,' said Lulu. 'Their empathy does not extend to other species.'

'They will regret it one day,' she said.

'I like it without electric lighting,' said Hunter.

'I suppose you prefer sneaking around in the dark?'

'I catch more mice and rats. Everyone benefits.'

'I don't,' said Andy the cockerel. 'It gives me the shits when you creep up on me.'

242

'There's less for you to do now,' said Hunter. 'With no electric lights, they wake up at dawn. They don't need your racket.'

CHAPTER 42 SUPERPOWERS

After the missile crisis was over, the superpowers were content to posture. The eye of the storm that had hovered over Caruba moved away, leaving the animals with a future in which they could live, but were expendable.

The SR and DU had been drawn together by Algy's RED and the tension between the superpowers relaxed as they focussed on the challenge of restructuring their economies without carbon. President Natalia Alphancourt had restored nuclear electricity to the aluminium smelter but kept the power station at half capacity.

'Aluminium smelting requires carbon,' she said. 'We will allow it as an essential use.'

A trade delegation from Ceramica toured Caruba and showed interest in renewable energy investment. Caruba was a showcase for reducing fossil fuel use. Starting when the DU embargoed Caruba's oil supply, they learned to live without machines or electricity and grow their food by manual labour using rudimentary tools and materials.

Barry used the Internet to survey and analyse world events and updated the worker animals. The news was disheartening.

'Totalitarianism is growing,' said Barry. 'Each superpower has a domineering ideology, central control, isolation of individuals and mass terror. In the DU, since the attack on the World Trade Centre, the nation has moved away from democracy towards dictatorial presidency. The SR is recovering from collapse of socialism but central control has continued without conceding multi-party democracy. Ceramica has central control, with new tyrannies and increased external influence.

'People in those nations don't see it that way.'

'How do you know they don't?'

'They accept the changes.'

'Of course they do. Totalitarian change is too fearful to be rejected, even when the people don't want it.'

'Totalitarian development is being pursued in each of the superpowers with vigour, possibly with a secret goal of uniting to dominate the World. All three superpowers are frightening ordinary folk with fake news, contrived disasters, exaggerated conflicts, surveillance, torture, murder of dissenters, violent policing and military control. Governments are using misinformation about climate change to create alarm.

'We do not have full-blown World totalitarianism yet, but we have more domination and fearfulness than we did ten years ago,' he said. 'Societies in the SR, DU and Ceramica have been depoliticised, de-socialised and dislocated into a mass of angry individuals, superfluous and impotent, alienated from worldly affairs and ripe for totalitarian takeover. In this world, Animal Farm is a small island of independence situated at a point of friction between the SR and DU.'

'I hadn't realised we were independent,' said Laura. 'Maybe our pigs aren't so bad after all.'

'We are dominated, fearful and isolated,' Jack said. 'We lack self-identity, feel worthless and redundant.'

'We are humiliated by arbitrary and heinous laws, have to comply with the leader's edicts, are manipulated by propaganda and are routinely beaten into submission,' said Laura, anger in her voice.

Laura was Rose's daughter. She was white with black patches, more like Henry's half-Charollais from Earl, than her partner Jack's pure-bred Frieisian. Jack had assumed paternity. Rose had been consorting with Henry behind Jolene's back, until Dimitri's dogs killed him. Jack didn't mind because Henry had been herd bull at the time.

Jack had taken over as chief bull and Rose was his favourite until she was whipped and died in terrible pain. Laura had been a yearling then and she was always anxious now and angry. When Arnold, was purchased from another farm, black, large and fearsome, he and Laura became fast friends. She had explained to him customs on

245

Animal Farm and the tyranny of the pigs. He was appalled by her account of her mother's murder.

'When I heard I was going to a farm owned by animals, I imagined it would be a kinder place,' he said. 'From what you say, your pigs are crueller than humans. Why do the animals here put up with them?'

'They are well-organised and bully us. Any animal giving a hint of rebellion is murdered or sent to the abattoir. We have not been able to organise to resist them.'

'I want to help with that,' said Arnold. 'Barry has been telling me that you have a group planning liberation. I hope he'll ask me to a meeting.'

Arnold learned quickly and was popular.

He and Laura became lovers. He was besotted, admiring her beauty, from her classic head to her pert udder.

But it was her intelligence and communication in discussing the Farm and other matters that he most valued, for she was able to suggest responses he would not have thought of himself.

'We lack policy ideas, allow single candidate elections and elect leaders who promise to save us,' she said. 'We're surviving, that's all.'

'We could start a family,' he said.

'I never want to have a calf as long as these pigs are ruling us,' she told him.

'Maybe I should lead a revolt,' he said to Laura.

'It would have to succeed,' she said. 'Or you will be dead.'

Arnold had been on Animal Farm a month when he heard Jack complaining about the RED.

'What's the problem with it?' he asked.

'Everything,' Jack said and started to tell him the EGHE didn't exist.

'Of course there's a greenhouse effect,' said Arnold dismissively.

Jack told him how Raman spectroscopy showed CO_2's absorption of infrared was similar to the other gases. Higher levels of CO_2 had not harmed living things in the past, nor caused runaway warming.

'I don't believe it,' said Arnold. 'We have evidence of global warming all around us: melting ice, rising sea levels.'

'That may not be a change in climate,' said Jack. 'The ice melting and sea level rise could be sensational reporting of seasonal events.'

'Aren't you aware of what the rest of the world is saying?' said Arnold.

'Our opinion is based on careful study. Global warming is not large and probably caused by anthropomorphic heat. We have concluded that the RED is false. I would like to explain our thinking to you.'

Jack caught Arnold up with the scientific thinking of the Farm's animals. They spent several evenings going over it and Arnold was impressed by the home grown expertise on Animal Farm. Although he sometimes found his beliefs challenged, Jack was able to convince him of the falsity of the RED.

Lord Dimitri's regime was cruelly oppressive. With so many of the island's businesses closed, revenues dwindled and the islanders knew hard times. Hatred of the pigs was building among the animals and Barry was leading a group who were planning insurrection. When a pig spy overheard the animals' scepticism about global warming and told it in the farmhouse, there was a thought-crime pogrom. Under cover of darkness Algy's thugs beat up and killed several animals who had been overheard complaining about the RED. Animal bodies piled up in the farmyard, murdered by the Rottweilers. Barry was not amongst them.

Conditions on Animal Farm were stressful for the worker animals. Hard physical labour, poor shelter and bad food made the animals' situation seem hopeless. With coal mining halted, some animals were under-employed and starving. The internal dialogue each animal had between a voice of reality and a voice of hope for the future had become unbalanced by totalitarianism. Their fear destroyed their capacity to form convictions and they could only live from day to day.

The animals continued to whisper about the excesses of the RED. Domino and Blondie's filly Violet was overheard by a goose, who

247

blurted it out to a pig. A posse of pigs arrested Violet as she was hauling construction materials for the wind turbine. She was declared guilty of high treason and Algy shot her dead with Farmer Jones' shotgun.

'Those who oppose our government are traitors and will be executed,' he said.

Domino her father and Grace her sister were devastated. The workers grieved for their loyal friend Violet.

'Like Dongle and Henry, Violet has died for talk about climate change that was factual. They are gone but their concerns are still with us,' said Jack as they buried her by the dam. 'We will miss her.'

Algy discouraged the animal workers' growing discontent by invoking more terror.

'I warned you that the debate about global warming is over,' Algy said. 'We have evidence that Blondie and Rose have been talking about climate and they will receive 100 lashes each.'

Blondie had been overheard talking with Rose about the RED being based on theories without evidence.

The animals watched horrified, huddled together, as old Blondie and the kindly Rose were whipped mercilessly by pigs until they fell. Blondie, the older of the two, died where she lay. Rose lived on for two days in the stable and then died in great pain. The animals were distraught.

'I blame Algy and I want revenge,' Jack said.

'Myrtle, Earl, Milk Bar, Blondie, Rose and Violet have been murdered,' Laura said. 'None of us is safe.'

'Why did they kill them?' asked Arnold.

'You've come from a farm run by humans, haven't you?' said Laura. 'There every animal gets murdered. Our lives here are relatively long. We are well off.'

'Being brutalized here is worse.'

'Are you sure it isn't more natural? It more closely resembles being hunted in the wild. Being herded with an electric prodder and felled by a stun gun seems worse than being torn to bits by predators.'

Lord Dimitri expanded the Farm, coordinating neighbouring farms into a trading bloc. The farm was controlled by a pig oligarchy, each of them operating a part of Farm business. Away from public scrutiny, Lord Dimitri reasserted his dominating control over a population too fragmented and fearful to oppose him, with terror from his police and killer dogs. The Farm continued to be run by pigs in the traditional totalitarian communist style copied from the faraway SR.

For the animals, liberation was in the forefront of their minds, but it was too dangerous to complain.

'Unless we gain liberation, our destiny and that of our descendents on this Farm is forever to be eaten,' said Clarabelle.

'The pigs will never liberate us,' Jack said. 'Their only concession is to allow us the solace of religion. We will have to liberate ourselves.'

'Each superpower has an official religion, or in the Republic of Ceramica, a central party,' Patriarch reminded them. 'Morals are determined from religious or party teaching, although fewer than half the populations are followers of the official national religion. The pigs have racial and sectarian prejudices and religious freedom is precarious.'

'Paradoxy is making a comeback, I hear,' said Jack.

'It is resurgent in the SR, because the people are oppressed,' Patriarch said. 'Other religions are forbidden.'

'You Ravens inform on their proselytising,' said Jack. 'It's hypocritical.'

'We are doing it to survive,' said Patriarch.

'Materialism is displacing religions, races and nations,' said Barry. 'DU citizens consume more materials per person than in any other nation, followed by the SR, then by the Republic of Ceramica. Wealth in each superpower is almost entirely owned by a small group who control production, the media, politics, developments and public discourse. Ordinary citizens' participation in democracy is limited to 4-yearly elections in the DU, the same in the SR. Ceramica

249

is planning to hold an open election. All three superpowers have set ambitious national growth goals.'

'Why?'

'Growth allows the leaders to expand their budgets and give jobs to their cronies,' Barry said.

'Growing their economies has become a religious crusade uniting the superpowers,' said Barry. 'They have been able to gloss over their political, economic and social differences. Scientists' predictions have been appropriated, misrepresented and exaggerated. Expert deliberation has been side-lined as epistemic elitism. Climate policies are decided by populism.'

'You make it sound like a conspiracy,' said Hugo the steer, brother of Jack.

'Algy's policies *are* a conspiracy, a secret plan to restructure the World by false observations, false theories, false association and exploitation of peoples' fear,' said Barry. 'Already the SR and Ceramica are actioning the RED.'

'What is their overall plan?' asked Hugo.

'To increase private wealth of the controlling elite.'

Worker animals on Animal Farm could conclude that neither the SR, nor the DU, nor the Republic of Ceramica, would improve their living conditions, which are getting worse. They would be better off if they expelled superpower influence from their lives while they still had strength. They realised they only had themselves to rely on. Their revolt would be do or die.

CHAPTER 43 THRESHOLD EXCEEDED

The animal workers were docile until the pigs' cruelty provoked resistance. Several animal workers attacked the pigs, or tried to escape from the Farm. They were caught and killed by the Rottweilers. Jack was planning a mass revolt and met his group almost every day. They trusted and supported each other, valuing each other's strengths, forgiving weaknesses, closing ranks and sharing information about the pig enemy.

The privations of the Renewable Energy Deal (RED) had disrupted living and without electricity, conditions had worsened.

'The pigs are unaware of, or disinterested in, the cruelty they impose on us,' said Jack. Working conditions on the Farm had worsened. Work with repetitive actions and uncomfortable body positions was exhausting, but the pigs were oblivious to their suffering. If they detected lowered quality of output, the pigs would punish them brutally. Poultry were adept at picking faulty materials but were not allowed to control the quality of produce in case they sabotaged marketing wantonly. The Government regulated against cruelty, but the pigs stayed under their radar. President Natalia Alphancourt was inculcating voluntarism on the island to cope with the oil embargo, but on Animal Farm pigs stood over the labouring animals with whips.

The burdened animals' perceptions had been affected by the whipping to death of Blondie, Rose and Violet for misdemeanours. The workers reframed the Farm as a concentration camp and their work as forced labour, the only exit being by death in a slaughterhouse. The workers outnumbered the pigs, with some

251

animals larger in size than their guards. To force a large animal to comply, a group of pigs would attack it with whips.

'Do not allow them to single you out for punishment,' said Jack. 'We need to act as one, with an animal to lead us in a fight.'

'Who?'

'We are lucky to have several possible leaders.'

It didn't seem as though Jack would lead them. He was getting old and losing his edge.

'When?'

'Soon. Our group is almost ready.'

Arnold, the import, was popular, commanding but not bossy, firm with incompetence but kind. He shared their vision of liberation and his counsel was wise. His weakness was to be impatient and abrupt with horses, whom he actively disliked, contemptuous of their simplicity. His favourite cow was Laura and she helped him deal with the horses.

'Horses are lovely,' said Laura. 'They are always reliable and honest.'

'They are dim-witted and slow,' said Arnold.

'They are just as smart as we are,' she said. 'The problem is that you try to bully them and they become passive aggressive. You can lead a horse to water, but you can't make it drink. They are on to you and you don't like it.'

'I need them to take part in our group,' he said.

Arnold, Domino, Brandy, old Jack, Barry and Laura were talking during their midday respite from ploughing and cultivating. Arnold had taken over as chief bull from old Jack. Barry tried to get the larger animals to commit to a plan.

'How do you want to revolt?' he asked.

'We have to unite to meet opposition,' Arnold said. The workers admired him as a disciplinarian who expected a lot from them but who knew their individual weaknesses and made allowances for them. 'I can't imagine the pigs agreeing to our taking over leadership of the farm without a fight.'

'How long have you known we are going to fight them?' asked Barry.

'I have known for years that we should do something but I wasn't sure what, until they killed Blondie, Rose and Violet,' said old Jack. 'Then I knew we had to takeover.'

'Will we kill the pigs?' asked Barry.

'If we need to,' said Arnold.

'Are you sure we'll succeed?' asked Domino.

Arnold pondered his answer. *'Should I acknowledge the risks or would that seem foolhardy? Goliath wants certainty. Which should I give him, the reality of events which are uncertain, or the certainty of my own commitment? Our outcome is uncertain but I am certain I want to be in control. The outcome will be best with me in the lead. It is a huge responsibility, but I know that under my leadership we have the best chance of succeeding. This is what I was born to do.'*

His duty to them all made cowardice impossible for him.

'I am sure we'll win,' he said humbly, 'or I will die trying.'

'I hope it won't come to that,' said Domino.

'Thanks,' Arnold said. He respected Domino from then on.

The group wanted Arnold to lead in any fighting.

'Can we negotiate instead of using force?' asked Barry the ram.

'Pigs are uncompromising animals,' said old Jack. 'There is no stopping a pig when it has found a gap. It thrusts its snout in and shoves its wedge-shaped body through. Negotiating with them would be difficult.'

'I heard the way to turn a pig is with a flat surface, having no openings,' said Domino. 'Striking it on the softness of its snout will paralyse it.'

'Could we arm ourselves with shields to turn them and hit them on the snout with clubs?' said Barry.

'What can we use for shields?'

'There are some ply panels they use as sidings for pens in the farrowing house,' said Arnold. 'We can make holes in them, to hold in our mouths in front of us, to block pigs from pushing through.'

'We can stop them, but how can we subdue them?' asked Laura.

'We could ask them to give up,' said a hen.

253

They all looked at her as she rearranged a feather.

'We will demand they stop fighting. They will have to obey us.'

'We can tell them our revolutionary group has taken over the farm and they must vacate the farmhouse forthwith,' Barry said

'What if they won't come out of the farmhouse?' asked Laura.

'We will go in and kill the bastards!' said Arnold. 'We will use our forks, picks and hammers to fell them. Will you be in it?'

Remembering the years of oppression they gave an exultant shout: 'Yes!'.

'Hang on,' said Laura. 'Don't we want to minimise deaths and injury? We should offer them a choice of coming over to our side.'

'We should kill the leaders,' said Arnold.

'Lord Dimitri too?' asked Barry.

'He's the worst of them,' said Judy. 'Death would be too good for him.'

She had never hidden her contempt for Lord Dimitri. For her, he epitomised the tyrannical and corrupt face of pig power.

'Are we agreed it has to be a full-on rebellion?' asked Arnold.

'It would be better to get rid of Lord Dimitri without rebelling,' said Barry. 'With him gone the animals could reorganise. There may be a way to assassinate him.'

'We don't have guns and the assassin would be risking his own life. Who will do that?'

'I would,' said Barry. 'I have reached the age of indiscretion. I will work out a plan. Let me have your ideas.'

Barry investigated ways to poison the boar's food and reported to the group at a meeting. 'Since the ban on herbicides and pesticides, no chemical poisons are used on Animal farm,' he said. 'The only natural poison is green potatoes. Green coloring on potatoes indicates the presence of a toxic substance called solanine, also found in tomatoes and eggplants and can occur naturally in leaves, fruit, and tubers. Green potatoes are dangerous for pigs. Potatoes protruding from the ground became green and we earth them up or discard them. The more a potato is exposed to sunlight, the more solanine can form.

254

'Solanine intake may cause intense pain as it damages the cell membranes of the boar's intestines. Solanine is considered a neurotoxin and ingestion by humans can cause serious neurological problems, nausea and headaches, excessive salivation, sudden loss of appetite, hindering the production of essential enzymes, discontinuation of pregnancy and can lead to and even leasing to death if enough is consumed. Effects on the boar should be similar.'

'His pregnancy wouldn't be terminated,' Arnold said.

Barry wanted to prepare a dish of food containing enough solanine that Lord Dimitri would die when he ate it. Cooking did not reduce its toxicity. He would expose growing potatoes to sunlight by brushing off soil to uncover the shallowest tubers. He could cut off the green parts, but if the solanine was too concentrated, the food would be bitter.

Cookie told him Lord Dimitri was partial to savoury scalloped potatoes. He asked her to show him how she prepared them. He watched as she pre-boiled slices of potato in salted water with garlic and rosemary then layered them in a casserole dish. She covered them in a onion cream sauce made with flour, butter, milk, broth and seasoning. She stirred in shredded cheese and baked it until the top was golden brown.

Over a period of a month Barry cultivated and gathered enough green potatoes. Laura helped him obtain the ingredients and she prepared the savoury scallops in the workers' kitchen, which had a wood stove with an oven. His grown lamb with Judy, Christine, carried a basket held in her mouth containing the potato dish, innocently draped in a white cloth. She gave it to Cookie at the kitchen door.

'I have cooked these savoury potato scallops myself for Lord Dimitri,' Christine said as she handed them over. 'He is a good leader.'

The next morning Cookie sent for Christine.

'Lord Dimitri is very ill. How did you prepare those potatoes?'

Christine had helped Laura but they hadn't told her about the green potatoes. Cookie's suspicions of poisoning were assuaged and she assumed the affliction was from an infection.

255

Lord Dimitri didn't die as planned. He recovered after a week.

'I'll have to think of something else for next time,' Barry said. 'Perhaps one of us could do a suicide attack?' he said. 'I'm oldest and therefore best qualified to die.'

'It would not be honorable,' said Arnold. 'We are only animal workers, but our opposition should be dignified.'

The following day a lorry came and took Barry away.

'Do you think they realised it was the potatoes?'

'They may have suspected.'

'Do you think they worked out who did the poison?'

'He was talking down the RED and Algy,' they remembered, wondering who could have reported him.

'They could be slaughtering him as a warning to us.'

'They couldn't be sure it was him. Barry's was a good plan,' said Arnold. 'It almost succeeded.'

No-one said anything.

'Okay,' said Arnold mildly. 'We'll takeover, with a coup. If they quibble, we will kill them! Are you in?'

They hesitated, mumbled, then spoke out.

'Y . . .es, yes, YES. Aye!'

'Not too loud. Again, all together. One, two, three, Aye.'

'Aye.'

'And again.'

'AYE,' they yelled quietly.

Their conviction was urgent.

'We can do this bloodlessly,' said Arnold. 'We don't need to rage through the farmhouse buildings. We can go in quietly and deal with them firmly. Killing is not how we want to dispose of our enemies; it would put us on the same low level as them, killing for convenience. Killing a pig is a last resort, when it is intransigent or violently opposed.

'We are fighting for control over the Farm property and our community. There can only be one winner, us. The pigs are going to lose control.'

'I don't think an uprising is the way to go,' said old Goliath. 'We should simply push them aside. They will realize they are outnumbered. If we show they have no option they will surrender.'

'They will fight,' said Arnold, 'until we get the better of them.'

'Physically they will be finished here. The pigs' farming business is legal and cannot be acquired by force. The pigs will have to wind it up themselves.'

'What are we going to do with the pigs?'

'If they make a new start with us, so much the better.'

'Could they change?'

'Yes, they will have to, or be killed.'

'What about Lord Dimitri?'

'If he is compliant, we will keep him locked up. If he isn't, we will kill him.'

'This is going to be fun.'

Lady overheard the pigs talking about the possibility of a worker rebellion. They decided to buy a cow to infiltrate and discover worker insurrection activity. They would extort her compliance by threatening to harm her calf. The new cow informed of a group meeting and the pigs planned to raid it. But Lady informed the animals in time and thwarted their raid. The pigs guessed Lady's betrayal and Lord Dimitri turned his dogs on her. It wasn't the end Lady wanted or deserved for her loyalty to the workers. She had saved them and they held a wake in her honour.

Now Jack's group was planning their liberation, the oppression of their slavery lifted off them. Morale spiralled headily and even the horses began to hold dances. Even the most obscure explanations of technology attracted their interest, for they wanted to mine coal, use electricity and spread the bounty of the resource across Caruba.

257

CHAPTER 44 ADDING SOLAR HEAT

One evening after they had eaten, the workers gathered secretly in an old cattle byre, an outbuilding on the farm. Meeting there would be away from pig scrutiny.

'The question we need to consider is whether we should cooperate with this RED nonsense,' said Arnold. 'The pigs' interest in the RED is to get more government spending, whereas we will be out of work.'

'What is there about renewable energy that can be renewed?' asked Hugo, son of Jack and Rose, castrated by the pigs. 'Energy can't be renewed can it?'

'Not literally,' said old Jack. 'It can't be reused but it can be replaced from the Sun, which is supposed to have an infinite supply.'

'Is the Sun's energy readily accessible?'

'No,' said Arnold. 'It has to be collected, is less convenient to convert, difficult to store, unavailable at night and less easily transported than fossil fuels.'

'What are the best ways to supply renewable energy?' asked Hugo.

'Photoelectric panels and wind turbines lose most of it,' said old Jack. 'Better technologies lose less. A clock invented in 1864 in New Zealand has never been wound, requiring little input energy to work. An airtight box inside the clock expands and contracts throughout the day with air pressure, pushing on a diaphragm. It takes only a six-degree Celsius temperature variation over a day to raise a one-pound weight an inch. This in turn descends, powering the clock.'

'So changes in the atmosphere are enough to keep the clock going,' Arnold said. 'But you can't get something for nothing. Energy has to be input.'

'Renewable energy is input,' said old Jack. 'Changes in the atmosphere power the clock but could they power an electric generator? The airtight box and diaphragm would have to be enormous.'

'Could autos run by clockwork?' Arnold said.

'No, but trains would run on time,' old Jack quipped.

'Haha.'

'Another device, called a hydraulic ram, pumps water, using the energy of water falling in a stream,' he said. 'If the discharge pressure is high, the efficiency of energy extraction is low. The advantage is that there are no moving parts, operation is automatic and the energy is renewed.'

'I thought rams were expensive,' said Amos, laughing. With Barry gone, he had taken over as chief ram

'Why?' asked Judy dully, grieving for Barry.

'Because they charge!' he said.

Everyone laughed, except Judy. She managed a small smile.

'Juliet, you have studied energy technologies,' said Laura. 'Why is renewable energy flavour of the month?'

'The big picture is that Earth's resources of non-renewable energy, coal, oil and gas are being used up,' Juliet said. 'Renewable energy is an alternative.'

'How attractive is renewable energy?'

'There have been many inventions but only a few devices are widely used,' she said. 'River sites for hydropower are nearly all taken and hydrogen for cars uses a lot of electricity.'

'Some are able to compete economically with fossil fuels and their costs are reducing,' Old Jack said. 'Could there be a breakthrough?'

'There could be small local applications,' Juliet said. 'A recent discovery was the photovoltaic pv cell used in solar panels discovered in 1839. I've made a list of the advantages and disadvantages of renewable energy for Caruba. The major advantage of solar pv energy is that it is supplied from the Sun, so there is plenty for the future. Another is that solar pv energy does not endanger workers as coal mining does, nor does it reduce the health of local populations from dust, fly-ash and toxic substances in air and water. Nor are the generating facilities as large and as vulnerable to terrorism. Less water is needed for cooling. Rehabilitation of mined lands is not needed. But solar pv panels take large areas of land, cause glare, are unreliable and vulnerable to weather, need electricity storage and warm the environment more than fossil fuels.'

Old Jack said: 'You are right, there are some advantages. but electricity from renewable technologies usually require more expensive converters and storage.'

'A supposed advantage of renewable technologies was that they do not produce greenhouse gases that cause atmospheric warming,' said Juliet. 'But it was a straw man fallacy, for there is no evidence that greenhouse gases even exist.'

'Scientists claim that the evidence is global warming,' old Jack said.

'It *a priori* to say that the evidence for greenhouse gases is global warming,' said old Jack. 'It is circular. Explanations of global warming without greenhouse gases are possible.'

'Renewable technologies have serious disadvantages,' Juliet said. In most situations, collecting, extracting, converting, storing and distributing electricity by renewable technologies would be more expensive than from fossil fuels. Renewable technologies are less efficient, cause about twice as much warming of the environment as coal, take up much more land, cause more visual pollution and are more offensive to local humans and fauna.'

'How insidious has been the invasion of solar panels on suburban roof tops and how misconstrued by the populace!' thought old Jack. *'They have interpreted their adoption as evidence of generating prowess, when in fact they are economically unattractive in most situations, before subsidies. The public authorities have used subsidies to foist them onto unsuspecting electricity consumers, to absolve themselves from public provision of electricity in bad*

260

weather. Hail, storms, snow, ice and cyclonic winds will still occur, but people will be on their own, unprotected by a public grid.

It gave old Jack a feeling of empowerment to oppose wrong ideas so vehemently held by the pigs and human leaders.

'Have you heard that wind turbine blades kill birds, reflect light, can make a whistling sound, can break and have to be replaced?' said Judy.

'There is a steady harvest of dead birds,' said Ranger the cat.

'Won't the birds learn to avoid the blades?' said Missy, who had replaced Lady. The pigs had hired a contractor to install a wind turbine on the old windmill.

'They don't learn much after they're dead,' EEyore said.

'Maybe they will hear the turbine whistling and stay away,' said Arnold.

'I've never heard a turbine whistle,' said Judy.

'Just as well: you can't fly anyway,' said Arnold.

'Birds might see the blades flashing sunlight,' said Ranger.

'Not at night they wouldn't,' Missy said.

'Do birds fly at night?' asked Judy.

'Not many,' Arnold said. 'The slaughter would be in the daytime.'

'What if they stopped wind turbines during the day?' said Judy.

'The danger to birds would stop but so would electricity production,' Arnold said.

'I would miss getting those birds,' said Hunter.

They all looked at him.

'Evil cat!' said Missy.

'The main advantage of a wind turbine appears to be it can supply cat food,' said Arnold.

Hunter was unable to control the barnyard mice population and the pigs had obtained Ranger, a young tom, for Hunter to train.

Near them an engineer was installing a wind turbine on the old windmill.

'Excuse me, please,' Missy asked the engineer. 'How efficient is this wind turbine going to be?'

261

'I heard the blades capture about 25% of the wind's energy.'

'Where does the other 75% go?' she asked.

'The blades warm by friction and the air takes the heat away.'

'How much of the 25% of blade energy is converted into electricity?' Arnold asked.

'My guess is about 80%,' said the engineer.

'80% of 25% gives 20% efficiency overall. That is only half as much as the 40% of the energy they get out of coal at a power station,' said Missy.

'It doesn't matter that wind turbine efficiency is low,' the engineer said. 'The energy is free and they can take as much as they want.'

'It does matter,' said Missy. 'The wind may not cost anything directly, but 80% of the incoming solar energy is wasted, all 100% has to be replaced and it has a cost to the environment. The heat output is at low temperature and is replaced with more heat from the Sun at higher temperature. This causes more warming of the environment than combusting the equivalent quantity of coal.'

'Hang on,' the engineer said, scratching his head. 'Energy taken from the wind doesn't have to be replaced!'

'Yes, of course it does,' Missy said. 'Energy can be neither created nor destroyed. When solar energy is taken by a renewable energy device on Earth, radiation from the Sun restores it, including the heat it wastes. Where could it come from except the Sun?'

Missy paused. The engineer seemed baffled.

'I'll tell you,' Missy said. 'Renewable energy is replaced by hotter solar radiation in greater amount.'

The engineer scratched his head, bested on his own turf. He was surprised to be talking with such knowledgeable farm animals and to understand what they were saying. He was annoyed by their criticism of the turbine he was installing, because it contradicted the information he had from the turbine manufacturers. He thought: *If the animals thought a wind turbine was without benefit, why were they having this turbine installed?'*

'Why is renewable energy being installed in many places?' he asked.

262

'They are wanting to sell turbines and solar panels and people have no way of holding them to account for their lies,' Judy said.

'Renewable energy could be okay for some situations,' said the engineer, ignoring the insult to his company. 'What about the rest of Caruba?'

'Lord Dimitri is following Algy's RED,' Missy said. 'He wants fossil fuels replaced because of a greenhouse effect. But there is no evidence that one exists.'

Lord Dimitri had told them at the Farm meeting they would have abundant renewable energy as soon as funds promised by the SR arrived. The funds had not come and they were going into winter without heat or light.

'Lord Dimitri has let us all down,' said Arnold. 'Adopting renewable energy as a blanket policy is absurd. It's true that the Sun's energy is virtually limitless, but the equipment to capture it is expensive. Huge areas of Caruban land would be taken from food production. Electricity won't replace the food production it takes. What will happen to the glass panels and wind turbines when there are gusting cyclonic winds, freezing rain and snow, or large hail? They need to store electricity or have an alternative supply. Worst of all, solar panels cause more warming, not less.'

'Publicly subsidised solar panels and huge batteries are proposed,' said Arnold. In developed countries, people can afford them, but in undeveloped countries, only the wealthy can afford them.'

'That is an exaggeration.'

'It is generally true,' Arnold said. 'The RED zealots will need fossil fuel power to back up their renewable energy. Natural gas has been burned heedlessly as a transition fuel, when it is a precious feedstock for manufacturing plastics and chemicals. We are turning our backs on a rich fossil fuels legacy, that has funded public programmes and has been our economic mainstay. It has sufficient resources to continue supply for many years into the future.'

A week later, President Natalia Alphancourt addressed a meeting at the Farm, with Lord Dimitri and most of the animals present.

263

'We must transform Caruba's economy to renewable energy,' said President Natalia. 'Renewable energy has been available for centuries but is little used today. Power supply has evolved from animal power, from steam and internal combustion engines and from nuclear fission. Technologies like wind turbines and solar hot water were previously rejected because they were more expensive but recent public subsidies have made them competitive. Technology has advanced and understanding of individuals' rights, usage of resources, pollution and economic knock-on effects have increased, with the result that there has been a reappraisal of old technologies. Some renewables previously dismissed are looking good.'

Arnold raised a foreleg.

'Yes,' said the President.

'If we are progressing backwards,' Eeyore said mournfully 'What is in front of us?'

There was laughter.

'Civilisations do sometimes revert to resources previously discontinued,' said President Natalia Alphancourt. 'The DU is still using oil and coal, whereas other nations have reduced their production.

'Missy tells me your science class has concluded that combustion is almost certainly the main cause of climate change,' she said. 'This is an opinion which differs from the conventional view that heat of combustion isn't enough to cause global warming and therefore solar forcing must be the driver. Arnold has informed me that the heat from combusting fossil fuels globally is at a rate 8.3 times higher than the heating up of atmosphere and oceans.'

There was a shocked silence.

'Yes, yes!' Arnold called out exuberantly. He was delighted the thermal pollution problem had been acknowledged by the President. Perhaps Missy had communicated the findings of the science group to Lord Dimitri and he had passed it on the President Natalia Alphancourt. He could hardly believe hearing it from a leader and applauded enthusiastically. Others joined in.

'We don't need to install new electricity generators,' President Natalia said. 'We need to get more electricity out of the ones we already have.'

Applause.

Lord Dimitri thanked Natalia.

'We have found out the bigger picture for Caruba,' he said. 'Animals, at our next meeting I will tell you my proposed energy plan for Animal Farm.'

As they walked back to their quarters, Arnold said: 'That was good. Natalia is seeing some sense at last. I think she has realized shutting down the coal station and installing renewables would trample on Carubans' freedom. Only the pigs want it. We animal workers won't get our freedom that way.'

'The message is to reduce excessive energy use, but the response in developed countries has been to shoot the bearer of this message,' said Arnold. 'I wonder what Lord Dimitri will want us to do?'

'We'll find out soon - he is going to tell us his plan.'

CHAPTER 45 ANIMAL LIBERATION

'I used to believe we would be liberated soon,' said Clarabelle, as she stood with the other cattle in the shade of a tree. 'Now that I've seen President Alphancourt doesn't care about our needs, I don't believe it anymore.'

'Lord Dimitri has taken away the hope Lord Miguel gave us.'

Arnold said: 'It has taken a long time for farm animals to reach the state of subjugation we are in and could take us a long time to get out of it. We have been bred in domesticity for thousands of generations and it is doubtful whether our offspring could live wild again, because our skills have atrophied. But recent research into epigenetic inheritance gives hope we can re-adapt quickly to living in the wild. They think animals can pass on, in their gametes, acquired forms and learnings to their offspring, without a process of natural selection. Thus, a giraffe that stretched its neck repeatedly could father a long-necked offspring. This theory, proposed by Lamarck, was displaced by Darwin's, but it is having a comeback.'

'Our deference to pigs may have been acquired.'

'Submission of the oppressed does not justify tyranny,' said Clarabelle.

'The pigs' oppression has to stop.'

'Let's run amok in a rout,' said Judy with enthusiasm.

'We won't succeed unless we unite.'

'Many of our animals may not be able to break away from the past. A few worker animals have bonded with the pigs, in a Stockholm Syndrome.'

'Hatred of them as our captors is more prevalent and that will unite us.'

'Some of our animals lack rebelliousness. They may be too beguiled or resigned to revolt. The seed of liberation may have to come in from outside.'

'Could someone like Sopher help us oppose them?'

'Yes. Animal liberation is not a defined course of action,' said Clarabelle. 'We will have to somehow merge into a new relationship with humans. Imagine our animals shopping in a supermarket. The different species would want their traditional foods and goods. For example, sheep could want wool cleaning treatments that other species wouldn't want. Liberation could be complicated and animals' rights might be obtained only gradually.'

'Why hasn't it already happened?'

'The pigs have copied humans. It says in the Bible that God gave animals to humans as meat. Genesis 9:10 says:

2. And the fear of you (Noah) and the dread of you shall be upon every beast of the earth, and upon every fowl of the air, upon all that moveth upon the earth, and upon all the fishes of the sea; into your hand are they delivered.

3. Every moving thing that liveth shall be meat for you: even as the green herb have I given you all things.

'Bloody hell!' said Judy. 'That shit about us being meat doesn't allow much liberation!'

'It authorises humans to eat beasts.'

'They think God created animals for humans to dine on,' said Arnold. 'Animal liberation is not one proposal nor a set of ideas. It encompasses proposals for small changes on many fronts. Animals will take whatever freedom is granted. The ending of animal imprisonments and murders will be gradual, as humans eat less meat, less dairy products and fewer eggs. Humans prefer meat, even after they have experienced a famine and survived without meat. Meatless diets have become more accessible, vegetarianism and veganism have become more common, but meat eating is deeply entrenched in

267

the human psyche. Although people would like to stop animals being killed, they won't stop eating meat overnight.'

'There are beginnings,' said Clarabelle. 'In a few places humans have adopted moral restrictions on eating animals. Eating of pets and very young animals is abhorrent and eating of pigs and cows is forbidden in some religions. Phil Sopher has wanted equality between humans and animals based on individual capacity for suffering, with the greatest amount of pleasure and least amount of pain for the greatest number. Neither humans nor pigs are entitled to kill other animals any more than they can kill their own kind.'

'Should an ant suffer no more than me?' asked Judy.

'Buddhists don't like to harm any living creature. Conflict with competitors is not inevitable. For us farm animals, the joy of our existential freedom is subtracted from by our awareness of immoral treatment of animals. We are oppressed by tyrannical pig and human regimes, who use us in their persecution of wild animals.'

'Then the outlook for livestock is bleak?'

Clarabelle spoke sadly. 'To counter meat eating, an appeal for fewer animal deaths loses its persuasiveness when there is no other way to dispose of the many livestock animals held on farms. It is easy to imagine animals not being killed but more difficult to contemplate them being freed from slavery, feeding themselves and defending against predators. Even if they could revert to the wild, there would not be enough wilderness for them to live in.'

'Could there be a future without animals being eaten?' asked Judy.

'Dougal the mule buys lottery tickets,' said Arnold. 'His only hope is buying his freedom. Unfortunately, there is no panacea. Prospects for domestic animals to live in freedom with humans, or to somehow achieve freedom living wild, are almost non-existent. Animals' ability to communicate with humans is too limited for mutualism. At best collaboration is no better than that humans achieve with their infants. In every interaction with an animal, human hegemony prevails. Animals' adaptations prohibit their survival without humans.'

268

'The idea that livestock can somehow be freed is far-fetched then?'

'Acknowledging their sentience is merely symbolic when there is no solution, like showing concern for long term refugees, or for prisoners doing life sentences, knowing they will never be freed.'

'What can be done?'

'Humans could breed fewer livestock,' said Clarabelle. 'If those bred are well cared for and live contented lives, total happiness would increase. The soldier who went to war and suffered was not unlike an animal sent to the slaughterhouse: it was his lot in life to be killed, because deaths were necessary for the community to survive. Death in abattoirs need not be traumatic and might not invalidate the happiness of young ones. The Aztecs sacrificed girls and boys as religious offerings. In times past, human lives were often cut short too, but early death was not considered to negate lives regarded as worthwhile and happy.

'Would a domestic animal's lot be happy enough to be worthwhile?' said Grace, the other daughter of the murdered Blondie, sister of murdered Violet.

'Look over there,' Arnold said. Several lambs raced through a puddle, again and again, their tails straight, leaping into the air and kicking. 'There's your answer. When lambs play, the life of a sheep could be as happy as a human life.'

'Would you tell Lord Dimitri that we protest slaughter of the Farm's worker animals,' Arnold asked Missy. 'The number of killings has to decrease.'

She accepted the message with reluctance. 'The pigs won't like it,' she said.

'Lord Dimitri says it's not possible,' Missy said when she returned. 'He said the animals' work doesn't earn enough for their food and the Farm has to sell animals to the abattoir, to keep from bankruptcy and starvation.'

'If the pigs did their share of the work, the Farm could be self-sufficient without selling comrades to the abattoir,' said Arnold.

'Perhaps the pigs send us to the abattoir mainly to terrorise us and maintain their authority,' Clarabelle said. 'It sucks.'

269

The worker animals puzzled over their future.

'Could we liberate ourselves by force?'

'We need a forceful leader.'

'Someone to lead us and govern after liberation?' asked Judy.

'The leader should be able to efface his or her ego,'

'Many would start like that, but would be corrupted by power, as happened with humans and pigs,' said Arnold.

'Do we have to choose a leader at this stage?' asked Judy.

'Yes,' he said. 'It is paramount. We need a leader who could join in a democracy with humans.'

'How would we choose our representative?' asked Judy.

'One who would represent all the species fairly,' Juliet said.

'Who could do that?'

'There are many who could lead us,' said Arnold. So far, he had led them. They knew old Jack lacked the energy needed for an uprising. 'We could ask for nominations.'

'Everyone should have a say,' said Brandy, Domino's ploughing partner.

Brandy seemed to be throwing his hat into the ring of a leadership contest.

'We need a say at the next election,' Juliet said. 'We need to have a representative we can vote for.'

'I'll ask Lord Dimitri when our candidate can nominate,' said Missy.

'Only pigs can run for the Farm Council,' Missy told them.

The worker animals were too fearful to protest.

'The pigs' treat us like they treat the mentally disabled or animals too young to be responsible.'

'As dependents.'

'They are stopping us being independent,' said Arnold. 'They won't give up their privileges.'

On most afternoons, the pigs went to the farm's beach house they had purchased.

'Animals like to see their betters enjoying wealth,' Lord Dimitri said. 'It gives them something to work towards.'

'Humans' relationships with animals, such as horses, must change before there can be equality,' said Arnold. 'Humans have cruel devices such as curb bits, martingales, double bridles and crops to force their mount to obey them.'

'Will humans and pigs ever grant true equality to other animals?' asked Juliet.

Brandy shook his head. 'Pigs have no concept of equality with us,' he said. 'They are more numerous, do no work and eat more than half the food grown. They are grossly overweight, their limbs protrude stiffly from their obese bodies and their eyes are sunken in their fat faces.'

'They have traded off hard work for cunning,' said Missy. 'Humans and pigs have oratorical skills that the rest of us are unable to match.'

'Could species achieve equality by sharing their lives paired off, as horses do with their riders and elephants do with their mahouts, in a symbiosis?'

'I could team up with a shepherd,' said Missy. 'Or perhaps with some sheep?'

'Not with me you wouldn't,' said old Jack. 'You are too much in the pigs' pocket.'

'I don't know what you're talking about,' said Missy, leaving without a backward glance.

Arnold, who was listening, swished his tail in annoyance and turned away.

A lorry came and took old Jack and Judy away. She had been active in the community and would be badly missed. His life had been damaged when he lost Rose in the whipping savagery. He had never recovered.

'To be free we have to become independent and oust the pigs,' Arnold said to Clarabelle. 'We can run this Farm better than they do.'

'I agree,' said Arnold. 'I am preparing a plan.'

'What are you going to do?' Clarabelle asked him.

271

'I'm making a list of principles for our revolution,' said Arnold.

CHAPTER 46
CONFIRMATION BIAS

Arnold felt a great weight of leadership upon him, as if his role would be pivotal in their liberation struggle.

He was with Laura, Judy and Amos, the ram who had replaced Barry. They were loading hay and waiting for a Shetland to bring a put.

'The pigs are being misled, as is President Alphancourt,' Arnold said. 'There has been a hysterical reaction to climate fears, whipped up by technology interests.'

Arnold was concerned that data was properly sampled, selected without a confirmatory bias and transparent. It was a nerdy approach, but he deplored the boots-and-all approach of the RED.

'They can't seem to decide what to do about climate change,' said Judy.

'They want to spend money bigtime,' said Arnold. 'The RED will be expensive.'

'The big shots have to shoot, or they lose their jobs.'

'We worked out climate change is caused by excessive energy consumption,' Arnold said. 'That says it all. Why can't they agree?'

'The climate scientists are stuck in the EGHE paradigm,' she said.

'They have the wrong data and they won't change because it's not in their personal self-interest,' Laura said.

'Yes, that's how I see it.' said Arnold. 'They can't decide and they turn to faked science. In the case of the fraudulent hockey-stick graph, unscrupulous people falsified climate data to cause alarm and self-serve.'

'The big picture is corrupted and our small government is trying to balance the climate alarmism with local energy provision,' said Barbara. She was Amos' favourite ewe.

'The evidence for climate change here is inconclusive,' said Arnold. 'The case for renewable energy on Caruba has not been made. Our pigs are kowtowing to Algy and the RED people. They should listen to President Natalia Alphancourt. She's more practical.'

'Changing those piggy minds will be difficult. Alarmists have their foot in the door.'

'The Panel Investigating Global Warming (IPCC) collects climate data. But in the Hockey Stick matter they had a confirmatory bias,' said Arnold. 'Climate prediction has been in the hands of people who have gained by predicting doom and gloom. Climate change is their starting point, not a reasoned conclusion. A culture demonising carbon has developed, a religious devotion. They are not to be trusted. Not even with weather forecasts.'

While they had been talking, Clarabelle and Missy had arrived and listened attentively.

'You animals are sitting in the cheap seats and haven't been able to see what's been going on,' said Missy. 'Lord Dimitri has cleverly set it up so the Farm will benefit from renewable energy, whether there is climate change or not.'

''Certainly having a flexible strategy could be an advantage,' said Arnold. 'I am concerned about confirmatory bias and wrong alternatives. Moderate scientists have been unable to counsel caution in reacting to climate change for fear of reprisals from colleagues. They have allowed themselves to be misrepresented.'

'It was a consensus of scientists that agreed fossil fuels cause global warming,' said Missy.

'No, not even close,' said Arnold. 'Scientists' positions were misreported. A survey for the IPCC claimed that 'Of the approximately one-third of climate scientists writing on global warming who stated a position on the contribution of humans to global warming, *97% of the one third* agreed humans contributed *somewhat* to global warming. It was falsely reported that a *majority believed that climate change was caused by humans*, as if there were no belief in any other causes. The scepticism of most climate scientists was falsely represented.'

'How could so many scientists get it so wrong?' said Missy.

'The IPCC has a vested interest in anthropomorphic climate change and fearing it would lose the debate, it declared a consensus and stifled it,' Arnold said. 'There was no consensus. It should have been called out of order because it was political manipulation. Scientists were too fearful to dissent. Rather than too much debate, there has not been enough! Declaring consensus, without a secret ballot of opinions, is worthy of fascism. The idea of vesting a survey consensus with justice, even if it had been done honestly, was ridiculous. Scientific objectivity isn't decided by voting. When science is thwarted by complexity, the correct response is to observe and measure until a pattern emerges. This was not done.'

'Are you labelling this attempt to dominate policy: 'fascism'?' asked Amos.

'Fascism is a harsh word, I know,' said Arnold, 'but it is justified here because of the nationalism and authority in the IPCC's declaration of a majority in agreement, which in fact was false,' said Arnold. 'A finding that would have reassured ordinary citizens was corrupted by sleight of hand to promote their activism. It was corrupted to cause anxiety in the totalitarian way, generated in military confrontations, trade disputes and refugee policies. The totalitarianism in climate policy-making was the same.

'The superpowers dominated their populations with central control, leader ideology and mass terror. The spontaneity, arbitrariness, cohesion and lack of conscience at the highest levels has been chilling and spilled over to terrorise Caruban energy supply.

'I blame the leaders,' said Arnold. 'The three superpowers: Republic of Ceramica, the Democratic Union and the Social Republic, all rule by totalitarianism. They keep their ageing urban populations politically isolated, socially lonely, superfluous, desperate, their thinking dominated by leaders with grandiose and

275

vague visions. Younger people are led to vent their energy in angry mobs. On Caruba the well-being of working people is sacrificed to counter minor climate change with technology that is worse than we already have.'

'What can be done?' asked Clarabelle.

'A more considered analysis is required to lead society forward, to understand climate change,' said Arnold. 'We need school children to study radiation physics and become climate scientists. We need informed discussion. Youngsters shouldn't be led by professional activists to vent prejudices, emotions and sentimentality in public demonstrations, as they have been.'

'A solution won't be found overnight, but the sooner the better.'

Carts and drays followed Lord Dimitri's car as he drove around the Farm followed by a car filled with his spin advisers. The animals had to turn out and cheer the procession. When a bullock turned its back in protest, Dimitri's dogs slayed it. The animals were superfluous, dispirited, malleable and beaten into compliance by the dictator.

CHAPTER 47 SAVING YOUR ENERGY

While they waited with the other workers for Lord Dimitri to speak to them, six sheep formed a line, side by side and danced a routine they had been practicing. They bleated the words of Sloop John B and stepped as one to a salsa beat, with their leader Barbara calling the steps: forward, back, forward, left, right, right, left. When Lord Dimitri arrived, they stopped immediately and lay down attentively.

Arnold sat with Laura in the middle of the audience. He was flanked by half a dozen prominent pigs, standing erect importantly behind him, all of them stuffed into suits and shirts.

'Good evening, animals,' Lord Dimitri said. *'Up at the farmhouse we have been deciding how to supply the farm with energy in future years. We are going to reduce usage and wastage. This afternoon I will explain our plan.'*

'Reducing energy would be good,' said Arnold to Laura quietly. 'If there is global warming, that should fix it.'

'We have been waiting for the SR to fund installation of solar panels,' said Lord Dimitri. *'They would be more attractive than coal, having less mineral resource depletion, using less water and losing fewer lives in mining accidents. Coal has a higher cost of environment destruction, pollution of the air, heating of rivers and lakes, noise, dirt and chemical pollution.'*

'Pig's ass,' said Arnold to Amos on his other side. 'Solar panels have worse problems.'

'Rich countries can make mistakes with renewable energy and pay the bill,' said Lord Dimitri. *'Poor countries like Caruba and India cannot afford to get it wrong. Nor can we.*

'When we don't know the cause of climate change, we cannot risk investing in expensive renewable energy. Comrades, we do not have a choice. Our Caruba Government is obliged by RED to reduce energy entering the environment from all sources: combusting fossil fuels, from nuclear fission, from food consumption and from renewable energy replenished from the Sun. These sources of energy cause global warming and in our opinion warming is not caused by carbon gases trapping radiation. It is caused mainly by heat of combustion and released when work is done. Energy releases must be reduced.'

'Hear, hear,' said Arnold loudly. He was excited because it was the same conclusion he had reached in his climate class. It was thrilling to hear their ideas used by captors with whom he had thought they had nothing in common.

'Energy has many forms woven into the fabric of life: heat; movement; fuels; and radiation,' Lord Dimitri said. *'The amount of energy an individual uses varies from country to country, place to place, time to time and depends on affluence. An individual can reduce their energy release by more efficient living, benefiting the community and gaining a sustainable future.'*

The muttering earlier had stopped. The animals were listening.

'We are going to reduce energy release on Animal Farm.'

Lord Dimitri announced: 'I'll stop there for a short break.'

278

'I hope he won't reduce personal energy consumption,' said Arnold. 'We don't consume enough energy to waste much. To stop emissions he will have to lower the whole community's energy consumption.'

'Turning down energy consumption rings capitalism's alarm bells,' said Arnold. 'Without energy growth, investment and profits could stop.'

'Bugger capitalism,' said Grace, Blondie's replacement. 'Energy growth must stop. The halcyon days of electricity at the flick of a switch are over.'

Dimitri had walked back on to the stage. The animals listened in the farm yard as he resumed his talk.

'Combustion produces energy emissions that warm the environment. We have to reduce energy production and wastage. One way is to reduce the number of animals; the other is that everyone has to use and waste less energy.'

The animals began talking with each other.

'I don't like where he's going with this,v' Arnold whispered to Laura.

'I like humans cutting back energy, but we animals shouldn't have to cut back,' Laura said. 'We hardly use any.'

'Energy use is a natural part of life,' said Clarabelle, whispering from his other side. 'We use energy to grow food, we use food to gain energy and we use energy to do work. Even when we are sleeping, we use energy. To reduce energy is to reduce living.'

'I agree,' said Arnold. 'We workers cannot reduce energy consumption. We are already at a bare minimum and it would mean starving.'

'Shh,' said Barbara.

'Comrades,' said Lord Dimitri. 'Only essential energy will be allowed to be used on our Farm from now on. It all ends up as heat in the environment, so we must use no more than is necessary.'

He turned to President Alphancourt.

'Ma'am, I believe you have an announcement.'

'Yes,' she said. 'For humans on Caruba, meat eating will end, because it infringes on animals' rights, without benefitting human nutrition.'

'Whoopee-do,' yelled Judy.

The animals applauded loudly and chattered noisily. Lord Dimitri waited for quiet.

'Fantastic!' said Laura to Arnold. 'At last we're getting our rights.'

'Each of you will have a personal energy quota,' said Lord Dimitri.

'Shit,' said Arnold.

'At least we'll be getting some energy,' said Laura.

Lord Dimitri sipped from a glass of vodka. His tone was severe.

'I will assign to each of you an energy quota that you may not exceed. You will be allowed one journey each week on the public dray. Any animal who fritters away their quota will be without transport. Pigs need to travel for their important work and will be allocated enough petrol to use the car for their travel.

'Animals must stop their slack habits that pour heat into the environment. Most likely, if there is global warming, you animals are causing it. Energy has to be transformed in our activities from a commodity in endless supply to a sustainable resource. We will get rid of those animals that contribute least to the food we grow.'

There was a stunned silence.

'Get rid of the pigs,' said Hugo-the-steroid quietly.

Only the audience heard him, but no-one dared to laugh.

'Animals must conserve their energy,' said Lord Dimitri. 'Rams may not butt, poultry are forbidden to beat their wings and dogs may not bark. Lambs are forbidden to skip.

'Energy use of all types has to decrease, especially food consumption. The right things to do are going without or using

something else. Instead of electric light, do your reading in daylight. Share a farm wagon and join with others to go places. Wait for a full load before setting off. When you must move, do it smoothly and efficiently. Do every task in one smooth motion, such as hoisting up a hay bale and stacking it. This uses less energy than frequent stops and starts. When a vehicle has to be restarted, stop it facing down a hill. You have to get the most useful work from every drop of petrol and every joule of food.

'You will follow these rules all day every day,' he said, pausing for another sip of his vodka.

'Does this make sense?' whispered Barbara to Amos.

'The science is correct,' he muttered, 'but we worker animals would be making the sacrifices. The pigs won't do these things. They are the biggest energy users and the worst offenders: their hypocrisy is blatant.'

Lord Dimitri continued: 'There isn't enough electricity for heaters, nor for air conditioners, nor for electric motors, except in the farmhouse. We pigs need energy saving appliances to support our high quality leadership. If you are cold, you can close windows and doors, or wear something warm. If you do not, you will have to die, preferably quickly. When you die, you cannot be cremated because this would use too much energy. Your ultimate value will be achieved when your body is composted for horticultural fertiliser.'

The animals' fear was silent. A hen began sobbing hysterically, until her companions stopped her.

'Every animal must grow as much hair, wool and feathers as possible, to insulate themselves. They must eat little and move hardly at all. When moving is necessary, they must proceed at a slow and even pace, by the most direct route, which is normally in a straight line.'

281

'It's stupid,' murmured old Juliet, who had been kept because of her fine lambs. 'Growing wool is okay for Barbara: she's part llama with a big fleece. But I am a Suffolk, with short hair. The best way to insulate me is with a decent amount of food to put on some fat.'

'Shh,' said Clarabelle.

Lord Dimitri spoke more quickly now.

'Electric motors will cease to operate the milking machines, grain augers, grain driers, mills, sewage pumps, hay elevators and threshing machinery. The machines can be operated by animal power, as they were before the electrical age. Stationary power will come from water wheels, treadmills, horse mills and steam engines.

'Without diesel, tractor work will be replaced by our strong horses and oxen, doing the ploughing, cultivating and hay making. We can bring into use the old machines stored in our sheds.

'Electricity for pumping of water must be minimised by reducing water consumption. Hot water from boiling eggs and potatoes is to be reused to make tea, or for washing. Pigs can bathe every day, but other animals, if they apply in writing, can have a cold shower lasting under 2 minutes once per week. The only other use of hot water will be for my daily bath, which has no time limit. Water from washing will be reused to irrigate our gardens.

'Our essential nutrition will be high yielding vegetable crops, requiring a minimum of work to grow and easy to prepare, like potatoes.

'Our horticulture will grow varieties requiring little manure, little water, no pesticides, no tractor energy and all animal energy,' said Lord Dimitri. 'Potatoes, grains, corn and rice are best. Pumpkins, corn, lettuce and root vegetables require moderate energy to tend and are permitted to be grown. Strawberries, tomatoes, beans, radishes and tulips require intensive energy and are forbidden. Only the pigs can display cut flowers.'

'You can take a 10-minute break now,' said Lord Dimitri.

'There's more?' asked Arnold. 'What is the arsehole going to put on us next?'

'Don't forget he's promised liberation,' said Juliet. 'We're ahead.'

CHAPTER 48 UNETHICAL AMBIGUITY

During the break the workers talked in a group about Dimitri's energy saving plan.

'It is draconian,' said Arnold. 'Borat restored religion as an instrument of totalitarianism. Lord Dimitri further oppressed us with climate policy, limiting our energy use as the means and ends of his tyranny. His creed is evil: domination, centralisation and terror. His goal is pig supremacy worldwide.

'Our control was first by humans and latterly by pigs. We have accepted their control as protection and as a condition of our slavery. The pigs on this farm have done nothing to improve our living conditions or liberate us. Dimitri's energy reduction nonsense is going too far.'

'Don't we want to reduce energy consumption?'

'Yes, but not just here, everywhere. The Farm is going to be the only place suffering.'

'Shh. He's coming.'

Lord Dimitri walked back onto the stage. He viewed his audience with satisfaction.

'I am the best leader they could possibly have and they are fortunate to have me deciding their lives,' his demeanour suggested. *'I have made a good start as President and have many years of ruling left in me. I embody the spirit of Animal Farm, the same determination to survive that drove out Farmer Jones and kept the farm occupied by animals, despite attacks by humans to try and regain control. There is a possibility that I am immortal. In the*

meantime, my presidency is getting easier with the passing years. The squalor of their lives is of their own making. If I take heed of their petty concerns they will want me to live their lives for them. Their role is to cope as best they can.'

From the centre of the audience, Arnold watched Lord Dimitri basking in his self-adulation and gave a shudder of loathing. Lord Dimitri had rigged elections to rollover the presidency he had extended by manipulating the constitution. His rule had reverted to the totalitarianism of his revolutionary predecessor: Napoleon.

'Animals, you have heard how you must conserve energy supply,' said Lord Dimitri imperiously. 'Now I will apply the same approach to food energy. Remember, our purpose is to reduce heat energy from entering the environment.'

'An animal's species determines how much food it is allowed to eat. Sheep and cattle will be able to graze for up to two hours per day. Poultry will receive a peck of corn each at 8 am. The goats are not allowed any food at all and will have to leave the Farm.'

Wizard looked at Arnold, his face a mask: 'Why is he victimising us again?' was his silent question.

'Patriarch told me they pick on goats because you lead us astray,' Arnold had told him earlier.

'They are using us as scapegoats. They always do.'

'They are prejudiced against goats,' said Arnold. 'The pigs don't want us to have an escape option.'

Lord Dimitri continued to recite his energy policy.

'All animals must do fieldwork, such as ploughing, haymaking, or weeding, or farmyard duties, or making vodka. The most efficient workers are required to do most work. The least efficient will be sent to the abattoir. Horses are efficient at many tasks and will receive extra food enabling them to work longer hours. The cows' milk will continue to be supplied to the farmhouse.'

285

'Pigs eat as much as they want,' said Arnold to Laura bitterly.

Laura's derisive snort got the dogs up from Lord Dimitri's feet to glare at her, drooling.

'Thanks to my leadership of Animal Farm, you will have the satisfaction of reducing Caruba's per capita thermal pollution to a level comparable with the SR, as required by our island Government. On my Sunday drive around the Farm, my human guests have been impressed by the crops you are growing, which testify to your learning and my management.

'Under my energy policy, the future is bright for all of you,' he said. 'You will be playing your part in reducing global warming.'

With sadness Arnold recalled Rose, Violet, Blondie, Henry and Myrtle, all killed under orders from Lord Dimitri. Dongle and Norman had been sent to the abattoir as punishment. Barry might have gone there too — they weren't sure where he had been taken.

'On this Farm we are immersed in disappearances and deaths. It is an awful situation. Lord Dimitri has gone too far,' thought Arnold. *'We must find a way to get rid of him.'*

Dimitri brought his energy saving speech to a conclusion.

'We have resumed coal exports. The coal mine is producing at capacity and the Farm's trading empire is rebuilding. Our coal exports are enabling electricity reticulation in India, with improvement in lifestyles and jobs. Our coal resource won't last forever. We might be able to sustain it by finding more coal and eking it out with renewable energy.

'We will shut down the wind turbines. Although climate science has not yet accepted carbon dioxide is benign, carbon alarmism is known to be false and we need to get the public trusting in coal again. When the generation steeped in greenhouse mythology dies, there will be fewer people using less fossil energy more carefully. Coal's reputation was besmirched by the alarmists and it will take some time to restore it to public esteem, as the bedrock of energy supply.

'Emissions are a problem which has been seen too narrowly. The focus has been on electricity generation, neglecting auto, aeroplane, air conditioning and other sources of heat emissions that cause warming.

'That is all. We will meet again in a week. Any animal who offends against my plan will be severely punished. I have eyes and ears everywhere. Now go back to work.'

Silently and in fear, the animals returned to the fields and lowered their heads to toil. In the following weeks they realized the far-reaching adverse consequences of Lord Dimitri's plan.

Arnold worried that if he could remove Lord Dimitri somehow, their next leader would also be a tyrant. If a panel could select the new leader on the strength of his qualities for the position, the result would be much better than obtaining the animals' preferences in an election that was rigged. The method of selecting the candidate who received the most votes, by the process they called democracy, had let them down badly in the past. Votes went to the most solicitous candidates, who lacked understanding of the problems. A series of presidents had garnered votes by corruption and intimidation.

'No,' thought Arnold. *'Any other leader would have a more humane interest in the community.'*

Late one night Arnold addressed a secret gathering of animals in the Dutch barn. They huddled together considering how to oppose Lord Dimitri's energy plan, whispering to prevent being overheard by pig guards.

'We have to do something about him.'

'Some of the changes are good. He is restoring coal production.'

'Not for our benefit. We will be worse off.'

'He's crazy.'

'How can we overcome the pigs?'

'We can rise up, all together.'

'Let's meet to plan it,' said Arnold. 'How about we get together at the dam tomorrow an hour before dark'

287

They crouched along the water's edge, side by side, gazing at their reflections and drinking from the clean water. The pool was theirs, with enough for all and it united them.

'I hate to break the spell,' said Arnold. 'Does Lord Dimitri's plan share energy fairly, as fairly as we share this water?'

'Definitely not,' said Arnold. 'We don' t have to guess to know the future. The pigs will hog most of the energy. They have consistently taken most of farm resources and output for themselves, as if they have a right to do that. Their responses to climate change and animal liberation have been totalitarian, terrorising us with arbitrary and nonsensical ideologies.

'We are here to decide what to do about Lord Dimitri's energy policy,' he said. 'It is not an easy matter. World authorities leading the climate movement have admitted that their policies may be based on unscientific theories and could have a political agenda. Ottmar Edenhofer, lead author of the IPCC's fourth summary report released in 2007, stated in 2010 as follows.'

'One has to free oneself from the illusion that international climate policy is environmental policy. Instead, climate change policy is about how we redistribute de facto the world's wealth.'

'I find this shocking and disturbing. I can see how the wealthy nations will be pulled down, but I can't see how that will benefit the poor nations,' said Arnold. 'Without rich markets, we won't be able to build up.

'The next quote is from the U.N. climate chief Christiana Figueres. She said the true aim of the U.N.'s 2014 Paris climate conference was:

'to change the (capitalist) economic development model that has been reigning for at least 150 years, since the Industrial Revolution.'

'I don't think capitalism is perfect but the alternatives are worse.'

288

'Another climate policy maker, Christine Stewart, Canada's former Minister of the Environment, has said environment benefits, justice and equality are more important.

'No matter if the science is all phony, there are collateral environmental benefits. ... Climate change (provides) the greatest chance to bring about justice and equality in the world.'

'I don't think we will accept phony science. Without sound science, justice and equality won't have a chance.

'My final quote is from Tim Wirth, former U.S. Undersecretary of State for Global Affairs and the person most responsible for setting up the Kyoto Protocol.

'We've got to ride the global warming issue. Even if the theory of global warming is wrong, we will be doing the right thing in terms of economic policy and environmental policy.'

'No genuine economic or environmental policy could possibly justify its ends with a 'wrong' scientific theory,' said Arnold. 'The Kyoto agreement is not respectable.'

'All four quotes indicate that response to climate change has been motivated by political agendas with shoddy science, rather than by mitigating or remedying the physical impact,' said Arnold. 'I am quite frankly horrified. I see no prospect of the World's politicians doing anything other than filling their pockets with public votes and money.'

'Lord Dimitri's plan is flawed by pig self-interest and cruel disregard for our welfare,' said Simone. 'Whereas we animals will be without power in our cold damp sheds, the pigs in the farmhouse will have soft beds, a sauna, a jacuzzi, sun lamps and a home theatre system.'

'This energy plan of Lord Dimitri's is the final straw. It is high time we ousted the pigs.'

'Lord Dimitri boasted the other day that the Farm's achievements are due to the pigs,' said Grace.

289

'That is laughable,' said Barbara. 'We animals have done the work. In future, we will be better off without the pigs.'

'Karl Marx predicted that eventually the workers will take over the means of production from capital owners,' Grace said. 'The pigs must work like the rest of us.'

'It has been 100 years since we drove out Farmer Jones. That revolution didn't succeed and we are worse off now than before. We have to face it that it is the pigs who have brought our misery.'

'Think about it comrades,' said Arnold. 'We will meet again in a week and we will decide what we have to do.'

'Do you mean: go back to human control?' asked Laura.

There was silence as Arnold looked at each in turn.

'Never,' he said. 'This time we'll get it right.'

CHAPTER 49 BULLFIGHT

That night Arnold dreamed he was in a small pen with high wooden walls. Suddenly they opened the door out into the bullring. He galloped around the ring with his lethal horns held high and the crowd roaring. In his dream they were an audience of believers in the Renewable Energy Deal (RED). He was a climate sceptic, black, dangerous and angry. They had come to see him fight the RED leader, matador Algy, a Large White boar.

Picadors danced in and stuck darts in Arnold's neck and flanks, to weaken and madden him. In his dream he attacked the barrier, trying to get at the jeering crowd. As he thrust his horns into the matting protecting the flanks of picadors' horses, they probed his neck muscles with their lances.

He was enraged and blowing hard when the boar Algy minced into the ring, tiptoeing upright on his hind legs and wearing tights. He walked jauntily and light-footed, a scarlet cape draped over his rapier. Arnold would try his utmost to kill this evil impostor before he himself died, as fate decreed he surely would.

Algy struck a pose with the cape, teasing him. Arnold charged, alleging that global warming was not significant, which he knew was heresy to this audience of believers. At the last moment, Algy stepped aside and Arnold's horn brushed past his taught brocade vest. The crowd roared.

Arnold turned and pawed the ground, menacing. Algy offered the cape enticingly and the bull charged again, asserting that carbon dioxide was benign, contradicting a foundational truth of believers that the gas was the cause of warming. Algy stepped away from this too. The crowd roared again.

His next charge was that renewable energy would cause more warming than fossil fuels, which was anathema to believers. He surprised Algy, who had to jump back at the last second. The roar this time was subdued. They did not like to see their champion struggling.

The boar had hardly recovered, when Arnold charged again, asserting that warming was caused by humans' heat emissions, not by the Sun at all, contradicting the believers' catechism. This time Arnold caught him on his horns, but he slipped away before he could gore him against the ground. The crowd groaned with relief.

Algy recovered and held the cape folded and draped over his rapier, as Arnold pawed the ground angrily and charged, in the certainty that renewable energy technology was more expensive, a point believers rejected. This time his horn caught Algy's vest, tearing off buttons but he leapt backwards and got away.

The bull was tired, his head was down, his flanks were black with sweat and there was white foam at his mouth. The boar sighted along his rapier blade from a distance, aiming between Arnold's shoulder blades. The bull was tired, his head was lowered and piercing him would be easy.

Arnold charged against Algy's pretence that climate science is decided by consensus, rather than by reason. Algy, a leader of fake science, held his ground as the bull's momentum thrust the full length of rapier blade between his shoulders, impaling his heart as he sank to his knees.

But with the last swing of his great head the bull hooked the matador with a horn and threw him aside like a rag doll. The crowd was silent as they brought in a stretcher past the mound of the dead bull and carried Algy out.

Arnold awoke from the dream exultant that he had gored Algy. The bullfight was wickedly cruel and unfair. It was de rigeur that he had succumbed to the boar's advantages. He was satisfied that his six charges against the false RED would be taken seriously. He had gored Algy and his climate deceit was seen to be a fantasy.

CHAPTER 50 ARMAGEDDON

It was twilight when in ones and twos the animals stole furtively through a broad gulley invisible from the farmhouse, to a copse near the dam. It had a stand of trees, moderate in height, with twisted trunks and a canopy so dense that light did not penetrate. The air was cool and thick like pooled molasses. Nothing grew in the open spaces between the trees and the ground was carpeted with leaves, sloping gently. Most of the Farm's animals were congregated there around Arnold, who stood on raised ground, with Laura, Amos and Barbara.

Arnold was talking in the fading light. 'Thank you for coming. You have had a week to consider Lord Dimitri's energy plan. He has demanded we reduce our energy use, which is fair enough, but the pigs will continue to use the lion's share. It has taken us a long time to understand what the pigs are up to but now it is perfectly clear. They are using climate change alarm to subjugate us. We must stop them.'

'Lord Dimitri's energy plan is authoritarian by central control. We have had that before but now he has gone too far. We must refuse to obey. He was elected president but his term has expired. An election should have been called and he has become a dictator. We will have to get rid of him another way.'

'At recent elections voting was for Lord Dimitri or for his henchman Algy. The two have taken over and it won't be easy to get rid of them. An election won't do it.

'Lord Dimitri's term in office has been a travesty,' said Arnold. 'Algy beguiled the pigs with his shonky climate theory and they shut down our power station, smelter and coal mine, ending our employment and reducing Carubans to poverty. But President Alphancourt has back-flipped and restarted them, saying funds for

293

renewable energy hadn't arrived but I suspect she has listened to us and lost confidence in the EGHE theory. Now Lord Dimitri has embarked on energy saving by taking from us the little energy we have, while the pigs continue their profligacy unabated.

'Lord Dimitri has dealt with these matters woefully,' said Arnold. 'He has self-served the pig interest by exaggerating climate change and using it as a springboard to restore the totalitarian regime started by Napoleon when the pigs took over.

'Totalitarianism has increased since he became President.

'He has crushed the hopes of liberation that Lord Miguel allowed us. He has terrorised us routinely, bullying us, forcing compliance at work and during recreation. His ideology is harsh, arbitrary and unrelenting. Workers are suffering and when they have gone off sick, we have covered for them and it is dragging us down.

'The green technologies installed to replace coal will have even worse environmental effects. Good agricultural land has been converted to grow biomass and trees. Carubans will be forced to pay for electricity from uncompetitive generators. The pigs have appeased their political masters, without regard for the well-being of either us animals or the public.

'Our revolutionary ideal was: 'All animals are equal'. Now theirs has become: 'All animals except pigs are superfluous.'

'What is your question, Laura?' She was his favourite, a middle-aged Friesian cow.

'Indigenous peoples in other countries have rights not to be harmed, killed, nor eaten, to own lands and property, to have freedom of movement and vote for a representative,' said Laura. 'Why not us?'

'Do you have an answer, Missy?'

'Lord Dimitri respects you worker animals and your plans for liberation,' said Missy. 'He acknowledges that animals are the traditional owners of the land.'

The animals weren't sure whose side she was on and listened to her with respect tinged with disbelief. They were unaware of her double agency and were suspicious of this conciliatory talk.

294

'All animals are capable of both suffering and experiencing pleasure,' Missy said. 'Animals are morally equal and their interests ought to be considered equally. Using animals for food causes suffering disproportionately larger than the benefits humans derive from meat. There is a moral obligation to refrain from eating animal flesh or any products derived by the exploitation of animals.'

'I agree,' said Arnold.

'Lord Dimitri expects the human diet to become vegan, with animals employed in growing vegetables.'

'Missy, that is so much shit,' said Laura. 'Neither Lord Dimitri nor any of the pigs are going to do a thing to liberate us and you know it.'

'She's right,' Arnold said. 'Will you bugger off, Missy? You are not wanted here. We have had enough of your two-faced lying.'

Quietly Missy slunk away.

Arnold had maintained Missy's deep cover. She would continue to report the pigs doings to him and take back to them his disinformation. For several years now she had loyally served the workers as a double agent. Each generation of Farm sheep and cattle dogs took on the secret tradition of living with the pigs and informing the worker animals of their manoeuvring. She was their faithful decoy and part of it is was to be derided like this.

Arnold sadly recalled his family members Rose, Cynthia, Myrtle and Earl, all murdered under orders from Lord Dimitri. Comrade Dongle had been sent to the abattoir before his time.

'Dimitri's monstrous energy saving plan is too much,' Arnold thought. *'For 10 years I have tried to see it the pigs' way and made excuses for their laziness, incompetence and bullying. I have condoned their indolence, contempt and exploitation of climate fears, thinking those ways would lead us to freedom. We are subjugated now worse than ever. I used to hope the pigs would share control with us but they have relinquished no control to us and taken away the little dignity Farmer Jones accorded us.*

My anger tells me it is time to deal with these swine. I have thought endlessly how to improve matters but always reach the same

295

conclusion: the pigs are opposing our liberation simply because they want to keep us down.

Peaceful confrontation is not possible and this means we will have to take control by force. Although I am a bull and built for combat, killing and injury repel me. It might not take many lives or injuries to climb out of the pit in which we have all been living for so long. I have hoped the pigs can be quelled without bloodshed, but I would fight them until death rather than continue in subjugation. There is no turning back.

The pigs have dominated us because they are pushy and greedy by nature. They appear fierce and strong, but they are cowardly and soft. Their main strength is the cunning to push others aside and force into others' territories in close fighting. In the open they are ponderous, slow and easily overcome by cattle and horses able to horn and kick them.

I am confident that in a confrontation with the pigs, we workers would prevail because we would be fighting for our lives, literally. If we lose, I am certain the pigs' reparations would include our deaths.

'Lord Dimitri's energy plan goes too far,' said Arnold angrily. 'His disrespect for us is intolerable. The time has come to decide whether to get rid of him and the rest of the pigs.'

'I think passive resistance would be better,' said Brandy.

Brandy the stallion heavy horse stood above the burly volatile bull Arnold, a head and shoulders taller, with strength to match and feet the size of dinner plates. They eyed each other as if they might fight.

'Passive resistance won't win against the pigs,' said Arnold. 'They have to be removed.'

Barbara interposed, speaking to both Arnold and Brandy.

'Come on guys. We can't put it off any longer. I agree, we have to get rid of the pigs, all of them, right now. We have to takeover, assert our control. Passive resistance won't do it. If another pig takes control, it could be another tyrant, corrupt and bullying. Lord Dimitri has inveigled his way through elections and he has become a corrupt and psychopathic dictator. A panel could select the next leader, a

296

non-pig, on the strength of his qualities for the position, with service to the community demonstrated. The greatest service to the community will be to lead us against the pigs and it won't be successful until we have won. Then the leader must take responsibility for organizing to create a prosperous Animal Farm, producing food for us to eat and sell, earning to meet our needs by mining coal from electricity supply to the island.'

'Thank you Barbara,' said Arnold. 'That's a good plan. Are you okay with that, Brandy?'

Brandy realised he had been sidelined.

'Okay,' he agreed.

'Let's vote on ending pig rule now, with a show of legs,' said Arnold.

They raised their forelimbs, a few at first, then an avalanche.

'Almost unanimous,' Arnold said. 'Only Ranger wants to keep the pigs. Ranger, would you leave us now.'

The tomcat left. He was a newcomer to the Farm, but already he had taken sides against the workers. He seemed to be uncooperative by nature.

They were interrupted by Ravens, lackeys of the pigs, sensitive to insurrections, flying in and perching to observe the proceedings.

Arnold told the ravens to flock off, but they lingered until he and the others threw dung at them and they flapped away, protesting noisily.

'We must challenge Lord Dimitri with the shock of a sudden coup. If we act tentatively or half-hearted, he will set his dogs, police and militia on us,' Arnold said. 'When we rise up, we must do it all together, driving out the pigs and taking over the running of the farm ourselves. We have to keep our revolution as an internal Farm matter. If it spreads to other farms, President Alphancourt will come in and oppose us.'

'When do we takeover?' asked Jigsaw, standing beside Bella his partner. Her parents, Brandy and Grace, stood with them.

There was absolute silence as they all looked at Arnold.

'Now,' he said. 'We will do it now. Be quick and get your weapons. We will gather by the farmhouse. The dogs will alert the

297

pigs but we will take them by surprise, before they can barricade themselves inside. At exactly midnight, I will shout 'Now' and we will attack together.'

The worker animals had suffered together and now they were united beyond friendship and mutual support, going shoulder to shoulder into a battle for freedom. They had had too much of the pigs. To escape from slavery, for even a brief period, would be worth risking injury or even making the ultimate sacrifice. The prospect of a fight was empowering after so many years of inaction.

'Go and get ready.'

The animals dispersed quietly into the night, with purpose, some running. They did not have timepieces and coordination was intuitive, as it had been for their ancestors. They would watch Arnold to know when it was midnight, the way starling flocks wheeling in the sky at dusk know when it is time to turn as one.

Arnold suppressed qualms as he watched them leave. He reflected that his entire life was about to be exposed to thrilling scrutiny. He would do everything he could to bring this insurrection to the best possible conclusion for their community. He was resolved to oust the pigs at whatever cost was necessary.

CHAPTER 51 UPRISING

As Arnold went to his stall, his surroundings had vivid clarity he had never seen before. He smelled odours for the first time and noticed qualities in his companions' speech he had never heard. He imagined events and rehearsed in his mind his actions, delivering crippling injuries, receiving blows and coping with agonising pain. He made his preparations with deliberation, eating grain he had stored for an emergency and going to the dam to drink. He checked around the sheds where the animals were preparing. He answered the questions of the bold and reassured the timid.

He was fearless, operating with automaticity. Time was his, to do with as he liked. Events were occurring exactly as he expected. Matters were crystallising irrevocably, exactly as he wanted. This was his show. Success was uncertain but the action would be absolutely decisive, with the outcome to be determined by their intelligence and valour. If there were setbacks or even defeat, he would have done his best.

As midnight approached the animal workers arrived at the barn and assembled in waves of species: sheep, cattle, horses, poultry. It was a restless tide of animals close together, fretting at the delay, pushing forward here, recoiling there. They were mobilised by anger, anxious to revenge themselves on the pigs who had killed, tortured and mistreated them and their ancestors for so long. They surrounded Arnold, their leader, his massive body reassuring them, for they had never before been armed for violence. Animals without horns carried weapons, hay forks, scythes, hatchets, hay knives, pick-axes, spikes and pikes. They held shields, clubs, cudgels, chains, hammers, hand-axes and crow-bars. Arnold's was a large and fearsome presence.

'*He knows we will win,*' they thought. '*It's all or nothing, This is it.*'

'Thank you all for coming,' Arnold spoke with calm confidence. 'We are not here to wage violence but to subdue the pigs. I'm glad to see you have brought your weapons. The pigs have several guns, swords and knives. They will imagine they are fighting for their lives but we will engage in violence only when there is no other alternative. If you are injured, our donkey will bring you to safety.

'Getting the pigs to surrender will not be easy but our aim is to overcome them and hold them captive. There is no need to despatch them. We must not sink to their level of depravity. You cannot assume our ends will justify killing. Their deaths are not necessary. We want them to flee or surrender unscathed. Eventually they will return and be welcomed under our command.

'Are there any questions?'

'Supposing they make a stand in the farmhouse. Can we burn it?'

'No definitely not. It would be dishonourable to do something we wouldn't like done to us. There are enough of us to mount a strong attack on the farmhouse, breaking down the doors and bursting in on them. They will be formidable fighters at close quarters, but we will subdue them with our shields and hammers.'

'What if they try to escape?'

'That is exactly what we want. Chase them off the farm.'

'How long do we fight for?'

'I will shout 'Animals stop' when we have won, or when we need to regroup. Then you will come to the farmhouse lawn for further instructions.'

'What about prisoners?'

'Take them to the pig sties and lock them in. I have the key. Is everyone ready? It is midnight. Let's go!'

As the animals raced away, Arnold turned to Laura.

'How did that happen?' he asked.

'You mobilised Pidgin English and sent it into battle!' she said.

Arnold, Jigsaw and Amos and several others ran to the farmhouse and banged on the front door.

'Who is it?' they heard grunted from inside.

'We are the Animal Army. Come quietly and no harm will befall you. If you don't come out, we will break down the door.'

There was muffled talking within, then a shout.

'Go away. You will die for this.'

'Ready?' asked Arnold. 'All together now.'

He charged the door, putting his huge weight behind his shoulders, smashing the door, breaking the lock and splintering it, opening it.

'Come on.'

Arnold pushed through the opening, with the others close behind. As he did so, Lord Dimitri knocked him over and grabbed the bull's hind leg in his powerful mouth. He bit into it. Arnold's horn raked along Dimitri's side, piercing his abdomen, hooking him and throwing him down. He struggled to his feet but Amos charged and his horn smashed into the boar's head and he sank down stunned, with one eye blinded. He released his hold on Arnold's leg. Arnold slashed again with a horn, piercing Dimitri, impaling him against the wall, gouging his intestines as blood spurted from the wound. All around them workers were fighting pigs. When they saw Lord Dimitri vanquished, the pigs cowered and tried to get away out of the door. Turmoil ensued. There were screams, squeals, barks and blood. Workers had taken control in most rooms and pigs were fleeing from the farmhouse pursued by workers.

Although the pigs were numerous and large, with sharp teeth, they were no match for the horses' kicks, cattle gores, ram butts and waves of flapping poultry. Several oligarch boars half-carried Lord Dimitri outside. They tried to flee with him in his car until workers stopped it, dragged them out, kicked them into submission and threw them over the fence into a neighbouring farm.

'What casualties do we have?' asked Arnold.

'A sheep is dead.'

301

'She made the ultimate sacrifice, for us,' he said. 'We will remember her kindly.'

'Several animals are bitten,' said Amos. 'Three Rottweilers are dead.'

'They were doing their jobs and had no choice but to fight,' said Laura. 'All authority is violence.'

'It is good to be free of the parasitical pigs!' Arnold said.

'Fighting for my freedom after being oppressed for so long seems reckless,' said Laura, 'as if there will be a reckoning.'

'The pigs' brutality is ended,' said Arnold. 'You will not be oppressed again.'

'Let's hope our new leader will be better,' said Clarabelle.

'We are free at last!' said Arnold. 'The stable door is open now. I'm bolting!'

He cavorted around, bucking and kicking, together with carthorses Grace, Brandy, Jigsaw and Bella. Other animals joined in excitedly, racing around the home paddock. Arnold's bitten leg was bleeding and they staunched it.

Missy came out from hiding.

'It looks like the pigs have gone,' she said to Arnold.

'They'll be back,' said Arnold, 'on our terms. You can stay with us, if you want,'

'No hard feelings?'

'None,' he said. 'On the contrary, your loyalty has been important to our victory. Thank you very much. But you'll have to share in the work with the rest of us.'

'After the dangers of spying, I look forward to regular work,' she said.

The next day the animals elected Arnold as a governor on the Farm's board for the next three years. There was one board member from each of the species. Amos was the sheep's representative and Bella the horses'.

President Alphancourt accepted Arnold in the Caruban parliament as the first animal member, with others planned later.

302

The Farm buildings were modernised for comfortable worker accommodation. The farmhouse was converted into a study and leisure centre for all the animals to use. A lottery was drawn for rooms. Barbara won the former presidential bedroom.

'Do you want to share with me?' she asked Arnold.

'Yes, thank you. Our cria can sleep in my room and I'll come in here with you.'

'Will the others be okay with that?' asked Barbara.

'What's it to them?'

'We can't just raise our children where and how we like,' she said.

'Why not?'

'Offspring needs are paramount,' Barbara said. 'It's not allowed to seek one's freedom at the expense of others. That's where humans went wrong.'

'We can be more considerate.'

'Are our children going to have rights?'

'Definitely. We will leave enough resources for them.'

'Are we going to have a welfare state?'

'Yes. It will help bring the species together.'

'Is it my job to unite them.'

'No. Democratic processes will see to it.'

CHAPTER 52 FREEDOM

Workers initially had wanted to be cared for and relinquished their rights willingly to paternal leaders. An unfortunate consequence of them becoming dependent was that volition atrophied and they had capitulated to human and then pig control. The tyranny that followed was a natural progression, rather than malign at inception.

The animals had opposed 100 years of totalitarian rule, first by ousting humans and now by overthrowing the pigs. A central committee governed the Farm democratically. The RED was terminated when general growth was no longer wanted and renewable energy was of limited value. For the first time Caruba was able to self-govern and Animal Farm could self-sustain.

The workers had instigated their animal liberation insurrection when the pigs could not be persuaded to break ranks with the superpowers' climate science hegemony. The worker animals had realised they were being tyrannized as part of a worldwide totalitarian conspiracy in the guise of climate alarmism.

Dimitri and the pigs, who had been hiding on a neighbouring farm, returned to Animal Farm. They were rostered with the other animals and put to work in the fields. The worker animals were free, for the moment.

The animals celebrated their freedom with an afternoon party by the dam. Arnold spoke to the jubilant gathering, as their leader, with the other two board members, Amos and Bella.

'First I wanted to honour all those animals who have slaved, protested, fought and died for the freedom we enjoy today. In the coming weeks we will honour their memory with a participative

democracy set up to preserve equality between animals of all species.

'Scientists' have focussed on an Enhanced Greenhouse Effect Theory and it has been misleading, Unintentionally they have misled us. It has been explained as follows.'

> The strong moral sense that accompanies climate science, seeking to 'save the world' from catastrophic anthropogenic climate change, is part of the problem, because 'high moral purpose' can lead to questionable interpretive practices as moral purpose affects the psychology of the scientists. (22)

'There is a little warming, but not enough to cause alarm,' Arnold continued. 'The actions we take should not be to fight global warming directly. Our fight should be to oppose excessive energy production and consumption in developed countries, in all energy uses, regardless of supposed greenhouse gas emissions, unless they are substantiated. We must reduce energy use for electricity, cars, trucks, planes, ships, food, consumable goods, furnishings, construction of buildings and roads. A target of halving energy will halve heat entering the environment and halve the rate of global warming. Greater cuts must be applied until that is achieved. If there is economic growth, energy use must be steady-state, except in developing countries.

'Curbing energy use counters the main thrust of western civilisation since the Industrial Revolution, which has been to utilise energy resources for movement and control of the environment. Whereas high energy use has been a status symbol, materialism has to be rebuilt on the idea that energy is too precious to waste. The more happiness and comfort can be obtained without using energy, the more the community benefits.

305

'Low cost energy technologies should be adopted that minimise heat emissions and conserve energy resources. Solar panels installed on rooftops can shave peak demand and complement efficient use of coal power for many years into the future. Using the criterion of carbon footprint is false, taking attention from the issue of utility of energy, allowing technologies such as wind turbines to be wrongly promoted as better than coal power.

'Our fight against energy use has to be taken up by the whole population,' Arnold said. 'Dimitri was wrong to cut energy use at your expense alone. The SR and DU recognise the need for everyone to cut energy use and they are leaving it to energy markets to decide which technologies to adopt, as they should. Totalitarian selection of technologies has been ruled by climate hysteria and populist politics rather than reason. Now President Alphancourt will speak to you.'

Caruba's President Natalia Alphancourt stood on a rock, steadying herself with a hand on Arnold's back.

'I want you animals to become missionaries in Caruba, who will inspire people far and wide to join the fight to reduce meat and energy consumption. My main task in government will be to measure and record consumption, keeping score as high energy consumers strive for the victory of halving their consumption, allowing low users to catch up.

'Meat production uses more energy than other sources of protein that can be substituted. Caruba will be vegan and the abattoir will be pulled down,' she said. 'I have taken this view considering what will be best for the whole community democratically. Animals will be able to live out their days looked after by friends. Your board can organise food growing and coal mining with working hours and pay of your choice. When your fieldwork is done, you will have recreation time and will be able to take it easy.

'When Carubans accept meatless living, the abattoir threat will be removed and you animals will have democratic rights. Your new worker board must be careful not to allow any species supremacy,

306

as happened when humans domesticated you and again when pigs took over.

'I congratulate you on your freedom!'

President Natalia Alphancourt joined in the applause.

Arnold turned their attention to celebrating several worker animals' birthdays. The assembly sang Happy Birthday To Ewe for Barbara and then the sheep's chorus line swayed up onto the dray, where they sang and danced their version of Island in the Sun, with other animals joining in a calypso rhythm on several upturned drums.

'This is my island in the sun,
Where my people have toiled since time begun.'

They sang the whole song, casting aside the chains of domesticity and taking a place equal with humans in the Caruban community. It was an ongoing revolution.

END

BIBLIOGRAPHY AND REFERENCES

1. Climate Change 2001:The Scientific Basis, Intergovernmental Panel on Climate Change, Third Assessment Report (TAR).
2. Cook, John University of Queensland, Journal: Environmental Research Letters, May 16, 2013
3. Earl J Ritchie Fact Checking The Claim Of 97% Consensus On Anthropogenic Climate Change Dec 14, 2016 https://www.forbes.com/sites/uhenergy/2016/12/14/fact-checking-the-97-consensus-on-anthropogenic-climate-change/#3d8acdeb1157
4. Morano, Marc Climate Change, Salem, 2018.
5. Ibbotson, J; Planning Ahead, Australian Lighthouse Traders.
6. Plimer, Ian; Heaven + Earth; Connor Court Publishing.
7. Box, M.A. and Box, G.P. Physics of Radiation and Climate, CRC Press.
8. Blair D. Macdonald, Quantum Mechanics and Raman Spectroscopy Refute Greenhouse Theory, Principia Scientific, 2018-10-13
9. Rifkin, J The RED, 2019
10. Greskes, N. Conway, E., Shindell, M. From Chicken Little to Dr. Pangloss: William Nierenberg, Global Warming, and the Social Deconstruction of Scientific Knowledge. Historical Studies in the Natural Sciences, Vol 38, Number 1, pps. 109-152, Copyright 2008, by the Regents of the University of California.
11. De Beauvoir, The Ethics of Ambiguity (1947

12. Lev. 16.
13. O,Sullivan, John Dr Tim Ball Defeats Michael Mann's Climate Lawsuit! Principia Scientific, Aug 23, 2019
14. Altena, Louis. Examining deliberative discourse on climate change: A Deweyan perspective. Medium, December 2019.
15. J. T. Kiehl and Kevin E. Trenberth. Earth's Annual Global Mean Energy Budget, Bulletin of the American Meteorological Society,Vol. 78, No. 2, February 1997 p20
16. Marohasy. J.(Ed.) Climate Change, The Facts 2017, Institute of Public Affairs, 2017.
17. Intergovernmental Panel on Climate Change, First Assessment Report, 1990, Overview
18. Ritchie, E. J. Fact Checking The Claim of 97% Consensus on Anthropogenic Climate Change, https://www.forbes.com/sites/uhenergy/2016/12/14/fact-checking-the-97-consensus-on-anthropogenic-climate-change/#1fdf48511157
19. Gessen, Masha. The Future is History. How Totalitarianism Reclaimed Russia. Riverhead, 2017.
20. Knox, Z. Jehovah's Witnesses and the Secular World from the 1870s to the present, Palgrave, Macmillan, 2018.
21. Long, M. Forum for Church and Human Rights in East Germany, in Knox, Z. Voices of the Voiceless, Baylor University Press, 2019.
22. Marohasy, J. Climate Change The Facts 2020, Institute of Public Affairs, 2020.

Books by Martin Knox

Will Maxi be able to break the
World marathon record
using simple brain physics?

TIME IS GOLD

Martin Knox

*A thrilling running adventure with
optimal achievement through Flow*
- Brad Ahern, Science and Sports Educator

https://martinknox.com/time-is-gold

WHAT CAN HAPPEN IF A COUPLE ARE NOT ON THE SAME LEVEL?

$hort of Love

Satirical Fiction

' . . . a narrative alternately amusing, shocking, and deeply familiar.'
Vesna McMaster, Author, *The Fastro Connection*

Martin Knox

https://martinknox.com/short-of-love

THIS BOOK COULD CHANGE HOW YOU THINK
ABOUT PARTY POLITICS

PRESUMED DEAD

A political crime fiction thriller

Martin Knox

https://martinknox.com/presumed-dead

312

https://martinknox.com/love-straddle

313

https://martinknox.com/the-grass-is-always-browner

www.ingramcontent.com/pod-product-compliance
Lightning Source LLC
Chambersburg PA
CBHW070057120726
47909CB00002B/420